MOTIVE FOR MURDER

JASON M HANSON

MOTIVE FOR MURDER

CHAPTER 1

S aturday 6th May...9:00am

The smirk left his face quickly, the force of the blow lifting him clean off his feet, sending him sprawling to the floor. The unwelcome visitor didn't need an invitation as he advanced quickly towards the reluctant host, who was trying unsuccessfully to get back to his feet. His hair was pulled, lifting him off his feet, before he was struck again, causing a curdling shriek. The man fell harshly back to the floor. His pain was clear, but this wouldn't draw any sympathy from his attacker. There was no remorse and no relenting. This was personal.

'Get up.'

'What do you want?'

'I want you to stand up and fight like a man.'

'Fuck you.'

A grin illuminated the face of the tall figure standing over his victim, who was now lying defenceless on the floor. It was the first show of any expression. It was also a strong indication of his intentions. He was well-built and looked more than capable with his fists. He hit hard, but more importantly, he knew where to hit. This was a grave concern for the unsuspecting victim currently slumped on his own living room floor, who would be no match for his adversary in a straight fight. Now retreating on his hands and knees, the man crawled towards the corner of the room. He paused momentarily to wipe his mouth, noticing the blood trickling down each corner. The bruising on his face was already beginning to form; the well-groomed individual who had answered the door, quickly becoming unrecognisable. Before he had time to process the extent of his injuries, a vicious kick connected with his chest, which left him gasping frantically for breath. At best, it would leave severe bruising. At worst, broken ribs. He lay incapacitated; the fight was over, with a clear victor. It was now simply a case of how far his attacker was prepared to go to prove his point, whatever that point was.

The sound of a phone ringing disrupted the aggressor as he closed in on his target. It was brief, but the momentary lapse was enough to hand his opponent an opening, and fighting for his life, he didn't pass up the opportunity. The injured man grabbed a poker from next to the open fire and swivelled, swinging with what little strength he had left, connecting with the kneecap of his assailant. There was a loud shout as the unwanted guest winced in pain, knee buckling from underneath him. He wasn't afforded any time to gather his thoughts or attend to his injury. This time, the poker connected with his arm, which he had instinctively raised to defend himself and prevent a blow to the head, a blow which would have almost certainly rendered him unconscious, therefore at the mercy of his assailant. He lurched back, before screaming with pain as his leg reminded him of its trauma. His opponent, whose carpet was now showing up sporadic patches of blood, swung again, having now regained his feet. His progress, however, was halted as a large hand enveloped the weapon he had obtained from the fireplace. Now effectively operating on one leg, the man who was now likely regretting his decision to look down at his phone moments ago stared wild-eyed. The crazed look did nothing to reassure the wounded individual stood opposite of his safety. The unwelcome guest squeezed until the grip on the poker was relinquished, the sound of it hitting the floor echoing around the large room. Without weapons, this was now a fair fight, and there would be only one winner. The question was, where would this end? His motive was apparent, his goal a little less so. Was this a warning? Perhaps it was simply about releasing some of the anger that had been burning away in the pit of his stomach. He looked down at his hand and noticed he had been involuntarily tightening his grip. The man had a pained expression on his face and was groaning.

'Who are you, and what do you want with me?' he managed.

'Who I am isn't important.'

'There are cameras which overlook my drive. I have your image, and so will the police when the alarms are raised.'

More than anything, his words were filled with desperation and hope.

'I entered the same way I will leave...through the fields at the back of your garden. Nobody knows I'm here. Nobody's coming to your rescue.'

The man's face looked ashen as he contemplated his fate.

'I can give you money.'

'I have no need for your money.'

'Then what is it you need?'

A smirk slowly appeared on the face of the large man, with his opponent down on his knees, helpless, and begging for his life. There was no fight left in him; he was at the mercy of a man he had never laid eyes on.

'I don't know you.'

His voice was now scarcely more than a whisper. He sounded beaten, but this wouldn't stop the attack. The man on the floor looked frightened, but it was the look in the eyes of the person standing over him, which was perhaps more significant. They were devoid of emotion, his expression cold and sinister. Critically injured, having been attacked in his own home, the man tried desperately to scramble free. He looked his attacker directly in the eye.

'Please don't kill me,' he stuttered.

There was a stand-off as the attacker hesitated. He had a chance to end it, to walk away now. Yet as he stared at his victim, he suddenly realised that his words symbolised defiance, not helplessness. He wondered why anybody would antagonise somebody who had the power to spare or end their life before delivering a final blow. The force sent the bloodied man hurtling towards the fireplace, where his head came to rest on the marbled corner. He lay motionless as an eerie quietness fell on the house. There was no blood, but he looked in a bad way. There was a pause, followed by blind panic. The attacker placed his head in his hands. He'd killed him. This changed everything. He still lacked any insight into what he'd hoped to achieve by coming here, but he now knew this wasn't it. He didn't want to feel for a pulse. This would confirm what he feared, and he had no interest in contradicting the small part of him that believed this wasn't as bad as it looked. He strained to hear breathing but was met with silence. He'd avoided detection, but undoubtedly there would be traces of evidence which tied him to the scene. The choice was simple, yet stark. Stay and hand himself in or go on the run. Either way, this was bound to catch up with him. Regretting his decision, he turned and looked towards the door, which was still ajar. The house looked immaculate. Even the living room gave no indication of the struggle it had just witnessed. It now housed two figures. One was still as the night, the other stood tall, now visibly shaking like a tree on a stormy evening. As he moved towards the exit, he took one last look around at the scene behind him, which was chaotic yet tranquil in the same vein. He went to close the door before thinking better of it. Slowly trudging around the side of the house, he noticed the birds in full voice, as the morning sun had now broken through. The garden was large, the grass freshly cut, but he was in no mood to stand and admire. As he made his way through the hedge which would open out into the surrounding fields, he pulled his phone from his pocket and stared at it. How could he even explain this? His life would change immeasurably, yet he felt a numbness he simply couldn't explain. He wondered whether it was shock or the fact he felt little remorse for his actions. In the distance, he could see a spectacular tree in the middle of the field. It stood tall and proud, coming into bloom. He walked towards it with some misguided notion it would somehow provide him with a moment of clarity. Upon reaching it, his situation seemed no less grave. The surrounding tranquillity wasn't reflected internally. The shock was subsiding, reality taking its place. A lot was resting on his next move. He took a deep breath and paused for a moment, before dialling. As the familiar voice answered the phone, words came tumbling out of his mouth that he never imagined would pass his lips, even in the darkest depths of his nightmares.

'I've killed someone.'

CHAPTER 2

S aturday 6th May...10:00am

'You look great.'

'All these years together, Toby, yet still, you struggle with small talk.'

Though she smiled as she said this, Beth wasn't wrong. Strangely, he had always felt more comfortable conversing on a deeper level. He didn't lack the ability to enter superficial discussions, it just didn't come naturally to him. From a young age, he had learned conversations had a purpose. The cynical part of him viewed time exchanging pleasantries, talking about insignificant things, as a delay in getting to what really matters. In his time as a therapist, every session, every conversation, was purposeful. If his clients weren't specifically exploring the origin of their affliction, they were building towards it. But this wasn't therapy, and she wasn't a client. The woman sitting opposite him in the quaint coffee shop was his wife, his soulmate. She was the love of his life, the one person he had shown nothing but devotion to over the years. She was his everything and living without her for the last few weeks had hit him hard. Whenever he had needed her, she had been there. Supporting him through turmoil, nursing him through illness, and celebrating with him through his successes. He'd never taken her for granted, but he had wrongly assumed her resilience and patience were limitless. He hadn't only pushed her to the brink of her boundaries; he had stretched them beyond their capability until they had snapped. *She* had snapped. Now he was picking up the pieces and working tirelessly to save his marriage, which was hanging by a thread. Toby and Beth Reynolds sat opposite one another in a moment of silence. They were more resembling of two people on a first date, than a couple who had shared over a decade together. He reached for her hand. She took it, but tentatively. A reflection of the tumultuous journey she had encountered over the last year. Toby felt her reluctance. He could see her body language was closed off. This wouldn't be easy.

'I'm sorry.'

'I genuinely believe you are, but that's not the issue, is it?'

'I regret the decisions I've made.'

'You regret the outcome, not the decisions.'

'I regret hurting you.'

'It's not regret I'm looking for, Toby.'

'Then what?'

She shook her head slowly.

'You still don't get it, do you?'

'Help me understand,' he pleaded.

'You had doubts about Olivia Stanton, yet you ignored them. Richard had doubts and advised you to end the therapy, yet you ignored him. Professional ethics stipulate you don't attend a client's house outside of an appointment, yet you ignored these. Mike warned you not to get involved with George's kidnapping, yet you ignored him. That's before we even discuss the times your own wife begged you not to get involved. You always told me therapy wasn't about saving people, yet you've become obsessed with doing just that. But here's the real irony, Toby. The one person who needs saving more than anyone right now is you. You've lost yourself and you've been fighting for the wrong things.'

She was angry, but more importantly, she was right. Everything she had said was right. He had prioritised both Olivia and George over her. It hadn't been intentional, but he recognised it now. At the time, it hadn't felt like it had been a conscious choice, but now he could see it. He lowered his head with an overwhelming feeling of shame. He'd hurt her, and in this moment wondered whether he could ever repair the damage *he* had caused.

'I need you.'

'You need perspective. You need to find the Toby I fell in love with all those years ago because this isn't a version of you I recognise.'

'What if this has always been inside of me?'

'Only you can answer that.'

Toby was struggling to control his emotions as he gulped. He wondered whether, if faced with the same decisions again, he would take a different path. Suddenly, he understood as he weighed regret against remorse. He raised his head and looked Beth directly in the eye with an unmistakable warmth. It wasn't regret. Seeing the sadness in her eyes, the indescribable trauma she had experienced because of him, he realised his decisions weren't his concern. It was Beth. Nothing else mattered right now. What he was feeling was a genuine remorse at the effect this had had on her. As the clouds in his head slowly dissipated, he felt an optimism for the future he hadn't felt for some time. He squeezed her hand, but her reluctance hadn't disappeared.

'I'm still unable to really comprehend what happened with Olivia, no matter how much I try to make sense of it.

'How many clients did you work with during your time as a therapist?'

'Why does that matter?'

Whether she was so focused on making her point, she didn't hear him, or didn't give his answer much credence, Beth didn't acknowledge his objection.

'I can only imagine the things you must have heard, but tell me this...how many times did you work with a rape victim, a victim of domestic abuse, a victim of bullying, harassment, control and coercion, and think about saving them?'

'More than I'd be comfortable admitting.'

'And that makes you human, Toby. It's also what made you a damn good therapist. It would take one cold son of a bitch to face that sort of disclosure and not feel anything.'

'Thinking and feeling aren't necessarily problematic in their own right. I went beyond that, however, and crossed a professional line that should never have been crossed.'

'They didn't strike you off.'

Toby considered his response. He knew Beth's angle. She was trying to humanise him to ease some of the guilt he'd been feeling. She was pushing him down the route of a rash decision with good intentions, rather than the alternatives which could range from professional ineptitude to a more ethically questionable desire to save his clients.

'You went to that house under some misguided notion that Olivia Stanton needed saving, and you should be the one to do it. You were naïve, but Toby, I've seen nothing other than goodness in you.'

Toby's head dropped. The guilt was overwhelming. He'd carried a burden, a truth she was unaware of, for all these years. Hearing her words now, she deserved to know. She noticed the tears roll down his cheek and reached out to him.

'Toby, what is it?'

She was met with silence.

'Toby?'

His head came up slowly, his eyes meeting hers. Those beautiful, caring eyes he had stared into over the years were about to change in an instant. He squeezed her hand slowly as a trepidatious look replaced her warm smile. There was a reason behind his bitter tears of self-reproach. There was a reason he had walked away from psychotherapy after the Olivia Stanton incident. Denial had been his companion, his protector, but it had now left him with a bitter truth that he had kept from Beth, from everybody. As he sat there and studied his wife's body language, from the anxious look on her face to her slumped posture, he noted a resignation in her. At that moment, he finally recognised the damage his decisions had caused. This hadn't solely been his ordeal. She had lived it, breathed it, and had suffered alongside him with every step. Beyond the radiance, he could see she looked tired. He thought how much easier it would be if he could attribute this to physical fatigue, but there was no denying it was the product of emotional trauma. He was responsible for everything that was happening to her and was about to break the one heart he vowed never to break. But she had to know. She deserved to know.

'Toby, I am praying with everything I have, that the next words out of your mouth are going to reassure me, but something tells me those prayers are going to go unanswered.'

Toby took a moment to compose himself, drawing in an enunciated breath, as he battled to find the words to let Beth know he had kept a dark secret for several years. He knew this would ultimately lead her to question everything she thought she knew about the person she fell in love with. If he couldn't reach her with his reasoning, if he couldn't somehow placate her, his marriage was over.

'Do you know why I went into psychotherapy?'

'Because you love helping people.'

'Except you're limited as a therapist. Therapists don't fix people, they don't make situations better, and they don't have a magic ingredient. They simply provide a safe environment for a client to feel vulnerable and explore their emotional difficulties.'

Toby paused, acutely aware he was distancing himself from his profession, a further reminder of the actual cost of his decisions.

'Toby, you're doing yourself and your profession a disservice.'

'It's no longer my profession,' he interrupted.

She continued, paying no attention to his correction.

'How many lives have been turned around because of what you did? Everything you achieved through therapy, you did so through good practice, not good fortune.'

'Do you know how difficult it is to work with an abuse victim, powerless to change their situation? I cannot even begin to explain how it feels to look somebody in the eyes, knowing the chances are they are going to return to that which they appear to be trying so desperately to escape.'

'That was never your role, Toby. You can't hold yourself responsible for your client's decisions, only your own.'

He flashed her a brief smile, which felt forced and insincere. She was, of course, on point, and that was the problem.

'Perhaps that's why I really walked away from it.'

Beth didn't respond. He had her attention.

'Part of me wonders whether I knew exactly what I was walking into, and what the consequences would be. Maybe I'd simply reached my limit and couldn't handle it anymore.'

'Psychotherapy?'

Knowing where the conversation was inevitably going, he hesitated.

'Injustice,' he finally replied.

'I don't understand.'

Toby now faced a dilemma. If he continued, he risked losing her forever. Retreating, however, would leave him burdened by a dark secret he'd kept from her—a secret that could have altered everything. She had the right to know who she was married to. She had the right to base the decision on her future around the real Toby, not the version he was presenting.

'Do you remember when I first opened my practice?'

'We were a little younger back then.'

'And naïve.'

She looked at him, puzzled.

'Those early days were challenging. I was attempting to carve my own path, unaware that I was actually searching for my true self. There were times when I questioned why I got into psychotherapy. Sometimes I could convince myself it was for the right reasons, but other times...'

He tailed off. 'I had intrusive thoughts, and questioned whether I'd be able to suppress them,' he continued.

'Intrusive thoughts?'

'I wanted to save people. I can't even verbalise the experience of watching a vulnerable individual relive unspeakable trauma, knowing your only role is to sit and listen.'

'Olivia Stanton broke you.'

Toby screwed up his eyes and clenched his fists, trying to find the courage to continue.

'It ended with Olivia, but it didn't begin with her.'

Beth looked shocked as she recoiled.

'Toby, you're not making any sense.'

'Olivia wasn't the first time I flirted with the ethical boundaries within therapy.'

Beth Reynolds sat quietly, an expressionless face which didn't betray her thoughts. Whatever she was feeling right now, she remained guarded.

'There was a client. At the time, she was in her early forties. She was kind and affable, but there was a deep pain behind those eyes. Her life encounters were truly heart-wrenching, and I found it challenging to navigate my way through the emotions that were surfacing during her sessions. Eventually, she disclosed she was being subjected to bullying in the workplace. Her situation had deteriorated to such a degree that she began presenting with suicide ideation.'

Beth reached for his hand, taking Toby by surprise. She knew. She immediately understood something that had taken him months to fully grasp.

'An overwhelming feeling of injustice consumed me, but it wasn't just about that.'

Beth studied him but didn't speak.

'I was frightened of what she would do.'

'Frightened?'

'I've worked with many people who have talked about ending their own lives, and whilst I acknowledged the severity of disclosure of that nature, it never phased me. But something was different with her.'

'Toby, what did you do?'

'She worked in a restaurant. I drove there one Saturday. She, of course, wasn't working, but her manager, who had pushed her to the brink, was.'

'Jesus Toby.'

'I considered belittling him in front of his staff. I thought about confronting him after he'd locked up, but as you know, I'm not much of a fighter. Then I thought about sabotaging the place, knowing he would have to take responsibility. In the end, I simply finished my meal and slipped out unnoticed as just another insignificant paying customer.'

'Why didn't you come to me?'

'I was ashamed. Had I externalised it, I would have made it real. I couldn't bear to acknowledge it for what it was...a warning sign. So, I simply suppressed it. It remained below the surface for years until I met Olivia Stanton.'

She squeezed his hand tightly.

'Toby, when you looked at this client, who did you see?'

'Somebody who was vulnerable. Somebody who was suffering in silence, on the verge of doing something irreversible.'

'Who did you see?' she repeated.

He turned away from her, swallowing hard in a vain attempt to hold back his emotions.

'My mother.'

She smiled at him warmly. It had taken him some time to realise that there were similarities between his mother and his client. But as many similarities as they shared, there was one key difference. He had been powerless to prevent his mother from taking her own life. He had been oblivious to her internal suffering. Yet with his client, he was fully cognisant of her anguish, and had assumed the role of her saviour. He hadn't acted, and most likely had never intended to, but he had walked a line he should never have been close to. He hadn't told Richard.

'You know I hadn't thought about that day for a long time until...'

He paused. Had he needed any further proof that Beth understood where this was leading, he need only look into her eyes.

'Good people can occasionally have poor judgement, Toby, but it doesn't make you a bad person.'

'Then why have I been going to bed on my own every night for the last few weeks?'

Beth sighed. She looked exasperated, like she was tired of trying to make the same argument that continuously fell on deaf ears.

'For somebody with your intelligence, you're really struggling to read the room.'

'I've done nothing but listen, Beth.'

'I don't doubt that. But for all the listening you may have done, you haven't heard a word.'

Toby looked hurt.

'When you chose to go to Olivia's house, I have no doubt you did so for the right reasons, but to repeat myself, that which made you such a great therapist also made you vulnerable.'

Toby flinched. Though he'd accepted psychotherapy was behind him, hearing Beth refer to his career as something of the past felt like a blow to the stomach. It made it even more real.

'That decision I could live with. The ones that followed marked the beginning of my struggle. You knowingly entered a world where every step you took led you further out of your depth. You continued to ignore those around you, and for what? Some misplaced notion you're a detective? A hero? Whilst you were chasing your past, you seemed oblivious to the fact your present and your future were crumbling around you. That Toby, *that*, is the real reason I left.'

Toby closed his eyes tightly, hoping Beth would comfort him, embrace him, reassure him that everything was going to be fine; that *they* were going to be fine. As he opened them again, he saw a sympathetic look on her face, but she had now physically withdrawn. As the silence grew, Toby became immersed in his own thoughts. He had wrestled with the guilt of prioritising both

George and Olivia over his own wife, but hearing those words pass through Beth's lips hit with greater magnitude. He was suddenly alerted to an irony that, though sat within close proximity of one another, he and Beth were currently worlds apart. Toby tried desperately to find the right words to make things better. Whilst an internal monologue raged on, this didn't translate to anything coherent outwardly, with Toby struck by a temporary aphasia. The truth was, there were no words. There was no justification, and there was no grand gesture which would undo all that had gone before them. His phone ringing provided an opportune distraction. It was Jack. He studied it for a while, but decided not to answer. His friend could wait, but his marriage couldn't. He made a movement to take hold of Beth's hand, but hesitated as his phone again rang. Noticing it was Jack for the second time in quick succession, a sudden angst gripped him. Beth's gaze oscillated between Toby and his phone.

'Perhaps you should answer that.'

'I'll get rid of him quickly. Knowing Jack, it will be something irrelevant. Maybe he needs my muscle again,' Toby joked.

Beth smiled, but it felt like his attempt at humour had been ill-judged. He seemed oblivious to Jack's persistence as he studied Beth's face, noticing the warm, inviting look it had housed previously had now disappeared.

'Toby,' she exclaimed, lowering her eyes towards his phone, which had now stopped ringing.

He felt confused. Much of Beth's hurt had come from the fact she hadn't felt he had made her a priority, but now, as he tried to save their marriage, she was urging him to prioritise his friend.

'Nothing is more important to me than you.'

'I'll still be here.'

Toby didn't have the opportunity to return Jack's call as his phone again lit up. Dread filled him as he made a move to answer it. Heading towards a quiet corner of the café, the colour suddenly drained from his face. He stared at Beth from a distance as he closed his eyes and sank to his knees in disbelief. This was supposed to be over. George was safe, Olivia was dead. Mike would soon enough have questions for Eric Stanton. Toby could channel all of his energies into his relationship. He had no capacity for anything else right now, but the opening words of the phone call had changed everything. His nightmare was far from over. In fact, it had just taken a sinister and irreversible turn. As he removed the phone from his ear, trying desperately to process what he was hearing, Toby questioned if his future had just changed direction in an instant. More importantly, he questioned whether he would ever be free of the Stantons.

CHAPTER 3

Saturday 6th May...10:30am

'It sounds like you're having a panic attack. Presently, you're experiencing both an unhealthy heart rate and a disconnect between your thoughts and feelings. What I need you to do is to draw in deep breaths through your nose, and then exhale through your mouth, slowly.'

'Toby...'

'Don't talk Jack. Listen to my voice.'

Toby could hear Jack's breathing. Soon, he would be calm enough to speak coherently, but that wasn't a moment he was relishing given how the conversation had begun. Having stepped outside, Toby gazed back through the window at Beth, who was staring attentively at him. The look of concern on her face was unmistakable. With desperation in his eyes, he placed his hand against the window, silently pleading for her support. She offered an anxious smile, but it provided little solace. Jack was in trouble, and as his closest friend, this inevitably meant Toby would be affected. But it wasn't just about him. This would have implications for Beth, as well as George.

'How you doing?'

'My sinuses are clear, but my situation is still fucked up.'

Toby couldn't help but laugh. Jack had a habit of using his humour at the most inappropriate of times. He savoured this moment, wondering how long it would be before he could smile again. A sudden and uncomfortable silence fell upon the two friends, Toby bracing himself for the inevitability of a life-altering conversation.

'I've done something terrible, Toby.'

Knowing this wasn't a moment to interject, recognising that Jack was building up to something, Toby offered no response. Jack would have undoubtedly planned this conversation, perhaps running through it several times in his head. Toby's only job right now was to listen.

'I didn't mean to kill him. I went there to give him a warning, intimidate him a little, I guess. He's walking around, unaffected by the devastation he's caused. But when he opened the door and flashed that smug grin, I lost control. From then on, I was driven by a rage I didn't realise was even inside of me.'

Realising Jack's speech was getting more frantic, Toby decided now was the time to break his silence.

'Jack, I need you to walk me through what's happened, but before you do, I want you to tell me where you are.'

There was a brief silence on the other end of the line, Jack clearly considering his next words very carefully.

'I'm currently huddled up against a tree in the middle of a field.'

'At the farm?

'At Eric Stanton's place.'

Toby felt a shiver move through his body. In the weeks that had passed since George's kidnapping, he had fought to remove any trace of Eric Stanton from his life. Beth had left, his career was over, and the client he had almost gone to prison for was dead. Physically he was struggling, emotionally he was running on empty. His mind was making a desperate attempt to piece together an alternative scenario, but all thoughts arrived back at the same place...Jack had killed Eric.

'George hasn't been the same, Toby.'

'It's been a matter of weeks. It can take several years to recover from the type of trauma she endured. Some never recover.'

'She's always gonna be like this?'

'I can't answer that. Everybody's different. The one thing I can tell you, however, is that this will still be incredibly raw for her. You also have to remember the kidnapping isn't the only ordeal she has been subjected to. It was simply the most recent.'

'You mean it brought up the past for her?'

'I think George may have gone actively looking for that past.'

'What do you mean?'

Toby swallowed hard. The words had tumbled out, and not for the first time since he had picked up the phone, Toby braced for a conversation he didn't want to have. Acknowledging he was angry with George, hit him hard. Though she was a victim, this didn't absolve her from causing harm to others through her decisions. Perhaps his real frustration was the realisation that they were more similar than he thought.

'Toby?'

'I think we have more pressing matters.'

'You mean *I* have more pressing matters.'

'If you genuinely believed that, you wouldn't have picked up the phone. What are you involved in, Jack?'

'Understand, I didn't mean for this to happen. I didn't go there intending to kill him.'

'I believe you.'

'This morning I went for a walk into the woods. George goes there a lot. She says it offers her peace.'

'But it didn't offer you the same.'

'I didn't find the answers I was searching for.'

'Perhaps you didn't ask the right questions.'

'You know, after all this time, sometimes I still don't get your logic, Toby.'

He said this with humour, but the severity of the situation didn't allow Toby to share its warmth.

'What did you find in the woods?'

'Anger. I found anger. My farm was wrecked beyond recognition and I suffered physical injuries. My relationship with George stalled before it even began...'

He hesitated before a transitory silence ensued.

Toby felt wounded, but he didn't know why. He and George had been college sweethearts, but Beth was his love, his life. Still, the very thought of Jack and George being romantically involved elicited feelings of discomfort. But this wasn't about him. His feelings played no part here. Right now, his friend was in trouble and he needed him. This was about Jack.

'Toby, I'm sorry.'

'I'm not sure what you're sorry for.'

'I know what she means to you.'

'I am a tiny part of George's history, a mere dot in the rear-view mirror.'

'Still...'

'Where did you go after the walk?'

Jack exhaled loudly. Toby could sense his frustration and knew it was because he'd shut the conversation down. He was unsure if Jack felt the need to explain his feelings for George or if, in a simpler sense, by deflecting, he was avoiding thinking about the more serious matter of murdering Eric Stanton.

'I just continued walking and found myself here.'

'Here being Eric Stanton's house?'

'Yes.'

'Considering where you live, that's some walk.'

Toby was choosing his words carefully. There were around eight miles between the two locations. He knew Jack hadn't simply ended up there. Whether it was an attempt to protect himself, or a fear of being judged by Toby, Jack was lying.

'You don't believe me.'

'Jack, you told me you went to teach him a lesson. Now you're saying you just ended up at a place several miles from your farm. You're intelligent enough to recognise the contradiction in those two statements.'

'I didn't mean to kill him,' Jack repeated.

'Of that, I have no doubt, but it's not me you're going to need to convince. What happened when you arrived at Eric's?'

'I knocked on the door hesitantly, unsure of why I was even there.'

'He presented as charming, right?'

'How do you know?'

'He doesn't know you. Part of it is his narcissism. A desire to feel validated.'

'And the other part?'

'A façade that persuades you to look in the other direction.'

'Why?'

'Because he doesn't want you to discover what's below the surface.'

'It's astonishing how someone you've never encountered before can wreak havoc in your life. How is that even possible?'

Toby fell silent. Not because he didn't have the answer, but because, in a way, Jack's situation resonated with him. He had seen that same charm upon first meeting Eric. Even in the hospital, it had only been a solitary and momentary look in his eye, which had seen the mask slip. Toby questioned whether Jack had seen the evil lurking beyond those charming eyes, or whether the attack had been too swift to reveal anything. He knew Eric had reach, but had no idea how tough he was. Jack, on the other hand, knew how to handle himself. He had gone toe to toe with Dylan Sampson and held his own, which was no easy feat. Toby felt certain that any fair fight between Jack and Eric would yield only one winner. The question then became about how far Jack would go. As Toby lowered the phone from his chin for a moment, he realised he already had his answer. This wasn't self-defence, and he was struggling to believe it wasn't premeditated, either.

'I felt this anger, this rage. It took hold of me and had complete control. It felt like I was watching myself from a distance, powerless to intervene.'

'You disassociated. It's not wholly uncommon in times of extreme trauma.'

'What does that mean?'

'It means somewhere in that moment, you became detached from yourself and the world around you. You ceased being a participant and instead became an observer.'

'But I remember it all, Toby.'

'Dissociative amnesia doesn't occur in all instances. I'm assuming you've called the police?' Toby continued.

A silence on the other end of the line left him feeling cold. This added further complexity to an already intense situation. Without realising, Jack had now put him in an untenable situation. His first call hadn't been to the police, it had been to Toby, which meant Toby now had knowledge of a murder the police were unaware of. If he couldn't convince Jack to hand himself in, he would be faced with a stark decision. Either he called the police on Jack, or he himself was implicated in the crime when the police eventually linked Jack to the scene and checked his phone records. Toby noticed he was perspiring, but it wasn't because of the temperature. As he again glanced at Beth through the café window, he was overcome with guilt, knowing he may not be able to fulfil his promise to her. The voice in his head was screaming at him to choose Beth and focus on his marriage, but he couldn't abandon Jack. He had nobody else to confide in. If Toby turned his back on him, he was on his own.

'Are you certain he's dead?' Toby finally managed, breaking the silence.

'His eyes were closed, and he wasn't moving.'

'He may have been unconscious. Did you check for a pulse?'

'I'm a farmer, not a paramedic, Toby.'

That humour again. Jack was frightened, and with the gravity of the situation unfolding, Toby couldn't judge him for that.

'I didn't check for a pulse because I was afraid.'

'Of what?'

'Not finding one.'

Toby suddenly understood. Part of Jack was in denial, but this part would cease to exist if faced with irrefutable evidence. He couldn't risk that. It would make it real.

'I should have walked away, Toby. He was on his knees. I'd proved my point. He was beaten and begging for mercy. It could have been over. It should have been over.'

'Why didn't you end it there?'

'There was a defiance in his eyes as he grinned at me through his bloody mouth. I lost control, and I hit him...hard.'

'What did you hit him with?'

'My fist.'

'Where did you hit him?'

'That doesn't matter. What matters is where he hit.'

'I don't follow.'

'His head hit the marble fireplace. Well, it came to rest there, anyway.'

'Which one is it? Did his head make contact with it while falling, or did it just end up resting on it? This is important.'

'I don't know Toby. I'm sorry.'

Toby sighed, feeling the frustration swelling inside of him. Looking up, he saw Beth leave their table and stroll toward the exit near him. He saw her worry, but suspected it would escalate if she learned about his conversation with Jack. He panicked, knowing another difficult conversation awaited him.

'Jack, I need you to listen to me. The next call you make needs to be to the police. Then call your solicitor. I promise I'll be right beside you, but simply ignoring this won't end well for you.'

'Shit Toby, what have I done? I just ran. I didn't even close the door. Just ran and left him there.'

'I don't have that answer, and you cannot control what's happened. But your actions and decisions from now...those you do control.'

'I can't go to prison.'

Toby's head instinctively dropped. Out of the corner of his eye, he noticed Beth had now exited the café and was quickly approaching him. Placing her hand on his shoulder, she addressed him with concern.

'I can't do it, Toby.'

'Jack, listen to me...'

Silence.

'Jack? Jack?'

The line was dead. Jack had hung up.

'Toby, what is it?'

He sensed apprehension in her tone, yet it was her facial expression that was far more striking. Despite the trials he had subjected her to, she showed an unwavering loyalty that he had no right to demand. Lying to her wasn't an option. He wouldn't test that loyalty any further, but Jack was in trouble and Toby couldn't simply turn his back on him. Yet he'd trodden this path before and knew how it would end if he couldn't get Beth on side.

'Toby?'

He slowly lifted his head to meet her gaze.

'Jack's in trouble.'

'What kind of trouble?'

'He may have killed somebody.'

'Jesus Christ, Toby.'

Overwhelmed by shock, Beth could only whisper those words, her face pale and her speech gone. Toby, having been measured with Jack, was now feeling the emotions of the situation making their way to the surface.

'Was it an accident?'

'Maybe. I don't know.'

'Toby!'

She was becoming angry at his cryptic responses.

'I don't think he intended to kill him, but he went there for a reason, and it wasn't to talk.'

'Him? You know who it is, don't you?'

Toby cleared his throat and began nodding slowly.

'Eric Stanton.'

'Jack killed Eric Stanton?'

'I believe so.'

'Oh my God, Toby. Where is he now? Do the police have him?'

'He was out in a field at the back of Eric's house. I tried to persuade him to contact the authorities, but he hung up. He's frightened, Beth. He wasn't thinking straight, and there was little I could do to stem the panic.'

'What next?'

She said this rather nonchalantly. Toby felt the coldness wrapped in her succinct and emotionless response.

'Do you realise the position that phone call has just put me in?' Toby paused and drew in a deep breath. 'I'm tired Beth. Emotionally, I'm tired, and I want my old life back, but this changes everything.'

'Position?'

'You don't realise the significance of that conversation.'

He had meant this as a question, but heard the words sounding more like a condescending statement.

'Jack's facing a murder charge?' Beth asked.

'That's only part of it. The first call he made shortly after the time of death wasn't to the police...it was to me, a seven-minute conversation. If he doesn't hand himself in, I only have two options. Either I turn my best friend into the police, or I get pulled into an investigation when they eventually link Jack to the scene and pull up his phone records. To save myself, I have to sacrifice Jack. How do I live with that?

Beth reached out to Toby and pulled him close, squeezing him tightly. He hadn't felt this warmth from her in a few weeks; it felt much longer. But as much as he yearned for this closeness and desperately didn't want it to end, he knew time was of the essence.

'Toby, what is it?' Beth asked as he pulled away from her embrace.

'There's a third option.'

'Toby?'

There was an apprehension in her voice, which suggested she knew whatever that third option was, she wasn't going to like it.

'I can't be the one to call the police, Beth. I just can't.'

'Then what?'

'It will look better if this comes from him.'

'Toby, he's just hung up on you. What makes you think you can convince him to turn himself in?'

'At this moment in time, Jack has nobody else in his corner. I have to save him.'

'What exactly are you saving him from?'

Toby turned his head and pondered for a moment.

'From himself.'

Beth regarded him with doubt.

'Toby, part of me wants to beg you as your wife, not to get involved, but I see that look in your eye and I know you're already gone.'

Overawed with emotion, Toby closed his eyes. It was guilt; it was remorse; it was trepidation, but mainly it was about the fact he knew she was right. Then an intrusive and unwelcome thought entered his mind. Beth noticed the worried look on his face.

'Toby, what is it?'

'Jack also has a third choice.'

She said nothing. She didn't need to. The realisation that she understood what he was alluding to was, in itself, tragic.

'Jack wouldn't. Would he?'

'He knows he can't outrun this, and when I talked to him in the past about seeing Olivia in prison, he said he'd rather die than be incarcerated.'

'Jack used the word incarcerated?' she smiled.

'I didn't want to repeat his actual words,' Toby replied.

'I'm here for you Toby, just promise me one thing.'

'Anything.'

'Don't put yourself at risk and don't shut me out.'

'That's two.'

There was vague laughter, but it was brief.

'You know I have to find him, right?'

'Be safe, Toby.'

'It's not my safety you should be concerned about.'

With a tender gesture, he kissed her forehead before turning and walking away hurriedly, unsure whether he had just spoken to his best friend for the last time.

CHAPTER 4

Saturday 6th May...20:00pm

Emerging from the shadows, Mike Thomas startled the two women, who had been completely unaware of his presence. For a moment, there was a deathly silence as Olivia Stanton and Georgina Sampson locked, each contemplating their next move. There was no mistaking the diametrically opposed demeanours, however. George looked hesitant. Her body language resembled that of a frightened child about to discover her punishment for her disobedience. This wasn't her world, Mike thought. Olivia looked composed, displaying a confident smile. He was more experienced, however, and saw it for what it was...a defiant smirk. There was no need for introductions; they knew who he was, and it hadn't taken him long to identify them. He was fairly certain behind the door through which the two women had just exited laid Eric Stanton, who had met his demise. Once that was confirmed, in any other situation, charging the two suspects in front of him would be a mere formality, but this wasn't any normal evening. The dead had risen. His mind had to grapple with the concept of someone returning from beyond the grave to exact their ultimate revenge. The night was calm; the trees were now motionless. He felt unusually relaxed, considering the chaos he was certain was about to unfold. Yet strangely, as he stared at the two women in front of him, he was immediately drawn to thoughts of Toby, a man who had risked everything to save both of them. He had lost his career for Olivia and his marriage for Georgina, yet neither of them deserved his loyalty. He had made sacrifices, and for what? Olivia was heading back to prison regardless, and there was a reasonable chance Georgina would make that same journey. Everything he had done had been in vain, and this would hit him hard. A sudden movement by Olivia freed Mike of his thoughts, bringing him back to the moment with a shudder. She had lit a cigarette and was now looking at him with a rebellious grin.

'How may we help you, officer?'

She spoke with arrogance, not respect, but it wasn't Olivia's tone that caught Mike's attention. It was the way her accomplice regarded her as the words fell from her mouth. It was a look of disbelief, of bewilderment, of disdain.

Mike peered over Olivia's shoulder, pointing at the front door.

'When I walk in there, what am I gonna find?'

'Justice and freedom.'

She said this without dropping eye contact, but more tellingly, she said it without relinquishing her smirk.

Olivia had all but confirmed his suspicions. Eric Stanton was dead. Still, he needed to enter the house, and quickly, to see whether there was any chance of revival, regardless of every fibre in his body telling him he was too late.

As Mike entered, his eyes were immediately drawn to the scarcely visible figure lying on the floor just a few feet ahead of him. Not wishing to disrupt the forensic integrity of the scene, he reached into his pocket and placed a glove on his right hand, before switching on the light. This wasn't through choice, but more necessity. The house was falling under the shadows of the eerily quiet night, and he needed to establish what he was facing. He dashed over to the man lying motionless on the floor and felt for a pulse. The extensive cut on the back of his head, coupled with the amount of blood on the rug, suggested this was a formality, not an expectation of finding any signs of life. This was confirmed as he removed his fingers from the nape of the man's neck. Though the victim was lying face down, there was no mistaking his identity, nor what had occurred. Someone had murdered Eric Stanton. He glanced outside and saw Olivia and George staring back at him. Perhaps the only logical decision they had made this evening, he thought. He had been fairly certain they wouldn't make a bid to escape. It didn't fit Olivia's persona. She hadn't escaped prison to be free from her cell. She'd escaped it to be free from her abuser, her tormentor. As Mike called in the incident, he gazed around the room. Everything looked immaculate, undisturbed. There was no sign of a struggle, but then something struck him. There was also no sign of a murder weapon. Because he didn't want to disturb the scene and was mindful of the two suspects outside, Mike restricted his own movements. He would need to wait for the forensic team to arrive before executing any detailed search. He headed for the door where Olivia was just putting out her cigarette. As he approached her, he reached into his back pocket and retrieved a pair of handcuffs.

'Olivia Stanton, I am arresting you on suspicion of the murder of Eric Stanton. You have the right to remain silent. Anything you say can and will be used against you in a court of law. You do not have to say anything, but it may harm your defence if you do not mention when questioned something which you later rely on in court. Anything you do say may be given in evidence. Do you understand your rights as they have been read to you?'

Olivia nodded. She seemed unusually calm for somebody just arrested on suspicion of murder, to add to the attempted murder charge she had already been serving a sentence for. As he looked across at George, he wasn't sure whether he saw an accomplice or a frightened woman caught up in something she had no need to be anywhere near. He wasn't sure what her link to Olivia or Eric Stanton was, but that wasn't important right now. She was a suspect. The details would come later. The sound of approaching sirens, which were getting louder with every passing moment, disturbed his thoughts. Their lights came to rest on him and the suspects. There were two police cars and an ambulance, the latter nothing more than procedure. The last time an ambulance had been to this property, Eric had been pulled from the clutches of death. This time, he wouldn't be so lucky. His time had run out. After a quick exchange with one of the officers at the scene, Mike walked Olivia over to the car, opened the back door, and placed her inside. He turned to face the second suspect, who was standing with a startled look on her face. It was clear to Mike that the adrenaline had worn off, leaving her in a state of shock.

'I didn't kill him. He was already dead when I arrived.'

'You'll get your chance to tell your side, but right now, I'd advise you to think carefully about saying anything, as it may be used against you as evidence.'

Before she could respond, Mike had placed the handcuffs over her wrist and had begun reading George her rights. As he did so, he was met with a stunned silence. Olivia had a motive. She had a history with Eric, but where did Georgina Sampson fit into this? Toby had alluded to the fact Eric had been behind her kidnapping, but there had been no evidence to support this, and George herself hadn't identified him as having any involvement. Mike had been around for long enough to know the two men currently imprisoned for the kidnapping of George had taken the fall for their paymaster. Whether through blind loyalty or fear, they had remained tight-lipped and confessed to masterminding the whole thing. Their reasoning for this had remained hazy, but Mike had known at the time they were protecting somebody. If Toby was right, that somebody was currently lying dead, having met his fate in a place which should have been safe for him. The sound of sirens broke the momentary tranquillity outside as another police car raced up the long drive and screeched to a halt just feet away from Mike. A younger officer accompanied a familiar face, somebody Mike had known for years. Sergeant Chris Wilkins was a tall, well-built man, but it was his perception and attention to detail which made him an outstanding officer. He was barely into his forties, and whilst Mike had seen the potential in him, he had never wanted to progress past his current ranking, feeling there were too many sacrifices that came with it. Mike respected this, but often felt he was wasted in his current role.

'Good evening, sir.'

'Sergeant.'

A quick exchange of pleasantries was followed by a brief, yet warm handshake. The respect between the two was palpable, but the severity of the situation meant any conversation would be concise and purposeful. Chris was the kind of person who you could easily be drawn to, but when it came to a crime scene, his demeanour drastically changed. The laid-back persona took a back seat to a more stern and meticulous individual. At a party, you wanted him on your table, but in an interview room, you wanted him elsewhere if you were a suspect.

'Sergeant, I need you to take Georgina here in for questioning.'

'Yes Sir. Anything else?'

Mike shook his head. He felt troubled by the entire scene and was still coming to terms with the fact Olivia Stanton was alive. Everything seemed to point to her faking her own death to allow her to escape from prison and murder her ex-husband, but even for somebody as cold as Olivia, she appeared far too calm for somebody who had just committed a murder. As he turned to walk back towards the house, he was approached by the two ambulancemen who had only a few minutes previously, rushed by him frantically to see if they could revive the victim. The fact they approached him slowly and without a trolley in tow confirmed what Mike had suspected since he first entered the house. Eric Stanton was dead. He was beyond revival this time. The paramedics spoke briefly to Mike, little more than confirming his victim inside the house was, of course, deceased. Forensics would be on the scene shortly, which didn't give him much time. As both cars had taken away suspects, he was now waiting for an-other uniformed officer to arrive, who was to be posted outside the front door, logging those entering and leaving the scene. It didn't take long for Mike to hear an engine approaching, as the police car came to a halt just yards in front of him. The door opened, and a young officer stepped out of the vehicle. He was PC Sam Normanton, a youthful-looking twenty-nine-year-old who had been on the force for around seven years. He cut an anx-ious figure, though this wasn't his first murder scene. He smiled tentatively at Mike, perhaps mindful of his seniority.

'I need you to position yourself outside the front door, Mike said, pointing behind him. Keep a log of everybody who comes and goes, but other than forensics and the coroner, I don't expect many others to be honest.'

'What happened here, sir?'

'Either he pissed off the wrong person, or his past caught up with him.'

'I don't understand.'

'Never mind. Just make sure nobody gets in without the rele-vant ID. Any concerns, call me.'

'Where will you be, sir?'

Mike turned and studied the front of the house for a mo-ment.

'I'll be inside trying to figure out what the hell's gone down here,' he smiled.

As Mike gazed around the room, he was mesmerised by how grand it was. Of course, this wasn't the first time he had been here, but his focus on that occasion hadn't been this room. The décor of the walls was beautifully modern, which felt strangely out of place in a building which resembled a manor house. To the left was a marble fireplace, which was architecturally eye-catching, but Mike questioned its practicality considering the size of the room. Concluding it was likely more of a showpiece than a source of heat, his focus shifted to the far end of the room. He was again overwhelmed by its enormity. There was an arch-way that opened out into what appeared to be, at first glance, a dining area. To the right was a door, but until forensics arrived, he was mindful of moving around too much. This was a crime scene, not a house viewing, and regardless of his personal feelings, he would remain respectful of the dead. He also needed to protect the forensic integrity. Not for the first time, he wondered how a man who fixed printers could afford such a grandiose place as this. Memories of his previous visit resurfaced, prompting him to delve into what they might have overlooked. They now knew Eric had been pre-warned, an act that had lost a promising young officer her career before it had had any genuine opportunity to gain traction, but Mike felt there was more to it than simply distributing drugs. His gut told him that Eric had hidden depths, ones that not even Toby was aware of, but a hunch without evidence remained just that.

The forensics arrived on the scene and immediately set to work. Their efficiency amazed Mike, but guessed they had done this many times before. A body to them was probably as commonplace as a calculator was for an accountant. They worked at pace, yet meticulously. Like a well-rehearsed exercise, they effortlessly cordoned off their places of interest. Mike approached.

'That's not a large area.'

'The absence of drag marks and the pattern of blood spatter indicate the incident likely happened here.'

'Blunt force trauma, Jim?'

Jim Matthews was familiar to Mike. When you'd worked as many murder cases as he had, you got to see the same faces. Jim was in his fifties and had been around for a long time. At gatherings, Jim had exchanged the boiler suit for a leather jacket and a ripped pair of jeans. He enjoyed the rock scene; they had spent several occasions discussing musical tastes and bands they had seen. Jim was the kind of guy who let his hair down at parties and really cut loose. Mike figured you'd probably need to have some sort of release doing a job like his day in, day out. He was married and had three children, all grown up. He'd once confided in Mike his disappointment at his youngest daughter expressing an interest in following in his footsteps. The job, he had said, was grizzly and lacked reward. Forensics didn't change the outcome, and the sight of them at any scene was never a welcome one. They dealt only in bad news and spent most of their time around people who couldn't talk back to them. Jim stared at the body of Eric Stanton and then looked back at Mike.

'Difficult to tell at this point.'

'Oh?'

Jim Matthews knelt down in front of Eric's body. He pointed to a cut on his forehead.

'This is most probably from the fall. His position is close to the fireplace, so I believe he hit his head at some stage. The blood over there supports this theory. However, he also has a deep laceration to the back of his head, which shows he was struck with force from behind. The question is, was it the blow or the fall that killed him?'

Mike didn't answer. He was distracted by the room under the archway. Instinctively he had begun moving towards it, intrigue now getting the better of him. He pushed the door open and entered what had the look of a small library. Eric Stanton wasn't the reading type. Switching on his torch, he felt suspicion creeping over him. From George Orwell to Stephen King, there was an eclectic collection here. He didn't have Olivia Stanton for the reading type either, which further aroused his doubt. A library would be in keeping with the ostentatious manner in which Eric Stanton presented himself. Nevertheless, Mike struggled to shake the niggling feeling that something was out of place here. As he moved through the darkened room, only his torch for light, he couldn't hide his admiration at the little intricacies. The décor was pristine and clearly well thought out. The books, he noticed, were alphabetised rather than sorted by genre. He estimated there must be over a thousand books in a room which didn't seem big enough to house them. Yet floor to ceiling, he was faced with literature spanning from romance novels to thrillers. Then it dawned on him. Most of them looked new. He reached into his jacket pocket, took out a pair of gloves, and put them on. Slowly, he began pulling them out at random. Each untouched, seemingly unread. Then something towards the top of the shelf caught his eye. A grey book that had no right being in its current position. Unlike the others, it looked worn, like it had seen many readers. What was a book like that doing in here? Just as Mike reached up to remove it from the shelf, the door opened.

'There's something you need to see.' It was Jim.

Mike switched off his flashlight and exited the room.

'This was well hidden.'

Jim turned the body of Eric Stanton, revealing a knife embedded deep in his chest.

'There's not much blood.'

'Sometimes with stab wounds, there is extensive internal bleeding, but the wound edges remain well approximated, which means little makes its way to the surface.'

'Does this change the cause of death?'

'Until the autopsy is performed, I wouldn't rule anything out.'

'So, what you're telling me is that it could be blunt force trauma to the head, it could be the fall onto the fireplace, or it could be a stab wound that killed him?'

Jim nodded and smiled at Mike, placing his hand on his shoulder.

'Good luck with this one.'

Mike stood for a moment, taking in the fresh evening air. It was still light and would be for perhaps another hour or so. Though the sky was clear, his thoughts remained clouded. The scene didn't quite add up. There was no sign of a struggle or even a break-in, which meant the killer may have been known to Eric Stanton. Without realising it, he may have invited his killer into the house. It was the cause of death, however, that was playing on his mind. There were three possibilities, each conceivable. The knife wound may have proved fatal, but if it hadn't, it wasn't beyond the realm of possibility it was inflicted post-mortem. This made it personal, further supporting his theory that the killer was known to the deceased. But it wasn't this that troubled him. The thought he kept returning to was how contrived this all felt. A scorned ex-wife found at a murder scene should feel like an open and shut case, but her demeanour, even for Olivia Stanton, didn't match that of a woman who had just committed a murder. Georgina Sampson, on the other hand, looked startled, frightened. Toby had alluded to the abuse she had suffered at the hands of Eric, which may have provided a motive. Even so, this didn't seem like a world she was comfortable in. She had looked nervous, making Mike sceptical about her ability to plan and carry out a murder. It was, of course, conceivable that Georgina and Olivia had been co-conspirators, but it was equally conceivable that whilst present at the murder scene, Mike was in fact looking for another suspect. A chill passed through his body, down to the base of his spine as it occurred to him that whilst he had two suspects in custody, the actual murderer may still be at large, roaming the streets he was meant to keep safe.

CHAPTER 5

Saturday 6th May...10:45am

Knowing the right place to begin was the first obstacle facing Toby. Jack would have been smart enough to have moved as far away from the scene of the crime as possible. His home, once his sanctuary, the place where he spent his days and nights as a proud farmer, would be the first place they would come knocking. That was out. This was all conjecture, but the debate as to what Jack would see as his way out of the situation raged on inside of Toby. It had been a fleeting thought, but one that had now cemented itself firmly into his thinking. Jack had switched his phone off, probably concerned his location could be tracked. They would know soon enough; it was only a matter of time. Toby pulled over into a layby and switched off the engine. He could feel his heart beating at the walls of his chest, like a caged tiger rapping at the bars to find its escape. He stepped out of the car to better control his breathing. It wasn't a panic attack at this stage, but he knew if he didn't stem it now, it certainly had the potential to escalate into one. He buried his head into his knees and remained that way at the side of the road for a good five minutes. It was quiet, not because of the time of day, but more that it was a narrow country road that attracted scenic drivers rather than those wishing to get anywhere in any sort of haste. Beautiful yet impractical is how he would describe it. Toby hadn't chosen this route deliberately; he hadn't, and still didn't, have a specific idea of where he was going. The panic subsided, making way for a welcome dose of clarity. He needed help. He needed somebody who thought like him, but who wasn't emotionally invested in the situation. He knew just the person, but debated how his call would be received.

'Hello, Toby.'

'I need your help.'

'I'm well, thank you for asking. How are you?'

Though Richard was teasing, Toby felt bad for such an abrupt opening to the conversation. He was acutely aware he only seemed to contact Richard when he needed something.

'I'm sorry. How are you?'

'No need to apologise. It takes a little more than that to offend me,' Richard replied.

'I'm worried about a friend of mine. I need to find him.'

'And you think I can help?'

'I need somebody who isn't close to the situation.'

'And that person is me?'

'You understand behaviour better than anyone I know. This is really important. Life or death, you could say.'

'I'm listening.'

'I received a call from him a short while ago. He's in trouble and he's panicking.'

'What sort of trouble?'

'It's best you don't know that.'

There was a pause on the line, and Toby could sense Richard's hesitance. Richard was good, very good, in fact. But he was also by the book. Toby was pulling on a friendship chord he hoped existed. They had worked together professionally for years, but Toby felt their relationship had developed beyond something merely professional. There was mutual respect, and when Toby had needed some perspective, Richard had been there for him without questions or judgement. He would, however, have his limits, and out of that respect, Toby wouldn't test these.

'What are you feeling?' Richard asked, catching Toby a little off guard.

'I feel like every time I get my head above water, somebody else comes along and pushes it back under.'

'That's what you're thinking. I want to understand what you're feeling.'

'My feelings aren't relevant here.'

'Why not?'

'Because I'm not the one in trouble.'

'Aren't you?' Richard asked casually, in a manner that almost felt rhetorical.

Toby paused. Richard was right. Toby was in trouble. This call was as much about him as it was about Jack. He just hadn't realised it until now.

'Tell me about your friend,' Richard said.

Toby inhaled through his nose, readying himself. He wouldn't lie to Richard, but to avoid putting him in a difficult situation, he would choose his words carefully. Richard would pick up on this undoubtedly, but he would also understand why it had to be this way, Toby hoped.

'I would trust him with my life.'

'That's about you. I want to hear about him.'

Toby smiled to himself. He genuinely missed these conversations. Richard was the one person who could challenge him without Toby feeling like it was a personal attack.

'He's always had a laid-back attitude and mostly just gone with the flow until...'

Toby broke off.

'Something happened?'

'I asked him to do something he wasn't comfortable with, and it had consequences for him. For us all.'

'Is this the reason he's gone missing?'

'Partly.'

'Toby, I understand your desire to choose your words carefully, but these cryptic responses are giving me very little, and I'm still not entirely sure what it is you feel you need from me.'

'I want you to help me get into his head so I can try to figure out where he is.'

'Have you considered he may not wish to be found?'

'I've considered he may not wish to be found *alive*.'

'Do you think he intends to take his own life?'

'It's the option I can't help but keep coming back to.'

'What are the other options?'

'I can't answer that without putting you in a difficult position. I'm sorry.'

'Do you think he would go through with it?'

Toby felt his heart skip a beat. Richard had just done what he had done many times himself during therapy. He'd made it real. It was now more than simply an internal monologue.

'He's never struck me as the type, but he's panicking, and he's desperate.'

'There isn't a type, Toby. There's simply a limit. Some people reach it, others don't.'

'But not everybody opts to take irreversible action.'

'That's because those people haven't reached their threshold, not because they're not capable,' said Richard.

Toby wondered what Jack's threshold would look like. Nobody knew Jack as he did, and he felt angry at himself that he couldn't second guess his next move.

'Where is your friend's safe place, Toby?'

Toby considered the question for a moment.

'Had you asked me that question last year, I'd have said without hesitation it was his farm.'

'But not now?'

'I think he sees it as tarnished, compromised, if you will.'

'Whether your friend is planning to end his own life, or simply retreating, it points in the same direction.'

'What do you mean?' Toby asked, feeling somewhat naïve.

'He'll be somewhere he feels safe, perhaps somewhere that has fond memories, or even a place from childhood, where he can regress and hide from his present.'

'I just need to figure out where that place is.'

'Precisely.'

There was a momentary silence on the line.

'Toby, I have one question for you. If a client were to indicate they were going to leave your practice and make an attempt on their own life, what actions would you take?'

'I'd call the police,' Toby replied without hesitation.

He knew what Richard's next question was going to be, and also knew he couldn't answer it.

'Then why haven't you done so in this instance?'

'I appreciate your time. Thank you, Richard.'

Toby hung up. He wasn't sure whether Richard had given him something new or simply re-enforced what he already knew. Regardless, he was in a race against time, with no margin for error. Jack's life depended on it.

CHAPTER 6

Saturday 6th May...14:00pm

As the stream flowed quietly, a gentle breeze passed through the branches of the tall trees, creating a rhythmic sound. Normally, the tranquillity would have induced a calmness in him, drawn a smile even. But this wasn't normal. His life would never be the same. A moment of madness, or was it a moment of clarity? He didn't regret his actions, only their consequences. And there would be consequences. George, Toby, Olivia. He had freed them all, but in removing their shackles, he had now placed them on himself. He would never again enjoy the freedoms of the past. A life without complexities where he simply floated leisurely downstream at his own pace. The future was no longer something to look forward to; his actions would haunt him for the rest of his life. As he looked around and admired the natural beauty, he wondered how long that life was going to be. Prison wasn't for him. A free-spirited individual who loved the outdoors, he couldn't think of anything worse than having his every move scrutinised, his access to daylight restricted. If he had to leave his farm, he would lose everything he had worked for over the years. His father's legacy. It was so much more to him than simply his livelihood. The fugitive's life was one of perpetual fear, a life spent anxiously scanning the surroundings, questioning whether a stranger's gaze was merely polite or a sign of recognition. Learning to live by a new identity, living a lie. He couldn't imagine living with the anxieties which would present themselves every time there was a knock at the door. The sudden panic when he was in the presence of a police officer. No, that life wasn't for him. The net would close in on him soon enough. He'd evaded authorities so far and wondered whether the body of Eric Stanton had even been discovered yet. At what point would suspicion be aroused? The alarm raised? He wasn't a professional and had likely made several mistakes which would tie him to the murder. *Murder.* The very thought of the word sent a shiver shooting down his spine. He wasn't a murderer. There had been no intent. Or had there? He hadn't felt in control at any point, almost sleepwalking his way to the front door of Eric Stanton's house. Whilst he hadn't blacked out, details of the event just a few hours previous were hazy. He remembered a scuffle, a predominantly one-sided one. However, the pain in his arm and his throbbing knee were reminders he hadn't fled unscathed. But the one thing he hadn't been able to shake was the image of his victim, motionless, face down on his living room floor. The memory was vivid and a reminder that what had happened was very real. There was no escaping it. His heart beat faster as the stark choices he was facing became clearer. Did it really feel like a choice, though? Hand himself in and spend years in the confines of a prison cell, losing everything in the process. Flee and live in daily fear of being reprimanded. Or...Again his mind settled on that third option. It was unspeakable, unthinkable, yet still, it was the one option he returned to. It would be swift, there would be no pain, and he would be free. Some would say it's a coward's way out, but those people had likely never occupied his current position. He thought for a moment about Toby, his closest friend, the one person he could always depend on. He questioned whether Toby would be disappointed in him. The thought of letting Toby down saddened him, but he'd gone well beyond that point now. Then he thought of George. The best relationship he'd never had. Thrust together in traumatic circumstances, and ripped apart by the same trauma. At a different time and under different circumstances, he felt George was somebody he could have really fallen for. The connection had been undeniable, but ultimately, they'd never stood a chance. Smiling, Jack looked up at the afternoon sky through a small clearing in the tree. It was cloudless and unspectacular, offering only a slight breeze. As he glanced around the wood, once more mesmerised by its beauty, he suddenly found the moment of clarity he'd been searching for. A sense of peace washed over him as his thoughts garnered momentum. This was his haven. This was his safe place. Nowhere else did he feel so at ease, only his thoughts for company. He was away from civilisation, away from prying eyes. They wouldn't search here, not immediately anyway. He had time. Clasping his hands together, he now knew what needed to be done. Jack Newby stood up and took one last look around the forest before setting off, walking purposefully through the fields towards his farm. It wouldn't be long before he would be back, but next time...he wouldn't be leaving.

CHAPTER 7

S aturday 6th May...15:00pm

In a darkened room, a figure sat patiently in the corner, quietly contemplating. There was no evidence of the afternoon sunshine, the drawn curtains casting a dark shadow. Time was a mere concept. There was self-reproach, a frustration at the naivety, the misplaced loyalty. Anger, however, was the dominant emotion, and it wasn't directed inwardly. It had been a risk, a costly gamble that hadn't paid off. There had been consequences, consequences which would undoubtedly have a rippling effect. As sadness pushed its way towards the surface, a small tear became visible. But there mustn't be tears of sadness. He didn't deserve them. A thought occurred. Fleeting, yet provoking. An idea. It left as hastily as it had appeared, but after a moment, it returned. And it gathered traction. This felt uncharacteristic, but these were no ordinary circumstances. Boundaries had been crossed, lines blurred, and for what? A misguided loyalty to somebody for whom deception came so naturally. They had once had a close relationship, but not anymore. It had all been based on a lie. Of course, he hadn't admitted it, but the evidence was undeniable. It was more what he hadn't said. It had taken little, and after conducting a small investigation, the initial suspicions had been confirmed. The same question played on repeat. How could justice prevail? How could each of his victims find their peace, their closure? He had evaded the authorities for so long. Suddenly, there was an overpowering feeling of frustration. How could this have gone unnoticed? Hadn't there been signs? But if you're not looking in that direction, those isolated moments of suspicion remain just that. It was easy to piece things together now, but previously, there would have been no reason to do so. That thought returned. He must be stopped. A brief glance around the room brought a feeling of sadness. There was little to show for the years of hard work. It had been a somewhat lonely existence, with the absence of anything resembling a long-term relationship, aside from Amy. She had been the one who had penetrated the barriers; the only person who had been allowed in. Their love had felt pure and there had been an optimism that it would last forever. They had shared many wonderful times together, creating cherished memories. There had been no arguments and no betrayal. Ultimately, it had been a cruel and tragic twist of fate that had torn the lovers apart. Amy had dedicated her life to helping the vulnerable, but one fateful evening, she had paid the ultimate price. Whilst volunteering, a fight had broken out between two residents at the shelter. Amy had attempted to defuse the situation, placing herself in between the men, when one had produced a knife. She hadn't been the intended target, but had died at the scene with one fatal blow. In trying to save a life, she had sacrificed her own. The memories of Amy were enough to change the mood from anger to sadness. That night had taken so much. It took a best friend, a lover, a future spouse, somebody who would have unquestionably made a wonderful parent. Amy had been fond of *him*. He had fooled her like he had fooled them all. She, a kind and trusting individual, would feel a deep sorrow at the situation. But this was no time to reminisce. There were more important matters to attend to right now. Amy had been gone a long time, and nothing would change that. There was no control in that direction, but in here there was. A wry smile appeared as thoughts of exposure surfaced. It could be swift or prolonged. Either way, his reputation and his life would be sullied beyond repair. There would be nowhere for him to hide, and it was no less than he deserved. As a small beacon of light forced its way through a hole in the curtain, what had begun as a fleeting thought had now become a plan of action. This was really going to happen, and he wouldn't even see it coming.

CHAPTER 8

S aturday 6th May...17:00pm

Toby's search was becoming more frantic with each passing moment. Composure had turned to desperation as he battled to find and save his friend. He had been trying in vain to suppress the internal voice now becoming louder, that was telling him it may already be too late. He loved Jack like a brother. There had already been too much heartache and too much trauma in the last year. To others, Toby may have appeared resilient, but inside, he was in turmoil. His world was crumbling. He had no career, his reputation was in tatters, and his marriage was on life-support. The mere thought of Beth caused his stomach to ache violently. He missed her. He needed her. There had been many moments he had wished he could turn back the hands of time. This was one of those moments. There had been several decision points where, in hindsight, he would have chosen a different path. He knew, however, that he was judging himself solely on the outcome rather than on his decision-making process. You can't necessarily control an outcome when there may be so many unconsidered variables, but you have full control over how you get to those decisions, he would frequently tell Beth. He glanced down at his watch as his progress was halted by a set of temporary traffic lights. It was just after five - rush hour. He had been searching for Jack for close to six hours, but so far, his search had been fruitless. Plagued by a sense of doom, he rapped his hands hard on the steering wheel, wincing with pain as he did so. Where was Jack? Was he still alive? Had they found Eric's body? Was he really dead? The lack of answers frustrated him. Though it all tied together, he felt like he was missing a vital piece of the jigsaw. He'd known Jack for a long time, yet had never seen this vulnerable side of him. This concerned him as he now believed he was trying to second-guess somebody he didn't really know, a stranger no less. This added further complexity to the situation. 'Think Toby,' his words breaking the now silent car.

Jack loved his farm, but wouldn't risk going home right now. He liked tranquillity, so he would be somewhere which brought him peace. Naturally, he would be away from people; he didn't want to be found. At least not yet. When they eventually found him, it would be on Jack's terms. All of this would be on Jack's terms unless Toby could find him. Professionally, Toby had spent years deliberately not talking people out of their suicidal ideation, but this would be a unique proposition. This wasn't a client with whom he lacked that personal emotional attachment. This was his best friend. This was somebody he had a deep love and fondness for. Losing him wasn't an option, but with every minute that passed by, this was becoming more of a possibility. He squeezed the brakes hard, much to the annoyance of the driver behind, who swerved around Toby, angrily gesticulating as he did so. He sat in the now motionless car, gazing out of the window. Then, in an instant, he was gone, praying his instincts and his haste would be enough to save his friend.

Nothing could have prepared Toby for the sight that greeted him. His legs didn't feel like his own as he ran desperately to reach his friend. He'd already called for an ambulance, but had convinced himself this was a mere formality rather than something that offered any hope of changing the situation. Jack lay next to a broken branch, rope around his neck.

As Toby reached him, he quickly felt for a pulse. Nothing. Carefully removing the rope, he frantically began CPR.

'Come on buddy, don't you leave me.'

The chest compressions were aggressive, reflecting his desperation. Then he tilted back Jack's head.

Still nothing.

'Don't you leave me, Jack. Do you hear me? Don't you leave me.'

And just like that, he and Jack were in their youth again. They were sitting in a bar. They were driving to the cinema. They were drinking, joking with Jack's father. It all came flooding back as Toby realised just how much his friend meant to him. The stakes had never been higher. He couldn't lose his best friend. Toby took a deep breath and repeated the chest compressions, now visibly pounding on Jack's chest. He again switched to the resuscitation, blowing purposefully into his mouth to clear his airways. Suddenly, there was a faint rasping, followed by a choking sound. Jack's immediate reaction was to panic, unsure of what was going on around him. He focused his eyes on Toby, but there was a glazed look about them. Toby wondered how long Jack's brain had been deprived of oxygen, questioning how much of his friend was left. He placed his hands on Jack's cheeks to try to get his attention. But it was more than that. Toby wanted to comfort him, offer him some reassurance it would all be okay. But would it? Jack was facing a murder charge and there were now questions of what he would look like physically and emotionally on the other side of this.

'Jack, can you hear me?'

Jack didn't reply. Though he was awake, it didn't feel like he was present.

'Nod your head if you can understand me.'

Still, Jack continued to look straight through him.

Toby hugged him tight as tears rolled down his face. He hadn't lost his friend physically, but he had no idea what version of him he would have from here on in. Holding Jack close, he heard the sound of sirens in the distance. Toby rose to his feet and waved his hands as the ambulance came to a halt at the gate of the field.

'He's breathing, but I'm not sure if he's lucid. He hasn't spoken yet. He looks confused, but I expect that's natural, considering the trauma his body has just been through.'

The paramedics quickly attended to Jack. Toby could hear them speaking, but had moved out of earshot. His heart rate rose as his legs went numb. He sat quickly, fearing his legs weren't stable enough to allow him to continue to stand. The adrenaline was now beginning to wear off; shock was setting in. The branch snapping under his weight had saved Jack's life, though it was unclear how long he had been up there before he had fallen. This wasn't Jack, this was desperation. He wondered how he could break the news to Beth. Jack was the one friend who had always

had her approval. It was about more than simply her own relationship with him. Jack was important to Toby, and that meant
he was important to Beth. She had seen Jack as hard-working
and honest and knew when Toby was with him, he was in safe
hands. A noise from above broke his concentration. A moment
passed before he recognised the escalating sound of an air ambulance. Though the paramedics were already here, getting Jack
to the top of the field would be an arduous task. The air ambulance would be his quickest route to the hospital from here. The
grass fluttered manically, like it was bracing itself for the landing.
Toby held onto his hair, which was now at the mercy of the force-
ful gust of wind sweeping down onto the field. He stepped aside
as two paramedics hastily rushed past him with a stretcher. As
they carefully manoeuvred Jack into position, Toby strained to
get a visual. There was part of him, however, that was afraid to
look, fearing the sight he may be met with. Jack was a tough character. He'd encountered and overcome a lot of adversity in his
life, but he now looked a pale shadow of the resilient individual
Toby knew. He'd never seen him look so vulnerable, so helpless.
Though he'd saved Jack's life, Toby harboured an overwhelming
feeling that he had also failed him. There was no logic behind this
feeling, but it was there, and it was becoming more intense. He
removed his phone from his jeans pocket and noticed a missed
call from Beth. He studied his phone briefly before placing it
back. Not now. Then he thought of George. Toby had already
had his suspicions there was something between her and Jack.
Or at least there had been. Hugs that had lingered, exchanges of
looks. There had been a clear chemistry between them. Jack had
confirmed the pressure of the recently shared ordeal had likely

taken its toll. Toby felt relieved. His relief, however, didn't stem from jealousy. George's revelation that she had orchestrated the kidnapping and had planned to kill Eric had rocked Toby. Much had shocked him over the last year, but nothing more so than that. It was at that moment when he had realised she had been damaged beyond repair, and the innocent girl he had fallen in love with back in college had gone forever. What he now saw was something unrecognisable, something he didn't want for Jack. Jack would be good for her, but she wouldn't be good for him. Toby's concentration was broken by the paramedic, who was now positioned in front of him. She was tall, perhaps in her late twenties. She seemed so young to be doing this job, he thought.

'Are you his next of kin?'

'No, but I'm the closest thing he has.'

She offered a reassuring smile.

'Can you tell me anything about what happened?'

Toby froze. He didn't want to relive what he had just experienced. This would inevitably come out in therapy, but for now, he needed to protect himself.

'He's my best friend,' Toby stuttered.

'He's lucky to have you. We're just trying to find out a little more about his identity and any family he may have.'

'His name is Jack. Is he going to be okay?'

'His vitals are good, but he isn't communicative. Was he unconscious when you found him?'

'He was dead when I found him.'

The paramedic placed a hand on his shoulder and looked directly into his eyes.

'Then he has your quick thinking to thank for still being alive. You saved his life.'

'Why isn't he speaking?'

'The ligature marks around his neck indicate a possible lack of oxygen to his brain. The hospital will do further tests to assess the extent of the damage, but the main thing is he's alive, and that's because of you.'

Toby recoiled, not feeling in a self-congratulatory mood. He wondered whether Jack would view things in the same way as the paramedic. He'd saved his life, but if Jack was determined to die, he may resent Toby for the unwelcome intervention. He noticed Jack had now been secured to the stretcher and was currently making his way towards the air ambulance. As the two paramedics who had earlier arrived in the ambulance walked past Toby, they each offered him a polite smile. They had done their job. They had stabilised him. Toby walked to the side of the stretcher, exercising caution not to get in the way. As they approached, the helicopter's blades swung around with ferocity. Jack, now having been placed on the stretcher, suddenly raised his hand and signalled for him to approach. Toby moved towards the door and knelt down beside Jack, who had mustered a smile. He gestured for Toby to move closer.

'You look like shit, Tobes.'

As the doors closed, Toby fell to his knees with an outpouring of emotion. He had his friend back, but his relief was short-lived. This did nothing more than buy Toby some time. Jack's situation hadn't changed. If he was still intent on escaping this world, he would find a way. There were no other options. He had to find a way to save Jack from himself.

Encased in darkness, this resting place has a secret to hide. It's cold and soulless, yet spectacular in its own right. It sits in comfort, away from prying eyes and experiences a lonely, yet tranquil, existence. You wouldn't know it existed unless you got close enough, camouflaged perfectly by its surroundings. By night, its covert nature enhances the mystery surrounding it. Once it was needed, but not anymore. Once it was revered, its use unquestionable, but alas, that use has expired. Most walked past oblivious, others noticed but didn't acknowledge. But today was different. Today somebody realised the potential. Though unintentionally uncovered, the intent had been clear. It must never be discovered. There's a secret to hide, and nobody must ever know.

CHAPTER 9

S aturday 6th May...21:00pm

'Thank God, I've been trying to call you all afternoon. Where the hell have you been?'

Toby placed the phone on his chest, pursed his lips, and looked up to the sky, tapping his fingers softly on his cheek. The emotion of the day had caught up with him. Having avoided her previous calls, he now felt ready to speak. But it was more than that. Beth was the one person he could feel vulnerable around, and vulnerable was how he was feeling.

'Toby?'

'I'm here.'

'What's going on? Have you found Jack?'

'Jack's okay...for now.'

'What does that mean?'

Toby gulped, fighting back the raw emotion, which was currently consuming him.

'He's in hospital, but it's not his physical health I'm worried about.'

'Hospital. Jesus, what happened?'

'He tried to hang himself. The branch must have snapped under his weight, but by the time I reached him, he wasn't breathing.'

Those words, spoken aloud, were too much for Toby to bear. His lips began to quiver before everything he had been thinking, everything he had been feeling, came flooding out.

'Oh Toby, no.' The only words she could manage.

'I had to give my best friend CPR. He was gone, Beth. Gone.'

'You saved his life.'

'Did I?'

'I don't understand.'

'Don't you see? I've bought us a little time, nothing more. Unless we find a way through this for Jack...'

Toby stopped

'You think he'll try again?' Beth asked.

'The branch snapping was divine intervention for us, but for him, it was an oversight. If this is what he really wants, he won't make that mistake next time.'

Toby was crestfallen.

'I don't know what to say.'

He didn't respond, instead entering deep contemplation.

'You're driving. Where are you going?'

Toby exhaled loudly but didn't answer her question.

'I don't like that silence, Toby. Please tell me you're not gonna do anything stupid.'

'I'm heading to Eric Stanton's house. I need to see for myself. I need to know what Jack's got himself into,' Toby said, bracing himself for the inevitable disapproving response from his wife. She didn't disappoint.

'Jesus Toby, you're not a fucking detective. After everything you've been through, still...still you're putting yourself into situations you have no right being near. You did your bit. You saved his life.'

'I have to help him.'

'And you can, by being a friend.'

'None of this feels like Jack. Maybe he was mistaken. He didn't check for a pulse. Perhaps Eric was just unconscious.'

'Listen to yourself. What are you going to do if you discover Eric deceased?' She sounded angry. 'You then leave traces of yourself at a crime scene. Do you need me to remind you what happened the last time you did that? How many more times do you think Mike will bail you out?'

'Bail me out?' he replied with defiance.

He felt hurt, yet surprised at the insinuation.

'Don't be so naïve, Toby. He's turned a blind eye to things that in others he simply wouldn't have ignored. At worst, he's tolerated your maverick attitude.'

'I saved Jack's life, and I found George. Don't call me a fucking maverick because I care, Beth.'

There was a silence on the line. He'd never spoken to her in this manner before and regretted the words the moment they left his mouth. He was frightened; he was hurting, and he was lost. Everything he knew had crumbled around him. Toby felt he had lost his identity and not for the first time, questioned his decisions over the last year. As he accelerated through the picturesque countryside, he heard sobbing.

'I'm sorry Beth.'

'Fuck you, Toby,' she replied before hanging up.

The cooling engine alone broke the silence of the serene countryside, where an empty car sat in what could barely be described as a layby. A solitary figure sat meditatively in the nearby field, desperately seeking guidance. It wasn't forthcoming. The night air was crisp, the spring sunshine having disappeared a short while earlier. He was close to Eric's house, but something had made him hesitate. Or perhaps someone. He'd pulled over almost immediately after Beth had hung up on him. While Toby grappled with the state of his marriage, a strong sense of nausea overcame him. Though not perfect, their relationship had been envied by many of their friends. Their household had only sporadically been subjected to raised voices, but now it had become all too familiar with them. The decision for Beth to take some time away had been intended to reduce tensions between the two. Toby now realised her absence wasn't the issue. It was his inability to give her what she wanted. She yearned for the quiet life he had sold her when they had first fallen in love. She craved the simplicity, the fun, the spontaneity. Toby sat with his knees pulled tight to his chest, pounding the ground with both of his fists, a sign of his frustration at again feeling so torn. This time between his best friend and his wife. In his mind, there was a harsh reality emerging that Beth didn't need him, but Jack did. His life was hanging in the balance and though Toby had little insight into the options available to him, the one thing he knew was he couldn't sit idly by and wait to see if Jack succeeded with his next attempt. With the wind now slowing to a gentle breeze, the branches of the trees shook gently and rhythmically. In any other situation, it would have felt cathartic, but there was no disguising his panic, nor the severity of the situation he found himself in. This wasn't about solace. It was about perspective. He hadn't stopped through desire. He had stopped through necessity. His heart rate had spiked, quite possibly suggesting that without evasive action, he was on the verge of a panic attack. He tapped his head slowly with his fingers, desperately hoping to have some sort of epiphany which would free him of this burden. How had Jack, a mild-mannered and laid-back individual, allowed himself to get drawn into a world where he was now faced with a choice between a long prison sentence or death? It made little sense. None of this did. As a tear rolled down his cheek, silently spilling onto the grass, Toby yearned for his previous life. A life where Olivia Stanton had never walked into his practice. A life where Eric Stanton and Dylan Sampson were just two names. A life where he could escape to Jack's when things got too serious, and just hang with his friend. More importantly, a life where Georgina Sampson remained in his past. He bolted upright as a moment of clarity presented itself. He blamed George. Jack had gone after Eric because of her. Maybe not directly, but she was responsible. In the aftermath of recent events, he had lost sight of the fact that George had colluded with Olivia Stanton to stage her own kidnapping. But ultimately, she hadn't wanted to frame Eric. She had wanted to kill him and had used Toby as a way of drawing him out. Then there was that moment during the rescue when she had shown a cold and vindictive side he hadn't known existed. She had been merciless in her quest for revenge. Though Toby hadn't witnessed this himself, Jack had. He still had nightmares about what might have been had he not gone back to the house and intervened. There was a strange paradox that whilst George had been a victim, she was also a perpetrator. He began to shake as the internal conflict raged on. On the one hand, he still had feelings for her. Not on a romantic level, but the feelings you have for somebody when you care deeply about them, about their welfare. Initially, when he had looked at her, he had glimpsed that teenager, but it was becoming harder to recognise that girl still existed. When he looked at George now, all he saw was a reason behind the breakdown of his marriage. Beth hadn't agreed. She laid the blame firmly on Toby and had angrily told him on more than one occasion the choices had been his to make. Those words had cut through him, mainly because deep down, he knew it was the truth. Defiance, arrogance or naivety, the decisions *had* been his to make. The genuine hurt, however, sat buried in the careful manipulation he had been subjected to, not by a client, but by somebody who he had once loved and possessed such potent feelings for. He was angry at himself for missing it. Manipulative behaviour and fabricated stories from clients during therapy sessions weren't uncommon. But George was different. Even now, he struggled to grasp the extent of the trauma she must have experienced to change her so dramatically as a person. He felt a deep sorrow that her sweet innocence had been ripped away, damaging her beyond recognition. He again wondered whether she would ever return to the girl she once was, or whether that George had gone forever. He thought about how she was precisely the type of client he would thrive on working with. But that life was gone. And just like that, he realised he and George weren't so dissimilar. They had both lost their former selves, their previous lives. They had both changed, and not through choice. He felt with a fair degree of certainty that like him, George would look in the mirror, unsure of who was staring back at her. What sat beneath the reflection? As Toby rose to his feet, he knew this was no longer about George. It was about Jack. Her life wasn't in danger, but the same couldn't be said about him. Feeling the soft grass give way under the duress of his heavy footprints, Toby hurried towards his car. His next stop wouldn't be in the picturesque countryside, though the scene would be a picture in its own right. Feeling lonely, and full of trepidation, Toby headed off towards the one place he never thought, or hoped, he would visit again.

The scene seemed all too familiar. The flashing lights and heavy police presence, but something was different this time. There was an absence of any urgency or chaos. It felt almost serene, which painted a very bleak picture. As his eyes surveyed the surroundings, they rested on a sight which sent an icy shiver into the base of his spine. He squinted in the vain hope his eyes had been deceptive, but there was no mistaking what he was seeing. Slowly making its way away from the house was a coroner's van. He wondered why the paramedics were there. Perhaps a formality? Last time, Eric, against all odds, had escaped a frenzied attack with his life intact. This time he hadn't been so lucky, but Toby wasn't mourning his death. His thoughts lay elsewhere. This now all but confirmed Jack's fears that he had indeed killed Eric Stanton during their altercation earlier in the day. Toby felt nauseous, the urge to vomit spurred on by the carnage currently taking place in the pit of his stomach. He climbed out of the car hastily, but his legs didn't feel his own as they buckled from underneath him. His fall to the ground was halted only by the door of the car. Toby could feel the colour slowly draining from his cheeks. There was no more scope for denial. This was real. The black coroner's van meandered past him at a pace which seemed respectful to its deceased passenger. Toby ran his hands through his hair as the van disappeared slowly into the distance. Still, no remorse for Eric Stanton. He suddenly felt lost in the moment, lost in the environment. Like a tiny stone in a deep ocean. Irrelevant. There was movement, conversations, but it was all passing him by. Not for the first time that day, he felt out of control. He closed his eyes for a moment, perhaps to gain some perspective, perhaps to shield himself from his surroundings. He achieved neither. As he opened them again, he could just about make out a familiar figure walking towards the bottom of the drive. Though they were friends, with Toby's recent history, he doubted Mike Thomas would take kindly to his presence at another crime scene. More importantly, having been on the wrong side of a police interview before, Toby had no inclination to repeat such an experience. He quickly climbed back into his car, started the engine, and reversed back up the road. He was now out of view, but could still see events unfolding in the distance. There was no reason for him to still be at the scene, yet he had a burning desire to stay close. Eric was dead, his body had left the scene, and Jack was safe...for now. Still, there was a reluctance for him to leave. Something was willing him to stay, but what? Lost in thought, his phone interrupted him, vibrating. He stared at it for a while before deciding to answer.

'It's bad, Beth'

'How bad?'

'Eric's dead.'

A momentary silence on the other end.

'Jesus, Toby.'

Toby moved the phone away from his ear, staring blankly ahead. The scene had a serene feel to it. There was no urgency, but why would there be? Forensics would likely be here for some time. A set of headlights moved towards him from the distance. Instinctively, he ducked his head to conceal his presence. He had nothing to hide, but he'd been here before, and it hadn't ended well for him. He had come in the vain hope of discovering a lifeline for Jack, but was leaving with a death sentence. Eric was dead and, though the police didn't know it yet, Jack was their prime suspect. He wasn't a criminal, and this wasn't his world. He would have undoubtedly left traces of himself at the scene, and it was only a matter of time before the police linked him to Eric Stanton's murder.

'Talk to me Toby,' spoke the voice on the other end of the phone.

'I'm not sure what you want me to say.'

'How the hell did Jack get caught up in this?'

'There's more than one answer to that question.'

'What do you mean?'

'He lost control, but then there were things which perhaps weren't within his control.'

'This is a little too cryptic.'

'He allowed his anger to get the better of him. That part he could control. The way Eric fell and hit his head, if that is indeed what killed him, that was just unfortunate.'

There was a pause, followed by the sound of a deep breath being drawn.

'You sound cold and detached. What happened to you, Toby?'

'This goes beyond today. Only now am I beginning to realise that Jack has been heading down this path for some time. Only now am I beginning to realise the warning signs were there. And only now am I beginning to realise that it was I who pushed him down this path.'

'What are you saying?'

'That I'm as responsible for Eric's death as Jack is. I got him involved in something he never wanted to be involved in. I didn't fire the bullet, but I put the gun in his hand and loaded the chamber.' He paused. 'Metaphorically, of course,' he clarified.

'This isn't on you, Toby. Jack's a grown man and has to take responsibility for his own actions. You deplore violence. You'd never condone murder.'

Beth was right, but it didn't stop the feeling of guilt that was rising through his body right now.

'Can I ask you a question?' she asked hesitantly.

'Sure.'

'Would you take it all back if you could? Olivia, George, that night at the house.'

Toby screwed up his eyes. She hadn't said it, and he was fairly certain she hadn't meant to imply it, but she was laying the blame for everything that had happened at his door.

'If only hindsight were foresight...'

'We'd never make a mistake,' she interrupted.

He smiled, before realising she couldn't see it. He missed this. He missed her, but there had been a lot of damage. Damage he had caused.

'The first time I met Olivia Stanton, I saw a victim. That hasn't changed, but it doesn't tell the complete story. I still don't know why I went to her house that night. I've asked myself that question on so many occasions, but could never find the answer. Or at least not the answer I was hoping for.'

'What do you mean by that?' she asked with intrigue.

'I want to believe I did it for the right reasons, but I don't even know what those right reasons would be.'

'You wanted to save her? You believed she was in danger?'

Toby thought for a moment as he looked out of his window, admiring the tranquil night with the stars taking centre stage. He fantasised about how much more beautiful this would be in other circumstances. In a world where it was still just him and Beth.

'I wish George had never walked back into my life.'

'Toby...'

'It's important you know this. George is a part of my past. An important part. That relationship helped to shape me into who I am, but I never loved her like I love you. When I saw her at the prison, I was overcome with nostalgia, but I wasn't overcome with love. I care for her and I care about what happens to her, but when I look at her, I don't get those feelings I got over twenty years ago.'

'Why are you telling me this?'

'Because Olivia and George...I did what I thought was right at the time. I never once considered it a choice between you and them. I never saw it as prioritising them over you.'

'What's next?' she asked calmly.

'I need to know what happened here. There's Jack's version, but that's going to be distorted by emotion.'

'You're not a detective.'

'Jack's life is at stake.'

'Then be the voice of reason, be the shoulder to lean on, but please Toby, don't get yourself embroiled in his fight. This isn't petty theft. It's murder.'

'If I am going to help him, I have to know what's happened.'

'Jack called you to say he'd killed Eric. Eric left the house in a body bag. What do you think happened?'

'There's an eerie feeling to all this.'

'It's a murder scene. Is that not natural?'

'I don't know. Something just doesn't feel right here. It's late, and it's dark. There's nothing I can do right now. I came here hoping Jack was wrong, but that hope quickly faded.'

'Call me tomorrow.'

'Good night, Beth.'

Toby sat quietly in his car and stared aimlessly out of the window for a moment before setting off. Eric was dead; there was little to disguise that fact. Everything pointed to Jack, but it seemed so out of character. What had driven him to such a heinous act? As the crime scene faded into the distance, Toby contemplated whether he could keep Jack out of prison. If there were any mitigating circumstances, he had to find them and find them quickly. He knew Jack would never see the inside of a prison, which meant this wasn't about saving his freedom. It was about saving his life.

CHAPTER 10

Saturday 6th May...22:30pm

Mike Thomas closed the door slowly and moved towards the desk where PC Amy Walker was already seated. She was young, ambitious, and possessed everything he admired in an officer. She could be hard, but she remained fair. He considered her trustworthy, a quality he valued even more after the Natasha Jenkins incident. She offered only a transitory smile. This wasn't a social gathering; pleasantries would have no place here. The reason for this...the woman sitting at the opposite end of the interview desk. She'd been here before, but this time was different. This time, they knew her history. Olivia Stanton was going back behind bars. She could add a prison break to the sentence she was already serving for attempted murder. The question was, would she be adding a murder charge to this? Had she succeeded this time, where she had failed the last? Had she finally got her revenge? Mike recalled Toby once telling him that Olivia was also a victim. At the time of her initial interview, neither the two officers who conducted it nor Mike were aware of Eric's abuse. He had a feeling there was more of that story to tell, and now he was dead, they would begin to see the real extent of the terror Eric

Stanton had inflicted on his victims. If Toby was right, Olivia and Georgina may only be the tip of the iceberg. Pulling out a chair from under the desk, Mike glanced over at Amy, before exchanging a look with the defendant and her solicitor. He initiated the recording function and sat back, gently tapping his pen on the desk. He cleared his throat.

'The date is 6th May 2023 and the time by my watch is ten-thirty in the evening. I am Detective Inspector 5408 Mike Thomas in the major crimes department based at Oxton police station. Present is PC 3280 Amy Walker, also based at Oxton police station.'

He looked across the desk.

'Colin Chambers, defence solicitor.'

Mike focused on Olivia.

'Can you confirm your full name, please?'

'This sounds official,' she smirked.

Mike turned his attention to Colin Chambers. He looked fresh-faced, barely out of law school, and wore a suit that was too big for his slight stature.

'Perhaps you should advise your client of the severity of the charges she is facing,' Mike said sternly.

The man leaned over and whispered into Olivia's ear.

'My name is Olivia Stanton.'

'And for the purpose of the recording, can you confirm there are no other persons present in this room other than those mentioned?'

'I confirm there are no others present.'

'Before I ask any questions, I must remind you that you do not have to say anything, but it may harm your defence if you do not mention, when questioned, something which you later rely on in court. Anything you do say may be given in evidence.'

'I have nothing to hide.'

She seemed confident, but familiar with her deception, Mike was determined to remain one step ahead of her.

'Perhaps you can begin by telling us how you ended up at the scene of a murder?'

'He's dead then.'

'You seem surprised.'

'The only surprise to me is that this didn't happen sooner.'

'Why would you say that?'

'He had a lot of enemies.'

'Like you?'

Olivia sat back in her chair. She contemplated her response, a smile gracing her lips.

'Is that a question or an insinuation?'

Mike smiled, but didn't respond.

'Enemy is such an ugly word' she continued. 'I had nothing but disdain for the man, and won't mourn him for a moment, but I wouldn't describe him as an enemy.'

'Then how would you describe him?'

'I feel answering that question would taint your already dim view of me,' she replied smugly.

'Our views on anybody sat in your chair are based solely on supporting evidence. And right now, what we have is you and Georgina Sampson, found at a murder scene. What compounds this further is the fact a senior police officer discovered you.'

'Sounds like this is an open and shut case for you.'

This was beyond confidence. It was a show of defiance. Olivia Stanton sat there with an arrogance which was testing Mike's resolve. There was an uncomfortable feeling beginning to swell inside of him, but he wasn't sure why. He'd interviewed many suspects in his time, but something was different about the woman sitting opposite him right now. Then he realised what had been troubling him. There *was* a key difference. There was something which stood her out from all the others who had gone before her. She was a ghost. She was supposed to be dead. Yet here she was without a mark on her body, baiting them.

'Perhaps you would like to begin by telling us how you managed to escape a high-security prison?'

'I thought this was about murder?'

'Or perhaps how you convinced the prison warden that you had perished in the fire? This must have taken some planning,' Mike replied, ignoring her. He knew this wasn't about her escape. That was a separate issue for another time. He was goading her in an attempt to appeal to her ego.

Colin Chambers leaned over to Olivia, whispering something in her ear. She looked at him with a smile. More of a grin, really.

'I didn't start the fire, you know.'

'But you took full advantage of it,' Mike replied quickly.

'An opportunity presented itself, and it was one I couldn't pass up. But I'm sorry to disappoint you. Whilst I went to the house to confront Eric, I'm not the one who killed him.'

'Confront?'

'To show him he wasn't impenetrable, that I could still get to him. I wanted him to know that for the rest of his life, he would be looking over his shoulder, sleeping with one eye open. That whenever he looked in the mirror, he'd see my reflection.'

'How did he take that little speech?'

'Officer, you don't appear to be listening to me. That conversation never took place,' she said politely.

Mike shook his head. Her account didn't convince him, yet part of him wondered.

'I need you to walk me through your day. And don't leave out any detail,' he said sternly.

'I arrived at the house late afternoon. I don't know it could have been four or half-past. I knew he wouldn't be in...'

'How did you get into the house?' Mike asked, curiously, not waiting for her to finish.

'He keeps a key under the bronze statue next to the front door. It's a hideous thing. I never liked it. Perhaps that's why he kept it all those years. Anyway, I was able to let myself in and replace the key so he would be none the wiser.'

Mike glanced across at Amy Walker, who was busy scribbling on her notepad.

'What happened once you were inside?'

'I headed straight for the bedroom.'

'Oh?'

A smirk lit up her face as she focused her eyes on Mike.

'Tell me, officer, what does the thought of me in the bedroom do for you?'

Mike felt a sudden unease at her attempt at seduction, but didn't allow it to show. He glanced at his colleague, more concerned with her reaction, but she was seemingly unphased.

'My thoughts are the least of your worries right now. If I were you, I would give careful consideration to answering the questions. Your solicitor here will be only too aware that your refusal to answer questions can lead to inferences.'

'It wasn't difficult, you know.'

Mike regarded her with intrigue.

'Would you care to elaborate?'

'Escaping from prison. I know you're dying to know how I managed it.'

Colin Chambers again leaned over to whisper into his client's ear, but she waved him away.

'I have no interest in your prison escape right now,' he replied, not wishing to allow her to control the conversation.

He didn't believe she was in the mood for confession. He believed she was in the mood for goading them. Mike wouldn't hand her that victory. The smirk on her face disappeared, leaving Mike wondering whether his refusal to indulge her had been a mistake. It wasn't difficult to see that Olivia Stanton was somebody who enjoyed being in control, playing to her audience. It was more than that, though. She appeared to take pleasure in lighting the match and watching as the flames developed. Mike gave a subtle nod to Amy Walker, intended as a non-verbal permission for her to take the reins.

'Olivia, you've already told us you went to the house of Mr Stanton's and laid in wait for him...'

'I don't recall saying I laid in wait for him,' Olivia interrupted.

'You deliberately went into the house when you were aware he wasn't there, intending to confront him. What would you call that?'

'I wouldn't call it lying in wait. That sounds like I went there with the sole intention of murdering him.'

'Didn't you?'

'Look, I hated that son of a bitch for everything he did. You have no idea how many victims he left in his wake. None of us do. When you find the person who actually killed him, pass on my gratitude.'

'That sounds like somebody who wanted him dead.'

'I'm glad he's dead and won't shed any tears. But that doesn't mean I killed him.'

'Why don't you walk us through what happened once you entered the house,' the female officer said with a smile, which seemed like it was genuinely trying to placate Olivia.

'Like I said. I went to the bedroom. What can I say? I was overcome with nostalgia.'

'Why the bedroom?'

Olivia looked at Amy, almost offended by the question.

'Knowing your ex-husband wouldn't be home, you go to his house to confront him. You head directly up the stairs to the farthest room from the front door, through which he will probably be entering. Why?' she continued.

Olivia looked rattled. Amy Walker wasn't finished.

'Let me phrase the question differently for you. If your intention was to confront your ex-husband, why did you feel the need to enter and remain undetected? You did everything you could to conceal your presence, right?'

'Perhaps I wanted to take a peek at his new life. You know, out of curiosity.'

'Perhaps you wanted to maintain a level of surprise.'

Olivia pushed her chair back, which made an uncomfortable screeching sound on the hard floor. She grinned but didn't respond to the insinuation. She turned to address Mike.

'There were two of us at the scene, yet only one of us had blood on our hands. Mine are clean.'

'Thankfully, we rely on evidence rather than simply the word of the accused. If your hands are clean, as you say, then you have nothing to worry about. You seem to be going to great lengths to mimic someone with something to hide, given your claims of innocence. That alone raises suspicion.'

Olivia's smile faded. If she was innocent, she was playing a game...a dangerous one. If she was guilty, inconsistencies would soon appear in her story. Both Mike and Amy knew they needed to press her. Her confident demeanour was diminishing.

'Going upstairs wasn't planned. I heard him pull up on the drive. The car appeared to screech to a halt in haste. I heard two doors slam, followed by raised voices. I quickly decided it wasn't the best time to announce my presence, and ran up the stairs and into the bedroom.'

'What happened next?' Mike asked.

'The argument spilt over into the house, but it didn't last long.'

'What do you mean by that?'

'The voices just stopped. Then there was this deathly silence, and the door closed.'

'Did you recognise the voices?' Amy asked.

'As you've probably already guessed, one was Eric's, but the other, I have no idea.'

'Were you able to decipher any of the conversation? Any detail at all you can remember?' Amy asked softly.

Mike glanced over at his colleague. She presented as incredibly confident and composed. He liked that. She was also reassuring. He struggled with Olivia and didn't have the patience that Amy did. Antagonising her would serve no purpose. He decided to take a back seat...for now.

'Through the floor, it was just a loud murmur. At the time, I didn't want to move through the fear of giving away my presence.'

'Again, I return to the question, I am struggling with the most. Why go to the house to confront Eric, yet spend your time doing everything you could to mask your presence?' Mike interrupted.

'Listen, I didn't care much for the idea of walking into the middle of a heated argument, having just broken into his home. It already seemed volatile. I didn't think a reunion at that point would be well received,' she responded with a smirk.

'I thought you said you let yourself in?'

'Whichever way you look at it, I sure as hell wasn't fucking invited,' Olivia snarled.

'At what point did you leave the bedroom and go downstairs?' Amy asked.

'I can't remember how long I was up there. The lack of any sounds or activity led me to believe they were gone, so I slipped downstairs, quietly.

'What did you see?'

'Not what, but who.'

There was an uncomfortable silence as both Mike and Amy stared intently at Olivia. If she wasn't the killer, she was about to tell them who was. Olivia glanced between the two officers and grinned.

'Georgina Sampson.'

Mike felt a surge of disappointment. They already had Georgina in custody. He'd been hoping she was about to provide a revelation, give them something which would further their investigation. They already knew George was at the scene of the murder. This proved nothing.

'Have you met Georgina Sampson before?' asked Mike.

'I'm sorry?'

'Georgina Sampson, the woman you were at the scene with. The one you have just told us you discovered downstairs. Have you met her before?'

'Why is that relevant?'

'I'm just interested to know if you've met her before.'

'I've met her a few times, but don't know her particularly well.'

'Before today, when was the last time you met with her?' Mike pressed.

'She came to visit me a couple of months or so back.'

Mike shuffled back in his chair. He turned towards Amy, who was wearing a look of confusion. She wouldn't know where this was leading, but he did. Mike gave a gentle nod of the head in her direction.

'Olivia, where was Georgina when you saw her?'

Olivia drew in a deep breath and clasped her hands together.

'She was kneeling down beside Eric. I think I startled her.'

'Did she say anything?'

'Not at first. Her eyes were wide with shock, and she looked right past me as if I wasn't there.'

'Then what?'

'I edged back towards the staircase. I wasn't sure what to think.'

Mike tapped his pen on the desk. He was also unsure what to think. Both women were at the scene; it was inevitable at least one of them had murdered Eric Stanton, but this all seemed too convenient. Olivia Stanton presented as somebody who was manipulative and would stop at nothing to get her own way. By her own admittance, she had escaped prison to track down and confront her ex-husband. Was he supposed to accept that she fled when she heard voices, then froze in terror when confronted by someone who posed no threat? He wasn't buying this narrative.

'Olivia, when I encountered you at the crime scene, you were talking calmly with Georgina Sampson. You certainly didn't look uncomfortable in her company. In fact, you looked rather friendly. Almost jovial.'

'Is there a question in there?' Colin Chambers interjected.

Mike stared at him as though he had spoken out of turn. He didn't care for him much. Truthfully, he didn't enjoy dealing with solicitors, especially the ones who worked for the defence. He found them to be pompous and deliberately obstructive. He gave a strained smile, deciding to try a different approach.

'Olivia, what were Georgina's first words to you at the scene?'

'She asked if he was dead.'

'Did that not seem like a strange question to you?' Mike asked.

'Why would it?'

'You arrived on the scene after her, right?'

'Yes.'

'So why would she ask you if he was dead when you couldn't possibly have known?'

'Perhaps she was in shock.'

'Perhaps you're lying,' Mike snapped.

Olivia's face turned stony as she regarded him with a look of disdain.

'What are you implying?'

'My interest lies more with what you are implying.'

'And what's that?'

'You plan and execute a prison escape intending to confront Eric. You break into his house and lie in wait for him. Then suddenly you have second thoughts when you hear him enter the house amid an argument, with somebody whose voice you don't recognise. Then remarkably you find your courage and head downstairs, where you happen to see Georgina Sampson standing over his body. Sometime later, you walk out of the house together, seemingly without a care in the world, whilst your husband...'

'Ex-husband,' she smirked.

Mike closed his eyes and inhaled slowly. He was too experienced to rise to her baiting, and she *was* baiting him. Yet something about her got under his skin.

'Ex-husband,' he continued. 'Whilst your ex-husband laid dead just metres away from you.'

'What do you actually have, officers? Because all I've heard so far is circumstantial. I can tell by your line of questioning that you have nothing on my client, so either charge her or we're done here.'

Mike scowled at Colin Chambers. In his mind, he reached over the desk, grabbed him by his scrawny neck, and choked some manners into him. In reality, he allowed a wry smile to form before addressing Olivia again, who was clearly revelling in her solicitor's performance.

'Olivia, was the other voice that of Georgina Sampson?'

'I don't believe so.'

'So, you're telling us there was a third person at the scene?'

'You're the detectives. All I'm telling you is that I didn't kill Eric, and I didn't recognise the other voice. Perhaps it was Georgina, I don't know, but there's something else.'

Amy looked up from the notepad she had been scribbling away on. Olivia had their attention. Mike gestured for her to continue.

'When I first met George, she revealed she carried a knife with her everywhere after he had raped her. She said if she ever saw him again...well you know.'

'Go on.'

'That she'd make sure he never had the chance to hurt her again.'

Mike and Amy studied one another for a moment. Though she'd stopped short of saying as much, the insinuation was clear. Olivia was attempting to deflect the attention from herself by presenting George as a suspect. A knock at the door broke the momentary silence, as another officer motioned for Mike to join him outside the room. After a brief conversation, Mike reappeared and asked Amy to join him, leaving Olivia looking un-comfortable, sitting forward in her chair. The confidence she had exuded had vanished. Olivia Stanton, for the first time, looked rattled. She was clearly hiding something, and they were about to find out what.

CHAPTER 11

Saturday 6th May...12pm

Dylan rapped at the door with an anger he had no intention of hiding. A fire had been lit inside of him, a fire which had raged on since the moment George had spoken of her ordeal. For her, he had kept his composure. For her, he had tolerated Toby Reynolds and his more passive methods. Despite finding George, the thought of her tormentor still being free brought a profound sense of injustice. But it ran deeper than that. He was aggrieved that Eric Stanton was still breathing. That was about to change. He'd had time to reflect and rather than that time pacifying him, it had merely allowed him to become more entrenched in his thirst for revenge. His plan had been well thought out. He would make this quick, not too quick though, as he wanted to look into Eric's eyes and watch the life slowly seep out of him. He wanted to savour the moment and make damn sure Eric knew he had fucked with the wrong person; that his mistake had ultimately cost him his life. Dylan would make sure Eric knew the name of his killer; he would afford him that courtesy. Once it was over, he would slip away and begin his new life. He didn't have friends and nobody really knew him. He could disappear with little concern. He would contact George eventually, but initially, he would need to lie low for a while. She'd understand. He was doing this for her. She would never have to look over her shoulder again. Never have to sleep with a knife under her bed. He would finally release her from the shackles she had been wearing for all these years. He banged harder at the door, his frustration at being kept waiting now boiling over. He wondered whether a place like this had security cameras. He questioned if he'd scared Eric with his erratic behaviour, regretting what now seemed like a lost opportunity. It was more than that, though. Eric would now be forewarned. If there were cameras, he would have the identity of his visitor. He could go to the police, and that would bring unwanted attention. Considering his observations of Eric, he doubted whether Eric would call the police. He tried the door. Locked. He took a few steps back and looked through the windows to see if he could see any signs of movement. Nothing. Dylan slowly made his way around the back. He wasn't sure what he was looking for and was now almost certain the house was empty, but still, there was a curiosity burning away under the surface. The first thing that struck him was how vast the garden area was. It seemed to stretch for miles. Removing a stick of chewing gum from his pocket, he wondered what secrets a place like this held. The whole area looked orderly. Then his eyes were drawn to something on the edge, just a little way down the garden. It would have been easy to overlook, but once you'd seen it, you couldn't unsee it. It looked like part of the shrubbery, blending in with its surroundings. But there were tiny reminders of the building that sat underneath. This was anything other than orderly, which in itself drew suspicion. If this was a deliberate attempt to camouflage, they had been sloppy. It didn't fit in with the persona of the rest of the garden, or the grounds in general, for that matter. It was unkempt, abandoned almost, but Dylan felt sure that was the intention. He wondered what sinister secrets lay inside and smiled at the irony that any attempt to conceal had only succeeded in drawing attention to it. Whatever was in there, Eric didn't want people to know about it, and that raised Dylan's doubt further. He slowly made his way over, fighting through the greenery that had been guarding its secret. With no obvious way in, he moved to the rear of the building. It took some work, but he finally located the door. A perfect position, he thought, with no uninvited scrutiny. Everything about this screamed detail. There was a small part of him that couldn't help but be impressed by the secretive nature of what was unfolding before his eyes. But Eric had been careless. Dylan's training had taught him to study every last detail of an environment and leave nothing to chance. He expected the unexpected, his default setting permanently switched to suspicious. The door was locked, but proved little challenge for him. After some gentle persuasion, he was in.

The first thing that grabbed his attention was how disordered it was. Though the dishevelled and neglected appearance reflected its exterior, it didn't reflect the rest of the surroundings. It didn't reflect Eric Stanton. What he knew, what he had heard of Eric, suggested he was measured and precise. This felt anything but. It felt rushed. It felt abandoned. That did nothing to quash the suspicion, which continued to rise inside of him. But what was he looking for? What did he expect to find in here? Then he realised it didn't matter. This was personal. He wouldn't be handing over anything to the police. The only thing he would be handing out now would be his own brand of justice. The man who had hurt the one person who meant more to him than any other was about to pay the price. The moment Eric Stanton had harmed George, he had put himself on death row, and now his execution date had arrived. Dylan had killed before, but had never really taken pleasure in it. It had simply been a job. This time, however, he would be sure to savour the moment. He had already established his motive. Anything found in here now would simply add to Eric's charge sheet. He was doing this for George, but he was also doing it for the other victims. He felt no remorse for ridding the streets of danger. He perused the building. It was awash with cobwebs and dirt. Over in the corner lay a crisp packet, which had faded to the point of being barely recognisable, a sign it had clearly been there for some time. He wondered when this place had last been used. Had it been simply forgotten about, or intentionally hidden? He approached the desk. There were some old newspaper clippings, but they were business-oriented. A dirty mug with the remnants of a past drink sat towards the back of the desk. That, too, looked like it had been there for quite some time. The more he explored, the more he felt this place had simply been abandoned. Finding nothing to shine a light on Eric Stanton's double life left him slightly disappointed. He wasn't sure what he was hoping or expecting to find, but this wasn't it. It was nothing more than a disused shed. As he turned to exit, he noticed a picture hung on the wall, close to the door. It hadn't been a focal point when he had first entered, but now it had his attention. It wasn't the picture itself, but something much more subtle. Something which most people would have missed, but not him. There was a key detail that drew suspicion, but only if you knew what you were looking at. The picture didn't sit flush against the wall. It was hiding something. As Dylan drew closer, he reached out and removed the picture from its hook. His instinct had been right. Facing him was the unmistakable sight of a safe. He smiled as he inspected the lock. It was a simple pin tumbler lock, which would take little time to crack. In a house this size, why have a safe in an outbuilding? The question was a simple one. The answer even more so. He had a secret to keep. As Dylan opened his bag and pulled out a small case, he wondered what he was about to find. Money? Drugs? A body part, perhaps? It didn't take long before the safe door creaked open. His eyes widened as he gained visibility of its contents. Slowly, his mind processed what he was seeing. He felt sick as an icy shiver made its way through his body. He had his answer. He'd finally met the real Eric Stanton.

CHAPTER 12

S aturday 6th May...22:30pm

George looked nervously at the clock, which now showed ten-thirty in the evening. She looked forlorn, a bundle of anxiety, who was more resembling of a victim than somebody who had just been discovered at the scene of a murder. The two officers facing her were Sergeants Carl Webb and Amanda Stone. George estimated they were perhaps both in their thirties, but looks could be deceiving. They had introduced themselves briefly, advised her of her rights, and laid out the charges she was facing. The very sound of the word murder had left her weak at the knees and feeling sick to her stomach. She wasn't alone. Next to her was the duty solicitor, who had been appointed to represent her. Catherine Hague seemed friendly enough, but George thought she looked inexperienced and rather nervous.

'Georgina, now the formalities are out of the way, would you like to begin by telling us what you were doing at a suspected murder scene this evening?'

George froze, terrified of opening her mouth for fear of incriminating herself. The confidence she had possessed just a few hours ago had now disappeared. She knew how these things worked; Toby had been very detailed about his experience in a police interview room. They subtly influence your answers to support their agenda. If she refused to answer, they would draw their own inferences. Either way, she was in for a rough ride. She wished Jack was here. Somebody strong and dependable to hold her, to protect her. She allowed her mind to wander for a moment and thought about if she and Jack had met under different circumstances. She wondered what the future would have held for them as a couple. But *he* had ruined it. She was glad he was dead, but she wouldn't tell them that.

'Georgina?'

'I didn't kill him.'

'Then help us understand who did. What were you doing at the house of the deceased?'

'I didn't intend to go there.'

The two officers exchanged a look but made no comment.

'That doesn't answer our question.'

'This morning I took a walk. Headed down to the stream at Jack's.' She paused briefly. 'That's the friend I've been staying with,' she added.

'We're familiar with Mr Newby.'

What was that supposed to mean? Why would they be familiar with Jack? Though recently a victim of crime on more than one occasion, the tone didn't portray him as such. George felt confused and realised her face was likely betraying her thoughts. The officers were staring at her expectantly.

'The next thing I knew, I was in the neighbourhood.'

'So, you expect us to believe your countryside stroll randomly led you to your alleged rapist's home, both hours and miles away?'

'It's not alleged,' she snapped. 'I know how this must sound.'

'And how is that?'

'Far-fetched,' George replied sullenly.

Carl Webb and Amanda Stone grinned simultaneously. George wondered how crazy this must sound to them.

'Do you remember the time you got to Eric Stanton's house?'

'I don't know. It was maybe around five. Could have been later, though. I didn't check.'

Amanda Stone stopped writing on her pad and looked up at George.

'So, after you randomly found yourself in the vicinity of the deceased's house, what happened next?'

They didn't believe her. Who could blame them? The story didn't even sound believable to her. She could barely convince herself. What chance did she have of convincing them?

'I took a stroll up the drive, but stayed close to the tree line.'

'Why would you do that?'

'To stay hidden.'

'I think Sergeant Webb's real question was why you went to the house initially,' Amanda Stone clarified. 'Sounds like you were there for a reason,' she added.

George placed her head in her arms and sobbed. Nothing she could say would make this better. They had already assumed her guilt and would go all out to make the evidence fit.

'Would you like a minute, Georgina?'

George slowly removed her head from her hands and looked up at the officers with tired eyes. She shook her head gently.

'Then perhaps you'd like to continue and tell us what happened when you got to the house,' Carl Webb said.

'The door was open. Not just ajar, but wide open. I stayed hidden, as I feared he was about to leave the house. But there was no movement, no sounds at all. The quietness felt eerie. Then I saw somebody emerge from the house and light up a cigarette.'

'Did you recognise that person?'

George took a deep breath and turned to her solicitor for guidance. Catherine Hague gave a cursory nod.

'Georgina, this is important. Who did you see exit the house?'

'Olivia.'

'Olivia Stanton?'

'Yes.'

The two officers scribbled away frantically.

'Can you tell us what happened next?'

'I waited until she had gone back inside. Then I walked towards the house.'

'Is Olivia Stanton known to you, Georgina?'

'I've met her a couple of times.'

'Friends?'

'I wouldn't say that.'

Carl Webb thumped his pen on the desk with enough vigour to make George jump back in her seat. He seemed frustrated. Amanda Stone glanced over at him but didn't speak.

'George, what you've told us so far is you just happened to randomly go to the house of somebody you were afraid of. You did everything you could to disguise your presence in fear of meeting that person. You state you found the silence eerie, which would further suggest you were in an anxious state. You then see somebody who you've only met briefly, somebody you wouldn't consider to being a friend, right?'

'Yes.'

The officer looked at his colleague open-mouthed, as though there was a joke only he understood. He then stared at George with a bemused look on his face.

'In that situation, why the hell would you actively choose to approach the house?'

'I don't know. Perhaps intrigue got the better of me.'

'Or perhaps that's not how it happened at all. Perhaps you were the first one on the scene.'

'That's not how it happened,' she protested.

'Or maybe this was something you planned together. Two women, spurned by the same man,' he snarled, ignoring her objection.

'No.'

'You had a common enemy, and that enemy wound up dead, Georgina.'

His voice was rising with every point he made. He had now stood up, towering over her, frustration boiling over.

'I didn't do it. I didn't fucking kill him,' George screamed, rising out of her chair to face him.

'That's quite a temper you have there,' he smiled.

If they were trying to get a response from her, they had succeeded. She felt angry, but not at them. She was angry at herself for letting them get to her. This is what Toby meant. They grind you down until you begin to doubt your own truth. Here, it was likely referred to as a police interview technique. Anywhere else, it was gaslighting.

'Is there a question in there?' Catherine Hague asked confidently. 'Because all I am hearing are accusations with no substance.'

'Your client was found at the scene of a murder scene, Miss Hague.'

'I once had the misfortune of finding myself at the scene of a bank robbery. That doesn't automatically mean I was the one wearing the balaclava and waving a gun, though, does it? What you have here is circumstantial. My client has already answered your question, so I suggest you move on.'

George smiled inwardly. She liked Catherine. Her look of inexperience was deceptive; she was tenacious, and George needed someone like her fighting her corner.

Amanda Stone cleared her throat.

'Georgina, what happened once you entered the house?'

George paused for a moment, inhaling slowly through her nose.

'She was standing over him.'

'She?'

'Olivia.'

'What did she do when she saw you?'

'She looked surprised, but strangely calm, considering. She just smiled at me.'

'Did she say anything to you?'

'Not at first. I was in shock. I thought she must be too, but looking back, she seemed...' George broke off.

'Seemed what?' Carl Webb probed.

'Content. She seemed at peace.'

'So, you walked in through the front door, which was already open. Olivia is standing over the body of her ex-husband and just smiles when she becomes aware of your presence. What happened then?'

'She said just one word...justice.'

'Justice?'

George nodded.

'She knew about his past with me. I knew about her past with him. I guess she thought he deserved everything he got.'

'Do you?'

'Do I what?'

'Feel like Eric Stanton got what he deserved?'

'You don't need to answer that,' Catherine Hague interrupted, placing her hand on George's arm. 'Her opinion on the deceased is irrelevant,' she said regarding the officers.

The tall sergeant smiled, looking down at his notes.

'She said she wished she'd done it,' George whispered.

'I'm sorry?'

George looked up at Amanda Stone and looked her directly in the eyes.

'Olivia. She said she wished she had been the one to do it.'

'Kill Eric Stanton?'

'I'm assuming that's what she meant. She despised him.'

'You seem to know a lot about somebody who you claim to have only met on a couple of occasions.'

'You don't get it, do you? Olivia sought me out a long time ago when she suspected Eric was a sexual predator. He was the only thing we talked about. When you realise your spouse is a serial offender, it's going to affect the way you think about them, the way you feel about them.'

'Enough to kill?'

'Perhaps.'

'So, what you're telling us is that there was a third person at the scene?'

George grinned. She was tired of the insinuations and she was tired of Carl Webb.

'What I'm telling you is that I wasn't the first person on the scene. What I am also telling you is that, according to Olivia, nor was she. The rest is for you to figure out.'

She was angry, but more than that, she was defiant. She was worn down and faced a choice: crumble or resist. She was done with being a victim and feeling vulnerable. Imagining Dylan, she contemplated how he'd handle things. He'd resist any attempt at manipulation or bullying in her situation. He wouldn't relinquish control, and neither would she. Confidence swelled inside of her...and then it vanished in an instant as the female officer opposite her pulled out a bag containing an object she immediately identified.

'Georgina, do you recognise this?'

They hadn't needed to ask. The moment she saw it, she knew her body language had answered the question. More importantly, they knew it. But how had it found its way into evidence?

'Georgina?'

'Yes, I recognise it.'

'For the purpose of the recording, can you please clarify what you are identifying?'

'It's a knife. It's my knife,' she added. 'Why does it have blood on?' she asked, somewhat naively.

'We were hoping you could tell us that.'

'I don't understand.'

'Then let me explain it to you,' the imposing officer said as he rose out of his seat and placed his hands on the back of his chair. 'The blood on the knife belongs to Eric Stanton. It was found deeply embedded in his torso at the scene. But do you know what's even more interesting?'

George shook her head slowly. She tried to speak, but a barely audible squeak was all she could manage. She was visibly shaking and felt nausea like nothing she'd ever experienced before. Carl Webb leaned over the desk and smiled. It felt like he was circling his prey, preparing to move in for the kill.

'There was only one set of prints we pulled off, and they belong to you.'

George met his gaze.

'I haven't seen that knife in years,' she finally managed. 'I don't understand.'

'There were no other prints found on the knife, Georgina,' Amanda Stone repeated softly.

Catherine Hague leaned over and whispered into her ear. George turned to look at her sullenly.

'I don't want a plea deal,' she shouted. 'I know how this looks, but I'm not taking the blame for something I didn't do.'

She felt angry, but more importantly, she felt abandoned. Her solicitor was supposed to have her back and now George questioned whether she actually believed in her innocence.

'The knife was for my protection. I kept it hidden in the bedroom I once shared with him. He'd already raped me once. I couldn't go through that again. But believe me when I tell you, I never used it. Until today, I'd forgotten it even existed. I left it behind the day I walked out with little more than a suitcase. I left all my memories and any reminder of him in that house.'

'Did you touch the body?'

'No.'

'Is there anything at all you can tell us about what you saw? Did you notice the knife?'

'I didn't go near him. I was freaked out just seeing him lying there. He looked limp and lifeless. I didn't stay in there long. We didn't stay in there long,' she corrected.

'How long were you inside?'

'A few minutes.'

Amanda Stone reached out and poured herself a glass of water. She looked over at George and held out the jug. George politely shook her head.

'You spent time with Olivia in the house, and you were found outside casually conversing. What did you talk about?'

'We didn't speak inside the house, really. Just what I already told you.'

'Whose idea was it to leave the house and go outside?'

'I said I needed some fresh air. I needed to understand what I'd just witn...'. She stopped.

The two officers looked at one another with intrigue before Amanda Stone spoke.

Go on.'

George looked down at the floor with a worried look on her face.

'I didn't see anything. I told you. He was already on the floor when I arrived.'

Carl Webb cleared his throat and rubbed his hand across his chin.

'Georgina, I don't need to remind you how serious this is. You're a suspect in a murder case, where if found guilty, you'll face a very long time behind bars. I'd think very carefully about where you place your loyalties here. If there's anything you're withholding, now would be the time to come clean.'

'Olivia was standing over his body. She had this smirk on her face. She was looking right through me. I feared what she was going to do next.'

'Next?'

'I thought she'd killed him, and I'd interrupted her plan. I thought she may kill me too.'

'Georgina, I'm confused. You previously stated that Olivia admitted to wishing she had killed Eric herself. Now you're telling us you believe she actually did it?'

'Maybe. I don't know.'

'When you were outside, what did you talk about?' asked Carl Webb.

'You've asked me that already, twice,' she said defiantly.

'And yet, still, you haven't provided us with a satisfactory answer,' he replied, somewhat frustratedly.

'She talked, I just listened.'

'Okay, so what did Olivia talk about?'

'She said karma had a funny way of working, and that his past finally caught up with him. Then she told me we needed to leave. That was when the officer found us.'

'If you had nothing to hide, why didn't you call the police?'

George looked down at the floor and closed her eyes momentarily. She was suddenly feeling vulnerable and struggling with reliving the ordeal. She wasn't sure whether or not they thought she was a murderer, but she was convinced they didn't believe her story. Hell, did she?

'Though I've only met her twice, I quickly established Olivia Stanton is not somebody you want to cross. At that point, I didn't know if she was a killer or not. If she was, I couldn't risk antagonising her.'

'So, you played along?'

'I'm not entirely sure what I was playing along with, officer. I simply remained quiet and allowed her to do the talking. It felt safer that way.'

Carl Webb looked irritated. It wasn't clear what he had hoped for out of this interview, but what was clear was that it wasn't this. He rose out of his chair once again, placing his hands on the table and leaning in towards George. He stared at her for a moment before sitting back down and addressing her.

'Tonight, at around eight, you were arrested at the scene of a murder. You have admitted to deliberately approaching the house, though the reasoning behind that remains unclear. You have stated Olivia Stanton was already in the house, standing over the body of the deceased as you entered. You have openly admitted there was a moment you feared for your life, as you believed she may have killed her ex-husband. But here's where I'm having trouble. There was only one weapon found at the scene; A knife, which had been plunged into the victim with force. A knife which you admit to being the owner of. A knife which contained only one set of fingerprints...yours.'

Catherine Hague leaned over to whisper in George's ear, but George waved her away in frustration, drawing a sigh from her solicitor.

'I suggest you listen to what she's saying,' he said, pointing at Catherine Hague rather aggressively. 'We're gonna take a break now. If I were you, I'd use that time productively to think about your story, as the evidence doesn't support your statement. Furthermore, I'd say with a fair degree of certainty that over at Oxton right now, neither does Olivia Stanton.'

That last part. What did he mean? Was Olivia putting this on her? She couldn't have planned it. She couldn't have known George would arrive at that moment, but perhaps an opportunity had presented itself and she wasn't for turning it down. George lowered her head into her arms and began to cry. Amanda Stone leaned over and spoke gently.

'Take this time to talk through things with your solicitor and think about whether there are any details you may have left out that could help us with the investigation. All we want to do is uncover the truth about Eric Stanton's death.'

She sounded kind and sincere. George felt reassured by her, but didn't like him. He was brash, having clearly taken a dislike to her. As the two officers paused the recording and exited, George gazed around the room. Its emptiness was almost intimidating. She wondered how many secrets a place like this had to tell, and then smiled to herself as she thought about the secrets she herself was hiding.

CHAPTER 13

Saturday 6th May...23:00pm

'What are your thoughts on Georgina Sampson?'

'She's inconsistent. There are signs of nerves, yet occasional glimpses of defiance. She's definitely hiding something, that's for sure. How are you finding Olivia Stanton?'

'She's arrogant and composed. Her story seems contrived, and so unbelievable that there is a part of me that wonders whether she is actually telling the truth, if you get what I mean.'

'Any news on the cause of death?'

Mike hesitated before answering. Something was telling him the evidence was going to support Olivia's story, and that frustrated him. *She* frustrated him. There was a smugness he didn't appreciate, and whilst she was going back to prison, there were too many coincidences for her to be entirely innocent. Bad things seemed to happen where Olivia Stanton was involved.

'Not yet,' he replied, pensively.

'Georgina owned up to the knife being hers, but I don't know.'

'You're not convinced she was the one who used it?'

'The prints are hers, but I watched her body language when we questioned her. Either she's a very compelling liar, or...'

'Or she's telling the truth,' Mike interrupted.

'That then leaves us with a third option.'

'There was a third person at the scene at some point. The real killer. I suppose the key question is did Georgina Sampson and Olivia Stanton stumble upon the aftermath of the crime, interrupt it, or carry it out?'

Mike fell silent for a moment, deep in contemplation.

'There's something else.'

'What's that, sir?'

'At the scene, Jim Matthews said something, and its relevance has only just dawned on me.'

'What did he say?' Amanda Stone asked.

'He said the cause of death could be the stab wound, the fall, or blunt force trauma.'

'I don't follow.'

'Only two of those can be explained. The knife was embedded in him, the cut on his head and the position of his body support the theory of a fall, but the blunt force trauma...' He tailed off, trying to make sense of it.'

'Sir?'

'There was no weapon found at the scene. Why would you conceal that, yet leave a knife in clear view?'

'Maybe somebody wanted us to think that Eric Stanton was stabbed to death?'

Mike removed the phone from his ear. This was all beginning to make sense now.

'Why would Georgina Sampson stab Eric to death, and then leave the weapon with her prints for us to find?'

'Perhaps she panicked?'

'Perhaps she isn't the killer. I think you have it right. Who knew that the knife belonged to Georgina? Who had access to the house? Who had a vendetta against the deceased, and had failed on a previous attempt?'

'Olivia.'

Mike closed his eyes and thought for a moment.

'I think we need to get a better understanding of the relationship between these two women. Something's off here. Olivia seems to implicate Georgina to us, but I can't figure out whether that's down to an animosity she holds towards her, or if she is simply diverting the attention away from herself. Either way, I think we need to press both of them hard on that relationship. I'll be making an application for ninety-six hours of remand to allow us time to get to the bottom of this. Something just doesn't feel right.'

Mike ended the call and prepared to walk back into the interview room. The uneasy feeling he'd had remained, and regardless of his position, he still felt he was about to, once again, enter the lion's den.

CHAPTER 14

Saturday 6th May...13:00pm

The chaos of the room reflected his mood as Dylan smashed his way through the outbuilding. Though disorganised previously, it was now unrecognisable as the fury inside him overspilled. He spared nothing and his message was clear. *I know what you've done, and I'm coming for you.* Kicking the door open, leaving it hanging from the hinges, he made no attempt to mask the mess he'd left in his wake. Hell, he'd just made the police's job easier, but they would never get to Eric. Not before he would, anyway. With no idea of when he would return home, and in no mood to wait, Dylan set off to seek his own justice. Whilst he didn't know Eric's whereabouts or indeed anything about his movements, he thought there were a couple of people who might. A couple of people who he would like to get reacquainted with. There would be no reminiscing, however, and the meeting would be anything but cordial. He would stay on foot, which, whilst adding time to his journey, would mean he was less likely to be detected. He felt a vibration in his pocket and looked down at his phone. It was George, but he had no time for distractions. His aim was clear. He was doing this for her, for all of them. He placed the phone back into his pocket, allowing his answering machine to do his bidding for him, and sauntered down the long drive, being careful to stick to the tree line. Towards the bottom, he would climb the small fence into the field adjacent, and pick up the road further down. He wasn't afraid of the police, but he couldn't finish what he'd started if he was in custody. He was already known to Toby's friend in the police, and a man of his stature wouldn't be hard to identify. He was angry, but in control, and that control was vital. The afternoon was bright, the only sounds being those of nature. There was a calmness about the conditions, but that wasn't replicated internally. Under the composed exterior raged a burning desire to rid the streets of a man who wouldn't be missed. He'd raped George, but not content with that, had orchestrated her vicious kidnapping, happily placing her in the hands of two men who he could only describe as the dregs of society. Two men who saw her simply as a plaything, a pay cheque. They had paid for their part in this. Their suffering would have been much more had it not been for the interference of Toby Reynolds. But Eric was a different matter. He had so far eluded Dylan, though his time was running out. It would be painful and prolonged. Eric Stanton would know the identity of his killer. He would know the stakes he was playing for. He would pay the ultimate price for his crimes. Eric Stanton's reign of terror was ending; he just didn't know it yet. As the road at the bottom of the drive came into view, Dylan scaled the fence and entered the field, being mindful not to catch any of his clothing in the process. It would be his last act in this town. Once it was over, he could never return. This would be his parting gift to George. The death of her tormentor would allow her to once again sleep comfortably and no longer live her life in fear. The field was dry and seemed to go on forever. The longer he remained in there and away from the road, the more inconspicuous he would be. It was difficult for him to blend in, as his size meant he, all too often, stood out. He would need to be smart and remain irrelevant. As he made his way slowly through the freshly cut grass, he could see a farmhouse in the distance. He immediately thought of Jack. They hadn't spoken since that eventful evening. He respected Jack and deemed him a worthy adversary. He was glad they'd ended up on the same side and still felt a little bad that Jack got pulled into this. His livelihood, his home, and his very existence had all been compromised. He knew from snippets of information George had disclosed that Jack had really struggled since the events that took place that night. Dylan didn't have friends, and aside from George, he didn't form relationships. Nevertheless, there had been a temptation for him to reach out to Jack, though that temptation had passed relatively quickly. He paused for a moment and thought back to the last time he had killed a man. He hadn't used his weapon. The man had instead died by his hands. He'd taken no pleasure in it, but when the man had attacked him from behind and put a gun to his head, it had left Dylan with little choice. He didn't believe in guns and had only used his when forced into it. He lived by the mantra that real men use their fists and don't require weapons. His willingness to regularly voice that belief was another reason his commanding officers appeared less than disappointed when he was ultimately discharged. There was camaraderie. In fact, that was probably the last time he allowed people to get close to him. But now he operated alone, and that was just the way he liked it. Above all else, it allowed him to fly under the radar as he remained largely insignificant to people. A gentle breeze made its way through the trees. The sound of the leaves brought Dylan back into the present. Without realising it, he had almost approached the end of the field. Turning sharply to his right, he followed a path, only scarcely recognisable through the grass cuttings. It was early afternoon, but the road seemed quiet. He wondered how many people had taken advantage of a warm weekend and headed away for a family break. As he approached the end of the path, he saw a small gate. A public footpath. Perfect, he thought. He wouldn't have to cut through a hedge or a bush after all. Before he knew it, he was walking down the road, blending in as just another civilian. He saw a bench and walked towards it. As he sat for a moment, he contemplated his next move. His time of irrelevance was coming to an end. He would soon be watching over his shoulder. His next move would see him announce himself; there would be nowhere to hide after that. He took a deep breath and removed a mint from his jacket pocket. Deep in thought, he slowly got to his feet and walked away. His next stop was the hospital, but this was a visit the patient wouldn't welcome.

Dylan stood at the entrance, admiring the grandiose appearance of the hospital. A little cloak and dagger detective work had given him the information he required. 'A private room', he said to himself. 'I guess he's pretty messed up,' he added, grinning. Sporting a dark jacket, jeans, and a baseball cap, he strolled leisurely towards the entrance. The rucksack on his back was the only thing that would make the journey home with him. The rest of his attire comprised recent charity shop additions, paid for with cash to ensure there was no paper trail. Even his shoes were cast off by somebody who had decided to upgrade their footwear at the sight of a mere scuff on the side. He now found himself in the awkward position of having to remain insignificant and unremarkable in the hospital to all, aside from one person. He wouldn't see it coming; he wasn't expecting this visit. Dylan had envisioned this moment many times in his mind, with thoughts of choking, severe beatings, and even dismemberment, but these were all fantasies. The reality was he was here for information. He would undoubtedly dish out a little punishment, but he couldn't lose focus. As much as he despised the man he was about to pay a visit to, this was a mere sideshow. Eric Stanton was the actual target, and he would stop at nothing to get him. Making his way through the doors, he immediately moved towards the staircase. He found the quietness appealing and hated the confined space of a lift. It gave people time to stare, or worse still, to make small talk. The room he was looking for was on the third floor, which meant he wouldn't have far to venture when he made his hasty retreat. The fact the staircase was relatively close to the entrance was an unintentional benefit for him. Gently pushing open the swing doors, he headed for the main unit. It was a key card system. Only staff members could gain entry without having to announce themselves. He turned to see a cleaning cupboard open in the distance, with a trolley blocking the entrance. He walked casually towards the cupboard, keeping his head down. The cleaner peered out and smiled at Dylan. He was an older man, perhaps in his late fifties, with a large tattoo on his forearm.

'Can I help you?' he asked politely.

'I appear to be a little lost,' Dylan replied rather coyly.

'Where are you supposed to be?'

Dylan thought quickly.

'I'm meeting a friend in the café,' he replied.

'You're on the wrong floor. It's on floor five. I'm heading up there now if you want me to show you?'

Dylan smiled.

'Perfect.'

As the two men walked towards the lift, Dylan was studying his key card, which was currently sitting in the man's top pocket. As the lift arrived, Dylan positioned himself on the man's left, closest to his pocket.

'Would you mind?' he asked, pointing to the lift buttons.

As the man turned to press the button for floor five, Dylan quickly knocked a container, which he assumed to be housing some kind of cleaning fluid, onto the floor. The man instinctively dropped to the floor to pick it up, which gave Dylan the opportunity he needed.

'My apologies,' he said, crouching beside the man. 'Let me get that for you.'

The elevator came to a halt, and the door opened.

'It's just over there,' the man said, pointing the way to the café.

'Thank you. I'm a little early, so I'm just gonna make a quick call. Sorry again for my clumsiness.'

'It didn't smash, that's the main thing,' the man smiled.

Dylan pulled out his phone and held it to his ear as he watched the man disappear down the corridor. Once out of view, he hurried to the stairwell and descended the stairs back to the third floor. It wouldn't be long before the cleaner noticed he was missing his ID. Maybe he'd put things together, maybe he wouldn't. Either way, Dylan didn't want to hang around. The longer he was in here, the more likely something was to go wrong. He moved swiftly, but in such a way as not to draw attention to himself. Once again entering the third-floor corridor, he slowed down as he approached the door which led to the ward. Having waited for a quiet moment, he slid the ID out of his pocket and held it to the keypad. The door clicked open. He was in. He looked for room three. It was towards the bottom of the ward. Shit. He would have a longer distance to the exit than he would have liked. A nurse walked by. He smiled at her politely. It was visiting hours, which meant the ward was busy. He would use that to his advantage. He opened the door to the room, being careful not to be seen. The occupant was asleep. That was a stroke of luck. He wouldn't be able to raise the alarm. Dylan walked over to the bed and pulled out his knife, cutting the alarm cord. He then placed a hand over the man's mouth, who awoke with a muffled scream. With his free hand, Dylan reached for the IV drip.

'Have you heard of an air embolism?'

'The man shook his head slowly, still attempting, unsuccessfully, to cry for help.

'The contents of this pouch are running into your veins. If I detach this and squeeze, air bubbles are gonna form, and that's not good news for you. Do you know why?'

The man had now given up trying to scream. Dylan had his attention.

'Air bubbles will block your veins or arteries, preventing blood from passing through. If they travel to your heart, that's a heart attack. If they travel to your lungs, that's respiratory failure. They may opt for the brain. That's a stroke,' he grinned.

Dylan removed his hand, confident he'd done enough to scare his target into silence.

'The moment you unhook that machine, the alarms will sound.'

'Maybe,' Dylan replied, reaching into his rucksack and pulling out an object wrapped in cloth. 'Do you know what this is?'

'A knife.'

'It's not just a knife. It's a Japanese Deba knife. Do you know what these are used for?'

The man didn't answer. A look of terror had spread across his face.

'Gutting fish. They're extremely sharp. They would make very light work of say a finger, a toe. Perhaps even an ear,' Dylan continued.

His face broke into a grin, his eyes taking on a crazed look. The man in the hospital bed lay catatonic. He had no option other than to comply.

Dylan removed his hat.

What little colour the patient had in his face drained quickly as he recognised who was facing him.

'I can see you recognise me,' Dylan snarled. 'I'm here for information. Give it to me, and I may spare your life. Fuck with me, and I'll end it.'

'What makes you think I have the information you need?'

'Your life depends on it.'

The man glanced towards the alarm button.

'Disconnected,' Dylan gloated, holding up the cut wire. 'Where do I find Eric Stanton?'

'Who?'

Dylan lurched forward and, with one solitary action, grabbed the patient's wrist and twisting. As he did so, he placed his hand once again over the man's mouth to silence the involuntary scream rising from the pain. Dylan let go and stepped away.

'Let's try that again. The guy who paid you to kidnap my sister. How do I find him?'

'I can give you his address.'

'He's not home, and I don't have the patience to wait.'

'There's this pub he sometimes goes to. It's out of town. You could try there.'

'What does he have over you that you'd risk your life and your liberty for?'

The man looked puzzled.

'It was just a job. It was nothing personal. It never is. He pays well, but there's something else.'

'What's that?'

'He's a powerful man. He has contacts. He's not somebody to be messed with. Once you're in, there's no getting out.'

'He's a rapist. You know that, don't you?'

The man closed his eyes for a moment.

'That was never my scene. I tried to stop Carl at the abandoned house that night. Told him that's not what we signed up for. Listen, I may be a lot of things, but I'm not a rapist.'

'What else do you know about him?'

The man turned his head and stared blankly at the wall. Dylan moved closer, grabbing his chin and forcing his head to turn and look him in the eye.

'Whatever you fear Eric Stanton will do to you, I guarantee I will do significantly worse. I can hurt people in ways you couldn't imagine were possible. He doesn't have a choice in that matter, but you do. I'd think very carefully about your allegiance to him if I were you. What else did you see?'

The man drew several shallow breaths.

'There were others.'

'How many were there?'

'I don't know. I swear I didn't know at the time. I was just a fucking chauffeur.'

'You took women to him?'

Dylan felt a sudden anger rise through his body. This piece of shit in front of him had taken women to be abused.

'Answer me,' he roared, pressing his fist deep into the ribcage of the man, who grimaced in pain.

'I swear I didn't know what he was doing. That's not my thing, I told you.'

'You were paid to take women against their will to his house. What did you think was happening? Afternoon tea, you fucking idiot.'

'You don't understand. They went there willingly. I just transported them. You see, he has this image. Like I said, he's a powerful man.'

'When did you first find out?'

The man swallowed hard.

'When did you first find out?' Dylan repeated angrily, grabbing the man by his throat. It was only the sound of choking which made him relinquish his grip.

'I took the girls to the house, but I never picked them up. I never really questioned that. But one day, I was driving by when a woman whom I recognised ran down the driveway and right in front of my car. I nearly hit her. She turned to face me as I slammed on the brakes. Her clothes were ripped, but it wasn't that. I saw the look in her eye. I'd heard one or two things but hadn't wanted to believe it. But after I saw her, I knew.'

'But you continued taking women to him?'

'I had no choice. As I said, once he has you, he won't let go.'

'You son of a bitch,' Dylan snapped, seizing the man by the face and squeezing. He grabbed his bag and retrieved a roll of tape, placing a strip over the mouth of the patient laying helpless. He then calmly pulled down the bedcovers and applied a sharp pressure to the leg that was in a brace. The scream was inaudible because of the tape over the man's mouth. He reached for his knife as the individual laid at his mercy, becoming more frantic by the second. A sadistic grin twisted his lips as he made an incision above the kneecap. He then waved the knife slowly in front of his victim's face, taunting him with the threat of further torture.

'Nobody can hear your screams,' Dylan goaded. 'This is for every woman you served up to him, you sick bastard.'

Dylan struck the man hard on the bridge of his nose. The loud crack was the only sound heard as he was knocked unconscious. Blood quickly covered his face and began dripping onto his bed sheets. He would need reconstructive surgery and some stitches in his knee, but he'd survive. Dylan tapped him on the face as a final insult, and slowly edged out of the room.

He quickened his pace toward the door, aware that the alarms would soon sound and he'd need to be off hospital grounds by then. Making his way down the staircase and out of the main entrance, he experienced a wave of frustration. He hadn't got what he came for, but he'd had his suspicions confirmed. Twenty minutes later, he was back in the countryside. Dylan found a bench and sat on it for a moment, quietly pondering. Reaching into his pocket, he pulled out his phone and scrolled through the gallery, highlighting several images. He placed it face down for a moment as he considered what he was about to do. There would be consequences, and it would reunite him with somebody he wasn't overly fond of. Yet it needed to be done. The list of people he could tolerate could be counted on one hand. Those he trusted reduced that number further. He regathered his phone and forced a tentative smile as he thought long and hard about the chain of events he was about to trigger. His reluctance wasn't regarding the consequences, though. It was the fact he liked to do things alone, and he was inviting somebody else into the equation. But this was something he couldn't do on his own. It would require an element of investigative work he simply didn't have the patience for. His methods had their place, but they were flawed. He needed a more measured perspective, and there was only one person he knew of who could offer that. Looking down at the multitude of images on his phone, he screwed his eyes up tight and hit send.

CHAPTER 15

Sunday 7th May...9:45am

'So, your phone does still work then?'

'Dylan?'

Toby was caught off guard. A Sunday morning call from Dylan Sampson was the last thing he had expected.

'Dylan, what is it?'

'Eric Stanton. I went to his house, but he wasn't there. I looked around and that's when I found it.'

'Found what?'

'His secret hideout.'

'When did you go to his house?'

'Yesterday afternoon. Why?'

'Eric is dead. He was found at his home yesterday. The police are treating it as murder.'

Toby had no inclination to disclose all he knew about the case to Dylan. He didn't trust him, and in the short time he had known him, had come to realise he wasn't somebody he was comfortable being around.

'He's dead?'

'You sound disappointed.'

'I am. I wanted to be the one who put the nail in his coffin. I wanted to have a front-row seat as the life drained out of his body. Not just for George, but for the others, too.'

'Others?'

'The images I sent you.'

Toby felt a shiver pass through his body. He hadn't seen any images and something told him he didn't want to.

'Hold on.'

He removed the phone from his ear and scrolled through with haste. He saw an unopened message from an unknown number. The number he now knew to be Dylan's. A terrifying premonition washed over him as he steeled himself for a sight so unforgettable, it would be forever etched in his mind.

'Dylan, what am I looking at?'

'A sick fucker who got what he deserved.'

'Are these...Are these?' he repeated.

'Women in their underwear, from what I can make out.'

'Where did you find them?'

'There's an outbuilding. It looked suspicious, so I decided to take a look around. These were hidden in a safe behind a picture on the wall.'

'Suspicious?'

'The grounds and the house seemed well looked after. The bits I could see, anyway. But this place. It was a mess. It didn't fit in at all. Like it was deliberately trying to stay hidden. A few more weeks and that likely would have been the case. It was close to being camouflaged by the surrounding shrubbery.'

'Did you see anything else?'

'No, the house was locked.'

Toby froze. This made little sense.

'Locked?'

'Yes.'

'Are you absolutely certain it was locked?'

'I tried the door. It wasn't shifting. Why?'

'No reason. I'm just trying to put a time frame together. What time did you leave?'

'After one.'

Toby felt a silent relief as a realisation dawned on him. Jack hadn't killed Eric Stanton. The timeline didn't match up. Jack's altercation with him had been in the morning. He had admitted to fleeing the house, leaving the door wide open. When Dylan entered the premises later that day, the door had been locked. Eric's body wasn't found until later that evening. None of this made sense, but from the complexities rose some clarity...neither Jack nor Dylan had killed Eric.

'Toby, what are you thinking?'

'Why me?'

'Why you what?'

'Why did you send those images to me? Why not the police?'

'You're smart, and you know my feelings towards the police. They simply get in the way.'

'That gives me only a superficial answer. What exactly are you hoping to get from me?'

Dylan breathed in loudly.

'The fact that the son of a bitch is dead changes everything, yet nothing. It's evidence this runs deeper than any of us thought.'

'Could these possibly be trophies from past affairs that he hid from his wife?

'No,' Dylan replied assertively.

'You sound sure.'

'Let's just say I paid a visit to one of his associates yesterday and found out more than I'd bargained for.'

Toby didn't reply. Though he'd only known Dylan a short time, reading between the lines, he knew exactly what paid a visit meant.

'I'm assuming he didn't volunteer any information.'

'What makes you say that?' Dylan replied in a transparent manner.

Toby, already feeling uncomfortable with the direction of the call, chose not to engage Dylan any further in that line of questioning. He knew Dylan had beaten the information out of somebody. He wasn't averse to instigating conflict, and on the rare occasions trouble found him, was equally willing to engage. Toby had come close to being on the receiving end of Dylan's temper, and had it not been for Jack, it would have been a very different story. Not that he disliked him. He just wasn't the type of person Toby would usually associate with. It was fair to say they didn't operate in the same social circles.

'Who did you go to see?' Toby asked.

'Who it was doesn't matter. It's what he told me that's important.'

Toby had questions, but nothing he wanted to hear the answer to. Dylan had contacted him for a reason, and that reason was about to be revealed.

'He said he used to drive women up to Eric Stanton's place. Apparently, he never questioned it, aside from one time.'

'He saw something his mind wasn't able to refute, but I suspect he knew all along.'

'What makes you say that?'

'Call it a hunch.'

It wasn't a hunch. It was his experience. His strength was he knew people, and he knew behaviour.

'He denied it, but a little gentle persuasion soon got him singing.'

'Something really got to you during that conversation. What was it?'

'I knew he was lying.'

'You weren't angry with him.'

'People used to pay you for this wisdom?' Dylan asked sarcastically.

'People paid me for several things. Wisdom wasn't one of them.'

'You know Toby, I can't figure you out. You seem smart, but you're not at all streetwise.'

'Something tells me right now you don't need streetwise.'

Dylan laughed down heartily, but Toby didn't feel its authenticity.

'What did he tell you?'

'This one time, he nearly hit a girl in his car. She ran straight out in front of him. He recognised her as somebody he had recently taken to Eric's house. The most important thing is that she recognised him. The state of her attire and the expression in

her eyes told him the story he claimed he hadn't wanted to believe.'

'You're angry because he had a chance to stop this and turned
a blind eye?'

'Aren't you? My sister risked her life to take that asshole off
the street, to make it a safer place for women. This piece of shit
coward knew it was happening and said nothing. Worse still, he
continued to take women to that place, knowing what was going
to happen to them. He's worse than Eric Stanton.'

'What did you do to him?'

The question appeared to catch Dylan off guard.

'There's going to be a warrant out for my arrest soon enough.
It's only a matter of time before the hospital releases CCTV
footage with my image heading into the ward.'

Toby took a deep breath as a thought occurred.

'Did you wear gloves?'

'At the hospital? Yes, but that doesn't matter.

'The hospital isn't my concern, Dylan.'

'What do you mean?'

'You've admitted to ransacking Eric Stanton's property. So,
you were searching for something or somebody. If you left the
place in a state, it would imply anger was a key driver. Later the
same day, Eric Stanton was found dead. If your prints are at the
scene, the assault in the hospital may be the least of your worries.'

'Fuck! How could I have been so careless?'

'Where are you now?'

'Keeping a low profile.'

Toby knew he may regret what was about to come out of his mouth. He was still wary of Dylan, but he had played an integral role in George's rescue, and he felt indebted to him for that.

'I'm heading home now. Meet me there.'

'Why would you help me?'

'Because I know how it feels to be a prime suspect in a crime you didn't commit.'

'How do you know I didn't kill Eric Stanton?'

'I'm smart, remember?'

'I'm counting on it. See you in about half an hour,' Dylan replied before hanging up the phone.

As Toby neared home, he thought about the last year of his life, and how much things had changed. This wasn't an isolated occurrence. Every time he returned home to an empty house, he was reminded of what he'd lost. Beth was still at Lara's, no closer to returning. It was times like these when he realised how insular his life had been, and just how much he and Beth had done together. He didn't have an overflowing social life. Quite the contrary, really. He had been happy with him and Beth living in their own little bubble, only occasionally stepping out to dip their toes in the outside world. But Olivia Stanton had changed all that; had changed him. His evenings were spent alone. Days merged into one another, and weekends painfully highlighted the gaps in his life. He hadn't acclimatised. Not because he couldn't, but because acclimatising meant accepting the situation for what it was. It was that which he struggled with most. Consciously, he refused to see this as anything more than temporary, but with the magnitude of some of the feelings he was exhibiting, he questioned whether there was an unconscious part of him that felt somewhat differently. A part more accepting of reality. A part that didn't live a charmed life embedded deep in the bosom of denial. Toby had realised on the journey home that helping Dylan allowed him to fill a void in his life. He didn't like injustice, but that wasn't the main reason he had agreed to help. He'd lost his identity, his purpose. He was struggling to find himself and was desperately seeking a way to once again feel relevant. It wasn't psychotherapy, but there were similarities. Beth was right. He wasn't a detective, but being involved in locating and rescuing George had ignited something inside of him. Something which had burned brightly and powerfully ever since. He hadn't known it then, but it had been the first time since turning his back on his profession that he'd felt like he had a purpose. He'd felt alive. But that had come at a cost. Beth had called it an addiction. She believed he had no control over resisting the urge to get involved. She had said it wasn't a life she could lead. Toby had since concluded this had always been inside of him. A somewhat insular existence had, at some point, spawned a need for excitement. Psychotherapy had never completely fulfilled him. Beth had struggled with that, questioning whether she had ever really known the real Toby, and whether their entire relationship had been based upon a misconception of who she had married. That one statement had been a hammer blow to him. Emotionally, it had reaped cataclysmic consequences for him. If there was one truth in his life, it was his love for Beth. Above all else, that had been his constant. She had been his constant. She had been his purpose. She had been his sole focus, and he resented her for suggesting otherwise. As he made the obligatory turn onto his road, as always, he did so in brief hope that Beth's car would be sitting outside the house. Once again, an empty drive met him, causing disappointment. The disappointment was fleeting, however, as something caught his attention. The bin had been moved and the gate at the side of the house was ajar. Subtle enough to go unnoticed by most, but Toby was well-versed in studying minor details. It was one of the things that had made him such a successful therapist. A skill which had also played a crucial role in finding George at the farm that night. Toby brought the car to a stop and sat quietly, engine idling. There could be several explanations, but a surge of trepidation had made its way through his body. He considered calling Mike, but worried about wasting his time. It was likely nothing, but he couldn't shake the feeling of dread that was now consuming him. Switching the engine off, Toby made his way tentatively towards the front door, looking over his shoulder as he did so. Turning the key, he made his way in, making sure to close the door swiftly behind him in case anybody was lurking in the background. Once inside, he relaxed a little, but still felt something wasn't quite right. He made his way into the lounge and looked out of the window. Out of the corner of his eye, he saw something move. He squinted to get a closer look. As he did so, he suddenly heard a set of footsteps approaching from behind. He turned just in time to feel the full force of a blow to the side of his cheek. Wincing in pain, he stumbled backwards. The man grabbed him by the throat and threw him down onto the chair.

'Who are you? What do you want?' he whispered, putting his hands up to defend himself.

The assailant remained silent, instead picking Toby up off the chair and throwing him down onto the floor. Toby felt a crack in his arm and wondered if it was broken. He wasn't a fighter and was fairly certain there would be no reasoning with his attacker. He was on his own. He was in trouble. He held his hands up, in a desperate bid to show he was submitting, and provided no threat. But the man's fist struck again, this time on the side of the head. Toby let out a shriek as he was overcome with pain. The attacker grabbed his head and prepared to land what would inevitably be a devastating blow. A knock at the door offered a temporary reprieve as the intruder was distracted. Toby saw his opportunity to scream for help. It was the only thing that could save him. This was a personal attack; the intruder was here for a reason and it wasn't about his possessions.

'Toby?'

'Help me,' Toby shouted, feeling disorientated.

He hoped he'd done enough to raise the alarm and stop the assault. Suddenly, the door flung open with ferocity. The intruder looked up in surprise as Dylan hurtled towards him with a look in his eye which clearly suggested he was in no mood for any sort of conversation. He let go of Toby just in time to feel a blow to the head. Toby, who was crouched down, gathering his thoughts, didn't see it, but he heard it...and he heard the resulting scream. Dylan had now lifted the man back to his feet by his hair and had his hand around his throat. Only a horrifying, choking gasp, as the trespasser struggled for air, could be heard. Dylan could easily kill him, and would likely think nothing of it. The attack wasn't Toby's primary concern. It was the reason behind it which worried him. Since Beth had left, he had been close to becoming a recluse. He could think of no reason anybody would want to harm him. Eric was dead; this was over. But still...something didn't fit. He needed answers, and he certainly wouldn't get them from a corpse.

'Dylan, stop!' he exclaimed.

Dylan turned to Toby, involuntarily releasing his grip. His momentary hesitation gave the assailant the opening to shove him, causing him to lose his balance, before fleeing through the front door. Dylan, regaining his composure, sprinted after him, but the man's athleticism allowed him to get away with relative ease. Dylan briskly jogged back to the house, disappointment and anger clearly etched on his face.

'What the hell was that all about?' he asked Toby angrily.

'I was afraid you were going to kill him. I think he was too.'

'He was supposed to. How else was I gonna get him to talk? Did it look to you like he would be a willing participant in any line of questioning?'

Toby walked over to Dylan and placed his hand on his shoulder, smiling.

'I'm really glad to see you.'

Dylan looked at him, stony-faced.

'You're welcome.'

This was as close to a heart-warming moment as you were likely to get with Dylan. There was only one person Toby had seen him drop the mask for, and that was George. He used the term mask because he felt much of Dylan's anger came from pain and fear, and questioned whether there was a frightened individual perched beneath the bravado. He'd clearly been hurt. Despite that, Toby was very wary of him, and placating him was always at the forefront of his mind. As he'd just shown, Dylan was a very useful ally. However, he would make a formidable enemy, and it would be a grave mistake to cross him. Toby had instantly seen that Dylan was driven by emotions, not logic. He couldn't argue that his approach had played a role in George's rescue, however, he couldn't help but feel that had he not reined Dylan in, the outcome may have been very different. He paused for a moment, wondering whether he was judging Dylan harshly, considering the impulsiveness he showed with Olivia Stanton. Although he'd convinced himself his decision was rational, replaying that night revealed otherwise. Emotion had led him. Beth knew. He hadn't realised it at the time, but she knew, and that's why she had struggled so much with this.

'Wanna tell me what's going on?' Dylan asked.

Toby shrugged his shoulders.

'I came home, walked into the house and suddenly he was on me. I knew something wasn't right when I pulled up, but I managed to convince myself otherwise.'

'You seem to have a habit of pissing people off.'

He said this with a sly smile, but it did little to reassure Toby that a full interrogation wasn't coming.

'I'm not somebody who makes enemies.'

'Eric? Olivia?'

'Both are deceased.'

'Olivia Stanton is dead?'

'She perished in a fire at the prison.'

'They'll be reunited in hell,' Dylan said, grinning.

Toby didn't reply. He was once again immersed in his own thoughts. The only two people who had made threats towards him were now dead. An icy shiver passed through his body as he contemplated when this would end for him. It should have been over. Eric was dead. Olivia was dead. George was safe. He was responsible for saving the kidnappers from the clutches of an out-of-control Dylan. What would anybody want with him?

'Why me?'

'You think this was personal?'

'It's the middle of the day and nothing was taken. When I came home, he had the chance to flee but instead chose to attack me. He only fled when you arrived. Nothing about this seems random. This was a targeted attack. But the what is the simple part. The why is what I'm having difficulty understanding right now.'

'We could have found that out, had you not interrupted me.'

Toby forced an uneasy smile. He was reluctant to dance this dance with Dylan; it would serve no benefit. He needed him on his side, but it was more than that. He felt a gratitude for his timing. He wasn't sure what his attacker had wanted, but it would have undoubtedly been much worse for him had Dylan not arrived when he did. As he gazed out of the window with a blank look on his face, Toby realised whatever this was, it wasn't over. Somebody out there had a score to settle with him, and Dylan wouldn't always be around to protect him. Just like that, he found himself positioned in a situation he had wanted to avoid at all costs, but this time he wasn't just battling to save somebody else's life. He was also battling to save his own.

CHAPTER 16

Sunday 7th May...12:15pm

After Dylan's departure, Toby's reluctance to remain in the house alone became apparent. He didn't want company. He needed some thinking time, but he felt the need to be surrounded by people. Historically, the natural choice would have been the coffee house, but ever since he had been ensnared by Eric, Toby had struggled to return there. Meeting Mike had been the exception, and simply because he felt safe with him. He had since stumbled upon a quaint café a little further out, where the staff were friendly and the coffee aromatic. The twenty-minute drive would provide the opportunity for quiet deliberation. As he drove, Toby thought about Olivia. He thought about her last moments and wondered whether she had suffered. His thoughts then rested with Tyler, who was such a sweet boy, now orphaned. None of this was his fault, yet he was about to endure indescribable pain. Toby knew the trauma would stay with him for many years. Sadly, he was old enough to remember. Some would believe Tyler was better off without parents like Olivia and Eric Stanton, but he differed from this view. Olivia had admitted Eric was a good father, and she herself had lived for her son. Toby could differentiate between the Stantons as people and the Stantons as parents. He'd stared into their eyes, engaged with each of them on more than one occasion. They were vengeful and narcissistic to a degree, but they weren't sociopathic. He was convinced their love for their son had been genuine, and Tyler hadn't been a mere pawn in a game to mask their real identities. Though it would be easy for somebody on the periphery to come to that conclusion. As he pulled up outside the cafe, he noticed it was a little busier than usual. Joining the back of a queue he wasn't accustomed to seeing, Toby scanned the room to look for a vacant table. The ambient setting, with the low set music, meant there was little appeal in purchasing a coffee to consume in the confines of his car. Besides, he really liked it here, and this setting was just what he needed right now. After a few minutes, he found himself at the front of the queue and soon searching for a place to enjoy his freshly prepared beverage. Then something caught his eye. Not something, but someone. There was a look of familiarity about her, but Toby couldn't place the face. As their eyes connected, it appeared that she, too, was struggling to make the connection, like two long-lost acquaintances verifying if they had the right person. She was slim, attractive, perhaps in her thirties, but Toby couldn't be sure. As perceptive as he was, estimating ages had never been his forte, and after one particularly uncomfortable incident, he had resolved to never get dragged into such an awkward situation again. Finally, he recognised the face, but as he did so, his smile disappeared. He turned to walk away but managed only a couple of steps before he was stopped in his tracks.

'Toby, right? Toby Reynolds.'

He turned slowly back to face her.

'Natasha?'

'Would you like to join me?' she asked hesitantly.

'I should be going, but thank you anyway,' he replied.

'I know what you think of me.'

Toby, having turned to walk away, paused before turning back to face Natasha.

'And what's that?' he replied.

'You see a disgraced former police officer who defended a criminal.'

Toby remained expressionless and wondered whether his initial refusal of a seat had caused offence. He smiled, pulled out the chair opposite, and sat down, wondering what kind of conversation he was about to get into.

'Tell me, would that bother you?' he asked.

'If it's not justified.'

He pondered his next words.

'I'm sorry for your loss, Natasha.'

'Many people have said that to me, but I wonder how many people actually mean it.'

'What makes you say that?'

'I know what some people thought of my brother. If I thought the same about a person, I certainly wouldn't be sorry they were dead.'

'I wonder if the phrase is more about a show of empathy?'

'Is that what you're doing?'

Toby hesitated as he thought about the potential consequences of his reply. That hesitation gave Natasha her answer.

'It's okay. I know you and him weren't exactly friends.'

Toby didn't respond. He was wary about where the conversation may lead and had little trust in people at the moment.

'That looks painful,' she said, noticing the bruise on the side of his face.

Toby instinctively put his hand to his cheek, like somebody who was trying to hide evidence of a vicious attack from an abusive partner.

'I sound like a police officer, right?' she smiled.

'Do you miss it?'

'Every day.'

Toby stared at her for a moment.

'Did you always want to be a police officer?'

'I used to work in the victim support field. It grew from there, really.'

She halted.

'I'm deeply regretful of what happened, you know.'

'Regretful or remorseful?' Toby asked.

'Is there a difference?'

'Regret is a phrase often used when people are caught out. They regret the outcome, not necessarily the action. Remorse is more than just regret. It's a sadness over the hurt you've caused another.'

'Can it be both?'

'I'm sorry, I sound like a psychotherapist,' he grinned, not answering her question.

'Can I ask you something?'

Toby nodded.

'How did Olivia manage to drag you into her web of deceit?'

'Natasha, I'm unable to talk about clients, past or present.'

'That confidentiality expires upon death. You're safe.'

'Actually, that's not correct. A therapist still has a duty of care to honour the wishes of their client even after death.'

'I thought you said you were no longer a therapist?'

'That was something you inferred, but you are correct. I am no longer practising. Even so, I'd rather not talk about past clients publicly, whether they're alive or not.'

'I didn't mean to make you feel uncomfortable,' Natasha said apologetically.

'You didn't.'

She flashed him a rather awkward smile. Toby wasn't sure why this was difficult. She hadn't been involved in any of Eric's misdemeanours. She hadn't made threats or orchestrated a kidnapping. She wasn't a serial rapist. But she had defended him, and ultimately it had cost Natasha Jenkins her career. Blind loyalty, or naivety, it all added up to the same thing. Yet, he was in no position to judge anybody for being naïve. He had been taken in by a Stanton, also costing him his career. As the thought of their similarities passed through his mind, he suddenly felt sorry for her. She, like him, had made a judgement call and paid dearly for it. As he stared at her, he noticed how different she looked. There was a natural beauty to her he hadn't consciously acknowledged the first time they had met. Her hair was a little darker now, which she wore down. She looked elegant.

'It's remorse, by the way.'

'I'm sorry?' Toby asked, feeling embarrassed by his moment of distraction.

'You asked me if I was remorseful or regretful. I was just saying it's remorse. You know, when I found out yesterday at teatime, I didn't know what to feel. He was my brother, but all those things he's accused of. All those years, he held a dark secret. We all lived a lie. Looking back, I doubt that I ever really knew him,' she continued.

Toby considered his response as he gazed directly into Natasha's eyes.

'I wonder if it's possible to ever really know somebody.'

'Are you speaking from a personal or professional perspective?' she teased.

'As a therapist, I could only ever work with what was presented to me. If clients chose to lie, that was on them.'

She leaned forward, placing both hands around her cup.

'Do you miss it?' she smiled, returning his earlier question.

'Perhaps not in the same way you miss the police,' he replied diplomatically.

'Your job must have been fascinating. I can imagine you worked with some really interesting people.'

'Everybody's interesting in their own right.'

'Can therapists tell when somebody is lying?'

Toby smiled. This was a common misconception when it came to the perception of the profession, though he'd had more training on the subject of body language than most of his peers. His discomfort at discussing the topic stemmed from a fear that people would become overly self-conscious and act strangely around him. There was a certain irony in the fact that trying so deliberately to act naturally could look wholly unnatural.

'Sometimes it's more about knowing when to look rather than where to look.'

She looked at him blankly.

'If you have reason to believe somebody is being disingenuous, you'll begin to look for inconsistencies.'

'So, you allow them to talk and wait for the contradictions?'

'Not necessarily. Sometimes it's about what's not being said. That's where body language becomes a factor.'

'It sounds complicated.'

Toby took a sip of his coffee. He was feeling more relaxed. There was something quite alluring about her, and he found himself intrigued.

'Why did you change your name?' he asked, moving the conversation on.

'Excuse me?'

'I was just interested why you dropped the family name. I'm sorry, I didn't mean to offend you.'

She smiled as she began rubbing her thumb on her cheek gently. He couldn't be sure, but Toby thought she was flirting with him.

'Why does any woman change her name? I got married. We had a great marriage for ten years, but separated just before Christmas. It's still pretty raw.'

'I'm sorry.'

'Don't be,' she replied, waving his apology away.

'Can I ask you something?'

'Sure,' Toby said, feeling a little anxious as to where this might be leading.

'Do you believe all of those things they are saying about my brother?'

'Do you?' he deflected.

'When I told him about the search, I just figured he'd got himself caught up in something and had a stash of illicit drugs. Nothing heavy. Good people make bad decisions, right?'

Toby didn't externalise what he was thinking. Eric Stanton's criminal background wasn't public knowledge. Anything she had heard could have come from a variety of sources. He needed to tread carefully, as he didn't wish to either upset her or disclose something he shouldn't. Currently, he knew more than he should. More than the police. He needed time to piece things together, and that would inevitably mean remaining guarded.

'You said you feel remorseful over your actions. What prompted the change after you risked your career for him?'

'As I said, I started to hear whispers about other stuff. It made me question whether I'd made a grave error in judgement.'

'Other stuff?' Toby asked, feigning ignorance.

She took a deep breath and swept her hair away from her eyes. 'The rape.'

Toby swallowed hard, but was more concerned with Natasha's body language. She had closed up. Like she was protecting herself. A small tear had made its way down her face. She looked anxious. She looked vulnerable. He had his answer.

'Things that resonate with you are always the hardest to ignore.'

'What's that supposed to mean?' she asked defensively.'

He leaned in closer to her.

'Discovering your brother was responsible for inflicting the very pain on others that you yourself had been subjected to must have been awful.'

He stopped.

'How did you know?' she stuttered.

Toby smiled warmly at her. He felt truly sorry for what she'd endured. It also echoed with him on a personal level, due to what George had suffered. He ignored the question and change direction. When most people realise you observe their body language, they tend to shut down through fear of what you may uncover. He didn't want that here.

'Natasha, I'm sorry for what you've been through. What you're feeling right now...'

'Right now, I'm enjoying a nice coffee in good company. Let's just leave it at that,' she interrupted. 'I haven't seen you in here before. Is this a fortuitous find, or a planned escape?'

'Definitely the former,' Toby replied, laughing. 'I took a drive one day and stumbled upon it. They did enough to persuade me to return, but it isn't local for me. I used to visit the coffee house until...'

'Until what?'

'Let's just say the place brings up one or two unwanted memories for me.'

'Oh. That's a shame.'

'Actually, the last time I was in there was with Mike Thomas.'

Toby watched as her smile faded. It contained a mixture of regret and disappointment.

'I miss him, you know. He was a good boss. Our last conversation wasn't so pleasant for me, but he did what he had to do. I'd have done the same in his position. I never held it against him.'

'How's your wife?' she added.

Toby bowed his head and breathed out loudly enough for her to notice this wasn't a conversation he wanted to get into right now.

'I'm sorry, I didn't mean to pry.'

'It's fine,' he said, waving away her apology. 'She's staying with her sister for a while.'

'A holiday?'

'More of a separation,' Toby replied before realising how uncomfortable Natasha looked.

An awkward silence ensued, with both of the table's occupants reaching for their respective drinks. Toby sat back in his chair and began looking around the café. The décor was warm and inviting; the pictures were apt, probably quite typical for a coffee shop. But it had a real charm to it, and it was that charm that had drawn Toby in the very first time he had been here. He placed his cup down on the table and flashed her a lingering smile. She had been kind enough to offer him a seat, and yet on more than one occasion during their brief conversation, he had made her feel uncomfortable.

'People tell me I never stopped being a therapist,' Toby said, breaking the silence.

'As in you're always wanting to help others?'

'More the way I interact with people.'

'Is there a certain way therapists speak?'

'It's more of a style. I ask a lot of questions.'

'So, you're nosey?' she teased.

She ran her hand through her hair. She *was* flirting with him, although he couldn't be sure of whether or not she was consciously aware of it.

'Would you excuse me for a moment?'

'Sure.'

Toby pulled out his chair, stood up, and made his way across the floor to the toilet. He didn't require a comfort break, but he needed some time to reflect. Speaking with Natasha had evoked some strange sensations in him, causing him to need some time alone with his thoughts. He washed his face with cold water and stared into the mirror. He wondered whether he was simply a safe person for Natasha who he imagined was feeling incredibly vulnerable and alone right now. Did she see him as a therapist? Client attachments to him, though rare, weren't unheard of. He took a deep breath and pushed open the bathroom door. As he walked back towards the table, he noticed it was empty. He felt a tinge of disappointment but didn't know why. As he approached, he saw the cup Natasha had been drinking from planted down on a napkin. There was something written on it.

'Thanks for the company. See you soon? Natasha.'

There was a phone number written underneath. Toby sat down and finished the rest of his coffee, all the while staring at the napkin in front of him. A strange feeling overcame him as he sat, reflecting on their conversation. She had disclosed little, but yet had given away so much. She was a fascinating person, some-what closed-off, yet carrying a heavy burden of past and current trauma that Toby understood could have serious consequences. He wasn't her therapist though, and there was no hiding the fact she was not only Eric's sister, she had also helped him to evade the police. He would proceed with caution. Toby placed his cup back down on the table and stared long and hard at the napkin before placing it in his pocket and exiting the café.

CHAPTER 17

Sunday 7th May...14:00pm

The incoming call interrupted the loud music which had been reverberating around the car. Toby loved nothing more than listening to his favourite soundtracks, though wasn't known for playing music at an anti-social level. The events of the past few hours, however, had left him distracted. Firstly, somebody had attacked him in his own home for reasons unbeknown to him. But strangely, this wasn't what was occupying his mind. He had only met Natasha Jenkins twice, yet the last hour in her company had left him feeling uncomfortable for more than one reason. Her allure had undeniably captivated him. He hadn't felt this the first time he had laid eyes on her, but the circumstances were very different back then. It was more formal; she was at his house in an official capacity. He had Beth. Thinking about his relationship with Beth in the past tense was like a dagger through his heart, but the reality was he didn't know what, if anything, remained of his marriage. She'd left the family home, with no sign of when, or indeed if, she would return. He pressed to answer the call.

'Did you get a chance to look at the images?'

It was Dylan. There was an air of disappointment. Not because of who it was, but because of who it wasn't.

'Sorry, I got a little tied up.'

'Jesus Toby, what's more important than this?'

He sounded frustrated. Toby wondered what his interest was in Eric Stanton's past. He was dead, so it wasn't about retribution. Dylan didn't strike Toby as a compassionate person who wanted closure for the victims, either. So, why was he so keen for Toby to see the images taken at Eric's outbuilding? It wasn't a question he could ask directly, as Dylan would almost certainly interpret it as an interrogation, which would do nothing other than antagonise him. It wasn't simply that Dylan had already come to his rescue that day. It was also about the powerful enemy he would undeniably make should Toby venture to his wrong side. When you combined his size with his state of mind and volatile behaviour, you got something you really didn't want to cross. He walked a line, and Toby had known from the first time they had met that it would take very little for him to deviate from that line and lose control.

'I bumped into Natasha Jenkins and we got talking.'

'The bent cop?'

'Eric's sister.'

'I hope you passed on my condolences,' he said sarcastically.

'She didn't really mention him.'

'Would you? She's probably glad he's dead, like the rest of us.'

'I'm almost certain she was still in shock.'

'I'd have been out celebrating. I can't think there are many people mourning his passing.'

Toby didn't respond.

'Listen, Dylan, I have to ask...It sounds like there's something in these images which has really unsettled you. What is it?'

'You're supposed to be the smart one. I suggest you take another look,' Dylan replied firmly.

Toby pulled over into a layby and cut the engine. Picking up his phone, he scrolled to Dylan's message and opened the media content. There were sixteen pictures in total. As he began flicking through, his body froze, accompanied by an intense feeling of nausea. He didn't have the urge to be sick, yet had been sickened to the core by what he was seeing.

'Dylan. What am I looking at?' he said slowly, scepticism now in full swing.

'Go to the twelfth image.'

Toby flicked through the images until he got to where he needed to be. He studied it intently.

'Jesus Christ.'

'Now, do you understand why I was so keen for you to see these?'

'Eric's in the photo,' Toby said. 'The angle, the position, the lack of any pose, suggests he didn't set a timer.'

'So, who took it?' Dylan asked.

'He had an accomplice? That means...'

'It didn't end with Eric Stanton.'

'This isn't over.'

'That son of a bitch at the hospital kept that little detail from me, but he won't make that mistake again.'

'You can't go back there. The police will already be involved,' Toby said, in a vain attempt to appease Dylan's anger.

'He'll keep his mouth shut.'

'He has nothing to gain by keeping quiet. Security will be intensified. You've effectively made him untouchable.'

As the words came tumbling out, Toby feared they may have sounded accusatory. Whilst that wasn't the way he had intended it, it was an accurate reflection of what he was thinking. Dylan had messed up, and this was one of the reasons Toby didn't like his methods. It was reckless and ill-thought-out. Dylan had ensured that the one person who could have shed some light on Eric's accomplice was now out of reach for the foreseeable future. That meant he was free to continue his reign of terror.

'What do we do now?'

'Call Mike Thomas. Let the police handle it.'

'Bullshit Toby. They have nothing to go on. You know as well as I do that even if he's found, there's little to no evidence against him. The defence will sleepwalk him out of any charge.'

Toby sighed. Not because he was angry or even upset, but because he knew Dylan was right. There was insufficient evidence for anything to stick. Toby also knew Dylan was going to pursue this, with or without him. He didn't need Dylan, but though he didn't realise it, Dylan needed him. Toby was the voice of reason that had prevented him from facing a murder charge. A man with a temper and no patience could be dangerous, given the wrong set of circumstances. But controlled, he could be a real asset.

'Talk me through what you found.'

'That building is deceptively big inside.'

'Is that where it happened, do you think?'

'No, it's not that big, but it's bigger than it looks from the outside,' Dylan replied.

'What did you find inside?'

'At first, nothing. But as I was about to leave, I noticed this picture that didn't hang right. It seemed to be in an obscure place and wasn't flush against the wall. When I looked behind it, I discovered the safe. It didn't take long to crack open. That's when I found the pictures.'

'Were they time stamped?'

'Why is that important?'

'It gives us a time frame, which may help us locate some of the victims. One of them may be able to identify the second person.'

'That sounds more fucked up each time you say it.'

Toby found himself agreeing with his unlikely ally. When this had all begun, it had done so as an isolated incident. Now, it had escalated into something that involved meticulous planning and more than one perpetrator. The behaviour had evolved. George had described something which appeared almost impulsive. Now, what they were witnessing was something premeditated. Something designed with cruelty in mind, in some sick and twisted quest for control.

'They're time-stamped,' Dylan finally answered.

'I need to see the building,' Toby said tentatively.

'The police will be crawling all over it.'

'Do you have the photographs in your possession?'

'Yes. I didn't want the police to find them.'

This wasn't a humble gesture on Dylan's part to protect Eric from the law. He simply didn't want them involved. He wanted to dish out his own justice, and Toby was convinced prison would have been the better option for Eric had he been faced with that choice.

'Okay. I need some time to process all this. I'll call you tomorrow.'

Toby was about to hang up when Dylan sent him a stern warning, a stark reminder of who Toby was dealing with.

'Don't go calling your police buddy. I'm a loose cannon, remember?'

Frozen in place, Toby questioned Dylan's awareness of his past reference. While not explicitly threatening, it was as close to a threat as it could be. He was testing Toby's loyalties. He had difficulty trusting people and was clearly still sceptical. Toby believed Dylan only tolerated him because of George. But then she was the common ground between them. He and Dylan would never be friends or even acquaintances in any other situation. They simply wouldn't operate in the same social circles. George was the thread holding them together, and he felt pretty sure Dylan also realised this.

'Did you find anything else?' Toby asked, before realising he was continuing a conversation he was now desperately seeking an exit from.

'Like what?'

'Serial rapists like to keep mementos. It can be arousing for them to reflect on the moment they had total control over a victim.'

'I saw nothing.'

'Then it's in the house.'

'How sure are you?'

'He went to the trouble of installing and hiding a safe in an outbuilding where he hid photographs of his victims. That tells us he wanted to keep reminders of his accomplishments. This was about massaging his ego. We also know that the building isn't big enough for the incidents to have taken place in. The police have searched his house previously and didn't find anything remotely suspicious. And yet the man in the hospital admitted to driving women up there. None of this adds up.'

'Eric's hiding something.'

'Whatever it is, the police weren't looking in that direction,' Toby added

'It's a murder scene. The police are going to be crawling all over it. What are you suggesting we do?'

'I'm not suggesting anything. I'm simply stating that however deep this runs, the answers are contained somewhere in that house,' Toby clarified.

'Are you sure?'

'I'm certain.'

Toby fell silent for a moment.

'What are you thinking?' Dylan asked.

Toby looked down at his phone and began scrolling through the images.

'All these images show the background in detail. It's the same background in every image. In fact, it's the same angle. Precisely the same angle. Shit. It's precisely the same angle,' he repeated slowly.

'What does that mean?'

Toby didn't answer as he sat deep in thought.

'Toby?'

He slowly looked up from his phone and gazed out of the windscreen.

'It means we need somebody who knows the layout of that house.'

'Why?'

Toby exhaled slowly.

'Because somewhere in that house is a room that was set up solely for the purpose of carrying out the attacks.'

A shiver escaped to the foot of his spine as the words left his mouth. This had just become a lot more complicated, but as he hung up the phone, an inner conflict ensued. If there was any chance for him and Beth, he had to consign Eric Stanton to his past and return his life back to some normality. As the extent of Eric Stanton's brutality and the likelihood of a second attacker became apparent, the ongoing danger to the streets compelled him to consider his next move. Their discovery had meant this was no longer solely about victims in the past. At that moment, Toby realised this wasn't something he could simply walk away from.

CHAPTER 18

Monday 8th May...16:00pm

It was the call he'd been expecting and hoping for, yet still, it was a call which had left him feeling frustrated, and seemingly with more questions than answers. He had a strong feeling Olivia Stanton was responsible for the death of her ex-husband's death. However, substantiating this feeling was proving more challenging than he'd hoped. The scene itself made little sense. Several potential causes of death and the body's arrangement suggested a staged crime scene. The presentation of the house itself didn't wholly fit with the struggle that had been suggested. Mike had revisited the scene to take another look around the grounds to see if he could find anything which would shed any light on the events of Saturday 6th May. Olivia was still being held and had so far been interviewed twice. Her second interview had seen her even less cooperative than the first. She had a defiance about her, but it was subtle enough to avoid verging on arrogance. Mike doubted her confident demeanour, suspecting it concealed guilt instead of genuine innocence, but cases weren't prosecuted on feelings, they were prosecuted on evidence. Right now, the evidence wasn't supporting his theory. As he stood with his back to the front door, he peered out over the grounds, admiring the privacy. After a few minutes of quiet consideration, Mike slowly made his way around the back. He stood for a moment admiring the well-kept garden, which seemed to stretch for miles. As he made his way down the path, which bisected the garden, he noted the outbuilding, inconspicuous in its surroundings. It wasn't the first time he had laid eyes on this, but previously it hadn't particularly grabbed his attention. This time, however, it did. As he drew alongside, he noticed the door was open, hanging from its hinges. On the day of the murder, he hadn't been part of the team searching the grounds, and was left wondering why a detail like this hadn't been reported to him. He cautiously made his way over, switching his torch on as he did so. The building wasn't large, so it took him little time to realise he was the only occupant once he'd entered. The place looked like a mess. Empty crisp packets and a couple of empty bottles occupied the desk. There were some scraps of paper, but they were more resembling shopping lists, than a detailed piece of evidence that would crack the case wide open. The desk drawers were empty and the clock on the wall had stopped. In fact, it looked like the hands hadn't moved in quite some time. There was nothing of note in here. As he turned to leave, he swung round too quickly and knocked a picture off the wall, leaving it to shatter into pieces. His attention, however, wasn't on the picture's demise. It was on what it had been hiding. A safe lay there, door ajar. Upon closer inspection, he noticed whatever contents had been stored here had since been removed. Whoever had been responsible for ransacking this place had got what they came for.

The question was, what did they find, and what was its relevance to Eric Stanton's murder?

'Detective Inspector.'

'Mike's fine,' he replied, wishing to dispense with the formalities. 'What are your thoughts on Georgina Sampson?' he added.

'She appears frightened. Her story has inconsistencies.'

'Oh?'

'She claims she just found herself at his house, yet it's several miles from where she had been staying, and not somewhere you would randomly walk to. But what really struck me was her decision to enter the house. She described feeling anxious, seeing an open door, and sensing an eeriness. In most instances, that would send you running in the other direction.'

'Did you push her on her relationship with Olivia Stanton?'

'She said they'd met a couple of times, but weren't friends. She said Olivia was standing over the body when she entered the house.'

Mike placed the phone on his chest. He'd feared they may have collaborated to concoct a story, but clearly, this was not the case. This gave them a focal point.

'One of them is lying.'

'What makes you say that, Mike?'

'Olivia said she heard voices in the house and when she got downstairs, Georgina was already inside, standing near the body.'

'So, Olivia implicated Georgina?'

'Indirectly. She didn't exactly rush to her defence, shall we say.'

'My gut feeling is that Georgina Sampson is telling the truth, but her story is wild, and let's not forget, the fingerprints on the knife were hers.'

'That adds further complexity to the case.'

'Why is that?'

'The knife wasn't the murder weapon. It was inserted post-mortem.'

So, what was the cause of death?

'Blunt force trauma. The blow to the back of the head proved fatal. The coroner believes he was likely dead before he hit the ground.'

'So, Georgina Sampson stabbed Eric Stanton to make sure he was dead?'

'There's another scenario,' he said tentatively.

Amanda Stone didn't reply.

'That the only other person who knew that house, who could have known Georgina had kept a knife all those years, delivered that blow, serving us up an obvious prime suspect in the process.'

'Olivia Stanton.'

Mike was slowly piecing things together in his mind, but still, he felt uncomfortable with the whole situation. Everything lined up with Olivia Stanton being the killer, but they didn't have a shred of evidence to support this theory. Then there was the minor detail of a missing murder weapon. Reviewing the timeline, he found it hard to accept the women had enough time to hide the murder weapon. None of this made sense to him.

'There's one other thing,' he added. 'The outbuilding was ransacked. The scene suggests they were looking for something…and they found it. Either that or they were sending a message.'

'Could there be an accomplice?'

'Either that or we have the wrong suspects in custody,' he replied.

'Eric seemed to have a lot of enemies.'

'Widening the suspect pool doesn't make this any easier. If anything, it makes our investigation harder.'

'Olivia Stanton and Georgina Sampson?'

'They seem more concerned with implicating one another.'

'You don't think it's them?'

'The break-in and the murder may not be related. My gut tells me we're not looking for the same person.'

'What makes you think that?'

Mike paused, scratching his forehead. It was difficult to explain, but sometimes in his job you just got a feeling. It wasn't about evidence or even circumstance; it was just a feeling that told you a story that made sense.

'Revisiting a murder scene would be incredibly risky, if indeed that's what happened. Currently, we don't have a timeline.'

'So, the person we are looking for took a calculated risk?'

'Perhaps. But if I'm wrong and we are looking for the same person, the break-in would likely have taken place after Eric Stanton was dead,' Mike replied.

'Could the killer have been interrupted during the search?'

'There was no sign of any struggle in there, or anywhere else on the grounds, for that matter.'

'So that would point to something premeditated, then?'

'Blunt force trauma to the back of the head feels more spontaneous. Like a heated argument where anger has built to a dangerous level and then boiled over.'

Amanda didn't reply. She appeared deep in thought. The more Mike became immersed in his thoughts, the more complex the case became. He tapped his finger on the base of his bottom lip, desperately trying to find some inspiration. He was now back outside the front of the house, looking around for any tiny detail the forensic team may have missed. His eyes rested on the front door. Considering what had unfolded inside, it was in pristine condition. This further suggested the killer was known to Eric Stanton. He let them in. There was no sign of force. Olivia had also stated she had let herself in. His eyes widened as he frantically searched the ground and the bushes next to the front door.

'Mike?'

'Holy shit, that's it.'

He couldn't find what he was looking for, but that was the point. It wasn't there.

'In her interview, Olivia expressly told us that she had let herself in using a key.'

'So, we know how she got in?

'The key was under a bronze statue. She specifically mentioned this as she said she had always hated it.'

'I'm not following the relevance,' Amanda said, somewhat naively.

'The statue isn't here. There's an imprint on the ground where it has clearly rested for some time, but the statue itself is gone.'

'What does that mean?'

'He was hit with a heavy object from behind.'

'Like a statue?'

'Precisely. Its absence only serves to enhance its significance. I think we may have identified our murder weapon. The problem is, we now need to locate it.'

It wasn't long before the forensic investigators were back at the scene. As they worked on every last detail of the outbuilding, Mike searched the grounds just to see if the killer had got sloppy and left anything they may have missed the first time around. He was sure they'd identified the murder weapon, but locating it would prove challenging. The grounds were vast, with plenty of places to hide. He was fairly certain the killer wouldn't have risked keeping the murder weapon in their possession, so the likelihood was it was close by. But resources were limited, and time wasn't on their side. He still felt sure this was the work of Olivia, but proving this was a different matter. She had been very composed in her interviews, giving little away. She had maintained her innocence and reaffirmed the first person she saw on the scene was Georgina Sampson, who was standing close to the body when she descended the staircase. They'd been granted an extension for holding her, but that would expire in a little over twenty-four hours. The case was time-sensitive, but he was about to be thrown a curve ball as one of the forensic team approached him.

'What have you got for me?' Mike asked in a more abrupt manner than he'd intended.

'We managed to get an instant match through the national fingerprint database.'

Mike waited expectantly.

'Dylan Sampson.'

Mike's eyes widened.

'You know of him?'

'Our paths have crossed before.'

The man patted Mike on the shoulder and turned to walk away, leaving him silently thinking. He had no idea how deep this ran, but it was becoming more complicated at every turn. He wondered what Dylan had been doing here. What was he so desperate to find? He pulled out his phone and called the station.

'Put out an arrest warrant for Dylan Sampson. You're gonna need a team.'

'Why is that, sir?'

'When you see him, you'll know.'

The call was succinct. He felt little in the mood for conversation. There were now three suspects, all with motive. A mild breeze blew through the trees, but it did nothing to elevate his mood. He liked open and shut cases, but it felt like at every turn, this one was becoming more complex. He had an uneasy feeling about the whole thing. It was possible that one of the three had killed Eric in isolation. It was equally possible they had colluded. However, he couldn't rule out that perhaps none of them had committed the murder and the real killer was still at large. There sat the problem; the case was ambiguous, the possibilities equal in plausibility. He looked down at his watch. It was just before five o'clock. He would have good light for the next two or three hours, after which the evening would begin setting in. The key to the case would come in one of two forms. Either a confession or the retrieval of the murder weapon with conclusive evidence. At this moment in time, both seemed elusive. The murder weapon could be anywhere, and it appeared neither Olivia nor Georgina were in the mood for a confession, each preferring to implicate the other. He stood for a moment and considered his next move. He wanted to get inside the mind of the killer. He needed to delve into the secret life of Eric Stanton in the hope he would find a clue. He needed to understand what Dylan Sampson had been searching for. How did Georgina end up miles away from home at the murder scene by accident? Then it hit him. He needed to understand how all of these parts linked. He needed somebody who knew the suspects and their history. He needed somebody who knew behaviour. He needed Toby. He reached into his pocket and retrieved his phone, preparing to call in a favour.

The wind blows gently, yet it remains closed to the elements. Protected by its surroundings, hidden away by a natural beauty most would kill for. Somebody is close, but they will never discover the truth hidden in the depths. There are voices in the distance. Sound is the natural enemy of tranquillity, yet this hiding place remains unharmed, undisturbed. Traffic is a distant and faint murmur, sporadic in even its busiest moments. Somebody is calling, but who or what is unclear. It won't be long now. Soon, the clearing will vanish and the secret will be lost...forever.

CHAPTER 19

Tuesday 9th May...14:00pm

'Do we have enough to charge her?'

Hope or desperation, the conclusion was the same. The case had generated a lot of media attention, and naturally, this carried much greater scrutiny by those in charge. The media could either make a case or destroy one. They had a similar influence on careers in his experience. He'd seen officers promoted, perhaps above their ability. Officers that lacked integrity, but who said the right things and appeared to be liked by the press. Then there were people like Jim Goodhall, who were hounded by them for not closing a murder case. Ultimately, this had cost him his job as the attention on the police constabulary had magnified to an uncomfortable and intolerable level. There had to be a fall guy and Jim was it. He was one of the good guys who cared about the victims. What distinguished him, however, was his commitment to ensuring they had the right perpetrator. He wouldn't be bullied into placating public opinion. He was a principled individual, and his refusal to compromise on those principles led to his swift removal when the papers had begun baying for blood. Mike thought about how similar to Jim he was, though he perhaps entered the grey area more than Jim had. For Mike, it was never about doing things right; it was about doing the right thing. Yet here he was, desperately wanting Olivia Stanton to fit the crime. She had motive; she had opportunity, and she was at the scene. The difficulty was so did Georgina Sampson. The media only saw Georgina as a victim, however. Olivia, on the other hand, though a victim, was seen in a very different light. Eric's abuse didn't appear to be public knowledge, though the fact he had been murdered suggested somebody had seen him with his mask removed. The case was filled with complexity, which was becoming harder to decipher the longer it went on. Then there was the matter of the murder weapon. The cause of death was blunt force trauma, yet the lack of a murder weapon and any conclusive prints merely added to the challenge. There had been no sign of a break-in, and Olivia knew where the key was kept. She had also admitted to letting herself in the house. There was a whole heap of circumstantial evidence, but a lack of anything concrete. It would now be down to whether or not they felt confident enough that Georgina Sampson's testimony, along with that circumstantial evidence, sufficed to bring charges against Olivia.

'You're convinced it was her.'

Mike wasn't sure whether this was posed as a question or a statement. Either way, she hadn't answered his question, which meant she was delaying an answer she knew would inevitably frustrate him.

'Not yet,' she replied, finally.

'Keep me posted.'

Hanging up the phone abruptly, he slammed it against his leg in anger. While he wouldn't be the next Jim Goodhall, he knew external pressure, and thus, hierarchical pressure, was coming. The public would always sympathise with a victim, and the truth was, that was how Eric Stanton was seen. Mike sensed even among those who knew him, it would be difficult to find anybody who would speak ill of him. He stopped briefly, wondering what would happen if the public perception was different. This was a small town, which meant crimes like these were rare, and therefore even more shocking in nature. If people knew the death of Eric Stanton had actually taken a serial rapist off the street, sympathy for him may wain. The media and the public could be relentless...but they could also be manipulated.

CHAPTER 20

Monday 8th May...17:15pm

'I wonder if you need look past the fact that Eric raped George?'

It came out harsher than he'd expected, but the message remained the same. If Mike was looking for a reason why Dylan would want to harm Eric, it was difficult to look past the fact Georgina appeared to be the only person Dylan cared about, and she had been brutally assaulted by her former lover.

'So, you think he's capable of murder?'

This felt like a loaded question. He would need to choose his words carefully, but if he was overly selective or hesitant, Mike would notice. He would know Toby was being evasive, and his wrath was something Toby was keen to avoid, considering their history.

'You asked me why Dylan may have felt angry with Eric. Anger to murder is quite a leap,' Toby replied.

'Cut the bullshit, Toby. You know as well as I do that Dylan Sampson is a ticking time bomb, just waiting to go off. If somebody lit his fuse, he's more than capable.'

'I don't think Dylan's your man.'

'We know he's been at the scene. His fingerprints and handy work are all over the place. We also know he has a temper...and a motive. It wouldn't be a stretch to make the link.'

Toby was about to speak but stopped himself. He knew Dylan had been at the scene, and he knew why, but he wasn't prepared to share that information with Mike. Not right now, anyway. He considered how he could steer Mike away from looking in that direction without appearing too enthusiastic in doing so.

'Dylan's not your man, Mike.'

'Okay Toby, I'm gonna humour you. Given his motive, temper, and presence at the scene, why is it so hard to believe he may be our killer?'

'What do you know about Eric's death?'

'He died of a blunt force trauma to the head.'

'And where on the head was he struck?'

'The back. Why is this relevant?'

'So that would indicate he was struck from behind?'

'That's to be implied, yes.'

'Mike, a blow from behind represents haste, impulse. It doesn't reflect careful planning. Tell me, from what you know of Dylan, do you think he's the type of person who would want or need to strike somebody when they are vulnerable and without defence?'

'His prints were all over the scene, Toby. He's been here and we can't ignore that fact. I wasn't sure we were looking for the same person until I discovered Dylan had been present. Now it makes sense.'

'I just don't think he's your guy.'

The line went quiet, Mike clearly absorbed.

'I wouldn't have had him down as the friend type,' he said frustratedly.

'Perhaps he'd agree with you,' Toby replied nonchalantly.

There was another lull in the conversation with Toby scrambling to understand why Mike had called him. This didn't seem like a conversation out of choice. Perhaps necessity?

'What do you need from me?'

'How's Beth? I haven't heard from her for a while. You two not resolved your differences yet?'

'I don't believe you called me to ask about Beth. I also don't believe it's solely about Dylan, either. What's going on Mike?'

Mike let out a sigh.

'That right there is why I called you, Toby. You understand behaviour better than anybody else I know. We have criminal profilers who don't have that level of ability or expertise. We could use a guy like you.'

Toby felt flattered. He had been drowning in a sea of emotional trauma. This felt like somebody had thrown him a life jacket. Despite the traumatic nature of George's rescue, he couldn't help but acknowledge the surge of adrenaline he had felt. He was self-aware and quickly realised his emotional and physical crash immediately after the conclusion of the ordeal was because of the excitement fading. But he knew any role within the police would be limited, and he doubted whether he was the type of person they really needed.

'What's on your mind?' he asked, ignoring Mike's comment.

'Something's off about that house, Toby.'

'The outbuilding?'

'No, the house itself. I looked around while forensics were working the scene. I ended up in what can only be described as a library.'

'You don't think Eric Stanton was the reading type?'

'Do you?'

Toby pondered. Eric had blindsided him before, but Mike was almost certainly right. Whatever that room was about, it wasn't books.

'You saw something that aroused your suspicion,' he said, as more of a statement than a question.

'What makes you say that?'

'I'm good at this stuff, remember? It's why you called me,' Toby teased.

'Like the rest of the house, the place was immaculate. The books were alphabetised and sectioned by genre. I'm talking OCD here.'

'You know not everybody who enjoys order has obsessive-compulsive disorder, right?' Toby corrected. He believed as a condition, OCD was over-diagnosed. He'd worked with many clients who had incorrectly self-diagnosed, spending time unpacking their need to attach a label to something simply because they were unable to understand it. A societal misconception.

'Have I touched a nerve there?'

'I just don't like the whole concept of labelling. Most things will arise from trauma, but rather than spending time working through that, we seem more obsessed with categorising it, but that's irrelevant here, of course,' Toby replied, feeling somewhat defensive. 'What got your attention?' he added.

'There was this one grey book that looked lost. It was almost too thin to be a book. No writing on the sleeve, no rightful home. It felt like it had been put there randomly, which doesn't make sense considering the effort somebody went to keep that room so pristine and ordered.'

'It wasn't random. It may have looked out of place, but it would have been premeditated.'

'What makes you so sure?'

'Eric Stanton left nothing to chance. Everything about him was structured and calculated. He had a way of making things look coincidental, but they would have been carefully planned. The positioning of that book may tell you more than you think.'

'Meet me there? I could do with some insight on this one. Something isn't sitting right.'

Toby stood silent, thinking about Mike's proposition. He felt conflicted, knowing he had information on the case that he was deliberately withholding from him. This didn't feel right to him, primarily because Mike was a friend who had supported him when times had been difficult. He had risked his career for him, something Toby hadn't fully appreciated at the time. How could he consult on a case he was already personally embroiled in?

'There's something else. It's about Olivia Stanton.'

Toby felt his heart rate increase rapidly at the very mention of her name. He wondered how she still had the ability to impact from beyond the grave. He could never fully understand his feelings about her death. He'd felt relief, regret, sadness, and joy—the entire spectrum of emotions. Yet still, the sound of her name sent a shiver deep into his sacrum.

'She's still alive, Toby.'

His heart felt like it had stopped momentarily as he tried to process Mike's words.

'What? How do you know?'

'Because we have her in custody.'

'How is that possible?'

'She was found at the scene of the murder shortly before Eric was discovered. Toby, she wasn't alone.'

'She wasn't alone?' he echoed.

'Georgina was also there.'

Toby's body began to shake. None of this made sense. How was Olivia still alive? She had perished in the fire. It had been confirmed. But more importantly to him, how was George involved in this? She had no affiliation with Olivia. George had implicated her in her own kidnapping. They weren't friends, yet they had a common enemy. In their loathing of Eric, they had the one thing strong enough to unite them. Olivia and George, colluding, suddenly made perfect sense. The clarity didn't make it any easier. He closed his eyes in disbelief. She hadn't been able to just walk away. The pain had eroded her moral compass. She had yielded to her anger, and Olivia had been only too willing to assist in the process. Her companion, her co-conspirator.

'Toby? Are you still there?'

'I'm here. Just trying to take in what I'm hearing.'

He paused, silently trying to piece together the sequence of events.

'Was George complicit in Olivia's escape?'

'I'm not comfortable having this conversation over the phone, Toby. Come and meet me. If I put you on the books as a consultant, it gives me a wider scope to share details about the case. The little I've given you so far is a courtesy as a friend. The rest would need to be official.'

Toby thought for a moment. The prospect of consulting on a murder case brought about a wave of excitement in him that had been absent for some time. Mike was offering him the chance to again have a purpose. It would be foolish of him to decline, regardless of the situation with Dylan on the sidelines. He was almost certain the photographs and Eric's murder were intrinsically linked. He now had the opportunity to learn more from the inside. He stopped as a realisation hit him. He wasn't doing this for Mike. He was doing it for Eric's victims. His priority wasn't finding a murderer. It was finding Eric's accomplice.

'I'll be there in twenty minutes,' he replied, hanging up the phone.

A strange feeling consumed Toby as he found himself at a scene, memorable for all the wrong reasons. His lasting memory had been that night. The night when everything changed for him. In his more honest moments, he realised that was the mere crescendo, the road to decline beginning several weeks before he decided to rush to the house of a client. Confessing to Beth had forced him to confront the truth; this started long before Olivia Stanton. There had been something lying dormant in him for years. He'd questioned whether this was about his mother. Both victims had been suffering in silence, like his mum, though that was where the comparisons ended. The situations weren't comparable, yet he was unable to shift the lingering thought that there was a tenuous link somewhere. He'd worked with many types of victims, the sense of injustice always a battle to contain.

Yet on two occasions, there had been an unforgivable personal involvement, where the boundaries had been crossed. Upon reflection, he should have walked away after the first incident, but as a young and enthusiastic psychotherapist, he had convinced himself it was an isolated occurrence. With a more mature head, looking back, he now knew that to be a lie. Beth had accused him of caring too much. As difficult as it had been to admit, she had been correct in her assessment. His level of investment in his clients had been one of his biggest strengths, but it had also ultimately led to his downfall. Now, he had a chance to channel that emotional investment into the right areas. Areas where he wouldn't be required to operate within the same ethical boundaries as he had previously. As he made his way up the long drive tentatively, he found himself admiring the magnitude of the grounds once more. It expanded past the grounds, though. There was a natural beauty to the surrounding area. From the adjacent fields to the quaint farmhouse in the distance. The geographical isolation served only to enhance its appeal. The weather was mild, with sunset still a while away on what had turned out to be a pleasant spring day. A gentle breeze stirred the trees, yet the air remained comfortably warm. As Toby approached the front door, he saw Mike studying the ground intently. Upon seeing Toby, Mike stood up and held out his hand with a smile. As the two embraced a warm greeting, Toby's eyes fixated on the ground Mike himself had moments ago been methodically investigating.

'The house is off limits for now,' Mike said regretfully.

Toby stood for a moment, wondering why he was there. What necessitated an in-person discussion?

'The scene doesn't make sense.'

'In what way?'

Our findings all suggest that Eric Stanton was a diligent and organised individual. Look around you,' Mike said, waving his hands. 'Everything about him and this place screams ostentatious.'

'But?'

Mike lowered his chin before looking Toby directly in the eye. 'Walk this way.'

Toby and Mike moved around the back of the house. Toby knew what Mike was about to show him. He also knew who'd been inside. He hoped his face wouldn't betray him. Mike couldn't know Dylan's level of involvement. He again felt that pang of guilt, but reasoned his furtive approach was for the greater good. Mike didn't know how deep this ran. It wasn't simply about a murder. Toby remained cautious about assuming Olivia's guilt, and he knew George wasn't capable. That meant there was a murderer and a rapist still walking the street. Or perhaps they were one and the same. Either way, there were complexities Mike wasn't aware of, and if he knew of Toby and Dylan's involvement at this stage, there would be repercussions. He was already gunning for Dylan. He didn't like people who dished out their own version of justice, and Dylan didn't play by the rules. He would be a thorn in Mike's side, and Mike knew this. Toby, on the other hand, had been warned on more than one occasion not to play detective. He could only play the friendship hand so many times before he ran out of cards. He could still assist Mike, but right now he needed Dylan, and that meant protecting him at all costs. Toby knew he needed to find a way to point Mike in another direction.

'Dylan Sampson's handy work,' Mike said, pointing at the door swinging loosely on one hinge.

Toby smiled. This wasn't about a lack of diplomacy; it was a show of anger. Dylan had made no attempt to hide his disdain for Eric.

'Are you sure it was him?'

'His prints are everywhere.'

'Mind if I look inside?' Toby asked.

Mike gestured. 'We have everything we need from here, but still be careful about touching anything.'

Toby walked inside and gazed around the room. He closed his eyes tightly as he wondered what secrets were being held within the four walls. What had they seen or heard? As he opened his eyes slowly, he was drawn to the shelves. One of them was loose. They looked old and dishevelled.

'What are you thinking?'

Toby moved closer and reached out to the top shelf, then spun round to face Mike.

'You were right about one thing, Mike.'

'Just one?' Mike replied with a wink.

Toby smiled, relieved he'd not caused offence.

'This is out of place.'

'He was trying to keep this place a secret. That's obvious.'

'Maybe...but there's an alternative explanation.'

'And what's that?'

Toby paused for a moment as he looked around the room again, before resting his eyes back on Mike.

'He wasn't the one using the building.'

Mike looked stunned.

'What are you implying?'

'Whoever was using this room, it wasn't Eric Stanton.'

'How can you be sure?'

'The exterior is overgrown, but that's a deliberate attempt at a clandestine existence. In here, though,' he said, gesturing around the room. 'In here doesn't have any markings of Eric.'

'So, it's a little untidy,' Mike replied somewhat sceptically.

Toby walked over to the corner of the small room.

'They say it's the little things that give you away,' he said, pointing at several empty coke cans in the corner.

'A penchant for soft drinks isn't exactly a crime, Toby.'

'It's not a crime, but for a man who only drinks water, it's suspicious.'

'How could you possibly know that?'

'Olivia once dropped it into conversation. She felt he was obsessive with his diet.'

'And you believed her?'

'It would have been an unnecessary lie. When you are creating a false narrative, you keep details to a minimum. The more you must recall, the greater the risk of your deception being exposed. That fact did nothing to either enhance or diminish her story. Why risk it?'

Mike breathed out through his nostrils. Toby had clearly piqued his interest, but he could tell Mike still needed convincing.

'Mike, Eric is dead, and somebody came in here and took something of importance. Something incriminating, perhaps. Is it possible that what you're looking at is a falling out between co-conspirators?'

'Dylan Sampson was here, Toby. Do you think he and Eric were into something together? That sounds a bit of a stretch considering how they are connected, wouldn't you say?'

He sounded dismissive, but it didn't feel personal.

'You need to look past Dylan. He may have been here, but he's not the person you're looking for. Dylan would never blindside anybody. To have killed Eric, he would have needed to witness the life fading from his eyes. Whatever you think of him, Mike, this just doesn't sound like Dylan.'

'What is it with you and this guy, Toby?'

Toby recoiled. He didn't like what was being implied, but largely because it had an element of truth contained in it. He was protecting Dylan, but not through any loyalty. He was protecting him because he knew whoever had killed Eric; it wasn't Dylan. He was protecting him because he knew he and Dylan were about to become immersed in their own investigation. He was protecting him because whatever was about to go down, he would rather have Dylan on side.

'What's the significance of the area next to the front door?' he asked, ignoring Mike's remark.

Mike, who had been studying something on the floor, looked up at Toby.

'I believe the murder weapon is missing.'

'The statue?'

'How did you know?'

'I know Olivia hated it. I noticed it the night I was here.'

'Olivia said she used the key from under the statue to gain entry to the house.'

'So, the killer entered after her?'

'If she's telling the truth.'

'You don't believe her?'

'As I said, there's a lot about this case that doesn't add up. She was at the scene. She had a motive, and she'd tried to kill him previously. The woman had just faked her own death to escape prison. She hardly epitomises integrity.'

Toby laughed, but then questioned its appropriateness given the situation. Mike placed a hand on his shoulder.

'Toby, there's something else you should perhaps know about our enquiries.'

Observing the serious look Mike was wearing, Toby felt a wave of anxiety come over him. Olivia had risen from the grave. What else could there be?

'Eric was found with a knife inserted into his abdomen. A knife that belonged to Georgina. A knife that contained only one set of prints...hers.'

'I thought you said he died from blunt force trauma?'

'He did, but that doesn't change the fact he was also stabbed. It just turns out it was post-mortem.'

Toby looked up at the sky, struggling to process what he was hearing. None of this sounded like George, but he'd been wrong about her before. Was he still judging her as that sweet teenager, rather than the damaged woman she had become? Could she really have gone after her ex-lover in a rage spurred on by a thirst for revenge?

'Sounds like she may have stabbed him to make sure he was dead,' Mike continued.

'You have both Olivia and George in custody?'

'They don't corroborate each other's stories.'

'They're blaming one another?'

'Not exactly. Olivia implicated George, but not directly. It seems George was more concerned with clearing her own name, rather than implying Olivia's guilt.'

'I don't understand why George was there in the first place. Especially with Olivia Stanton. There's no relationship there. They are only linked by...'

'By Eric Stanton, who had viciously attacked them both. They were found together at the house of the man who had subjected them to heinous abuse. As his limp body lay on the floor, they stood over him. Still having trouble joining the dots?'

'The very fact you brought me here suggests you have doubts.'

'I was part of Olivia's interview. She came across as very assured.'

'That troubles you, doesn't it?'

Toby was in a precarious position, yet Mike's call was for more than just theory confirmation. He knew Toby would look at it from a perspective that went beyond experience and intuition. There was something about the murder of Eric Stanton that troubled Mike.

'You don't believe it was George, do you?' Toby asked, mindful it sounded like a leading question.

'She had a motive. She was at the scene. Her prints were found on a knife embedded in Eric's torso...a knife which she admitted belongs to her.'

'Did you ask her that question directly?'

'Why is that relevant, Toby?'

'It's relevant. Did you ask her directly?'

'I'm led to believe she owned up to being the owner of the knife after being shown it in her interview,' Mike replied, looking puzzled.

'Why would she admit to owning the knife?'

'Pardon?'

'Why admit to owning the knife? It holds no relevance. It's not something that could be easily proven. She willingly volunteered that information. Why?'

'I'm not sure what your point is, Toby, but you need to be mindful of your tone.'

'Respectfully, Mike, does this not all seem a little too contrived?'

Mike cleared his throat. This time, Toby *had* offended him.

'The evidence doesn't lie.'

'No, but it can be manipulated to tell a different story.'

'She was at the scene, Toby. I arrested her.'

Toby could feel his frustration rising. Mike seemed intent on making this fit George, regardless of having doubts.

'Wouldn't you agree that a stabbing post-mortem is about proving a point?' Mike asked.

'It's certainly about proving a point, but perhaps not the one you're thinking of.'

'Oh?'

Mike now sounded annoyed, likely regretting his decision to involve Toby in the case.

'There are two possibilities here. Either George is responsible for Eric's murder...'

'Or?' interrupted Mike.

'Or somebody is working very hard to convince you of that very fact. Everything you have told me so far would suggest that both women have something to hide. But have you ever considered the possibility that neither of them delivered the killer blow? Two women found at the scene of a murder, both with motives that would keep you from looking in any other direction.'

'What are you saying?'

Toby bit his lip. He knew what he was implying, but he had to be very careful. He wasn't a criminal profiler, but he knew people and he knew behaviour. He smiled at Mike, before patting him affectionately on the shoulder.'

'I should go,' he said, turning to begin the walk down the long drive. As he briskly strolled, he again admired the field to the left of him through the trees. It looked desolate. He thought for a moment about the tranquillity it offered, but that thought was only transient. He had more concerning matters after the conversation with Mike. Why had George been at the scene, more importantly, if neither she nor Olivia had killed Eric, who had?

CHAPTER 21

Monday 8th May...20:00pm

Up to this point, the conversation had been somewhat un-comfortable for Toby. When they spoke now, it no longer felt how it used to. He yearned for things to be the way they were, but that seemed a distant memory now. They cared for one an-other deeply, but the trust and the shared interests that had once been the pillar of their relationship had slowly dissipated. Toby had previously believed they were strong enough to survive any-thing, but recent events had pushed their marriage to the brink of collapse. He hated not being with her, but considering her disapproval of his involvement with George's kidnap ordeal, he had no inclination to open up to her about what was currently holding his attention. She could perhaps just about forgive his work consulting for the police, but the knowledge of his back-ground work with Dylan would be enough to send her into a furious tirade, where she would undoubtedly question his de-cision-making and his judgement. The very thought of keeping things from her upset Toby. It was tantamount to lying for him, but for now, his priority was identifying Eric's accomplice, be-cause that one photograph had changed everything. He felt both anger and sadness for all the victims, but as much as he tried to reason with himself to the contrary, there was a personal investment in this case. He'd wondered how Eric seemed to know so much and stay one step ahead. Now he knew. He'd had eyes and ears on the ground. On his house, his wife no less. The frightening encounter in the countryside. There was somebody else. All along, there had been somebody else. Eric and his associate shared a mutual penchant for luring women with deceitful promises, only to strip them of their humanity. Seeing the pictures, the building, and hearing Dylan detail the process, as told to him by a less-than-savoury character, had turned his stomach. Though ordinarily a meek and reserved individual, this had ignited something within Toby. A determination fuelled by disdain. But Beth couldn't know about any of this. At least not yet. His marriage was important to him, and he was still trying to figure out a way to save it. This wasn't it.

'You still haven't told me how you know about the break-in.'

'That doesn't matter, Toby. What matters is I didn't hear it from you. Have we become strangers?'

Toby wanted to tell her it was she who left the family home. He wanted to point out it was she who had kept contact to a minimum. He wanted to highlight the fact she was the one who had refused to give a time scale for how long she would be at her sister's. Instead, he remained silent, deliberating a more measured response that had less risk of antagonising her and escalating an already difficult situation.

'I've missed you,' he finally managed.

'Toby, I'm not one of your clients. You don't get to evade questions with me. I'm your wife,' she snapped back.

'I'm not sure what you want from me.'

'You could start by telling me what you're involved in.'

'Why do you feel I'm involved in something?'

'What did they steal?'

'Nothing.'

'Did they vandalise anything?'

Toby was on the back foot, and he knew it. Beth sounded more and more aggressive with every question. He knew where she was going. He'd led her there without thinking.

'Why does that matter?'

'When somebody breaks into your house, takes nothing and inflicts no damage, they aren't there for something...they're there for someone.'

Toby stayed quiet. Beth was astute, and she was also accurate. He'd known this was personal from the moment his intruder was gifted a chance to run, but instead, chose to attack him. He wondered how far it would have gone had Dylan not entered the scene. He also wondered how far Dylan would have gone had the opportunity presented itself. She was uncharacteristically angry. Something was wrong.

'Beth, what's going on?'

'Nothing's going on.'

The slight hesitation aroused his suspicions. The faint, almost surreptitious exhaling through her nostrils confirmed it. She was lying. But what was she hiding? More importantly, why was she unable to tell him? He bowed his head as he questioned what their marriage had become. A sudden shift had occurred; they had gone from open communication to secretive behaviours that now came far too easily. Perhaps she had been right. Perhaps they had descended into a place where they walked the path as strangers. He wondered if they were destined to drift apart like he and George had done years earlier. Consumed by sadness, he considered whether their story ended here, or whether it had simply been paused. This was no longer even small talk. It was a painfully uncomfortable situation which at best felt like an awkward first date, and at worst, an interrogation. With every passing moment came a reminder of what he was missing. Every conversation only served to highlight how he had brought them here. *He* had brought them to this point. She had been a reluctant passenger throughout, but out of love and loyalty had remained...for a time, anyway. But that reluctance had escalated. Her patience had been eroded, and she had simply stepped out, prompting him to make a decision. Either he got out with her, or continued alone. He hadn't actively made that decision, but what he had done was overestimate the distance she was from reaching her threshold. He had taken her for granted, and that had led to self-reproach. However, he was also angry. He felt abandoned by her.

'I didn't mean to keep things from you.'

'We have a very different definition of lying, Toby.'

He was on the ropes, caught between throwing in the towel and fighting back. He felt the attack was unjustified, but he also knew there was something else fuelling it. This didn't feel like it was about him, but he had to tread carefully. Deflecting now may antagonise her, and the last thing he wanted to do was upset her further. In her mind, this was about him. He needed to keep it that way while he figured out what was really going on.

'Have you heard from Jack?'

'Not for a day or two.'

The line went silent again. The conversation had shifted from uneasy to strained.

'Beth?'

'I'm fine, Toby. Just tired.'

'Come home?'

The words had just slipped out. A question that he could, or indeed should, have asked on several occasions, yet had not...until now. He wondered why he had struggled so much to open up to her about how he was feeling. How much he missed her, and how desperate he was to have her back. How he missed the simpler times, the times when they would spend the day cocooned in one another's arms, oblivious to the outside world. He wanted to tell her, yet only now realised why he couldn't. He was angry with her. She hadn't doubted his intentions or his integrity, but she had cast doubt on his decision-making. He had been unable to convince her he had set out to save the lives of two people. For Beth, it had come down to one thing. Trust. He hadn't been truthful with her; he wasn't even sure why. Perhaps it had been because one was an ex-love, the other a client. Perhaps it had been because he felt out of control and was afraid, ashamed even. Perhaps it was because it had unlocked a part of him she hadn't seen. A side of him he was afraid she wouldn't like. He questioned whether the deceit had arisen from a fear that she would leave him, before letting out an ironic sigh upon realising the deceit was what had ultimately caused her to leave him.

'I can't Toby, not right now,' she replied after a moment, breaking the silence.

'I spent years helping people work through marital problems. Yet here I am, unable to save my own.'

'Toby...'

'I understand,' he interrupted. 'I've broken the trust and I know this is all on me. But please listen when I say this. I will never stop trying to make this up to you. I love you more...'

'You're not the reason I can't come home right now,' she whispered.

The words should have been reassuring, yet they induced a trepidation inside of Toby that he hadn't felt in some time. He'd known something was wrong. The oscillating between confrontation and distance had set alarm bells ringing. This wasn't Beth. She was troubled. But as Toby questioned whether she would open up to him, the line went dead. A nauseous feeling washed over him as he desperately tried to reach her, but the phone call went unanswered. She hadn't lost signal. She'd hung up. Nothing about Beth during the conversation had felt right. She had been close to erratic, a word you would never ordinarily associate with Beth Reynolds. She had been angry, yet distant in the same vein. She wasn't at risk; he would have known. They had developed a code word for if either were in imminent danger. She hadn't used it. But it was clear something had happened, something she hadn't felt comfortable confiding in Toby with. That hurt him more than anything, providing further evidence of the distance that now lay between them. As he sat pondering whether he had lost Beth for good, a call came through. It was an unknown number. In the past, this would have been a referral partner, but that chapter had closed, and recent experiences had made him nervous whenever he didn't recognise a number. As he answered the call, the feelings of angst amplified and an icy shiver ran through his body at the sound of the voice on the other end of the line.

CHAPTER 22

M onday 8th May...18:45pm

His anger intensified with every picture he examined, vexation now burning through his veins like an uncontrollable fire. Eric would never answer for his crimes, a reality that irked him. Death had spared him from facing a justice unrivalled by anything dished out by the legal system. Compared to facing Dylan, life in a maximum-security prison would have seemed like a vacation. The whiskeys were disappearing quickly, but the alcohol wasn't providing the escape he had hoped. He was growing impatient, and without meeting him, had found somebody he detested as much as he had Eric Stanton. But so far, this person remained elusive, masked behind a camera, with no clues as to his identity. He was the silent partner, lurking in the background behind anonymity. He started walking toward the bar, but something in his peripheral vision caught his attention. As he walked backwards slowly, he felt a sudden jolt. As he turned, he was faced with a well-built individual, with a shaven head, and tattoos for eyebrows. On any ordinary day, Dylan imagined he would look unfriendly, but the look on his face signified something way beyond this. As Dylan looked down, he could see the man's glass was half empty, the rest of his drink identifiable on the front of his white tee shirt. He glared at Dylan with a face which seemed to redden by the second.

'Watch where you're going, idiot.'

Dylan grinned but said nothing.

'You owe me a drink,' the man said sternly.

He was met with continued silence.

'I said you owe me a goddamn drink, you prick,' the man bellowed, now moving a step closer towards Dylan.

Before Dylan could respond, one of the doormen, who Dylan recognised from the last time he was here, made his way over.

'I'm not gonna have any trouble from you two, am I?'

Dylan smiled and turned to walk back to his table. The bar was quiet, but after his last visit, he realised the doormen weren't there because it was a busy pub. They were there because of its reputation. There were two types of people who frequented a place like this. Those who liked to drink, and those who liked to fight. Dylan considered himself more of an observer and wondered which category his new acquaintance fell into. He would soon find out.

He looked up at the clock and saw it was now after seven, just over twenty minutes since the altercation. He caught sight of the man responsible for the tirade of verbal abuse heading towards the toilets, which were tucked away in the corner. They were out of view of the main bar area, but more importantly, they were out of view from where the doormen were positioned. Dylan carefully slid his chair back, stood, and purposefully followed the man. Pushing the door open, he noticed it was just the two of them. The man had little time to turn around before Dylan grabbed him by the head and smashed it against the wall. There was a piercing shriek as blood gushed down his face from a nose that was clearly broken. Dragging the man to his feet, he grabbed him by the scruff of his neck and buried his head deep into the urinal, not to punish, but to humiliate him. As his opponent gasped for air, Dylan picked him up and threw him against the basin. The man was now little more than a crumpled heap on the floor, but Dylan was relentless. He placed a hand around the now barely conscious individual's throat, forcing him to look in the mirror.

'Remember this face,' he said with an unmistakable coldness, before thrusting the man's head into the mirror, tiny shards of glass quickly filling the bathroom floor. Dylan looked down at the motionless figure, remorseless. A sadistic grin spread across his face.

'The next time you see me, I suggest you keep your head down and keep walking...you fucking prick.'

At that, Dylan casually exited the toilet and left the bar. That would be his last visit. His first scuffle had been outside and hadn't been instigated by him. But there was no mistaking what this was. It was nothing less than a vicious attack that had allowed him to jettison some of the fury which had been building slowly. He knew exactly what this was about, and the man at the bar, as confrontational as he was, had played only a minor role in Dylan's anger escalating as quickly as it did, and to a level that seemed disproportionate considering the situation.

Dylan made his way down the backstreets, regretting his actions. He had no remorse and gave little consideration to the condition he'd left the man in. His regret came from the impact this could have on him. There would be unwanted police attention, and he wouldn't be hard to identify. Whilst there was no evidence linking him directly to the attack, the earlier altercation, coupled with the fact he may have been seen walking into the toilet shortly after the victim, would be enough to certainly make him a person of interest. This wasn't explainable as just a fight. The man had stood no chance. It was a frenzied attack that went beyond any disagreement. This had been about more than proving a point. It had gone beyond humiliating somebody who had provoked him. This was about all the victims. It was about Eric Stanton, the man in the hospital, and George. It was about the accomplice. That second person who'd been Eric's loyal partner all along without them realising it. They had only one lead, but getting to him would prove difficult. Toby had warned him there would be a police presence, but he didn't care. He'd find a way. With that thought firmly lodged in his mind, he pulled his hat out of his pocket and placed it carefully on his head. This wasn't for warmth, but a hollow attempt at concealing his identity. The country roads seemed to go on forever, but the picturesque sunset, along with the warm spring temperature, made the journey palatable. The walk gave him time to reflect, but he hadn't used it for this purpose. Instead, he had been considering his next move, imagining squeezing information from somebody he would rather see dead. As far as he was concerned, the scumbag in the hospital had turned a blind eye to what was happening. That made him equally culpable in Dylan's eyes, and he would much rather see somebody like that in the morgue than a hospital bed.

He didn't hear his phone ring, but he felt the vibration.

'Mike Thomas is looking for you.'

'There's a warrant out for my arrest?'

'That I don't know, but your prints were all over the outbuilding at Eric's.'

'Shit, that's all I need.'

'You may need to lie low for a while.'

'There might be a slight problem there,' Dylan replied.

'What's going on?'

Dylan thought about the best way to answer that question. Toby would know if he lied, but he also had no inclination to hear Toby take the moral high ground after he hadn't heeded his warning.

'I just got into an altercation with a guy at the Tavern.'

'Jesus Dylan, how bad was it?'

'He was unconscious and bleeding heavily, laid on a pile of broken glass when I left.'

'That's your idea of lying low?'

'No, that's my idea of blowing off a little steam.'

'Where are you now?' Toby asked.

'Heading towards the hospital.'

'Are you crazy? Mike is already gunning for you. I mean this with the greatest of respect, but you're not hard to identify.'

'He's the only person we have who knew about Eric.'

'Then let me talk to him. I can be there in twenty minutes.'

Dylan hung up the phone without replying. He had little faith in Toby being able to extract the information they required, but Toby had been right about one thing. He was easily identifiable, and security would have been strengthened after his last visit, which meant only one thing. He would need to act swiftly and go undetected.

Dylan had a visual on him. The fact he was outside made life much easier for him. He could now avoid entering the main hospital, eluding both staff and security. Slipping on a cap and a pair of sunglasses, he moved with haste across the car park, finding his way to the greenery. He shook his head as he noticed it was a smoking area, questioning why hospitals continued to treat people who didn't help themselves. His ire was transient, as he drew close to the intended target, who was in a more secluded part of the garden area. He was with another man, though the two didn't look deep in conversation. Dylan walked a wide circle to get to the back of the garden but had to be careful not to be seen. A non-smoker in a designated smoking area would draw suspicion. He sat and waited. His hunch was right. They hadn't come out together; the other man was now walking back towards the building, gown flowing in the cooling temperature as the sun began to set on another mild spring day. His window would be short. There was no room for error. Mindful not to draw attention to himself, Dylan crept up on the hospital patient briskly. Grabbing him on the shoulder, but applying pressure in a way that made the man grimace, he spun him around so they were now face to face.

'Before you think about shouting for help, you might want to consider how easily I've been able to get to you.' He paused. 'Twice,' he added.

'What do you want?

'A little chat,' Dylan grinned.

'I've told you everything I know.'

'I can put that to the test if you like?'

The man just stared at him. Dylan could see the fear in his eyes. If he didn't realise it before, he realised it now. Dylan was somebody you didn't fuck with.

'Now I have your attention. Keep it that way and you can walk back in there in the same condition you walked out here in.'

He was met with an anxious silence.

'Eric Stanton had an accomplice. I need to know who he is, and where I can find him.'

'I never saw anybody else. Like I told you before, it wasn't until that one incident with the woman who ran in front of my car that I questioned anything. Women used to love him. They loved his money more, though, I think. What makes you so sure there was somebody else involved?'

'Let's just say some fresh evidence has come to light.'

'As I said before, I've done some bad things in my time, but I draw the line at rape. That girl we took to the house...'

'My sister?' Dylan interrupted.

The man gulped so loudly it was audible to Dylan.

'I tried to stop that. It wasn't part of the plan. If it had been, I would never have got involved. I know I convinced her otherwise, but I wouldn't have done that.'

'Why are you telling me this?'

'Because if I'd have known what was really happening at Eric's place with those women, all the money in the world wouldn't have persuaded me to get involved.'

'You admitted to having suspicions. You admitted to continuing working for him even after you were faced with the gruesome truth behind what was really happening up there. You're as guilty as he is, and the only reason you're not laid in a casket is because you're more use to me alive than dead. But listen very carefully when I say this. Your usefulness will only last so long, and when it runs out, I'll be coming for you.'

'If I help you find him, will you leave me alone?'

'I can't make any promises.'

'Then what's in it for me?'

'Right now, you're a marked man. If you help take that sick bastard off the streets, I may spare your life. Those are the best odds you're likely to get.'

The man regarded Dylan with a look of concern. His choice was stark.

'He had this one friend I saw him with a couple of times. His name was Troy. I can't remember his last name.'

He screwed his eyes, desperately trying to retrieve the surname escaping him.

'Galen,' he shouted. 'Troy Galen. There was something about him that gave me the creeps.'

'How so?'

'Comments he would make. I only really met him once, but Eric was different around him.'

'In what way?'

'Like he was trying to impress him. It was like they were speaking in code or something. Eric always did right by me, but on those occasions when Troy was around, he spoke to me like shit.'

'And yet, like a loyal lap dog, you continued to go back for more.'

'My name's Carl, by the way.'

'I'm more interested in Troy Galen, and where I can find him.'

'I never went to his house.'

Dylan stepped closer to Carl, not even attempting to hide the gesture of a threat. Troy Galen could be the man they were looking for, and Carl may be his only lead. He smiled, realising he wouldn't get another chance if he blew this one. Even he understood that some situations demanded a more subtle approach than violence. Much to his annoyance, this was one of those occasions. He closed his eyes and took a deep breath.

'Eric Stanton had an associate. You know what he was doing to those women. You know what *they* were doing to those women. Think about the woman who looked you directly in the eye. Think about how many more there were just like her. Eric is dead, but the threat to other women in this town didn't die with him. Do you believe Troy Galen was his partner?'

Carl thought for a moment.

'At the time, I just thought he was a creep, but now, yes, I think he could be capable of it.'

'When people talk in code, they don't trust you. You know that, right? You know they didn't respect you, and saw you as nothing more than a subservient lackey? You can retaliate. You can have the last laugh and knock the smile right off this sick bastard's face. Think hard. Give me something I can leave here with.'

He was playing Carl. He knew what to say. People like him readily accepted their place without really complaining until you drew their attention to it. Then pride would take over and a defiance would arise. You just needed to poke the bear a little, and that's exactly what he was doing. Of course, the added incentive for Carl was he was in a fight to save his own skin. Dylan wouldn't allow him to simply walk away without reproach, but he didn't know this.

'I heard them talking about meeting at a pub out of town. I got the impression it was somewhere they regularly visited. That's all I know, I swear.'

Dylan strode towards Carl, who flinched, but this time he simply patted him on the back.

'I'll be in touch,' he said before turning and disappearing in the same clandestine manner in which he had appeared moments earlier. The last thing he wanted to do was to draw further attention to himself, but this visit had been necessary. The information was minimal, but he felt certain Carl had told him everything he knew. Whether his conscience had been pricked, or he was afraid for his life, didn't concern Dylan. All that mattered to him was that they had a starting point. The hunt was on, but time was becoming a crucial factor. This was no longer simply about seeking justice for the victims. It was now about preventing that list from having any other names added to it.

'The sirens in the background...'
'They're not for me. At least I don't think so.'

'Did you find what you were looking for?'

'I found *who* I was looking for, but he didn't give me much.'

Toby felt a surge of disappointment. He didn't like Dylan's methods, but couldn't deny he had hoped a more threatening approach would yield a better outcome for them.

'I'm not doubting your methods, Dylan, but is there a chance he was holding out on you?'

He did doubt Dylan's methods, but that wasn't a conversation he neither wanted nor needed to engage in right now.

'I saw the fear in his eyes. Believe me, anything he knows, we know.'

'Did he give you anything at all?'

'Does the name Troy Galen mean anything to you?'

'Should it?'

'It's a name he mentioned. Though they'd only met twice, he found him shifty, claiming Eric acted differently in his presence.'

'Different how?'

'Does that matter?'

'More than you think. It would give us an insight into the dynamics of that relationship.'

'He said it was like they were talking in code or something.'

'It's not just about what they said.'

'Oh?'

Toby wondered how best to expand without appearing condescending. As he had learned previously, Dylan was a person you wanted on your side.

'A person's body language can say a lot about how they're feeling, particularly when in the presence of others.'

'There was one thing. He said Eric and Troy would meet at a quiet pub out of town, but that doesn't exactly give us a silver bullet.'

Toby's heart skipped a beat. He was fairly certain he knew the place Dylan was referring to. Dylan picked up on his hesitation.

'What is it?'

'I was in a country pub with Beth a while back. I got talking to somebody at the bar and then in the toilets. I later discovered this to have been Eric Stanton. He gave the impression it was somewhere he liked to visit.'

'You think it's the same place?'

'It's out of the way and somewhere he feels comfortable.'

'I think we need to pay this place a visit.'

'We need to tread carefully. If we ask the wrong questions of the wrong people, they'll shut down.'

'There are ways around that,' Dylan said in a manner that unnerved Toby.

'Dylan, people like Eric, as you may have seen, can appear charming to others. They want people to look in another direction. Maintaining a persona that is inconspicuous is vital.'

'And?'

'Troy Galen, like Eric, will probably surround himself with people who see him in a different light than his victims. Either that, or they are afraid of him. Either way, persuading them to drop their silence may not be that easy. We need to think carefully.'

'You're not thinking about running to your cop friend, are you?'

He didn't like Dylan's tone. He was tiring of his resentment towards the law, and the continuous questioning of Toby's loyalties. Though he was consulting on the Eric Stanton murder, this had now been superseded by the urgency of catching a rapist. Not just any rapist, but a rapist who had bought into Eric's world of torture and control. He wanted this as much as Dylan, and became more offended, every time Dylan questioned his methods. There was an urge to rise to the bait, but instead, he responded in a way that would make more of a statement. He remained silent before hanging up the phone.

CHAPTER 23

Friday 12th May...19:30pm

She rarely did this, but dating had been tough the last year because of her demanding work schedule. She reached for a dress before placing it back, opting instead for a more casual, more conservative look. A blouse and a pair of jeans would do fine. She looked in the mirror and saw the apprehensive smile of a 37-year-old woman who had chosen a career over family. She had avoided marriage, with children never entering her agenda. She had enjoyed the single life, perhaps a little too much, but watching friends around her get married and start families had served as a reminder of what she was missing out on. She owned her own home, possessed a collection of luxury cars, and could afford to go on several holidays per year, but the appeal of materials had waned over time. She now felt ready to take the step and enter the minefield that was dating. They had been speaking for a few weeks now, and having had some previous experiences that could only be described as cringeworthy, he had felt like a breath of fresh air. They had much in common, and he had shown more interest in her than himself, which was something she had learned not to take for granted. 'That'll do,' she thought to herself, before heading down the newly installed spiral staircase into the hallway. As she reached for her shoes, she studied the key rack, deliberating which car to take. She didn't want to feel ostentatious, so elected to take the Range Rover. The table was booked for eight, and she loathed being late. They had agreed to meet at a local Thai restaurant, something they both had a love for, though these days she was better acquainted with a take-away menu. Making her way out of the door, she switched off the light and headed towards the car. She felt strangely calm, considering the time that had passed since her last dating experience. She carried no expectations, simply hoping he was as good-natured in person as he was behind a computer screen. After a couple of conversations over the phone, she was eager to get to know him better, so had readily accepted his dinner invitation. The electric gates opened smoothly as she activated the switch from her phone. Technology. How she loved it. Something else they appeared to have in common. As she left the grounds, the butterflies began. A mixture of excitement and trepidation, she concluded. She felt like a schoolgirl about to go on her first date, anxiously awaiting her first kiss. Looking in the mirror, she noticed her cheeks were flushed. The reflection smiled as she allowed herself to get swept up in the moment. With excitement and hope, she looked forward to what the night held. The time felt right. *He* felt right. She screwed up her eyes, realising she was placing too much pressure on herself. Slamming on the brakes, the car came to a sudden halt as she exited the car and took a moment to collect herself in the fresh air. The long and drawn-out breath was stressed, but necessary. She couldn't meet him like this. Everything about her as a professional epitomised composure, but in this moment, it eluded her. The giddiness had now subsided, replaced by an anxiety that seemed to be gathering traction. Pausing, she considered turning back and heading home. She was successful, independent, and ambitious. She didn't need anybody, yet there was something about him which was strangely alluring. Something she felt sure many women had gravitated towards in the past. The nerves would subside once she arrived, she felt sure. That was usually how this worked, right? As the gentle wind blew on her long blonde hair, she got back into the car and started the engine. The roads were quiet at this time in the evening, which meant the journey would likely carry little stress. A few minutes later, the smile had made its way back onto her face as she drew closer to her first date with Gary Tolen.

CHAPTER 24

Tuesday 9th May...17:45pm

'Please don't hang up.'

Toby felt his blood turn to ice as he was rendered almost catatonic. The last time he'd felt like this was *that* night. Finding out she was still alive had induced feelings he was struggling to understand. Regardless of the nature of their relationship, in a short time, Olivia had impacted his life profoundly. There was something strangely alluring about her, something that had been there from the beginning. It had troubled him then, and it troubled him now. He'd spent every day since that night trying to understand how he had allowed himself to come under her influence. Her 'death' had been closure for him and allowed him to very much consign her to his past, but here she was, alive, and very much in his present.

'Olivia.'

Every fibre in his body was urging him to hang up, yet he felt powerless to do so.

'I need your help.'

What could Olivia possibly need from him? He didn't respond. Not because he was unwilling, but because he was unable.

Numerous thoughts skipped through his mind, but none he was able to verbalise at that moment.

'They've charged me with murder.'

Toby still said nothing. He was experiencing an emotional numbness he wasn't familiar with. He was ambivalent, but still...

'Where do I fit into this?'

'That's not the first question I expected you to ask me.'

'Then what was?'

'I thought you'd want to know whether I did it.'

'I already have the answer to that question.'

'Oh?'

'The reason you've used your phone call on me is because you know I don't like injustice. Unless I believe you're innocent, that approach won't work. So, either you're about to take an enormous gamble on me not living up to my reputation, or you're telling me the truth.'

'I have never doubted your professional capability.'

'Were that true, you and I wouldn't be having this conversation now, and our therapeutic relationship would have been brief.'

'I'm sorry, I feel genuine remorse for what I've put you through.'

'That's the second lie you've told me on this call. What you're feeling is regret. Most likely due to the inconvenience this whole situation has caused you.'

There was a brief pause on the other end of the line, and for a split second, Toby wondered whether Olivia had hung up.

'You're right, and I deserve that. But what I don't deserve is to be charged for a crime I didn't commit. I'm already facing a long time away from Tyler. It's hard knowing I'll miss his first day at high school. He'll barely remember me anyway by the time I'm released.'

'What makes you think I can help?'

'I believe you may be the only person who knows I didn't do this. That has to count for something.'

Toby swallowed hard. Deep down, he believed she was innocent, and as much as it pained him to agree with her, she was right about one thing. She didn't deserve to be punished for a crime she hadn't committed. However, it was more than that. He now knew Jack hadn't killed Eric, and the method simply wasn't Dylan's style. The only other suspect would be George, but she wasn't capable. Besides, she had been trying to move on with her life, and this was anything other than moving on. That meant the real killer was still at large.

'Will you help me?'

She sounded genuinely desperate. Hearing Olivia in such a vulnerable state shocked him, yet still, he struggled to sympathise.

'Where would I even begin?'

'The murder weapon.'

'They haven't retrieved it?'

'No. They kept asking me where I'd hidden it.'

'They're either stalling for time because they're sure they'll find it, or they think they have enough evidence already, however circumstantial it might be. Alternatively, they may believe they have a watertight eye witness testimony.'

'The only other person at the scene was Georgina.'

Toby grimaced. The very mention of George's name injected him with discomfort, reminding him that he and Olivia were linked tenuously through her.

'Why do they think you did it?'

'I was at the scene. I had a motive, I guess.'

'That same rationale applies to George, but she hasn't been charged with murder. There must be something else.'

'Perhaps she was more believable in her interview.'

Toby was certain Olivia was keeping something from him. Both women were at the scene of a murder. Both women had been victims of Eric, therefore giving both a motive for murder. Yet they seemed fixated on Olivia. Before he made any decision, he needed to understand what she was keeping back from him.

'Perhaps we are asking the wrong question.'

'What do you mean?'

'Well, rather than asking why you, perhaps we should be asking why not George?'

'What's the difference?' she asked in a somewhat frustrated manner.

'The area of focus. There's no weapon and the circumstances are almost identical. So why not her?'

'I don't know, and to be honest, I don't care. I know that might piss you off, but I'm only concerned with my own situation. I feel sorry for the girl, of course, but that's her trauma to come to terms with. It's her battle, not mine.'

If nothing more, he admired her brutal honesty. He smiled upon realising even as she reached out with one hand, she had no problem lashing out with the other. This encapsulated Olivia Stanton. Vulnerability wasn't her thing. She would only show a glimpse before going on the offensive. She had refused the label of victim previously, and that wasn't going to change now.

'Tell me what happened that day.'

'Do you want to know how I managed to escape from prison?'

She sounded smug.

'Is it relevant?' he asked curtly.

'I thought you may be intrigued.'

She was gloating, but he had no intention of stroking her ego.

'I don't need to know,' he replied dismissively.

'I got to the house late in the afternoon. It was maybe around four o'clock. I heard him pull up, but there was somebody with him. They were arguing. I decided that wasn't the right time to announce my presence, so I went upstairs and hid in one of the bedrooms.'

'How did you get into the house?'

'He kept a key under the bronze statue at the front of the house.'

He knew this already, but there was a reason for the question.

'When did you see George?'

'When I went downstairs after the arguing subsided.'

'George and Eric were arguing?'

'Maybe. I don't know. All I know is she wasn't there when I arrived, and the first time I saw her, she was standing next to his body.'

Toby shook his head, not that Olivia could see him doing so. If everything she was saying was true, George would be the obvious suspect, not her. There was more to this than she was disclosing. He was certain she wasn't the killer, which left him confused as to why she was withholding information that could potentially exonerate her. He was convinced something else had happened in the house that day, but for some reason, she was reluctant to let him in. He wouldn't probe but would remain cautious.

'When you left the house, did you notice the bronze statue?'

'Why?'

'I believe that may have been the murder weapon. More importantly, so do the police.'

'I didn't notice it on the way out.'

'That's because it wasn't there. Whoever killed Eric took it. It will have been discarded close to the scene.'

'How do you know?'

'When you arrived Eric's car wasn't there?

'No.'

'When you left it was?

'Yes,' she replied tentatively.

'If as you say you heard two doors close, that would imply his killer arrived home with him. Yet his car wasn't taken. We can safely assume they didn't call a cab, which means the murderer left on foot. An argument suggests this was spontaneous and not pre-mediated. It's unlikely they would have brought a bag, which means they are left fleeing the scene with a heavy, blood-soaked statue.'

'You should have been a detective,' she teased.

'You know that area well. We are looking for somewhere close to the house, where you could make something disappear without drawing attention to yourself,' he replied, ignoring her remark.

There was a silence as Olivia contemplated. Toby knew finding the murder weapon could be crucial in Olivia proving her innocence. This all had a rushed feel to it, which meant inevitably, the killer would have made mistakes. The evidence would be there, they just had to find it.

'There's a field right next to the house,' she suddenly exclaimed. 'It's overgrown. You can access it from the drive if you follow the tree line about halfway down. Climbing the fence would allow you to remain undetected. There's no public access to that field until further down the road.'

'Who would know about that access point from the drive?'

'I don't know, why?'

'Because it may suggest that the killer wasn't simply somebody who knew Eric, but somebody who was close to him. That would narrow the suspect pool further.'

'So, what now?'

Toby removed the phone from his ear and stared up at the sky. He had promised Beth that Olivia was in his past. She had played a pivotal role in the breakdown of his marriage, his career, and fundamentally his character. Yet here he was on the precipice once again, about to take a dive. He reminded himself that finding the killer would get him closer to discovering who the rapist was; that proving Olivia's innocence may help to prevent other victims suffering at his hands. He reasoned with himself that Olivia wasn't the main show, but simply the warm-up act. It was that thought which lingered as he hung up the phone and headed back to the scene of the crime.

As the line went dead, she wasn't sure how to feel. Had she underestimated the inevitable disdain he felt for her? Had she overestimated his desire to find a killer? She had undoubtedly taken a gamble, but had that phone call sparked Toby Reynolds' interest? As she was escorted back to her cell, at the prison she had only recently escaped from, she suddenly realised she wasn't relying on Toby's forgiveness. That would never come. She was relying on his need to fix. A need he would almost certainly deny, but it was there. It was there that night, and it still burned inside him now. She just hoped that need, that desire, would burn strongly enough to allow him to put his feelings towards her to one side, at least for now. But forgiveness worked both ways in this scenario, she thought. There was no disguising the fact that, in her mind, had Toby not shown up at her house that night, she would be a free woman, actively nurturing her son, rather than watching from a distance. His role had been merely to provide a testimony of her abuse. Both his decision to blur the boundaries and his need to save his client had played a pivotal role in her incarceration. She hadn't wanted that desire then, but she was counting on it now. Everything she had despised in him then, she needed now. Regardless of her feelings towards him, he was smart, and he was tenacious. That much she had learned from their brief time together in a professional capacity. But as much as she had tried to paint him as a figure of hate, and as much as she had tried to apportion blame for her situation onto him, she had a degree of sympathy for Toby Reynolds. She admired who he was as a person and felt bad she had dragged him into a world he was clearly not acquainted with. But that was then. Now, it seemed, he had acclimatised. More than that, he was thriving.

She knew George's ordeal had ignited something within him, and the more time that passed, the more comfortable he was becoming in his new world. He already had all the required attributes, he just needed the incentive. Now, she believed, he had this. As the door on her cell slammed shut, Olivia Stanton looked dejected. There was little doubt her appearance had changed. She looked much older. Yet that dogged determination, that craving to get what she wanted, still remained. As she gazed around her confines, a tentative look made its way onto her face. The stakes were high, and she found herself relinquishing control. Uncomfortable as it was, the action was necessary due to her limited influence in this situation. The retrieval of the murder weapon was her best hope, but so far, the police had come up short. She was relying on Toby. Her future was in his hands, and that made her anxious. As she closed her eyes, she fixated on their relationship. She had used and manipulated him, yet now found herself at his mercy. If he decided to help her, he would be justified. Alternatively, if he opted not to do so, he would also be justified. That was her final thought of the night as she slipped into a deep slumber. The trepidatious look on her face had disappeared. For the moment, at least, she looked peaceful. Something reminiscent of her younger and happier self. Olivia Holmes had been a free-spirited and outgoing individual with little to worry about. Though one and the same, Olivia Holmes and Olivia Stanton were different in almost every way; Eric Stanton had seen to that. Now, he was laughing at her from beyond the grave as she careered out of control down a path towards life imprisonment. They didn't believe her. They liked her for this and would do all they could to make the charges stick. She now relied on a man whom she had wronged and taken so much from. She didn't need his mercy; she needed his brilliance. Then suddenly, the cell fell quiet, with only the faint sound of breathing disrupting the tranquillity. Olivia Stanton was at peace...for now.

CHAPTER 25

Thursday 11th May...19:00pm

The call from Olivia had rocked him, but the last year had thrown up more than one surprise. From George's history with Eric to Olivia's apparent resurrection, Toby had been left perpetually braced for the unforeseen. In his professional setting, he believed he had experienced almost everything. But nothing could have prepared him for what was to follow his first meeting with Olivia Stanton. Conflicted, he had ultimately decided against revisiting the scene of Eric's murder. His mind hadn't changed, it simply hadn't been made up in the first place. That decision wasn't based on his feelings for Olivia, but more a case of where he felt there was the greatest need at this moment in time. Olivia was already behind bars, and that wouldn't change. Everything about the murder had suggested it was spontaneous yet personal, which meant in his mind, they weren't dealing with a serial killer or even somebody who would likely kill again. But there was a serial rapist on the street who had been involved in luring women with the sole intention of defiling and dehumanising them. This wasn't about sex. Rape rarely was. It was about power and control. They were mere pawns in a sick and twisted game...playthings. The photographs highlighted they revelled in what they did. Perhaps they even competed with one another. Eric's death hadn't nullified the danger to women. Though it was no longer about him, it still felt like he had a certain influence, even from beyond the grave. But tonight wasn't about him. It was about his grieving sister.

'Thank you for coming. I do really appreciate it,' she said nervously.'

'My social calendar isn't exactly overflowing these days,' he replied with a smile, before regretting the way the words came out.

'I didn't mean it like that...'

'It's fine,' she interrupted. 'You were the last option.'

She winked at him playfully.

'Touché.'

'How have you been?' he asked.

'It seems to have suddenly hit me. Is that normal?'

'Delayed grief isn't uncommon. Perhaps you were in shock?'

'Or denial.'

'That's also common.'

'I've read about the five stages of grief. I think maybe I have entered depression. Only one stage left I guess.'

'It doesn't necessarily work like that.'

'Oh?'

'People often believe it's sequential. It's a common misconception.'

'So, I may jump back a stage?'

'Not everybody experiences all five stages,' Toby replied.

'How's things with your wife?'

Toby froze. Why was she asking about Beth? She had done the same the last time they had met. Was this polite conversation, or did she have an ulterior motive?

'I'm sorry, I didn't mean to be intrusive,' she added.

Toby smiled. This had a first-date feel to it. The awkward conversation, the tentative questions. He felt hesitant, but couldn't understand why. It wasn't a date. He still remained as committed to Beth as the first day he had met her. Infidelity wasn't his thing. Then it hit him. It had hit him the first time he'd seen her at his house, he just hadn't realised it at the time...or had he? Natasha Jenkins was captivating. There was something about her. What he was feeling was fear, and he felt certain that every moment he remained in her presence, that fear would intensify. He reminded himself that she wasn't Olivia, but couldn't deny there were similarities.

'She's still spending time with her sister. They're close,' he finally replied.

She nodded, before looking down at the table. Toby thought he saw her blush. Was she flirting with him?

'I hear you're consulting on my brother's murder case.'

Toby wasn't sure how to take her comment, and Natasha had clearly picked up on this.

'Relax. I think the force could use someone like you. From what I hear, nobody understands behaviour better.'

Now it was Toby's turn to blush. Another reminder he didn't take compliments at all well.

'There are many better than me,' he replied brushing off the praise. 'I'll go order.'

He wasn't in a rush for his caffeine fix, but he was beginning to feel uncomfortable and needed a distraction. On the surface, he'd come here because she had reached out to him, consumed with grief at the loss of her brother. On the surface. He didn't dare contemplate what may be occurring underneath. He'd never hated another person but came closer with Eric Stanton than anybody else. She knew Toby's feelings, so why would he be the one she called? Standing up to leave the table, he felt a bead of sweat drip down his forehead. As he wiped it away, he studied his surroundings. But mainly, looking back from the counter, he studied Natasha. She was presenting as friendly, but her body language told a different story. It went beyond sadness, beyond grief. She looked lost. She had lost her career over an impulsive decision, much like him. Now she had lost her brother. That was a significant amount of loss for anybody to sustain. He suddenly felt sorry for the slight figure, now relaxed back into her chair. Toby returned to the table and placed the two drinks down on the freshly wiped surface. Taking his seat, the look on her face suggested she had something to say, but was struggling to find the right words.

'Thank you,' she said politely.

'My mum always said a good coffee would shine a light on even the darkest of days.'

'She's a wise woman.'

'Was,' Toby corrected, feeling a sadness creeping in.

'I'm sorry.'

'It was a long time ago.'

She looked at him awkwardly. She seemed sincere.

'I was at university when she took her own life. She was one of the main reasons I went into psychotherapy.'

'That must have been awful for you.'

As she said this, she reached over the table and gently rubbed his hand. It took him by surprise, but he didn't rebuff her at first.

Having only met her twice before today he didn't know her well, but his instincts told him this was more of a compassionate gesture than a romantic one.

'It was so unexpected. Even looking back now, I still can't identify any signs that suggested she was suffering.'

He hadn't opened up to many people about his mum's death but felt strangely at ease doing so with Natasha. She let go of his hand and sat back in her chair, reaching for her coffee in the same movement. She rubbed her hands together and then reached into her bag, drawing out a pair of gloves and placing them over her hands.

'Raynaud's,' she said with a smile, but Toby noticed a pain sat behind it. He also noticed there was a natural grace to her mannerisms, not unlike Beth. She noticed his stare.

'The most frustrating thing is there is no consistency or method to it. It can just strike at any time. For me, it's mainly my hands that suffer. They can switch from warm to freezing cold in what appears to be an instant. I always carry gloves around with me just in case, though I don't need to use them every day. It's rather embarrassing, to be honest. Can I ask you a question,' she asked, quickly changing direction.

Toby nodded.

'Do you think Olivia killed my brother?'

Toby was caught off guard and wasn't wholly sure how to respond to such a question. Was he able to discuss any aspect of the case now he was officially consulting on it? He decided to exercise caution. He would share his opinion, but not the specifics. He had an inkling she would still have enough contacts in the police force to be able to elicit the facts of the case anyway, which meant her interest lay with his thoughts.

'The police seem to think so.'

'But you don't?'

He took a deep breath.

'Olivia had motive, opportunity, and had attempted previously.'

'But?'

'It feels a little too contrived.'

'Have you told Mike that?'

She grinned at him, but Toby felt a nervous sensation overcome him. This was beginning to feel more like an interrogation than a friendly chat over coffee, but she was seeking closure. He would remain sensitive to that.

'I never liked that woman. There was something about her that made me feel uneasy. But now I know what he did, I find myself having a degree of sympathy for her. God knows what he did to her. I didn't meet her until they had been together for about a year. I guess he'd already done the damage by then. But I can't hate him, Toby. You know? He was my brother and underneath all of this, he was damaged like the rest of us.

'Damaged?'

'Our upbringing wasn't easy. Eric had it worse than me. He saw more. She paused. 'I'm not trying to justify it,' she hastily added.

'Explanation and justification are very different. We seek to understand, not condone.'

She smiled, but it looked forced. Toby firmly believed there was a victim behind every perpetrator. Past trauma almost always sat in the background where any emotional unrest was concerned. Still, showing any degree of sympathy for Eric Stanton was proving difficult.

'Do *you* think she did it?' he asked.

'She had reason, but perhaps others did too. I heard they had Georgina Sampson, but released her without charge.'

Toby nodded hesitantly, remaining coy about his knowledge of the case.

'How did you find out?'

'About Georgina?'

'About your brother.'

'I overheard him on the phone. He didn't know I was there, but I heard enough to realise the whispers going around had substance. Suddenly, it all made sense, and I could no longer defend him.'

'Did you ever find out who he was talking to on the phone?'

'That's what creeped me out. The way they were talking, you know...'

She stopped, but it didn't matter. Toby knew how that sentence ended. He noticed a stray tear begin to make its way down her cheek. This was painful for her to recount. He wondered whether a subtle change of direction would be the best option, but quickly realised that without knowing it, she had moved onto a topic which was of greater interest to him than her brother's murder. Not that he would ever disclose that to her.

'If Olivia didn't kill my brother, then who did?'

'I'm only consulting on the case.'

'And what exactly does that entail?' she asked.

'It's effectively criminal profiling.'

'Sounds interesting.'

Toby didn't reply. Instead, he braced himself for the inevitable questioning he was about to face. She wasn't just here for closure. She was here to find out information about the case. She was hurting and needed an avenue to channel this when that hurt inevitably turned to anger. She needed a suspect. More than that, she needed the killer.

'So, you'll know who they like for this?'

Toby hesitated. She was becoming more forthright with her questions. He was beginning to feel under pressure and didn't have the answers she was seeking.

'I'm sorry, this is all still raw for me,' Natasha added.

'I can only imagine,' he replied with a sympathetic smile.

'Tell me about Dylan Sampson.'

Toby felt an uncomfortable feeling in the pit of his stomach. Why was she asking about Dylan? As far as he knew, she'd met him only once, briefly, at Toby's house the night Beth had called Mike. He was now convinced that Natasha had somebody close to the investigation feeding her information.

'What would you like to know?' he replied casually.

'I hear he was at my brother's house the day he was murdered.'

Toby didn't respond. His silence gave her the impetus to continue.

'He suspected my brother of being behind the kidnapping of his sister. His prints end up all over the scene. He had motive and opportunity, right?'

'Are you asking me or telling me?'

Natasha smiled.

'A man of that size with a temper like his could do some damage,' she continued.

'You think Dylan killed Eric?'

'I don't know what to think. My brother had a list of enemies. That list seems to be getting longer by the day.'

It wasn't his enemies Toby was interested in though. It was his friends. One in particular. It dawned on him that their conflicting goals were making it hard to continue the conversation with Natasha. He was treading a tightrope, and balancing his desire to find out more about Troy Galen with being sensitive to Natasha's need to find her brother's killer, was no easy feat. He knew Dylan had been at the house, and he knew why. Dylan was more than capable of killing Eric, and no doubt could have justified it to himself, but it simply didn't fit for Toby. Dylan wasn't a suspect, in his mind.

'You're correct with the assertion Dylan could do some damage. You're also correct he had motive, but you're looking in the wrong direction.'

'And what direction should I be looking in?'

'If I knew that, I suspect we wouldn't be sitting here having this conversation right now.'

'What makes you so sure it wasn't him?'

'Eric was struck from behind and that's not Dylan's style.'

'How can you be certain?'

'I've spent time with him. He enjoys inflicting suffering on those who have wronged him. A swift blow from behind doesn't fit that narrative.'

Natasha lowered her head, disillusioned. Toby could see how desperate she was to find her answers...answers that would provide her with some closure and allow her to begin moving through her grief. But as Toby knew only too well, life wasn't always that kind to you. He felt a deep sympathy for her situation but was now beginning to wonder what she wanted from him. As she took another sip from her cup, savouring the carefully prepared beverage, she looked around the room. Toby noticed her staring at a picture hung on the wall at the back of the counter. It depicted an isolated cabin set in wintry woodlands.

'I love that picture,' Toby said softly. 'Geographic isolation.'

She smiled, but somehow it seemed forced.

'I can see the appeal of living completely off grid. Beth, not so much.'

'City girl?'

'Not really, but she does like access to local amenities.'

'You must miss her.'

Toby realised as uncomfortable as he felt talking about Eric Stanton, the prospect of talking about Beth was even more daunting. Noticing his hesitation, she reached out and placed her hand on his arm in an affectionate way. Toby didn't recoil. He suddenly felt emotionally vulnerable.

'Events of the last twelve months have taken their toll on our marriage. Beth feels they have changed me.'

'Have they?'

He smiled. That's how he would have responded to a client in this same situation.

'Trauma has a tendency to change things.'

'You saved my brother's life, and then somebody else took it. How does that feel?'

'This feels like therapy,' Toby said politely.

Natasha looked sheepish. She was darting all over the place with her conversation. It was a sign she was nervous, but it made her difficult to read. He wasn't sure why he was trying to read her. Old habits perhaps?

'When you balance on a tightrope for so long, there's always the possibility you will fall at some point. Or even get pulled off it.'

'It sounds like you think there was an inevitability about his death.'

'Don't you?' she asked sharply. 'Don't you think that somebody who inflicts so much suffering onto people deserves their comeuppance?'

'You're asking me if I agree with the death penalty?'

'I guess so.'

'No,' he said firmly.

'Aren't some people just born bad?'

'Do you feel that was the case with Eric?'

She paused. The focus of the conversation had again switched.

'Yes,' she finally responded.

'I don't believe you mean that.'

'Oh?'

'A short while ago you told me your brother had been damaged during his upbringing. You said he had seen things, which I can only assume must have affected him profoundly. That suggests trauma may have been pulling his strings.'

'Sounds like you're making excuses for him.'

'Understanding one's actions is not justifying them.'

'I admire how you're able to stay so balanced. How do you remove your personal feelings?'

'That voice is always there. It just becomes quieter.'

Natasha leaned back in her seat, immersed in her own thoughts. Her warm smile had returned, and he was again reminded of her natural beauty. She had caught him off guard with her willingness to change direction in conversation in an instant, yet he felt a degree of comfort in her presence. Aside from Beth, she was the first woman he had felt like this around. Even George had elicited an element of caution within him.

'I don't know how I'm supposed to feel. I'm so conflicted after my own ordeal...'

She stopped, as though she had disclosed too much. But Toby knew what was about to come. He had known since their first meeting. Her inner turmoil was being driven by the fact her brother had committed the one crime that would resonate with her more than any other. She had lived as his victims had, just with a different perpetrator.

'I was nineteen and waitressing at a local restaurant. You know, trying to earn some money whilst I figured out what I wanted to do with my life. Anyway, there was this guy I worked with. He was older than me, but he was kind and everybody fancied him. I was tired of dating kids, so when he showed interest in me, I agreed to go out with him. I never questioned why me at the time, but looking back, he could have had his pick, and I was nothing special.'

She paused and looked up at the ceiling. She was about to re-live a trauma; this wouldn't be easy for her. He reminded himself she wasn't a client, though he wasn't entirely sure what she was to him. She clasped her hands together, smiled at him and continued.

'We went out a few times and I thought he really liked me. I was young, naïve, and flattered that somebody like him would pay me any attention. After about a month he invited me to a cabin in a secluded part of the country. It looked picturesque and I remember feeling so excited. When we got there, the first thing I noticed was that the place looked nothing like it did in the photographs. When we walked through the door, we weren't alone. He reassured me the other three men were old school friends he hadn't seen in years, and they were only there for the evening to catch up. As the drinks flowed, things started to feel out of place, and his manner changed. He was no longer the person I thought he was.'

She stopped again as tears began to stream down her face. Toby knew what was coming, but this was her story to tell. He reached out and placed his hand on her arm.

'It's okay. You're in a safe place now,' he said reassuringly.

'That night I was passed around. I lost count of how many times. I just became numb in the end. At first, I resisted. Then when I realised I had no control, I just let them do it. Once they'd passed out from all the alcohol, I grabbed my bag and just ran. It was dark, but I managed to somehow find my way to a road.

Some kind lady picked me up and took me to the local bus station. I only ever told one person. Eric.'

She looked up at Toby, and he suddenly saw the hatred within her eyes.

'I told him every last detail of what happened to me. I cried in his arms. He watched me struggle during the night-time, and become a recluse during the day. He saw it all, yet still, he did what he did. He saw the effect it had on victims, but he still chose to undertake those sickening acts. How do I feel any remorse for a man like that?'

There was nothing Toby could say to make this any easier for her, so he chose to stay silent. She rubbed his hand before wiping away her tears. He couldn't even begin to imagine the conflict she was experiencing. Her brother had become the very person she despised more than any other, yet he was now dead, and she was wrestling with her emotions. As he looked up, he caught a glimpse of the painting he had drawn her attention to. His face dropped as he realised why her smile had felt so forced. It had resonated with her, inducing powerful traumatic memories of a time she had likely tried hard to forget.

The conversation had become much more superficial after that, the emotion of her disclosure proving too much for Natasha. Toby felt a real sadness for her. Single, with a strained relationship with her parents, and now her brother whom she recently discovered was a serial rapist, dead. She'd gambled her career on him, a decision she was now openly regretting. She'd lost everything, but a feeling within Toby surfaced. What had begun as a niggling doubt had escalated into something he was now certain of. There was more. She was holding something back, he was sure. That feeling remained as the two said their goodbyes and headed off in different directions. The question was, did Natasha Jenkins have a secret to tell, or a secret to hide?

CHAPTER 26

S aturday 13th May...14:45pm

Toby looked outside. The climate was betraying the season. This was the height of spring, heading into summer, yet the cool temperature accompanied by the dark clouds felt like he had been transported back several months to the middle of winter. Despite his reluctance to acknowledge it, the weather had been having a noticeable effect on his spirits lately. Ever since his car accident, his moods had been darkened when it came to the winter months, or anything resembling them. Beth had tried to help, but Beth wasn't here. His inability to pick himself up served as a reminder of the distance between them, not just in the physical realm. The last woman he'd enjoyed conversation with had been Natasha. This had both saddened and worried Toby. He'd enjoyed her company, and that was the problem. He was now harbouring a deep guilt, which he hadn't previously experienced. He sat staring at the blank computer screen in front of him. He'd spent the morning torn between finding a rapist and finding a murderer, still with a niggling feeling that it could be the same person. Finally, he had come to a decision. Switching his focus to discovering the identity of Eric's killer hadn't been a choice based on Olivia's plea. It had been based on the anguish he had witnessed first-hand in Natasha. Locating a serial rapist wouldn't give her the sense of closure finding her brother's killer would, but it would remove a genuine threat to women. Both crimes struck a chord with her, just for different reasons. He removed his reading glasses and placed them on the table in front of him, but not before picking up the batch of freshly printed images, which had been haunting him since the day he had received them from Dylan. He thought that enlarging the photos might help him discover some detail, however small, that would help identify the women. Their best hope of finding the assailant would be to build up a picture of him. That would mean first tracing his victims, which in itself presented several challenges. Even if there was anything identifiable within the images, it would then take some work to track down that individual. Then, of course, there was the reticence of some victims not wishing to be found. Toby knew from experience that things suppressed were done so for a reason. Asking a victim to re-live a past trauma such as rape could be construed as insensitive. Some people preferred to just simply move past it. The need for justice was often felt to a greater degree by family members than the victims themselves. He stared down at the coffee table, more specifically the image staring back at him. A young woman with blonde hair. She was half dressed, on display like a piece of art, yet this was about fear more than grace. She had most probably been asked to pose like this to satisfy a thirst for control. This wasn't about sexual gratification. It was about wielding absolute power over another person. She had likely been forced to beg for her release, an act that in itself would further feed their insatiable appetites. He bolted upright grasping the photo and pulling it closer to his face. The detail he had been searching for had been staring right at him, he just hadn't known it. He stumbled out of his chair, almost tripping in the process, and sprinted up the staircase to the small room he used as an office these days. He waited impatiently for his laptop to spring to life. Finally, he was in. He began pouring through the archived files in his psychotherapy folder, frantically searching.

Seb T...

He clicked on the file and opened up the case notes, but the urgency had now made way for something more detailed. Although client disclosures aren't always fully recorded, therapists typically remember when therapy dramatically changes course due to a traumatic experience. Seb had presented with crippling anxiety about two years ago and had been progressing well. That was until his girlfriend had been brutally raped. Though Toby had never met her, he had heard a great deal about Abigail Crookes through his sessions with Seb. A young girl, vulnerable by all accounts. She had a young daughter and had been the victim of a tough upbringing. Seb had initially taken them on as a project but had confessed to falling hard and fast for Abigail. Sympathy had turned to love unexpectedly. Seb had ended his relationship shortly after the incident, unable to handle his own grief and support Abigail. He ended the therapy a matter of weeks after that. Toby had a face, and he had a name, but it would be the next step which would prove most difficult. Regardless, there had been a development and that meant one thing.

'I think I may have identified one of the victims.'

'Somebody you know?'

'Not directly.'

'Then how?'

'I can't go into detail, but one of the girls has two distinctive features, which on their own would perhaps mean nothing. Together though...'

'Do you know where to find her?' Dylan interrupted.

'I don't think that's the challenge.'

'Then what?'

Before responding, Toby considered the most tactful way to tell Dylan that asking a trauma victim to relive their trauma was difficult, no matter what the objective.

'How long did it take for George to open up about her ordeal?'

'This isn't about George,' he yelled.

'Actually Dylan, it is. In more than one way. This woman is just like her. Both fell victim to Eric. George was able to open up about her attack in her own time. All victims should be afforded that courtesy.'

'So, we just leave it?'

Dylan's frustration appeared to increase with every answer Toby was providing.

'That's not what I'm saying.'

'Then what are you saying?'

'This needs to be handled sensitively. But also, we need to be prepared for the fact she may not wish to talk.'

'When do we go?'

Now came the really difficult part of the conversation for Toby. The truth was he couldn't have Dylan anywhere near a victim. Quite simply, he didn't trust him, and it would only take one inappropriate comment or act to bring down the shutters and end the conversation. He couldn't risk that, and he couldn't put a rape victim through any further anguish. There was no way to dress this up. He would need to be honest but with as much diplomacy as possible.

'Dylan, I've never met anybody who has the ability to extract information from people like you do.'

He hesitated.

'But?' Dylan asked.

'You're used to working with perpetrators. We have very different skill sets, and this situation requires somebody accustomed to working with victims. I respect your areas of expertise and have trust in what you do. Now it's time for you to do the same for me.'

'Don't fuck it up.'

'I appreciate your confidence in me,' Toby laughed, but his composure above the surface wasn't reflected underneath. He was nervous, largely due to the expectations he knew Dylan had placed on him. There was also the small matter of locating Abigail Crookes. Realistically he had two options. Enlist Mike's help, or contact a past client. He stopped. There was a third option. He knew somebody who no longer had any affiliation with Mike but had inside information. Natasha.

'I'll keep you posted,' he said casually to Dylan before hanging up.

'You do realise what you're asking, right?'

He did, and had braced himself for an inevitable line of questioning he didn't feel comfortable with. But in his mind, this was the most viable option. Talking to Mike would alert him to the fact he was conducting an investigation outside of what he had been commissioned to do. Equally, he didn't feel comfortable contacting a former client to ask them about the whereabouts of an ex-partner. This would be uncomfortable but would carry the least chance of serious repercussions.

Toby nodded.

'What's her name?'

Toby looked down at the ground.

'Abigail Crookes.'

It was only a brief moment, but he noticed it. She had flinched; something had chimed with her. She either knew Abigail or she knew about the case. But why had she tried so hard to camouflage it? He didn't acknowledge it.

'How did you identify her?'

'There are two significant markings on her face. Isolated, they would mean nothing, but together they felt like too much of a coincidence.'

'How do you know of her?'

'That's a question, I'd rather not answer.'

'You don't trust me?'

'It's not about trust. Will you help me?'

'What makes you so sure I can?'

Toby studied her for a moment. Her darkened eyes looked like she hadn't slept for a while.

'Can you?'

'I'll see what I can do.'

'You're not sleeping.'

'Is that a question or an observation?'

Toby thought carefully for a moment. She was grieving, and he didn't feel good about having to come to her with this, but he reasoned with himself there were no other options.

'Are you taking care of yourself?'

'Are you?' she replied, somewhat defensively.

Toby smiled at her before reaching over the table, stroking her shoulder, briefly. He pushed his chair back and stood to leave, but as he did so, she grabbed his arm. Toby flinched, taken back to the last time he had tried to leave a conversation and been halted. A look of confusion spread across her face as she noticed his hesitation.

'Toby?'

How could he answer her? How could he tell her that looking into her eyes right now, all he could see was her abusive brother? The person she loathed, yet also grieved.

'I'm sorry. You just took me by surprise that's all.'

'I didn't mean to startle you. I just don't want you to go.'

The two sat staring at one another across the table for what seemed like an eternity to Toby, but in reality, was just a few seconds. A strange feeling overcame him, but that feeling was compelling him to stay rather than run. He smiled as he looked down at his watch.

'I have time for another drink, I guess.'

Natasha caught the eye of one of the baristas, who was busy cleaning a table nearby, and ordered two coffees.

'Beth was always uncomfortable ordering drinks. She felt like she was imposing.'

Natasha giggled.

'She's lucky to have somebody like you.'

Toby blushed. Yet another reminder of how much he struggled with compliments.

'I'm not sure Beth would agree with that.'

'Relationships are tough.' She looked down at the table. 'I lost my partner. Haven't dated since. She was killed by the people she was trying to help.'

Toby looked at her, unable to hide his confusion.

'I'm bi-sexual, Toby,' she replied noticing.

Toby felt both embarrassed and ashamed. He had no reason to assume her sexuality. Why had it been a surprise to him? More importantly, why did it matter?

'We were together for five years, but she's been gone a long time. I still miss her.'

'I'm so sorry,' he managed.

'We'd discussed marriage, though it had taken her a while to convince me. We'd planned to elope at Christmas of that year. She died in June.'

Words would have little effect here. He reached across the table and placed his hand on her wrist, offering a sympathetic look. He could see the pain in her eyes. Then he withdrew and studied her for a moment.

'Abigail Crookes.'

Toby's concentration was broken.

'You're assisting with my brother's murder. What do you need with a rape victim?'

Toby no longer felt comfortable with this dialogue. Not for the first time, he found himself desperately trying to find a way of exiting a conversation with a Stanton.

'I'm sorry to have bothered you,' he said sliding his chair back.

This time there was no attempt to keep him there. She looked dejected, but he wasn't her therapist. He wasn't even her friend. The truth was, he barely knew her, yet here he was clinging to whatever this was in some hope she may be able to help him. He didn't feel good about it. He didn't feel good about any of what was happening. As he turned to leave, he dropped a business card on the table in front of her.

'Give him a call. He's an excellent grief counsellor,' Toby said with a warm smile.

Scarcely ten minutes had passed before Toby received a message from Natasha.

07885 363229-Abigail. Thanks for the coffee. Tash x

The small house was nestled in the corner of a cul-de-sac on an estate which you perhaps wouldn't wish to venture out onto at night. He looked down at the notes scribbled on the pad sitting comfortably on the vacant passenger seat to ensure he had the correct address. He did. Tentatively, Toby closed the car door and made his way towards the house, still unsure as to exactly what he was hoping to get from the conversation. It had taken some time to gain her trust, but she had agreed to see him. Perhaps reluctantly. As he gently knocked on the door, he felt a tinge of trepidation. This intensified as he saw a shadowy figure approach the other side of the glass.

'Abigail?'

At first, she didn't reply, seemingly more concerned with looking over his shoulder to ensure nobody was watching. Satisfied they were not under the watchful eyes of the neighbours, she motioned for him to come in and quickly closed the door. The hallway was narrow with paint peeling off the wall. Sporadically scattered toys provided the only real indication there was a child living here. There was a serenity about the place not conducive to the presence of children. They were alone. The lounge was small, yet not without charm. It was well decorated with a fireplace nestled under a chimney which looked unusually big in its surroundings. She signalled for Toby to take a seat on the small 2-seated sofa underneath the window.

'Can I get you a drink?' she asked politely, now seeming more relaxed.

'No, thank you,' he replied. 'Thank you for agreeing to see me.'

'I know how much you helped Seb. He really trusted you.'

Toby let out a smile, but it was a reluctant one. He was still uncomfortable with any mention of past cases. The boundaries, however, had been blurred the moment he accessed case notes from a past client to confirm Abigail's identity. Tracking her down and questioning her went way beyond blurring.

'It was too much for him to handle in the end. He saw me as both a victim and a perpetrator, I think. He was right, wasn't he?'

It was rhetorical. Abigail Crookes wasn't looking for his validation. She had a story to tell, and his only objective was to hear that story.

'I loved Seb, but I was struggling with Leyla. That's my daughter. We didn't earn much. Suddenly this guy, Eric, ghosts into my life and shows me something I wasn't used to. I know it must sound strange, but the escape from being a mum merely scraping by, caught up in a routine, was really appealing.'

She paused and stared out of the window. A vacant look appeared on her face, like she was somewhere else. Toby wondered whether this was down to regret at losing Seb, or the ordeal itself. She took a deep breath and continued.

'It only happened a few times, four or five maybe. He took me out for lunch or coffee. Usually when Leyla was with my parents. We'd then go back to his place and have sex. You have to understand it wasn't about the physical side for me. It was just a way of escaping my life, and having a little excitement. Do you know what I mean?'

Toby nodded. He'd worked extensively with affairs but had no interest in them. Affairs didn't break relationships. They merely highlighted the fact there were problems within them. But this wasn't an affair, it was grooming. She had been targeted; she just hadn't realised. Eric Stanton had no interest in her as a person. His interest lay in her vulnerability.

'He seemed really nice until that last time. We'd been to a really lavish wine bar and had lunch and a few drinks. We then headed back to his place, but this time it was different.'

'Different?'

'He was different. Kind of on edge.'

'He was anxious.'

'What makes you say that?'

'What happened to you wasn't a spontaneous act. It had been carefully planned. He would have likely fantasised about that moment. That creates an internal pressure to live up to the fantasy.'

'I thought he liked me.'

'You were supposed to. It's how he gained your trust.'

Toby hesitated, aware of his sharp tone.

'I'm sorry for my bluntness,' he said, apologetically.

'It's okay. I guess I was naïve.'

Toby smiled, and this time it was genuine. Even though she had knowingly begun an affair, he felt sorry for her. She hadn't asked for any of this, and that decision had cost her much more than just a relationship.

'How much did you tell your partner?'

She smiled at him, and Toby knew she had picked up on his reluctance to refer to Seb by name.

'You can say his name you know,' she said reassuringly, before continuing. 'I told him I was in town, and somebody who I got talking to offered me a ride home. I couldn't bear to lose him. Turns out I did anyway.'

'What happened when you entered the house?'

'We weren't alone. I took an instant dislike to the guy. He was smarmy and had a look about him. He came and sat next to me and began to run his hand up my skirt. I told him to stop, but it was like I wasn't there. I looked to Eric for help, but he just stood grinned. I managed to free myself and got up to leave.'

'They prevented you from leaving?'

'Not physically.'

Toby looked at Abigail, confused.

Eric had text messages and pictures. He threatened to tell Seb about the affair. But it wasn't just that. He threatened to tell the parents and teachers at Leyla's nursery. He said my reputation would be in tatters. I had no choice but to stay.'

'You didn't consent.'

'Didn't I? I stayed and took part.'

'Consenting through fear after being threatened is not consenting.'

'Then what is it?'

'What you're describing is sexual coercion.'

Abigail wiped away a tear and stared at Toby for a moment.

'You understand now why I never came forward.'

Toby smiled and nodded gently.

'They took pictures and made notes. It was humiliating. They had me pose in different positions. I was nothing to them. Can I ask you a question?'

'Sure.'

'Do you think there are others?'

Toby bowed his head. His eyes had already given him away. Abigail didn't need any verbal confirmation; she had her answer.

'Shit,' she said softly, almost in a whisper. 'Why did you come here today, Toby?'

'Eric Stanton is dead, but his accomplice is still very much at large. I'm trying to identify who that person is.'

'I can't remember what he looked like. He wore a baseball cap, but I don't recall any distinguishing features. I guess I tried to block it out.'

'That's not uncommon.'

Toby smiled but didn't want to push.

'I'm sorry I couldn't be of more help,' she said regretfully.

'Thank you for your hospitality.'

Abigail Crookes watched from the doorway as Toby headed down the path. The trepidation around being seen appeared to have disappeared. Toby opened the car door but stopped just as he was about to get in.

'Did you tell anyone at all about what happened?'

'I spoke to a member of the rape crisis team. She was nice, but I never made anything official. I knew the world would only see somebody who consented and later regretted her decision. Isn't that how it happens? A woman has an affair, things get messy, and they cry rape?'

'I'm sorry.'

'May I ask you one final question?'

Toby nodded.

'Should I have told the police?'

'There are many reasons why crimes aren't reported. Try not to reproach yourself.'

Toby looked down at his watch.

'I should go. I've taken up enough of your time. Thank you for seeing me.'

He offered her a sympathetic smile as he turned to leave the house. Although she hadn't spoken much, she'd unknowingly divulged more than she had realised. This was how they had remained under the radar. This was why there had been no complainants. Sexual coercion was much more difficult to prove than rape. He now felt certain they had convinced each of their victims it was consensual. Toby drove away slowly, deep in contemplation. The further he got into this, the more he was becoming convinced the sexual assaults and the murder were linked.

CHAPTER 27

Monday 15th May...10:00am

Quiet contemplation was a close acquaintance of Toby's these days. His visit to Abigail Crookes had left him with more questions than answers, though he hadn't left empty-handed. He now realised how they had managed to avoid detection, and the likely reason for the victims not coming forward. Abigail had been frightened, but not of what they could do to her physically. The leverage they had held over her was enough to coerce her into complying. Of course, this was not due to a willingness, but a fear of the consequences should she refuse. They exercised complete control over her, and Toby knew that was part of the thrill for them. She was vulnerable, she was desperate, and she was at their mercy. The respite a country walk ordinarily offered was somewhat lacking today. He was struggling to gain any perspective, any real breakthrough. He needed a different viewpoint, and it suddenly dawned on him that it would come from an unexpected source.

'What do you have?'

'We're not looking at rape.'

'What do you mean we're not looking at rape?'

Toby felt himself begin to perspire, wondering how he could deliver the next part. The country pub was relaxed and inviting, the antithesis of the man sitting opposite. Toby placed his head in his hands and let out a sigh.

'I think I have the answer as to why nobody came forward.'

'They were scared. That's what usually happens with rape victims, right?'

'Not exactly. They were scared, but not necessarily of Eric and his criminal partner.'

'Then what?'

'Of what an investigation would uncover.'

'And what's that?'

'Infidelity.'

Though Dylan's puzzled expression was visible, he probably didn't realise it reflected Toby's internal state.

'Abigail wasn't raped. She was the victim of sexual coercion. She had begun an affair with Eric, and he used her existing relationship, and even her daughter, as leverage. He built up her trust and manipulated her.'

'She consented?'

'That's a grey area. She participated, but not willingly.'

'So, she didn't consent.'

Toby leaned back in his chair and let out a deep breath, highlighting a little frustration. This wasn't easy to explain. Dylan was a black-and-white person, but this was anything but.

'She didn't want to have sex with them, but they didn't force themselves on her either. She was threatened with the one thing that would hurt her most.'

'Exposure?'

'Precisely. I didn't leave there any clearer on who the other person is, but I certainly left with more clarity.'

'Like what?'

'I think they prayed on vulnerable women. This was an operation that would have involved intricate planning. The victims were sought out, charmed by promises of a better life, and then coerced into doing whatever was asked of them. This was about absolute power and control. It was about humiliation. But there's one more thing...'

Dylan gazed at Toby wide-eyed with a rising anger that was difficult to hide.

'Go on.'

'I don't believe Eric was the architect. I think he was the accomplice.'

'She told you that?'

'Not specifically. Just an impression I got from the way she described it all.'

'So, what now?'

Toby's shoulders slumped as he looked around the pub, desperately trying to draw some inspiration. He'd fallen flat. Knowing the techniques and the process the perpetrators had used to select their victims, still left him and Dylan no closer to discovering the identity of the person they now believed had been pulling the strings all along.

'I don't know,' he replied with a degree of resignation.

The table the two men were sitting at fell under an awkward silence. One looked deep in thought, somewhat desolate. The other smouldered with an intensity that was increasing with every passing moment. Toby picked up his glass of water and took a long drink. The warmer weather often meant he exchanged his obligatory coffee for something more likely to quench his thirst. He'd also resolved to maintain a healthier lifestyle, and water played a much more prominent role in that than coffee.

The journey home was dominated by an intense feeling of pressure. He could feel the weight of Dylan's gaze even when not in his presence. He knew the expectations he had, and Dylan Sampson was not a man known for his patience or understanding. Toby was almost certain he was on a timer, and that timer was quickly running down. What he knew, with a degree of certainty, was that the women were carefully selected. They were vulnerable, which made them easier to manipulate and coerce. Perhaps the hardest thing for him to accept was that if he was right, each of the victims would have consented. That didn't mean they willingly participated, but they weren't physically forced against their will. This didn't rid Eric Stanton of his label, but perhaps further substantiated Toby's theory he wasn't the one orchestrating things. The clues were out there, he just needed to dig deep enough. As he walked through the door and headed for the conservatory, he stopped at a picture hanging from the wall. It was one of his favourite photos of them both, and he'd found himself more and more drawn to it since Beth had left. It had been taken around three years ago whilst they had been holidaying in the Bahamas. Beth looked radiant. They both looked carefree, but then again, they were back then. Toby felt sad knowing he'd let down the loving couple staring back at him. This wasn't supposed to happen. Olivia, George, Dylan,

Natasha...his life didn't involve them. For so long it had just been he and Beth, and he missed that. He smiled, but it disguised a deep sadness at what his life had become. The enjoyment of consulting on a murder case seemed somewhat diminished without having Beth to share in it. Toby moved into the kitchen and poured himself a glass of water. Though the sun was shining, the temperature was deceptively low, encouraging him to opt against housing himself outside in the garden. He pulled out his phone and again turned his attention to the photographs Dylan had sent him, studying each one in detail. He was missing something. It was there; he just needed to search thoroughly. Suddenly, an ice-cold shiver entered his veins, running slowly into the base of his spine. For a moment he was incapable of any movement or even thought. Something had turned him cold. He opened the door to the garden and vomited, now on his knees. The colour in his face had disappeared and his lips were quivering involuntarily. His mind was racing, and he knew any attempt to get to his feet would be futile. As he sat on the floor unable to control his sickness, he tried to dispute what his eyes had seen, but he couldn't unsee it. It was there. It had always been there; he just hadn't realised it. He sat quietly for a few minutes with tears strolling down his cheeks, but they weren't part of the sickness. He was experiencing emotions that carried an intensity he wasn't familiar with. The truth was he didn't know how to feel at this moment. He was reacting unconsciously on impulse. He sat up and placed his hands on the top of his head, screwing his eyes tightly before allowing them to again look down at the image still displayed on his phone. The embroidery on the underwear was unmistakable. He desperately wanted to look away, afraid to see any more, but he had to know. Then he looked closer. Something was missing. A small scar at the top of her left leg, a reminder of the car accident she had encountered as a child, which had claimed the lives of both of her parents. This wasn't Beth, but that gave him little relief as he realised it could only be one other person. The victim in the picture was Lara. As the initial shock began to subside, an unfamiliar urge overcame Toby. He was angry. He reached for the glass he had moments ago been drinking from and threw it against the wall. His anger didn't subside at the sight of the tiny sharp fragments dispersing over the floor. He grabbed the small table which had been housing the now shattered glass and threw it against the wall. It was a little more resilient than the glass but was still left nursing superficial damage. Toby was wrestling with emotions so intense and unfamiliar that they frightened him. He understood these emotions in others, but not in himself. He felt out of control, and the anger showed no sign of abating. He screamed, but any hope of the now unbearable tension, alleviating, was quickly dashed. A thought passed slowly through his mind. That thought consisted of this sick son of a bitch locked in a room with Dylan, Toby observing and savouring every moment. He was a mild-mannered man, ordinarily opposed to violence of any kind, but this had just become personal. Objectivity had no standing here. Paying little attention to the shards of glass indiscriminately scattered throughout the room, he made his way to the sofa and sat down, head in hands. The tears were flowing. A mixture of hurt and blind rage. He remained that way for several minutes until the anger began to subside, the heavy flow of tears, reduced to sporadic sobs. This changed everything. Suddenly, finding Eric's killer seemed unimportant. His mind began to wander, taking him to dark places which made his stomach turn. He reached for his phone, screwing his eyes tightly as he braced himself to once again view the image which would no doubt confirm his fears. As he studied the photograph, he noticed something written in the bottom corner. He ran quickly to the kitchen, searching for his glasses. Magnifying the image would surely distort it. After rummaging around, Toby located what he was looking for and took a seat at the breakfast bar. Squinting, he was just about able to make out it was a time-stamp. Whatever device had been used, it had recorded the time and date of the image. It was recent. 'Holy shit,' he shouted loudly, closing his eyes tight. This one hadn't been about control, or fulfilling a fantasy. This had been about revenge and getting his attention. This was Eric's parting shot, and whilst perhaps not in this way, Toby believed his intent had always been for him to discover the truth. This is where the impact lies. His mind was awash with questions, each taking him further down the black hole which he had now inevitably entered. It was the final question, however, that lingered, inducing feelings of nausea and sheer terror...Had Beth killed Eric?

Each failed call to Beth further elevated his panic levels. He was at the point of frantic by the time the fifth call had gone unanswered. She wasn't out of a serviceable area; she just wasn't picking up. Desperation had become blind panic. Trepidation had transformed into terror. Toby paced around the living room, again trying to reach his estranged wife, again yielding no success. The sight of the damage in the conservatory, something which would have customarily sent him into a frenzied state, suddenly seemed insignificant. He felt neither regret, nor despondency. He felt nothing. He sat down, noticing his hand was now visibly shaking. Usually known for his composure, currently, he was showing anything but. He was frightened yet angry. More concerning, he had developed an insatiable appetite for revenge, something he hadn't experienced to this extent before. His feelings were extreme, and he was losing sight of himself. He was losing his grasp of objectivity. The stakes had been raised, as had the level of personal investment. Toby took several deep breaths and sat quietly, immersed in his own thoughts. After a few minutes, with his anxiety lessened, he began to piece together what had happened and strategise his next action. As a series of questions began to run through his mind, he became aware, this also provided him with a series of answers. She knew and likely had done from the beginning. This was the reason she had stayed away. She blamed him. He would be a constant reminder of an unspeakable event. He wondered how she could look him in the eye again and questioned whether she'd ever forgive him. He hadn't planned this. He hadn't planned any of this, yet here he was, seemingly at every turn, falling deeper down the black hole he had entered the moment he stepped into the Stanton household that night. He felt a tightening in his chest as it suddenly dawned on him that Beth may never come home. He sat staring into a room of broken glass and chaos, reflecting on how it mirrored his own life. They'd had it all, but very quickly it had been reduced to almost nothing. His mind returned him to a thought so invasive, it made him feel physically sick. Could the woman he had loved for so many years, the woman who knew him better than he knew himself, be capable of murder? In the eyes of the law, she had motive, but was it possible for somebody with such a kind and sensitive exterior to mask such a dark secret? It was unthinkable, yet it played over in his mind repeatedly until his concentration was broken by the sound of his phone ringing. Bleary-eyed, he looked down. It was Beth.

CHAPTER 28

Monday 15th May...13:00pm

'Why didn't you tell me?'

'Is that how we greet one another these days?'

He shared her frustration but for different reasons. This was going to be an uncomfortable conversation; one he could never have imagined he would be having with his own wife. There had been no time for preparation; he would be relying solely on impulse. He didn't want to upset or antagonise her, but he needed to know. He desperately wanted to see her, look her in the eye as he asked the many questions swimming around in his head. Yet he was afraid. Afraid of what he might see in those eyes. He wouldn't be able to resist studying her every movement, and he would know. He would know if she was lying to him. As he stared out of the window, he realised his biggest fear was hearing something he didn't want to. Suddenly, he no longer wanted to have this conversation, but he couldn't unsee what he'd seen, and he couldn't eradicate those thoughts.

'How did you find out?'

His head instinctively dropped. She had confirmed it. He'd hoped he had it wrong, that somehow he'd deciphered the information incorrectly. But deep down, he knew. He knew that Lara was one of the victims. Explaining to Beth that her sister had been photographed and dehumanised after her ordeal would prove difficult.

'Toby?'

Taking a deep breath, Toby braced himself.

'Dylan found some photographs hidden away at Eric Stanton's house.'

He'd deliberately referred to Eric by his full name to avoid Beth thinking there was any familiarity between the two. He couldn't risk provoking her any further. The situation was volatile, he was already walking a tightrope. He couldn't afford to lose his balance.

'There are others?'

Toby let out the breath he felt like he'd been holding in for a while.

'We believe so.'

'We?'

'Dylan and I.'

'What does Mike think?'

Toby hesitated.

'Jesus Christ Toby, you haven't told him, have you? When are you going to learn? Have the last twelve months not taught you anything?'

'It's not that simple, Beth.'

'That seems to be your automatic response whenever your poor decisions are questioned.'

'That's not fair.'

'Why Toby? Why is that not fair? Every time you make a decision which inevitably will come back to hurt you, you explain it away by trying to convince people they don't understand the complexity of the situation. It's fucking insulting.'

Beth's voice had risen, and her use of profanities was still something Toby was neither accustomed to nor comfortable with.

'But it's not just you they affect, is it?' she continued. 'I sat at your bedside not knowing whether my husband was going to live or die. Our home has been broken into. Jack was attacked by that thug you're now apparently aligned with.'

She paused, but Toby was reluctant to speak. She hadn't finished.

'Now my sister has been defiled in the most horrific way, as an act of revenge against you. Against you, Toby. Against you.'

Her voice tailed off as she began to cry uncontrollably. Everything she had said had been true, and he couldn't change any of it. The remorse he was feeling was overpowering. Never had he questioned himself as much as in this moment.

'Beth I'm so sorry...'

'You never answered my question,' she interrupted. How did you know it was Lara?'

'I told you. Dylan found some photographs.'

'Lara has recounted her nightmare on numerous occasions. She never mentioned anything about being pictured.'

'They didn't show her face.'

'Then how did you identify her?'

Toby swallowed hard. He'd desperately wanted to avoid intimate details, but he had been cornered and had no choice but to be honest with Beth, regardless of the impact it may have.

'The embroidery on her underwear. The unicorn with B&L which has been a regular exchange between the two of you at Christmas every year. It had been staring me in the face the whole time, yet I'd been blind to it. Perhaps there was an unconscious part of me wishing to protect my mind from what my eyes had cast over. There was that one fleeting moment Beth. That brief moment, where I thought it was you. Realising it was Lara gave little relief, though. I know this is my fault, but you have to understand I didn't intend for any of this to happen.'

'You never do Toby, yet people still continue to get hurt by your actions. I know you're a good person deep down, but this person you've become isn't you.'

'Why didn't you tell me?'

'Because I was afraid of you running off and doing exactly what you've run off and done. When we met in the coffee shop, it took so much to smile and pretend everything was okay. And then there was the incident with Jack. After that, the more I internalised it, the harder it became.'

'You could have come to me. I would have been there for you. I would have been there for you both.'

There was a silence on the line before Toby heard the faint sound of sobbing, which had only moments earlier subsided. The pain arising from the guilt he was feeling was becoming unbearable. The depth of his current feelings was unprecedented. Even the raw emotion he had felt in the hospital with Beth by his side, hadn't come close. The reality was everything that had happened to those whom he held close was on him. Toby's actions had resulted in devastating consequences for his best friend, culminating in a brutal assault, a home invasion, a deliberate car accident, and a suicide attempt. One hardship after another had befallen his wife: a break-in, a disturbing meeting with Eric Stanton, a near-fatal car accident involving her husband, and finally, the fallout from her sister's horrifying experience. His marriage now lay in tatters, and he was struggling for the right words to make it better. His eyes felt swollen, his heart heavy. Perhaps he'd already lost Beth. How could he even begin to atone for his poor decisions, his bad judgement? As the silence continued, he looked down at his watch. It was a little after one. They'd been on the phone for fifteen minutes, yet it didn't really feel like they had said much to one another. Was this how it was going to be? Floating further and further away from each other until even the exchange of cordial pleasantries on the occasions they happened to be in one another's presence became forced?

'Can I ask you a question?' she asked breaking the silence.

She didn't wait for him to answer.

'What do you know about what happened to my sister?'

Toby noted her use of terminology. This had a formal feel to it. Beth was trying to remove any emotion from the situation. He needed to be very careful how he answered. The feeling of apprehension passing through him saddened Toby as he wondered how the trust would ever be revived.

'All the victims were specifically targeted. They were all vulnerable. Lara doesn't match that criterion. I believe she may have been targeted for another reason.'

His voice tailed off as the reality of him being that other reason hit once again.

'How many others are there?'

'There were twelve photographs, but that's just what Dylan found. There could be more.'

'Jesus Toby. You antagonised a serial rapist and brought him into our lives. What were you thinking?'

'Beth, there's something you should know.'

'There's more?'

'I don't believe the others were raped...'

'You think it was consensual?'

Toby sighed heavily, but it was a frustration with himself, not Beth.

'I went to see one of the victims. She believed she was part of an exciting affair until she went back to Eric's house and found somebody else waiting for them. They threatened to expose her to not only her partner but also her young daughter's nursery. It's a grey area. She complied, but not willingly. Sexual coercion can be a little more difficult to prove than rape. There aren't usually the marks or any signs of force.'

'I can't believe people can actually gain sexual pleasure from such perversion.'

'It's most often not about sex. It's merely a vehicle used as a way of punishing or controlling somebody. In this case, I think it was about power. It was a game to them.'

'Toby, what you're describing isn't what happened to Lara. There was only one attacker.'

'This was Eric.'

Beth remained silent, waiting for him to continue.

'Lara didn't fit the criteria. She wasn't meant to be part of it.' He paused as he fought back tears.

'Eric targeted her because of me. This wasn't planned meticulously. It was impulsive, fuelled by an uncontrollable rage.'

'Can you imagine how that must have felt for her? He defiled her, and when he was finished, he urinated on her as a final insult, to compound her humiliation.'

Toby couldn't respond through the tears, but bubbling away inside of him was an anger which was rapping at the door to come out. Lara was like a daughter to him and had been since the day they had met. She was much younger, and he'd gained an insight into just how protective Beth was of her very soon into their relationship. Their shared grief at such a tender age had created an impenetrable bond which Toby couldn't help but admire. That admiration, at times, had become envy, a closeness he could only experience vicariously through Beth. Lara epitomised kindness. He'd rarely seen her display anything remotely resembling anger, and they had never exchanged any cross words. This was partly due to Toby being so mild-mannered, but largely owing to the fact that Lara only saw the good in people. She had dated, but nobody had been good enough in Beth's eyes. Lara's innocence had been snatched away from her for no other reason than her link to Toby. Eric had shown he could get to people when he had manipulated his way into their home with an unsuspecting Beth, at a time he knew Toby was out. But Toby could never have imagined the lengths he would go to in order to prevent his dark secrets from being uncovered. Despite his lack of foresight and intent, the end result was the same. Toby was responsible for what had happened to Lara. His involvement with

Eric and Olivia Stanton had forced the former into a desperate move that had produced cataclysmic consequences. For that, he would never forgive himself. The sniffling on the other end of the line had dissipated.

'You said you went to see one of the victims. How did you identify her?'

Toby paused. This was another of those moments where he needed to choose his words wisely but for different reasons.

'I noticed an identifiable mark.'

'Oh?

He'd aroused her suspicion. Knowing he couldn't risk any more deception, he chose to be honest with her.

'Can you recall when I mentioned that there may be occasions when I can't answer your questions due to confidentiality, but I still need your trust?'

'Yes.'

'This is one of those occasions. Something resonated with me, and after a little digging I had it confirmed.'

'How did you locate her?'

That was the question he had been dreading since the moment he had mentioned his visit to Abigail Crookes. The choice he now faced was clear. He either lied to her or confessed that he'd had lunch with the sister of Lara's rapist.

'I called in a favour from a friend of mine in the police.'

He'd managed to avoid either of these options but had perhaps exaggerated the level of his relationship with Natasha. He wasn't comfortable calling her a friend at this juncture. He still hadn't figured out precisely what she was to him.

'Did she give you anything the police could work with?'

This was Beth's diplomatic way of telling Toby not to get involved. She was subtle, but he knew her.

'Asking a victim to re-live their ordeal can have a damaging effect on them.'

'That didn't answer my question.'

'I didn't want to push too hard. I listened to her story.'

'Do you know how many times I have listened to Lara's story?'

Toby shook his head, before realising Beth couldn't see his resignation. She was angry, and it was anger directed at him. There was undoubtedly an unimaginable pain arising from what happened to Lara, but her anger was only heading in one direction.

'I'm sorry Beth. I didn't mean for any of this to happen.'

Awash with emotion, centred around remorse, Toby removed the phone from his ear and placed his head in his hands. The tears were now accelerating down his face, but it was the sniffling that would alert Beth to the fact he was crying. His heart began to beat faster, the tears continued to flow and distorted breaths had settled in. Intrusive images had now taken residence in his head, all relating to Lara's brutal torment. He fought desperately to rid himself of them, but this was his way of punishing himself. He needed to envisage Lara being brutalised. It would serve as a reality check that his decisions had consequences. He was responsible for this. Lara's rape was on him.

'Toby?' Beth asked in a concerned voice.

Toby didn't respond. He'd fallen so far into despair that there was no hope of recovery at that moment. Realising he could no longer continue with this conversation, Toby hung up the phone, wondering if he had just provided the hammer blow to his marriage.

CHAPTER 29

Friday 12th May...19:45pm

As the nerves enveloped her once more, Samantha Howard closed the car door and began the short walk to the restaurant. She paused for a moment, questioning whether she was doing the right thing. She was young, successful, and fiercely independent. She didn't need a man in her life. Perhaps this wasn't about need, but rather about want. She *wanted* to share her life with somebody. She *wanted* to have a life outside of her career. Taking a deep breath, she continued the final few yards and casually entered the restaurant. There was a nice ambience to the place, and though it was a Friday evening, it was relatively quiet. She appreciated this as it would give her and her date an opportunity to talk as the evening progressed. Looking around, her eyes rested on a man seated in the bar area, drink in hand. A wave of relief swept over her as she recognised Gary Tolen. Short dark hair, around 6ft and well presented. He matched his picture. Upon noticing her, he smiled and stood to greet her.

'Samantha?'

'Call me Sam,' she replied returning his smile.

Gary tentatively offered his hand, perhaps unsure of whether a hug would be inappropriate at this stage. Sam took his hand and shook it, before taking the seat he had offered her.

'Can I get you a drink?'

'Soda water is fine, thank you. I'm driving.'

'I must confess so am I, but I'm just having one to calm the nerves,' he replied a little coyly.

She studied him for a moment before catching the eye of the waiter.

'Can I have a Martini please and...' she said gesturing towards Gary.

'A glass of house red please,' he replied, with a look of intrigue.'

'I thought you weren't drinking?'

'To calm the nerves, right?' she laughed.

The evening flowed like wine, with Sam making the decision to opt for a taxi and then collecting her car in the morning. She was enjoying Gary's company as much as the food, feeling more relaxed around him with every moment that passed.

'A solicitor. That sounds interesting.'

'It's really not. I work in corporate law,' Sam replied.

'So, you don't get to work with hardened criminals?'

'I didn't say that,' she replied through a fit of laughter.

'Tolen?' she asked with intrigue.

'Irish ancestry?'

'I love the Irish accent, but I am ashamed to admit, I've never been.'

'Can I let you into a secret? Nor have I,' he said struggling to get the sentence out through the laughter.

Sam was enjoying herself, but the night was getting on. She looked down at her watch. It was close to ten, and she was feeling tipsy.

'I should be going,' she said politely.

'I've never been one for drinking alone, so I'll also make tracks.'

She smiled at him. He had been the perfect gentleman. Attentive, complimentary, and respectful.

'I'll call us a cab, where are you headed?'

'I live out of town in Bakersfield.'

'Anywhere near the old colliery?'

'Actually, just a few minutes down the road from it.'

'Would you like to share a cab? I live out that way.'

He had a sophistication about him, which really drew her in. A dinner jacket, with a black shirt and a pair of stressed jeans. He looked younger than his forty-four years.

The image of the two individuals laughing in the back of the cab suggested a familiarity not usually associated with a first date. The nerves had disappeared, and Sam was feeling completely relaxed in Gary's presence. The journey would take around twenty minutes. The restaurant was local in that it was one of the closest to them both, but in terms of distance, it certainly wasn't within walking distance. She pulled out her phone, but the battery had run down. Having realised she had forgotten to switch the charger on, she cursed.

'Don't worry, you can charge it at my place over a coffee if you like?'

She looked at him hesitantly, considering his proposition.

'I'm sorry,' he quickly added. 'I didn't mean to make you feel uncomfortable. It's just I've really enjoyed the conversation this evening and hoped we could continue it, but over something a little lighter,' he smiled.

'Maybe next time.'

'I understand.'

The tone of the evening didn't change for the rest of the journey, which quickly eased Sam's concern that she may have offended him. As the car came to a halt, Gary opened the door and turned towards Sam.

'The coffee is still on offer.'

Sam paused for a moment. She'd been advised by her friends to be less uptight and more carefree. She had struggled with trusting people, but maybe this was one of those moments where she needed to take a leap of faith she thought.

'Well, are you in or out?' the taxi driver asked impatiently.

Taking a deep breath, she opened her door and climbed out of the taxi. Gary placed his hand on the small of her back as they approached the small cottage at the end of a garden path that seemed to stretch for miles. The weather was chilly, but the shiver that shook her entire body didn't come from the cold as Gary Tolen closed the door firmly behind them.

CHAPTER 30

Monday 15th May...13:45pm

For the third time in a short period, Jack's phone illuminated. Until now, he'd ignored it, but a growing sense of dread overwhelmed him. Something was wrong. Drawing the phone closer to his face he tentatively pressed to answer the call. It wasn't that he didn't want to speak to her, he didn't want to speak to anyone right now. The last week had been gruelling. He'd spent several days believing he had killed somebody and had made an attempt on his own life. He felt an enormous sense of relief that it had been Toby tasked with finding him. Anybody else, and he felt certain he would have been dead. Toby knew him better than anyone. Jack would be forever indebted to his best friend.

'Have you heard from Toby?'

The voice had an urgency to it you wouldn't normally associate with Beth Reynolds. She was usually the calming factor, the voice of reason.

'I haven't heard from him in days. Why?'

'He just hung up on me, and now his phone is switched off.'

'That doesn't sound like Toby. Could his battery have drained?'

'Considering the context of the conversation, his battery wasn't the problem.'

Jack felt a tinge of sadness. These were his closest friends, and it was tearing him apart to see their relationship in the state it was. Once a marriage to be admired for its strength and commitment, it had now been overshadowed by deception and mistrust. Jack knew Beth was angry, and that Toby had made mistakes, but he believed Toby had acted with the best of intentions. He wasn't in the habit of deliberately hurting people. Ironically, he had spent years doing exactly the opposite.

'I don't want to get in the middle of whatever you guys have got going on.'

'I'm not asking you to, Jack. Something's happened, and I think Toby is really struggling with processing it.'

'What's going on, Beth?'

There was a temporary silence on the other end of the line as Jack braced himself for what he had already determined was going to be a tough listen.

'My sister was raped.'

'Jesus Christ. Lara?'

'Yes.'

'I don't know what to say.'

Jack felt numb. He had met Lara only a few times, but she had always struck him as a genuinely sweet girl.

'I know how Toby feels about Lara. He sees her as a daughter. This must have hit him hard.'

'That's not the reason he's struggling.'

Jack braced himself. Hearing Lara had been subjected to such a terrifying tribulation was tough, but something told him there was worse to come.

'It was Eric Stanton.' She paused. 'He did it to prove a point when Toby began looking into him,' she continued. 'This was on him.'

Jack screwed his eyes tight. Lara's rape was shocking, but hearing Beth blame Toby had blindsided him. They had enjoyed a relationship which was the envy of those around them. It pained him to see their marriage in tatters. Eric Stanton had caused unimaginable devastation around him. Jack was glad he was dead, but at this moment, regretful it hadn't been at his hands. That thought horrified him, especially since he'd recently made an attempt on his own life after believing he'd murdered Eric.

'If Toby had known Eric would personally attack one of his family members, he would have walked away. Surely you realise that?'

'He had plenty of opportunities to walk away, Jack. I warned him, Mike warned him, but he was so caught up in this misguided notion that he needs to save everyone, that any warning simply fell on deaf ears.'

'He saved George's life. He saved my life.'

'George manipulated him, and you wouldn't have been in that position had he not dragged you into this in the first place. Were it not for him, Eric and Olivia Stanton wouldn't be known to you. You wouldn't have had your house ransacked and been subjected to a savage attack from that thug that is Dylan Sampson. You would never have sheltered somebody who staged her own kidnapping, and your peaceful existence on the farm would still be intact.'

'George faked her own kidnapping?'

'That's irrelevant now.'

'Not to me it's not.'

'I never trusted her. I tried to warn Toby to tread carefully, but, that was another warning he chose not to heed.'

'It's difficult to believe she would do this. Are you certain?'

Jack became aware of a desperation in his voice. He'd grown fond of her and didn't want to believe everything had been based on lies. Had he ever really known her?

'She admitted it to Toby the night you found her. She used him, Jack. She used him to get close to Eric.'

'I was there Beth. I saw what those guys did to her. I have a scar as a constant reminder. Surely, she wouldn't have allowed that to happen?'

'Olivia Stanton helped her, but it appears Eric's reach was greater than hers. It didn't go down the way she planned it. Everything that happened from the point of abduction was genuine. That's when she understood the danger, and that's how you almost died. Regardless, she put you in that position.'

Not for the first time during the phone call, Jack felt numb. It wasn't often he was lost for words, but Beth's disclosure had rendered him speechless. But something didn't make sense. Beth had called him clearly concerned about Toby's welfare, yet all she had done was attack him.

'You seemed worried earlier, but now you just sound angry.'

'Perhaps it's both.'

'Listen, Beth, I know this must be hard for you, but you know Toby has always tried to do the right thing. Family and friends are everything to him. He would never knowingly put anybody in danger.'

'Toby saw the warning signs, Jack. He just chose to ignore them.'

'He's still that same person you fell in love with. You know how much he invests into those he loves.'

'He invests himself too much into the wrong people, and that investment took my sister's innocence away.'

Confused, Jack clenched his teeth, struggling to comprehend what he was hearing. Beth was clearly concerned about Toby but had spent the entire call launching an angry tirade. He contemplated how two people he knew and trusted could display a side to them he had never before seen. Yet, his loyalty would always lie with Toby. A mixture of sadness and anger washed over him as he battled with his emotions. He was still feeling vulnerable himself and had little space to take on other people's problems. But this was different. This was his closest friend and the only person who really knew him. Jack would loyally support Toby if he was in trouble, and would defend him without hesitation. He'd just never believed that the person he would be defending Toby to would be Beth.

'When was the last time you spoke to him?' Jack asked.

'A short while ago. We argued, and he hung up.'

'That's not Toby. This must have affected him really badly.'

'It's affected more than just him. I care deeply for him, and naturally, I'm concerned which is why I called you.'

'You abandoned him when he needed you most.'

The words just slipped out, but they were symptomatic of how he was feeling. He now recognised the anger he was feeling was directed towards Beth. This was more than a verbal attack. She had abandoned him for trying to help others.

'Toby was arrested and questioned on suspicion of attempted murder. I stood by him. He nearly died in a car crash when he was distracted by a client he'd formed an unhealthy relationship with. I sat by his hospital bed. He invited his college sweetheart into our home. I accepted her. He lied to me and disappeared for God knows how long, putting his life at risk for yet another woman who had manipulated him. I waited for him. Don't you dare tell me I abandoned him. Those were his choices, Jack. He abandoned me. I became an afterthought. He caused this. He caused all of this,' she replied, in a fit of anger, before breaking down in tears.

The sound of her crying induced a feeling of guilt inside Jack. He had known Beth a long time and would consider her one of his closest friends. He respected her and they had never shared an angry exchange before today. This made him feel uncomfortable. Suddenly his anger disappeared.

'I'm sorry, I didn't mean that. I'm just worried about Toby. You understand he's always been there for me.'

'I know. But you have to understand a lot has happened Jack, and I'm not sure if I can ever forgive him. But more importantly, I'm not sure if I can ever trust him again.'

Her words cut through him; the thought of Toby and Beth separated not something he ever imagined was possible. But their marriage wasn't his priority right now.

'I'm assuming he's not at the house.'

'I checked with the neighbours before I called you.'

Jack thought long and hard about the places he and Toby had hung out. Nothing sprang to mind.

'Jack, you're his best friend. Has he ever mentioned to you places he goes to reflect? I know he used to love the coffee house, but stopped visiting there after the incident with Eric Stanton.'

Jack closed his eyes, looking up as he did so. Suddenly it hit him.

'There's a country pub out of town. I believe he met Eric Stanton there for the first time, but obviously didn't realise it until later.'

'I was with him that day. I knew he'd taken a shine to the place, but didn't realise he'd returned.'

'A couple of times to my knowledge. He mentioned it was away from everything and nobody knew him. I'll head over there now. Do you want me to pick you up?'

'I love Toby with everything I have, but right now I can't see him. You understand that, right?'

Jack felt the disappointment return as the severity of Beth and Toby's marital difficulties became clearer. She sounded like she had given up.

'He doesn't deserve this, Beth.'

'None of us do. There's been irreversible damage. Lives have been changed...some forever. Trust has been shattered, confidence has diminished, and boundaries have been overstepped. This isn't a quick fix; that's if there even is a fix.'

'We shouldn't be having this conversation.'

'I wish with every fibre of my body that we weren't. I wish I had my Toby back, the one I fell in love with. I wish we could erase any memories of Eric and Olivia Stanton, and dare I say it, also Georgina Sampson. I wish my sister hadn't been viciously raped, and that I was back in my own home, a place I once felt safe.'

A feeling deep in the pit of his stomach consumed him, but this time it wasn't anger. It was pain. Hearing Beth sound so deflated, upset him. But the real pain came from knowing it was difficult to deny Toby hadn't played a role in what had happened. Perhaps where they disagreed was the choice Toby was faced with. Jack felt Beth had over-simplified this. He himself had made questionable decisions, which could have easily had catastrophic consequences, but he'd got lucky. Toby hadn't been afforded that same luck. Beth couldn't get past the fact Toby's actions had resulted in Lara's assault, and Jack understood this. But the very fact he was able to have this conversation with Beth was due to Toby saving his life. He'd known just where to find Jack, and his haste had allowed him to arrive just in time. Jack couldn't forget that. It was time for him to repay the favour.

'Do you think he's in danger?'

'Only from himself,' Beth replied quietly.

'Can I ask you a question?'

'Sure.'

'Will you and Toby find a way through this?'

'That question has all sorts of complexities I don't think either of us want to explore right now. When you find him, let me know he's okay.'

'Are you sure you don't want to come with me?' he asked almost pleading.

'Goodbye Jack.'

As Beth hung up the phone, Jack stared at the blue skies above him. Something about this whole situation made him feel unsettled. A thought passed through his mind and lingered. He'd never really known George, but that didn't bother him. What bothered him was he'd just seen a side to Beth he had never encountered in the years they had known one another. Then there was Toby. Had he genuinely changed, or had he simply hidden his true nature all along? As his mood darkened, Jack questioned how well he knew his best friend. The only thing he felt was real right now was that Toby was in some kind of trouble. His questions could wait, but he had a sinking feeling, Toby could not.

CHAPTER 31

Monday 15th May...14:00pm

The almost desolate pub reflected Toby's life right now. He felt empty and for the first time since the death of his mother, alone. His marriage was on life-support, Beth's finger hovering close to the switch. His best friend had almost died and would take years to get over the trauma he'd experienced in the last few months. His sister-in-law had been brutally raped, by a man whose death he was investigating, and his career had no real direction. He'd considered turning to Richard, but couldn't bear to hear the disappointment in his voice as Toby disclosed the inner turmoil that continued to plague him. He barely knew Natasha, couldn't speak to Mike, and Dylan offered little in the way of emotional support. He was on his own. Approaching the bar, he was suddenly reminded of the first time he had laid eyes on Eric Stanton, albeit, unwittingly. Neither the initial pleasantries nor the small talk by the bathroom sinks had offered Toby any hint of what was to transpire. He stared at the empty stool which had once seated Eric and felt an unusual moment of sadness. Eric had portrayed himself as polite and charming. There had been a warmth there, something quite alluring. He knew there was a victim under every perpetrator, and wondered how damaged he had been by his exposure to the abuse in the familial home. Olivia had alluded to the fact his childhood hadn't been the easiest, Natasha had confirmed this, and Eric himself had disclosed snippets in his brief encounters with Toby, but still, Toby was left wondering. He saw only a scattering of people in the pub, unsurprising given it was a Monday afternoon and not what you could describe as a local either. Its geographical positioning meant even those who resided closest would have quite a journey on foot. It wasn't within walking distance, but for Toby, this added to its appeal. Peering through the bar area and out of the window, he noticed the empty tables in the garden area. Within a few weeks, this deserted area would host a crowd of families, young children unable to hide their enjoyment as they ran around in a play area which was generous in size. Had he and Beth decided to have children, this was the type of place they would have brought them to. Good food, even better wine, and a great playground for those young enough to enjoy it. This place had everything. But for now, it had a different purpose for Toby. He'd been counting on its tranquillity. He needed time to reflect, but ruminating in the house had become counter-productive. His home wasn't the same without Beth, and these days he found himself spending more and more time away from it. The recently discovered coffee shop had been an option, but with popularity came crowds. He'd considered going for a walk, but after speaking with Beth, he realised how much he was missing her, and this was his way of keeping her close to him. Though it felt a distant memory, it hadn't been so long back they had shared a romantic evening together which had begun here in this very spot.

The jovial conversation and light-hearted banter then were a far cry from their exchanges now. He turned and glanced over at the table they had been seated at. A sudden cramp appeared in his stomach as Toby's feelings began to catch up to his thoughts. As he picked up his drink, which had been a picture of loneliness perched on the bar, he wrestled with the idea of taking a seat in the same spot, before opting for a smaller table in the opposite corner of the room. He removed his phone from the pocket of his jeans and tapped it on his knee. Studying the black screen for a moment, he considered turning it back on but thought better of it. He questioned how much more he could sustain, wondering if he'd finally reached the depths of his despair, or whether his fall would continue. Beth's words, whilst hurtful had been accurate. So much that had happened had been on him, and he needed to take accountability. Yet with that accountability came indescribable pain as the reality of the consequences of his decisions hit. The fallout was cataclysmic, and he feared it wasn't over yet. Consulting on a murder whilst surreptitiously investigating a rapist had its dangers and on more than one occasion, his mind had circled back to the same question. What if history repeated itself and Eric's accomplice went after him and his family? It hadn't ended with Eric, but he now questioned whether it had started with him, or he had played a mere supporting role. But Lara was on Eric. That wasn't a game. It was personal. It was retribution. It was about getting Toby's attention, but Eric hadn't lived long enough to see how his actions played out. He could only witness the devastation from beyond the grave. Sitting there, drink in hand, he again returned to thoughts of Eric and Dylan alone in a room. Even the pacifist in him smiled as Dy-

Ian tore him limb from limb, each blow representing each person he had wronged until nothing but a lifeless, blood-soaked torso remained. Unrecognisable to even those most familiar with him. He was snapped out of his daydream by the door opening close to him, a man making his way casually to the bar. He was a tall man with dark hair, dressed in a pair of trousers and a smart shirt. Toby caught the tail end of the strong scent of his fragrance as he made his way past. The barman smiled and a brief conversation took place. It was more than a simple exchange of pleasantries. They were familiar to one another. Toby recognised the barman from when he had been here with Beth previously. He looked friendly and had what you might call an infectious smile. Both men looked a similar age, perhaps in their forties. Toby sat observing the interaction for a while and realised he missed being a therapist. Watching for subtle changes in body language had been one of the things he had enjoyed the most about client work. Clients rarely realised that they could divulge so much without saying a word. As the two men finished their conversation, the patron, who had recently entered, made his way to a table. As he walked past Toby, he stopped and smiled.

'You're not a regular, are you?'

'What makes you say that?'

'The table you're sitting at has a broken leg. It's only a matter of time before your drink's in your lap,' he grinned.

Toby looked down underneath the table.

'Thanks for the warning.'

'They've known about it for a while, though I think it has become a source of amusement for them.'

Toby stood, picking up his drink as he did so.

'Roger White,' the man said holding out his hand.

'Toby Reynolds.'

It was only a brief look, but Toby was alert to it. Roger White knew who he was.

'Would you like to join me?' he asked politely. 'At a table that's not broken?' he added with a smile.

Toby nodded, and followed, but out of intrigue rather than courtesy. As the two men sat down, Toby was reminded of the last time he had engaged in conversation in this pub with somebody who on the surface had appeared friendly. Having witnessed Roger's response to his introduction, he proceeded carefully. Perhaps he'd heard Toby's name on the news. It wasn't beyond the realm of possibility. There was of course another option. Eric was known here, but Toby was certain, only on a superficial level. That meant people only saw the charming side of him, which would make him likeable. This, in turn, would make Toby unpopular in these parts. He suddenly found himself questioning whether he was welcome here. The location and tranquillity made it the ideal retreat, but among the wrong people, it could quickly descend into something unpleasant.

'I've never seen you in here before.'

'But you know who I am.'

'I'm sorry?'

'When I introduced myself, you recognised my name.'

'What makes you say that?' Roger replied, seemingly taken aback.

'Body language gives away more than you might think.'

The man stared at his drink, before looking Toby directly in the eye.

'Your name sounded familiar, but I meant no offence.'

'I'm not offended.'

Roger smiled, but it looked uncomfortable like he wasn't sure how to progress the conversation.

'A word of caution, Toby. Some in here were close to Eric Stanton. They bought into his charm.'

'But you didn't.'

Roger smiled, shaking his head slowly.

'I saw beneath that charm.'

Toby stared at his new acquaintance, contemplating his sincerity. He suddenly felt present and clear-minded, confident he would spot any falsehoods Roger White might utter during their conversation. Still, he would exercise caution.

'What did you see beneath?' Toby asked.

'I saw somebody who was deeply flawed. Eric portrayed himself in a certain manner socially. But I saw the mask slip.'

Toby stayed quiet waiting patiently for Roger to elaborate.

'Eric was a passive drunk. He didn't get lairy, he usually got more generous with his money. Perhaps that was another reason people liked him. There was this one night, however, where I walked in on an argument between him and Tony Regal over there,' Roger said pointing over towards the barman.

'Tony didn't like Eric?'

'On the contrary. They were close friends.'

'What did you see to change your opinion of Eric?'

'It was more what I heard.'

'They didn't know you were there?'

'I kept my presence concealed. It was late. In fact, I think I was one of the last to leave. I was driving so had limited myself to a single alcoholic drink at the beginning of the evening. I was heading to the back of the car park, where I'd parked when I heard a commotion in the compound.'

Toby knew precisely the spot he was describing. The only way into that compound was through the kitchen, somewhere customers wouldn't have access to. Unless, of course, they knew somebody who worked there. Roger was telling the truth. Eric and Tony were familiar with one another, but what was the nature of their relationship?

'Eric was incensed. Something had really riled him. This wasn't alcohol induced. This was absolute rage. Yet something didn't make sense.'

Toby focused intently on Roger, with an expectation he was about to discover something which could be pertinent to his investigation.

'Well, Tony over there is much bigger than Eric. He works behind a bar, which can present its own challenges. Though it's generally quiet in here, there are occasions when he has had to handle himself, if you know what I mean.'

Toby nodded.

'He's an easy-going guy, but there's another side to him,' Roger continued.

'What was the argument about?'

Roger smiled as he picked up his drink and took several gulps.

'A book.'

'A book?'

'Yes. From what I could gather Tony had taken one of Eric's books. It must have had some sentimental value to it, to elicit that kind of response.'

Toby sat back and pondered for a moment. Why would Eric be so precious over a book?

'Tony was trying to placate him, but there was no calming Eric. He was wild. It's the only time I've ever seen him like that, but it was enough to tell me there was something lurking underneath the surface I didn't like.'

'Did you notice anything else?'

'My view was obscured. I heard the sound of feet shuffling. I think Eric may have gone for him.'

'Did Tony retaliate?'

'Why is that important?'

'Just curious, that's all.'

Toby glanced over towards the bar, where Tony was now sitting on a stool reading a newspaper. He guessed this was what barmen did during quieter periods. He was quite well built, but nowhere near Dylan's stature. He was possibly a similar height to Jack, though less muscular. He looked meek, but then appearances could be deceptive. To form a solid opinion of the seemingly unassuming bartender, Toby required more time; however, this wasn't his immediate concern.

'How long ago did this altercation happen?' Toby asked.

'Relatively recently. Perhaps a month or so back. I never saw him again after that night.'

'Was that unusual?'

'Thinking about it, yes. I'd often see him in here.'

Toby ran his hand over his mouth, rubbing it gently as he contemplated. He knew the question he wanted to ask, but Roger White was still a stranger to him. He couldn't be certain he wasn't somehow involved, luring Toby into divulging any information which may allow Eric's co-conspirator to remain one step ahead of them.

'Can I ask you a question, Toby?'

Toby was jolted back into the moment.

'How did you come to form your opinion of Eric Stanton?' he asked, not waiting for Toby's reply.

'My opinion?'

'People talk. Your name is known around here, though perhaps not for the reasons you would like.'

'Should I be concerned?'

Roger shook his head with a smile.

'Not in my company.'

Toby felt reassured in one respect, yet still possessed that element of trepidation. Roger seemed nice, and nothing about his body language had made Toby believe he was anything other than genuine, but still...

'I actually met Eric for the first time over there,' he said pointing towards the bar. 'Later that evening, I found myself washing my hands in the toilet at the same time as him. He was engaging and seemed genuinely interested in the conversation.'

'What changed?'

'I went to see him in the hospital after Olivia had attacked him.'

Toby paused in anticipation of being interrupted by Roger, who looked poised to ask a question. It never came.

'One or two things he said didn't feel quite right, but it wasn't his words ultimately that changed my opinion of him.'

'Oh?'

'No. Just as I was about to leave, I noticed a look in his eyes. I was unsure of its significance initially, but it was enough to make me question his sincerity.'

'From what I can gather, that insincerity runs in the family. Anyway, this was a flying visit for me. I just popped in to see Tony before he sets off on his new adventure.'

He stood and dropped a card on the table.

'You're a PI?'

'It's not as glamorous as you may think. Good to meet you, Toby. If you ever need anything, give me a call.'

Toby got up and shook Roger's hand.

'Oh, and one more thing. I hear you've met Natasha. She's an interesting girl, but she shares more similarities with her brother than she would care to admit. Be careful.'

Toby looked down at his watch as he strolled towards his car, replaying Roger's parting words. What had he seen in Natasha, that Toby hadn't? Though a litter of free spaces, he had chosen to park in his usual spot, which was tucked away at the back of the car park, among the trees. He liked it there, though wasn't sure why. Had he become a creature of habit? He stopped as he reached the compound, and for a moment began to visualise the argument between Eric and the barman. The fact he hadn't been there didn't prevent him from trying to re-enact the disagreement between who he now believed to be two friends. He didn't doubt the validity of Roger's version of what had transpired, but he was struggling to understand why a book would anger Eric to such an extent that he became incandescent with rage. The list of people who had now seen Eric's more sinister side was growing, which meant so was the suspect pool. Ultimately, he'd antagonised the wrong person and paid for it with his life, but Toby was no closer to discovering the identity of the killer. The sun hid behind a cloud, sending a shiver down his spine and prompting him to look up at the sky. Though it was a mild, spring day, the clouds scattered periodically in an otherwise clear blue sky were responsible for sporadic cool bursts. Toby pulled out his car keys and approached his car. Drawing nearer, he could see an object resting at the front of the driver-side wheel. Bending down for closer inspection, he noticed it was a brick. A brick that hadn't been there when he had parked up. Picking it up for closer inspection, he suddenly felt a sharp blow to the back of his head. Hitting the deck, he winced with pain, but it was the shock that had his body trembling. The memory of being attacked in his home still fresh in his mind, Toby wondered how much more he could endure, physically and emotionally. His decision to leave his car in an area not overlooked by the pub or the main road may prove to be catastrophic for him. Nobody knew he was here; nobody was coming to his rescue. As he knelt looking down at the ground, gathering his thoughts, he felt a hand grip the back of his neck and pull him to his feet. With a sudden jolt, his head was thrown against the bonnet. Toby felt a sharp pain in his nose, which was now haemorrhaging blood. His vision was blurred, meaning any slim chance of identification had now all but disappeared. Sprawled across the front of the car, he was grabbed by the hair, feeling the warm breath of his attacker in his ear.

'It seems you don't learn your lesson, Mr Reynolds. This is your final warning. I'm sure you don't want to end up like Eric.'

The words were uttered in a raspy whisper, a deliberate ploy to camouflage the identity of their owner, however, that very tactic had given away more than the attacker likely had realised. The only reason you would mask your voice is if you knew the other person could identify it. That meant Toby either knew the attacker or had come into contact with him at some point. Either way, he was getting close to a discovery somebody didn't want him to make. He squeezed his eyes shut, readying himself for another strike. But it didn't come. Slowly opening them again, he rose gingerly to his feet and turned around. He was alone. The only sound, the quiet rustling of the trees in the gentle breeze. He rubbed his eyes as he desperately battled to gain some perspective. The attacker had left swiftly, yet covertly. Toby wondered if this had been the same person who had broken into his home. As his thoughts became disordered, he was overpowered with a haze that brought with it a nauseous feeling. Everything around him began to spin, as he struggled to maintain his balance. He felt a strange sensation but was unable to explain precisely what it was. He felt nervous and out of control, but had a brief moment of clarity before he fell to the floor. It suddenly made sense.

Grounding the car to a halt, Jack jumped out, pulse racing as the reality of the scene in front of him began to emerge. Was he too late? Then the still figure on the floor showed signs of life. Toby's slow movement was accompanied by a groan.

'Toby!'

Toby looked at Jack with a glazed look in his eye. He seemed confused, but Jack had no idea how long he had been out for.

'Don't try to move. I'll call an ambulance.'

Toby grabbed Jack's wrist.

'That's not necessary.' The words sounded slurred, which did nothing to reassure Jack of his friend's current physical state. 'I was struck from behind, I think. I stood up too quickly and had a delayed reaction.'

Toby rubbed the back of his head and studied his hand. 'There's no blood and no sign of a lump,' he continued. 'He didn't use a weapon.'

'Did you get a look at him?'

'It happened quickly. I never saw him.'

'Did you recognise his voice?'

'He only spoke once. Deliberately in a whisper, I think.'

Jack clenched his fists. He felt the anger surging through his body. Somebody had hurt his closest friend and left no trace of their identity. Visions of revenge entered his head, even though he'd never encountered his target. He wanted to make this right the only way he knew how.

'My mouth is dry,' Toby said, swallowing repeatedly.

'Well, we're in the right place,' Jack grinned.

Though the pub had become a little busier, Toby and Jack didn't struggle to find a table. Jack seated Toby in a booth close to the door and approached the bar.

'Your friend looks a little worse for wear,' the young girl behind the bar commented, regarding Toby who was currently slumped in his seat.

Jack glared at her.

'Compared to what I'll do to the cowardly bastard responsible for this, that's nothing,' he retorted angrily.

There was a momentary standoff as the bar worker struggled to know how to take the well-built angry customer standing opposite.

'What can I get you?' she asked gingerly.

'I'll have a lager, and my friend will have a glass of water,' Jack said impolitely.

He was in no mood for pleasantries. As he trudged back slowly to the table, he noticed Toby had now sat up and looked a little more present. Several cuts and emerging bruises marred his face. It would be hard to disguise.

'You need to walk me through what happened,' Jack said rather impatiently.

'A tranquil drink turned sour,' he smiled.

'Toby.'

'I met a guy in here. Turns out he was a private investigator. We had a drink and a chat and then he left. I exited not long after him. Then I got hit from behind as I approached my car. That's all I remember.'

'Could it have been him?' Jack asked.

'I don't think so.'

Jack thought for a moment.

'What did he whisper to you?'

'Whisper?'

'The person who attacked you. You said they spoke in a deliberate whisper. What did they say?'

Toby screwed his eyes tightly as he desperately tried to recall the words muttered to him only a matter of minutes previous.

'I don't remember.'

Jack felt certain Toby had just lied to him. Was it because he didn't trust him, or was he trying to protect Jack? He was still dealing with his own demons. Perhaps Toby didn't feel he had the emotional capacity to handle anything else right now.

'What's going on?'

Toby raised his head and looked at Jack. He still looked groggy.

'You've been beaten up twice in a short space of time. Somebody out there is trying to prove a point. Who is it, and what's the point they're trying to prove?'

'The break-in was opportunistic. Today, I'm not sure.'

'Bullshit. Opportunist thieves don't break into a place in the middle of the day, and they do everything they can to avoid detection...unless they aren't looking for something, but someone. I should know.'

Toby smiled, but as he did so, he broke into a fit of coughing, clutching his ribs. Jack wondered if an awkward fall during the attack had caused the pain. He was beginning to feel concerned. Toby looked unwell, and he wasn't sure what to do. He pulled out his phone.

'I'm calling Beth.'

'No,' Toby shouted, appearing more lucid all of a sudden.

'Toby, she's worried about you.'

'She has enough to deal with right now, Jack. I've caused her enough pain. I don't want to add to that.'

'Then you need to be honest with me. What have you got yourself into? As Toby was about to speak, Jack held his hand in the air. 'And before you answer, don't lie to me for a second time.'

'You've spoken to Beth. How much did she tell you?'

'I know about Lara,' Jack replied sullenly.

'I'm almost certain that was Eric, and it was done to warn me off.'

'Eric's dead. It's over now...isn't it?' he asked hesitantly.

'This didn't end with him. He had a partner, and he's still out there.'

Jack tilted his head back and closed his eyes. He'd hoped this story had come to an end, but now he was quickly realising it had only been the end of a chapter. Toby was in trouble. They, whoever they were, would stop at nothing to silence him.

'I think you should come and stay with me for a while.'

'That's not necessary.'

'Just for a few days until things settle and we figure out what the hell it is you're involved in. It's safer, and I'd feel better. It's either that or I call Beth.'

Toby smiled at him, perhaps knowing he didn't have a choice. Jack hadn't wanted to force his hand, but he knew Toby didn't want Beth involved, and the ultimatum left him with no other option but to comply.

'Okay,' Toby replied rather reluctantly.

'I'll be right back, and then we'll head off.'

Jack made his way across the pub to the toilet. Lost in thought, he splashed water on his face, only to be startled by the door bursting open. He turned instinctively to see a rather tall figure standing staring at him. At first, Jack wondered if he'd been recognised, but quickly realised this wouldn't be a friendly encounter. The grin on the man's face widened as Jack slowly dried his face and hands, not taking his eyes off him.

Their heights and general physiques were quite similar. To the observer, this looked like an impasse, each man measuring the other.

'Looks like your friend has had a rough day.'

'It's gonna be far worse for the guy responsible,' Jack responded without breaking stare.

'Is that so?'

Jack took a step closer to the man. He could feel the anger swelling around inside his stomach.

'Eric Stanton was a popular man in these parts. There are plenty of people lining up to take a shot at your boy out there.'

'Considering he's laid in a morgue, I'd say his popularity was questionable, wouldn't you?'

The man's smirk quickly disappeared.

'I'd be sleeping with one eye open if I were Toby Reynolds.'

Jack glared at the man opposite, struggling to contain the rage boiling inside of him.

'Perhaps it won't be him. Maybe that wife of his, or her pretty little sister.'

With the tension rising quickly, the door suddenly opened and in walked an older man. He regarded the two men with a courteous smile as he walked past them and into a cubicle.

Jack took a deep breath, smiled and brushed past the man to exit the toilets. The image of that grin persisted as he sat facing Toby. His laid-back demeanour was being severely tested, and he knew if he hung around, trouble would eventually find him. As he rose out of his seat, he made eye contact with the individual, who had now resumed his position at the bar. As they stared down one another, the man dragged his thumb from one side of his neck to the other. The gesture was clear. This was a threat and one he couldn't take lightly. Toby had clearly upset the wrong people, and it was becoming more apparent how far-reaching the consequences were. Toby and Jack moved slowly towards the front exit. Just as they reached the door, Jack turned around and noticed the man had exited through the rear door, which led out to the smoking area. He could just about make out through the window that the man was alone, aside from having the company of his cigarette. He handed Toby a set of keys.

'Go wait in my truck. I'll be along shortly.'

'Where are you going?'

'I have something to take care of.'

Toby looked him suspiciously but lacked the energy to interrogate. Jack watched him leave through the front entrance before turning and moving in the opposite direction.

F riday 12th May...23:30pm

Disorientated and dishevelled, Samantha Howard trudged aimlessly along the desolate country road. She felt only numbness as she struggled to conceptualise what had just happened. The night had begun with such promise but had descended into a horrific nightmare. He had brutally defiled her, taking photographs whilst doing so. She had fulfilled her role in his unhealthy fantasy, used as a mere plaything. But the hardest thing for her to grasp right now was the fact she had agreed to it all. It wasn't rape, at least not in a literal sense. It was coercion with him leaving her little choice but to submit to his demands. The charisma had been a front; the reassuring smile, a weapon to draw her into his false narrative. Alcohol had played no part, and she hadn't been drugged. He'd been very clever. She wondered how long he had been planning this. The fact he knew things about her she hadn't shared with him, suggested his research had been extensive. Sam wondered why her? Why had he actively sought her out? This wasn't about opportunism, and it wasn't about revenge. Perhaps she had been randomly selected. But the planning had been meticulous. He knew the right things to say to lure her in, and he knew the right things to say to make her comply when his intentions became apparent. His demeanour had changed in an instant, the friendly and sociable man she had shared dinner with a mere dot in the rear-view mirror. She regretted sharing a cab with him, but she couldn't possibly have known what lay ahead. There had been no red flags. There had been nothing to suggest he was anything but sincere. But when that front door had closed, she had seen it. His face gave him away long before his unforgivable actions. She knew at that moment she was in trouble, but she couldn't have imagined what that trouble would entail. Her pleading had fallen on deaf ears, her protestations fruitless. He had her in the palm of his hand. Her career, her family, and her livelihood were all on the line if she failed to comply with his demands. She had worked tirelessly for years, sacrificing her personal life. To see all that fall down around her would have been unbearable. He had her, and he knew it. His arrogance that she would give him what he wanted, brought a nauseous feeling to the back of her throat. Strangely, it hadn't seemed like the sex was the overarching thrill for him. He had seemed more excited by taking the photos and having her pose in various positions. The sex itself had been brief, her aggressor likely exciting himself so much beforehand, that he was left unable to perform for a sustained period. Small mercies, she thought. He'd ejaculated onto her clothes, perhaps as a final insult, before sitting back in his chair and lighting a cigarette. He hadn't spoken to her other than the occasional harsh words when trying to position her for a photograph. He had taken about a dozen she posited. As Samantha Howard drew closer to civilisation, only one thought ran through her mind, as she began to feel vengeful. Gary Tolen had fucked with the wrong person.

CHAPTER 33

Monday 15th May...15:30pm

The shelter stood peacefully out of view, hosting only one patron...for now. Its tranquillity was about to be disrupted in a way never seen before. Its positioning allowed for a stealth-like entry, which suited Jack just fine. He didn't take kindly to threats, particularly not where his friends were concerned, and the encounter in the toilets along with subsequent gestures, had left no room for misinterpretation. There was no mistaking Toby now had a target on his back, but Jack worried it wouldn't stop there. They'd already used Lara to prove a point. There were no scruples involved, no consideration as to who would get caught in the crossfire. Toby was close to something, something which perhaps even he didn't know the true depths of. Eric's killer was still on the loose, yet among his circle, Toby was the talk. Why did they have more interest in him than the killer? It didn't make sense. As Jack exited the pub, he glanced to his left and saw Toby in the distance, opening the passenger-side door of his truck, and tentatively climbing in. He didn't see Jack, which was probably a good thing. He didn't want Toby to be a part of what was about to happen. The less he knew, the better. Jack entered the shelter wanting his adversary to look him in the eye. He wanted to see how tough he was.

The man grinned as he turned and saw Jack, but Jack sensed a nervousness about him.

'You know there are others in there who would love to take a shot at you,' he goaded.

'And they'll meet the same fate as you,' Jack replied.

The man lurched forward swinging a fist at his face. Jack was able to side-step, but it had still grazed the side of his cheek. Before he could adjust himself, another blow came his way, this time connecting with his head. Jack staggered back. His opponent was quick for his size, but he'd been in this situation before, and he knew how to handle himself. He wasn't fazed. As the next fist came his way, Jack grabbed it, twisted it around, and snapped it backwards, which drew a piercing shriek from the man standing opposite. His wrist hung limp, but there was no relenting. Jack grabbed him by the throat and marched him back towards the glass shelter, his back hitting it with force, which elicited another pained yell. The man fell to the ground and stayed there for a moment. He clutched his wrist and closed his eyes tightly, making no attempt to hide the pain. Jack pulled him to his feet by his hair and whispered in his ear.

'I want you to walk back in there and tell your friends I'm waiting, and I'm in no mood to be fucked with.'

As his foe scurried off, Jack grinned, wondering whether he'd spent too much time with Dylan. Ordinarily, he would only settle trouble if it found him, yet here he was walking straight into it. It wasn't simply a case of walking into trouble, though. He was relishing it. The rage burned inside him. He wasn't done yet.

His concentration was broken by three men approaching, one of which was the individual he'd just had the altercation with. As they drew closer, they seemed to slow down and hesitate.

'So how we gonna do this?' Jack asked. 'You boys tough enough for one on one, or am I fighting you both?'

The men circled Jack. A smirk lit up his face as he rolled up his sleeves.

'I guess I have my answer.'

Jack didn't wait to invite an attack. He stepped towards the larger of the two men and hit him hard between the eyes. Before he could gather his thoughts, Jack grabbed him and threw him into the second onrushing attacker. The two collided with a thud and both hit the deck. Jack ran at pace and kicked the already injured man hard in the ribs. He screamed out with pain and clutched his midriff, gasping for breath. Jack had done what he needed to. He'd quickly evened up the fight and bettered his odds. He had no idea how long he had before the alarm would be raised. Perhaps it already had. Perhaps the police were on their way. No, people like this had their own form of justice. They wouldn't use the authorities. They'd simply deal with things in-house, but this also carried a danger. How many more were lining up to come out and take a swing at him? He was tough, but he had his limitations. As the smaller of the two men rose to his feet, he pulled something from his pocket, which shone in the sunlight. There was no mistaking what it was. He had drawn a knife, and not one from the kitchen. Jack suddenly realised the stakes had just been raised, and the intent was clear. The man standing opposite now circling him with knife in hand, had no qualms about killing him. He wondered if he had made a grave mistake. If this was a fight to the death, it had no winners, only losers.

'You seem to doubt your fighting prowess.'

'I'm trained in armed combat,' the man replied curtly.

'Tell me, what is it about Eric Stanton that commands so much loyalty?'

'He was well-liked around these parts.'

'He was a prick.'

The man jumped forward, but Jack was able to sidestep him.

'Touched a nerve, have I?' he asked sarcastically.

'Toby Reynolds was responsible for Eric's death. He'll pay for that.'

'Eric Stanton was a serial rapist who got what he deserved. With the amount of people he pissed off, it was only a matter of time before one of them fought back. The world is a better place without him in it.'

'And your issue is now with me, not Toby. Let's see how tough you are against somebody who knows how to fight, you fucking coward.'

The anger that had been swelling inside of Jack showed no sign of relenting. The man again jerked forward and flicked his knife. This time it caught Jack on the top of his shoulder. A small wound began to seep blood, but he wasn't hurt. He was enraged. When the adrenaline subsided, it may tell a different story, but for now, any pain he was feeling had been blocked out. The two men continued to move around one another slowly, neither wanting to overplay their hand. One wrong move could be fatal for Jack, so he had to be careful. He wondered how this would end. How far would he go? His intention had been only to make a point to the man from the bar that Toby was off-limits. He hadn't envisaged taking on a gang, and he hadn't imagined he would be facing down a knife. Though this wasn't the first time he'd been involved in a fight with an armed man, it didn't make him any less wary. If his opponent knew his way around a knife, he could kill Jack with a precision blow. If he wasn't accustomed to using weapons, he could kill Jack with a clumsy error. Either way, he was in danger and couldn't underestimate his adversary, who was currently closing in on him, wearing a sadistic grin.

'How about you drop the knife and settle this like a man? Perhaps you'd regain some credibility from your girlfriends over there,' Jack taunted.

He hadn't said this with any degree of expectation. He had merely wanted to goad his foe into making a rash move. If he was ruled by emotion, he'd be easier to read.

'I'm gonna shut that mouth of yours permanently,' the man said as he jerked forward, wielding the knife above his head.

Jack had anticipated his move and managed to grab his hand. As he squeezed it tightly, the man's grip on the knife loosened until it fell to the floor. Jack let go of his hand and grabbed him by the throat. He began marching him backwards until they both broke into a run, the man scurrying helplessly backwards. As they approached the back of the shelter, Jack thrust the man with everything he had straight into the glass, which shattered into tiny pieces under the weight. The ferociousness of the shove had caused Jack to lose his footing and tumble to the ground landing on tiny glass fragments. Pain shot through him as the cuts appeared on his hands. His pain was the least of his concerns, however, as he looked down and saw the other man motionless on the ground. He turned to look for the other two men, but they had disappeared. It wouldn't be long before a crowd formed, and that was the last thing he and Toby needed. A panic suddenly consumed him as he wondered whether he had killed the individual still stationary on the floor. He glanced over towards his truck. Toby was resting in the front seat, unsuspecting. He wouldn't have heard the commotion from his position unless he had his window down. Just as he was about to move, he heard a groan. The man was conscious. Jack thought about helping him up. He looked badly hurt and clearly required urgent medical attention. He wondered whether he should call an ambulance; the man now writhing in pain and visibly distressed. Regardless of who he was and what he'd done, that level of suffering was difficult to see. Jack pulled out his phone and stared at it for a while. He then placed it back into his pocket and bent down.

'Just so we're clear, this is over. Show your scars to any friends who are curious about what will happen if they go anywhere near Toby.'

As he got up to walk away, he kicked the man with force, connecting with his rib cage. The crack was almost as loud as the scream from the man, now flailing helplessly on the broken glass. Jack began walking at pace towards his truck, knowing time was of the essence. He needed to escape without being seen. He wasn't as conspicuous as Dylan, but he would still be relatively easy to identify. Regardless, as he entered the vehicle, he realised he would never be able to return here. Nor would Toby.

The sound of the door opening jolted Toby, who had closed his eyes briefly. The attack had left him shaken up, but more than anything, he felt exhausted. He turned slowly to look at his friend who was climbing hastily into the driver's seat.

'Jesus Jack, what the hell happened?'

'We need to get out of here,' he replied flinching with pain as he attempted to grip the steering wheel with his bleeding hands.

The car sped hastily out of the car park and onto the main road.

'Jack?'

'I had a little trouble with some guys. Don't worry, they look much worse than me.'

Toby stared at Jack. Psychotherapist or friend, it amounted to the same thing. It wasn't a stretch to conclude Jack was hiding something.

'What's going on with you?' Toby asked.

'What makes you think anything is going on?'

Toby lowered his eyes and took a deep breath through his nose, before turning to face Jack once again.

'You don't seek out trouble Jack, you avoid it, but back there something angered you enough to initiate conflict. Look at your injuries. That was some fight. You're also shaking which is adrenaline, but the grin on your face as you first got into the car, gave away the fact you enjoyed inflicting the punishment you have just dished out. Finally, aside from being your best friend, I spent a long time reading body language professionally. I know when somebody is holding out on me. Would you like to have another go at answering my question?'

Jack smiled at him.

'What's the world coming to when you can't even lie to your best friend?' he quipped.

The car was filled with laughter for a moment until Jack placed his hand on Toby's shoulder, leaving a bloodied hand-print.

'Do you know the real reason why I enjoy the farm life so much?'

Toby shook his head.

'I don't mix well with others Toby. It's more than just a little social awkwardness. It's a withdrawal from a society I want no part of. I have a very small social circle, and the farm is like a bubble for me. I get to pretend half the shit that happens in this world doesn't really happen. If I don't see it, it's not real right?'

Toby didn't respond. This was Jack's convoluted way of explaining what happened back at the pub, which now lay several miles behind them.

'Those who know me see me as laid-back and carefree. Those who actually know me, and there are very few, see something very different. I know you see it, Toby. You've always seen it. There are too many people in society who will use any means necessary to gain an advantage. Too many use fear as a weapon to manipulate others. Do you understand what I mean?'

Toby felt strangely anxious. In all the years of knowing Jack, he had never heard him speak so profoundly. He'd known there were hidden depths to Jack, but he'd perhaps underestimated just how deeply things affected him. He suddenly had his answer. His answer for what happened at Eric's, his answer for what happened at the pub. This had been building for some time, perhaps even years. He'd reached his limit and snapped. What was difficult to comprehend for Toby was the fact Jack seemed to be not only making a habit of getting into conflict, but he appeared to be enjoying it. It felt like a valve had been opened, and slowly the pressure was being released.

'What really made you go to Eric's that day?' Toby asked.

Jack slowed down the car, pulling over into a layby. He cut the engine and turned to face his friend.

'The day you found me...'

'Jack,' Toby interrupted.

'You need to hear this.'

Toby sat back, suddenly feeling uneasy. Jack didn't do serious conversation. The feelings of discomfort increased with every second that passed in anticipation of what he was about to hear.

'The last thing I said to you that day was that I couldn't do it.'

'I remember.'

The words had cut through him at the time and had continued to haunt him every day since.

'I told you I couldn't go to prison, but I wasn't afraid of prison, Toby.'

'Then what?'

Jack closed his eyes. This was uncharted territory for him.

'I was afraid of who I'd become. When I told you I didn't go to Eric's to kill him, I wasn't being entirely truthful. I didn't end up there by accident.'

Toby realised his response now was critical. Jack was at his most vulnerable, on the precipice of a breakdown. He needed a gentle hand to guide him back from the edge.

'Jack, I want you to listen very carefully to what I'm about to say,' Toby said offering a reassuring smile and placing his hand on Jack's shoulder.

'There are three things you should keep in mind. Firstly, and most importantly, those who are most lost in this world can still be found. What I mean by that is the changes you're experiencing aren't necessarily permanent.'

Jack lowered his head, the emotion of the situation beginning to get the better of him.

'Secondly, logic is filled with complexities, and doesn't co-exist with emotions.'

'What does that mean?'

'It means when your emotions are in control, logic and objectivity are absent.'

'That's why we can regret things after the event?'

'In a way, yes. There's a little more to it than that, but we won't get into the whole regret and remorse thing right now,' Toby smiled.

'What's the third thing?'

'Whatever your intention, you didn't kill Eric.'

'Do you believe I intended to kill him?'

Toby bit his lip, again contemplating how to deliver his response in a sensitive manner, without dismissing Jack's feelings.

'How tall are you, Jack?'

Jack laughed.

'About six foot three.'

'How much do you weigh?'

'Just south of sixteen stone. Why?'

Toby smiled.

'You also spent years in the ring, right?'

'Amateur champion in my younger days. What's your point?'

'My point is that if you intended to kill a man, you would know how to do it, and Dylan Sampson aside, I don't think there are many who could prevent that.'

'You're doubting my intentions?'

'You doubted your intentions, Jack. Whether it was a conscious decision or not, at some point you had second thoughts. If you'd wanted Eric dead, you would have killed him before leaving the house. You left him alive.'

Tears began to fall as Jack's face screwed up tightly. Toby unbuckled his seatbelt and turned to comfort his best friend. But his overarching feeling wasn't sorrow. What he was feeling was a deeply embedded guilt. No doubt there were past traumas that had brought Jack to breaking point, but Toby knew he had caused much of the damage which lay before him. The two friends sat silently in that position for several minutes, before Jack pulled away and patted Toby on the shoulder.

'About Lara,' Jack said, trying to regain his composure.

Toby placed his hand on his forehead and gently massaged it.

'So many people have been affected by my actions, and for what?' he said, dismissing Jack's comment. He didn't want to talk about Lara.

'Eric's dead. Doesn't that give Lara her closure?'

'There are others.'

Jack looked puzzled.

'There was a second perpetrator,' Toby continued. 'Eric didn't do this on his own. It was carefully coordinated, and had more victims than we thought.'

'We?'

'Dylan found some photos at Eric's place.'

Noticing the inquisitive look on Jack's face, Toby paused, knowing what he was about to say would likely lead to some awkward questions.

'He was there the day of Eric's death. It's how I knew you hadn't killed him.'

'It was Dylan?'

'Dylan said Eric wasn't there when he arrived.'

'And you believed him?'

'I believe he didn't kill him.'

'Why? He's certainly capable, and he despised the man.'

'Eric was struck from behind. You've met Dylan. Do you believe him to be the type of person who would strike someone from behind?'

'I guess not.'

Jack pondered for a moment.

'Then who?'

'I don't know. I've invested my time into finding his co-conspirator, not his killer.'

'Could you be looking for the same person?'

'I'm not sure.'

'Do you still have those images? Maybe a fresh pair of eyes will help.'

Toby didn't respond at first. He had fallen silent, deep in thought. Without looking up he reached for his phone and handed it to Jack who studied it intently, flicking through the images.

'Their smiles look forced.'

'Look at their eyes. They tell the real story. This was coercion. Each person in those images agreed to that.'

'Jesus, that's fucked up.'

'They believed they had no choice. Each had been carefully selected.'

'Lara?'

'Lara wasn't part of this. She didn't fit their criteria.'

Jack looked sullen. Toby didn't have to elaborate. Jack knew.

'What is the camera sitting on?'

'What do you mean?' Toby asked, moving into a position where he could see what Jack was looking at.

'It's in this one as well. In fact, it's the same on all of them,' he said quickly scrolling through and magnifying each image.

'Why didn't I see the reflection before?'

'Perhaps you were looking for people, not items.'

Toby studied the images closely.

'Why is the camera perched on something?' Jack asked. 'It doesn't seem necessary,' he added.

'Holy shit,' Toby shouted so loudly that Jack jumped back.

Toby magnified one of the images and turned the phone towards Jack.

'What does that look like to you?'

'An old grey book of some type.'

Toby's mind suddenly went into overdrive as he began piecing things together. The more it all began to make sense, the more convoluted it got.

'Toby?'

'Mike told me about a library in Eric's house. It was perfectly ordered, but for this one book that aroused his suspicions. A book be believed had no place in that library.'

'An old grey book?'

'Yes. I believe that's the same book in these images.'

'But you already knew Eric was involved. How does this help?'

Toby's eyes widened. He trembled, overtaken by nausea.

'Toby, what is it?' Jack asked, increasingly more concerned.

'The guy I met in the bar, Roger. He was a PI and told me he had witnessed Eric and the barman, Tony, in the midst of a heated argument one evening in the compound. They were arguing over a book that Tony had taken from Eric's house.'

'The grey book?'

'When you brought me back into the pub earlier, who was behind the bar?'

'A young girl. Why?'

'Was there anyone else there?'

'No, she was quite chatty and had just started her shift. I think I may have been quite rude to her, actually.'

Toby slammed the dashboard of the truck and clenched his teeth.

'Toby?'

'The barman was Eric's accomplice. He's also the one who attacked me. He remained hidden and hit me from behind because he didn't want me to recognise his face. It's the same reason the only words he uttered were in a gravelly whisper. He knew I'd identify his voice having spoken to him in the pub. He finished his last shift, attacked me and just disappeared.'

Toby became aware of his breathing getting heavier, more desperate. Images of Beth, Lara, and George began surging through his mind like a collage. His pulse was now racing as he hovered dangerously close to an anxiety attack. Yet he didn't feel anxious. He didn't know what he felt. Perhaps it was the shock of coming face to face with the man whom he had invested so much time in identifying. Jack took hold of Toby's head and looked directly into his eyes.

'You're safe now buddy.'

Toby smiled and began to take control of his breathing. He rested his head between his legs and inhaled slowly through his nose before exhaling out of his mouth. After a few minutes, he had managed to calm himself. He sat back in his seat and turned to Jack.

'I need to get my car.'

'We'll head back tomorrow. For now, you need to rest and I need to lie low. You're staying with me, no arguments.'

But Toby wasn't listening. Instead, he was preoccupied with something that Roger had told him. Something which became more disturbing the more he tried to make sense of it. The rest of the journey was spent in silence, owing to a solitary thought that had suddenly escalated into something alarming. Toby had connected the dots and could finally answer Jack definitively. They'd already discovered the identity of Eric's accomplice. He now believed he had discovered the identity of his killer.

CHAPTER 34

Tuesday 16th May...13:30pm

'Are you any closer to discovering who really killed my shit-head ex-husband?'

Toby couldn't help but smile at the welcoming he'd become accustomed to from Olivia. The fact she was also grinning put him at ease, though the dynamics of this conversation would be different. She needed him, but he was still cautious around her. She was deeply manipulative and had no agenda other than her own. If you wanted something from Olivia, there would have to be something in it for her. Altruism was a stranger to her.

'How often did you venture into the library?'

'The library?'

'At the house, Mike said there was a library.'

'Not when I lived there, and Eric doesn't read books.'

'Then why would he have a library installed?'

'You're the smart one, Toby. Haven't you figured it out?'

Toby looked at her curiously.

'He's hiding something. Even for someone as arrogant as Eric, building something purely for show would be excessive. I'd say whatever you're looking for is hidden somewhere in that room.'

Toby sat back in his chair and looked around the room. It was just as soulless as he remembered. Being here for one hour was difficult enough. He couldn't imagine how it must be for the prisoners who were to spend the rest of their lives in these confines.

'How does this help with getting me off a murder charge?'

Toby bit his lip. It was time for him to make his demands.

'Eric's criminality runs deeper than you think.'

'How much deeper?'

'He may only have been the supporting act. The victims were carefully selected and manipulated to such an extent they had little choice but to consent.'

Olivia's face dropped, and for the first time, Toby saw a genuine horror in her eyes. He'd reached her.

'Jesus, Toby. How do you know all this?'

'Did you ever go into the outbuilding?'

'It was his little workshop. He didn't like me anywhere near it. I didn't even have a key.'

'Did you not find that suspicious?'

'Eric could be a little precious over work-related things. He was rarely out there, so it didn't really bother me. Did you discover something in there?'

'There was a safe built into the wall. We found some disturbing images.'

Toby paused and closed his eyes.

'Of his victims,' he added.

'I lived a lie for all those years, Toby. I never really knew him. I'm far from perfect, but had I had any inclination he was involved in anything like this, I'd have called the police myself.'

'I believe you, but you do understand this changes things.'

'You're now searching for a sex offender as well as a killer.'

Toby nodded his head slowly, trying to gauge whether Olivia was comfortable with him now having an additional agenda. He didn't need her validation, but he did need her cooperation.

'There's something else.'

Toby looked up at her.

'I can see it in your eyes. There's something you're not telling me.'

Toby smiled, wondering whether Olivia could have had her pick of professions had she made different life choices. He exhaled loudly

'Eric raped my sister-in-law.'

'Toby, I don't know what to say.'

'It was after I began investigating him. He knew I'd piece it together. What he perhaps didn't know was that he'd be dead before I did.'

'I dragged you into all of this, and you didn't deserve it. For that I'm sorry.'

As he stared deep into Olivia's eyes, for the first time, he saw a genuine remorse sitting behind them. She meant it.

'Does the name Troy Galen mean anything to you?' he asked.

'Why?'

'Dylan tracked down one of Eric's associates who mentioned him.'

'Was it Carl by chance?'

'What makes you ask that?'

'He was always hanging around. He was the type of person who would walk into a room full of laughing people, never suspecting he was the source of their amusement.'

'Sounds like he was crying out for acceptance, and yearned to feel part of something.'

'That's perhaps a more polite way of phrasing it.'

'Is he trustworthy?'

'He was a lapdog. But if he's frightened enough, he'll sing.'

Toby laughed. Olivia had a way with words.

'Toby, I know of Troy Galen, but be very careful there. From what I've heard, he's not someone you want to cross.'

'Did you ever meet him?'

'No, but I heard Eric talking to him on occasion. They must have known each other for a while. Eric was always coy when I asked about him. Some of the conversations I heard made me think Eric was almost...'

She tailed off.

'Almost what?'

'Afraid of him, and Eric didn't scare easily.'

Olivia paused and then placed her hands on the table, moving in closer.

'Assuming you find Troy Galen. Then what?'

'I think that one would be best for the police to handle.'

'Why?'

'Because the alternative is letting Dylan handle it.'

'Considering what he's done, would that be such a bad thing?'

'Troy wouldn't walk away from that encounter alive, trust me. That leaves Dylan facing a murder charge.

'Why not let the police handle it from here?'

Toby studied her for a brief moment and wondered how such an articulate and observant individual could end up in her situation. He suddenly realised how close he had come to mirroring her journey. He too had made bad choices, and been fuelled by his emotions, yet he was a free man, she was incarcerated. He couldn't condone her actions, but he understood them, and there was a difference. He was snapped back into the moment.

'Toby?'

It was a valid question, he thought, but he already knew the answer.

'I'm consulting on Eric's murder. If I go to Mike with this, he will know I've been undertaking investigative work he specifically warned me not to undertake,' he smiled.

'You'll get told off?' she laughed.

'Something like that.'

'I may be able to help, but first, I need to know you're gonna find Eric's killer and get the charges against me dropped. What have you got so far?'

Toby thought for a moment. The truth was, he had nothing concrete yet, and had been preoccupied with locating Troy Galen.

'You have some swelling over your left eye. What happened?' she asked before he could answer.

Toby instinctively reached for his head. He hadn't noticed it before but could feel it now.

'I got into a little trouble at the pub.'

'You're not a fighter Toby, and you don't find trouble. Somebody attacked you, didn't they? Let me guess, one of my late ex-husband's lackeys?'

'You'd have made a good detective,' he laughed.

This Olivia reminded him of the woman he had first met in his practice. She seemed well-spoken and enticing. He wondered whether she had worn a mask on those occasions, or whether the vitriol and acidic tongue were simply to cover a more vulnerable side. Knowing how quickly she could turn, and her apparent penchant for manipulation, he would continue to tread carefully around her. He didn't know which Olivia he was dealing with and couldn't risk making the wrong guess.

'I believe it was Troy Galen.'

'You've met him?'

'Without realising.'

Olivia regarded him with puzzlement.

'He was the barman at the country pub I was in. I was struck from behind walking back to my car.'

'And you think it was him?'

Toby realised, that if he were to gain Olivia's help, he would need to be open with her about his recent discovery. However, time talking about Troy Galen was time taken away from talking about Eric's murderer, and one thing Toby was sure of, was that Troy Galen was not the killer.

'The library in the house contained a book, which seemed out of place.'

'In what way?'

'Everything was neatly ordered and looked new, aside from this one book. It looked well used, barely even passing for a book.'

'You saw it?' Olivia asked curiously.

'Mike Thomas did. At the time it didn't mean much until I was speaking to a PI in the pub who mentioned overhearing an argument between the barman and Eric.'

'Eric could be very argumentative. I wouldn't read too much into that.'

'Eric was incensed because the barman had taken a book from his house without asking.'

'Perhaps the book is of value?'

'In the wrong hands, of that I am certain. Whatever is contained in it, necessitated Eric confronting a man he was apparently scared of.'

'How can you be sure it's the same book?'

'When Jack and I studied the images, we noticed a book in the reflection. In every image it was underneath the camera, propping it up, yet it had no need to be there. Upon closer inspection, it was an old, grey book...just as Mike had described.'

'You know where he works. That gives you an advantage.'

'I know where he *worked*. He left the day he attacked me.'

Olivia screwed her face up in frustration. Toby felt her impatience but wasn't sure of its direction. He couldn't push too hard or too fast. He needed to make it about her.

'The field next to your old house. Are you still convinced that's where the murder weapon is hidden?'

'It makes sense. Why?'

'I searched it thoroughly, though that was some task considering how overgrown it is.'

'It's there, I know it. It has to be. Why would you carry something of that weight in a rucksack on foot?'

Toby stood up and looked behind him for a moment. He then looked back at Olivia and stared at her wide-eyed, as the realisation hit.

'Why would you have a rucksack in the first place?'

Olivia didn't answer.

'Everything suggests this was impulsive, not premeditated. So why would you carry a rucksack?'

'That doesn't tell us anything we didn't already know.'

'But it does. It confirms the statue was almost certainly carried by hand and dumped. It will have the prints of the killer all over it, and I'm certain it's in that field.'

'But you said you'd already searched it,' she interjected.'

'I missed something, and I need you to tell me what it was.'

Toby sat back down desperately hoping Olivia could fill in the gaps. He was convinced he was right on this one, but to date, the lack of findings hadn't supported his theory. He was startled by Olivia banging her hands on the table.

'The well. There's a well.'

'I searched that field, there was no well.'

'You wouldn't notice it unless you knew it was there. At the top left-hand corner of the field, there are some brambles. They've probably camouflaged it by now, but it's there. It's not a deep well either. They started to fill it in, but never finished.'

'Its position would make it ideal for the killer, as it's relatively close to the house, yet inconspicuous.'

'Toby, it's only inconspicuous to those who don't know the area.'

Toby gazed at her.

'You know what that means.'

'It was somebody close to Eric. They had to know the area.'

Silence set in once again as Olivia and Toby each processed the significance of their discovery.

'Of course, all of this remains mere conjecture unless we have the murder weapon,' Toby said, almost disconsolately.

'You need to go back and find the well.'

Toby nodded. Olivia was right. The murder weapon would release her from the murder charges. Then he could concentrate on Troy Galen.

'I hear you've met Natasha.'

Toby was taken by surprise. Though it had been strictly platonic, he possessed feelings of guilt, because he couldn't put a label on it.

'She's an interesting character,' she continued.

'Interesting?'

Olivia grinned, and Toby once again came face to face with the woman who had carefully manipulated him in the past.

'Her and I never saw eye to eye, though I guess when somebody spends so much time at your house, it's bound to become a little fractious. She's more like Eric than she'd care to admit, though.'

Toby felt a mixture of intrigue and dread. She'd grabbed his attention.

'She changed after her girlfriend was killed.'

'In what way?'

'She became mistrusting, paranoid to a degree. She locked herself away for a while, which was strange, as she'd been coming to the house regularly since Eric and I had first met.'

'That's not an uncommon reaction to such a trauma.'

'When she eventually came out the other side, she'd changed.'

'In what way?'

'She became very flirtatious, but only with men. It felt like she was denying who she was. She'd completely shut down that part of her that dreamed of finding a wife.'

'The thought of losing another female in her life may have been too much for her to bear.'

Olivia shook her head.

'She became promiscuous, leaving a string of men in her wake. Just be careful with her.'

'Because she's dangerous?'

'Because you're married.'

As visiting time wound down to a close, Toby found himself replaying his time with Natasha, analysing every word exchanged, every gesture, every smile. Just as the bell rang to signal the end of the visit, Toby had a solitary thought. Within seconds that thought had escalated into something much bigger. Olivia, picking up on Toby's sudden change in demeanour, reached for his hand. The room was now emptying, but Toby and Olivia remained seated, facing one another, her hand on top of his.

'What is it?' she asked.

'I need you to do something for me.'

Toby leaned in and whispered into her ear.

As he backed away slowly, she rose to her feet expressionless, before slowly nodding her head. Toby smiled tentatively as he watched her being led away by an officer. She looked back over her shoulder at him, before disappearing out of view. The visit had proved fruitful, though he now found himself faced with more questions. As he left the prison, he began to shake. It hadn't been an ordeal, but it had been emotionally draining. Olivia had been affable, but paradoxically, the clarity she had offered, had created further complexity. Toby drove from the prison, his destination clear, his mind anything but. If Olivia was true to her word, they'd just laid a trap that he hoped the killer would walk right into.

The footprints are intrusive, yet comforting. It's been a lonely existence for far too long. The visitors gradually lessened until there were none at all. Only one has shown any interest. The one who entrusted with their secret. A secret that has been guarded carefully. The sun burns down, yet darkness is a close friend. The brambles provide security, keeping any unwanted visitors at bay. Until now, only one has penetrated the barriers. Some have tried and failed, whilst others have been oblivious. The footprints are drawing nearer. The sound of the weeds giving way under the pressure is becoming deafening. Suddenly all is quiet. The darkness is lit up, the discovery is made. The secret is out. The burden is no more.

CHAPTER 35

Wednesday 17th May...11:00am

Toby entered the kitchen and reached for the kettle, thinking about the stories this place could tell. There were little signs of the preceding damage. As he waited for it to boil, he admired his surroundings. He'd always envied Jack's life up here, though at times had questioned whether it was a little too isolated. The farmhouse was stunning, a mixture of both modern and traditional. The wooden beams added an elegant touch. He recalled the last time he had been in this area of the house, faced with a wild Dylan Sampson, who had mistaken Toby for an intruder. Though not much time had passed since then, a lot of water had flowed under the bridge. George and Olivia had both been questioned on suspicion of murder, Lara had been raped, Jack had made an attempt on his own life, Toby had been attacked twice, and Beth had left him. A sadness clouded him as he found himself again yearning for his old life, wishing he could turn back the hands of time and make a different decision. A sinking feeling began to surface as he realised he couldn't pinpoint one decision that had been the catalyst for everything that had followed. It would be easy to assume this began with agreeing to see Olivia in the first instance, but she was just a client, no different to any other. She'd had an agenda of course, but he should have been able to see that. Perhaps it was continuing to see her when he began to have doubts? He now realised he should have stepped back and involved the police. Appearing at her house that night had arguably sparked the chain of events. Continuing to investigate Eric Stanton had been the mistake that had cost him most, however. It had cost Lara her innocence, and it had cost him the trust Beth had once had in him. As the remorse began to build, Toby saw his mood dip. Jack was out in the fields, salvaging what normality he could during these troubling times. This left Toby alone with his thoughts. The intrusive thought, which had grown considerably, remained unshared with Jack. He hadn't spoken to anyone about it He would keep that to himself until the time was right. Toby had been withdrawn for the last couple of days, but not due to the trauma. He and Jack had ventured back to the pub after hours to collect his car. He doubted whether the conflict at the pub had resulted in any police involvement. An individual who was happy to wave a knife around was unlikely to be the type of person who would actively seek out police protection. It was more likely they would pursue their own idea of justice, yet Toby wasn't worried. The heightened security offered reassurance that he would remain safe. He also doubted whether any of the attackers would approach Jack again after the injuries he had left them with. But right now, Jack wasn't his concern, not directly anyway. Replaying conversations had brought him closer to gaining clarity. Things were beginning to make sense, but that meant the situation was becoming more complicated, with increased fragility. A fleeting thought had gathered traction, now at a pace where it was difficult to slow it down. His challenge, however, was that the fallout would be potentially cataclysmic. He would undoubtedly put himself at risk. Toby poured himself a coffee and slowly moved into the living room where he stood at the window. The view was awe-inspiring, a solitude he could only dream of, even in the quaint village where he and Beth resided. The sun was shining, and the temperature was now at a level where you could put shorts on in the morning without feeling you were being overly optimistic. The grass lay still, with no hint of a breeze on the cloudless day. He smiled as he imagined how it would feel to live here permanently. Then his smile faded as he was reminded of his own living situation. Staying with Jack was as close to a bachelor life as he'd experienced since first meeting Beth. Whilst many married individuals yearned for that life, he was not one of them. The mundane things which had caused him frustration, things he'd taken for granted, he now missed. He'd resolved to give Beth some space and allow her some time to process the situation. Her anger towards him would reduce over time, but whether the love she'd once had for him would be waiting patiently underneath, was another matter. These were the moments he missed her most. She would provide that comforting reassurance that everything would be okay. That arm around him, the warm smile, the affectionate kiss. His heart ached as the reality of the situation began to hit. She may never return. His marriage may already be over. He had no control over that right now, but there was one thing he did have control over, though he continued to agonise over how best to proceed. He had to draw the killer out, but to do that, he first needed to raise the stakes and take a risk, which could have dire consequences for him. As his thinking became more ordered, he walked over to the chair he had been occupying earlier and reached for his phone. After placing it back down twice, he finally garnered the courage to make the call, he had been dreading since the moment the thought had first entered his head.

'What do you need?'

'What makes you think I need something?'

'You only ever call me when you need something, Toby.'

'Considering your position, I would imagine most people who call you need something on some scale.' Toby replied.

Mike laughed down the phone as Toby wondered how he was going to deliver what was inevitably going to set off a chain reaction.

'It's about Dylan,' he started.

'Dylan?'

'Is the warrant still out for his arrest?'

'Do you have information on his whereabouts?'

Toby hesitated.

'Toby?'

'I know where he's staying.'

'Why now?'

Toby had imagined how he would answer that question many times over, yet was still taken by surprise as it finally arrived.

'I believe he's hiding something, and you and I both know what he's capable of.'

'You think Dylan killed Eric Stanton?'

Toby ground his teeth. He'd known this would be a difficult call to make, but couldn't have imagined just how difficult.

'The question isn't whether I believe Dylan killed Eric Mike, it's whether you believe it. The fact you have an arrest warrant out for him would suggest he is certainly a person of interest to you.'

'His prints were found at the scene.'

'His prints were found in an outbuilding on the premises, but you wouldn't execute a warrant and deploy a search for breaking and entering.'

'You're not making any sense, Toby. You contacted me, remember. Am I missing something?'

Toby grabbed at his hair in frustration. The conversation wasn't going as he had planned. He reminded himself who he was speaking to. Mike had seen it all and worked with enough criminals to know when somebody was hiding something.

'I cannot tell you with any degree of certainty that I believe Dylan killed Eric. However, I can also no longer tell you with any degree of certainty that I believe he didn't.'

'When we first spoke about this, you were adamant it wasn't Dylan. You went to great lengths to explain to me why he couldn't possibly have done it. Now you're telling me I should look at this guy. I'll ask you again Toby, what's changed?'

Toby thought long and hard about the best way to answer this question. He felt sorry for Dylan, yet also feared him. But there was one person who Dylan would listen to, and Toby was hoping she would keep the wolf from the door. At least long enough to allow him to see this through. He had a plan, but it wouldn't be without its casualties. He would likely be the biggest casualty, but that was a risk he needed to take. Least harm, most good, he reminded himself.

'There was an intruder in my house. Dylan saved me. I guess I got blinded by the gratitude and perhaps didn't see what was beginning to take shape in front of me.'

'What was that?'

'You are looking for motive and capability. George and Olivia possess only one of those. Dylan possesses both.'

'We charged Olivia Stanton.'

'Then why is there an arrest warrant for Dylan?'

'Olivia was erratic in her interview. There were inconsistencies.'

'Mike, I know you. Without a murder weapon, you must have known it would be hard to bring charges against her. Either you had compelling evidence, or you went with your gut while you built a case. Is there any chance you may have been wrong about her?'

'Toby, you need to tell me what's really going on.'

'I don't follow.'

'I think you do. The police conducted a thorough investigation and an intense set of interviews, making an arrest off the back of that process. You're now trying to tell me you believe we got that wrong, whilst also implicating somebody who you went out of your way to defend previously.'

Toby was sweating. He'd underestimated Mike.

He ground his teeth as he prepared to deliver the hammer blow.

'Dylan confessed.'

'What?'

'I'm indebted to him, but I can no longer keep his secret. He gleefully told me that Eric had died by his hands. I have no compassion for Olivia, but I couldn't sit idly by and see her charged for a crime I know she didn't commit.'

'Toby, you realise what you're saying, right?'

Toby couldn't answer. This was too much for him.

'If he is charged, you may end up being called as a witness for the prosecution. You'd have to face him in court. Can you handle that?'

'A lot can happen between now and then, but yes, I'm aware of the potential implications,' Toby replied somewhat distracted.

There was a silence on the line, Mike seemingly considering Toby's cryptic response.

'What happens next?'

'Naturally, we will arrest Dylan and get his version of events. You will need to be formally interviewed,' Mike said softly. 'As a witness of course,' he clarified.

'But with his prints at the scene, his previous form, and his motive, we should have enough to hold him for a few days,' Mike continued.

'I'll send you the address now.'

'Does anybody else know where Dylan is?'

'Not even George.'

'He must really trust you.'

'I guess.'

'Toby, you know what that means, right? He will know it's you who turned him in.'

'I know,' but I need to atone for some poor decisions, and this is the first step.'

Toby placed his hand on his stomach as anxiety driven by intense feelings of guilt, began to surface. Only time would tell if he'd judged this one right. Never had he played such a dangerous game with such high stakes, and never had he felt so far out of his depth.

'Mike?'

'Yeah.'

'Go easy on him. He's not a bad person, he's just flawed.'

'Aren't we all?'

The line went dead, Toby recognising he now had no way of stopping the sequence of events he had just started. He placed his finger to his lip as the taste of blood ran through his mouth. He'd bitten his lip hard during the conversation without even realising. Closing the door behind him, Toby walked briskly towards his car. He'd call Jack later, but for now, he had more pressing matters. He didn't have long, and there was no margin for error.

CHAPTER 36

F riday 19th May...20:00pm

The restaurant was busier than he'd anticipated. Conversation would be a little more difficult, but not impossible. It had been a while since he'd done anything like this, and though he had tried to convince himself otherwise, he was mindful that to others, this would have the clear markings of a date. He'd arrived in a taxi, a decision he had wrestled with due to not having a swift escape should the evening not go as planned. It had been a while since he'd had a drink, which partially explained the anxiety he was feeling right now, though that could also have been attributed to the very nature of why he was here. He was dressed smartly in a dinner jacket and pair of stressed jeans, with a white shirt, loosely buttoned, which was more a sign of the warm evening than a fashion statement. Physically he felt comfortable, emotionally far from it. He was filled with conflicting thoughts and had questioned many times over whether he was doing the right thing being here tonight. He'd almost cancelled several times, but had realised that could do more harm than good. He stared down at his watch and noticed she was late. Had she also had second thoughts? It was only five minutes, but Toby felt the disappointment rising inside of him as an inner voice told him he'd had a wasted trip. All the planning had been in vain. He'd already experienced this evening several times in his mind, yet now feared in his mind was where this evening would remain. He caught the eye of the barman and ordered a small glass of wine. Drinking alone. He thought of Beth, wondering if she thought of him anymore. He thought about Lara and the brutality she had been subjected to. He thought about George, enduring a terrifying kidnapping and then being questioned over a murder. He thought about Jack in the woods, the imagery too painful to bear. He thought about Dylan and the trust he had placed in Toby. He thought about Natasha and her difficulty processing her brother's death, whilst also internalising unspeakable trauma. Finally, he thought of himself, a life now unrecognisable from the one he once led. He thought about how his familial relationships had changed so significantly and how his house, once a safe and loving place, had now become cold and compromised. As he sipped at his wine, he looked up at the clock above the bar where he was seated. It was quarter past eight. He was now convinced she wasn't coming. He would finish his drink and call himself a cab. Toby looked around the restaurant, noting how loud it had become. He considered the different conversations that were currently taking place. Romantic evenings, first dates, friends catching up, perhaps even business meetings. The restaurant would undoubtedly have an array of people, and each table would have a different story to tell. He smiled openly as thoughts of his past dinner dates with Beth passed through his mind. It was natural in most relationships to see a reduction in romance as the years went by, but he and Beth had remained in love for the entirety of their time together. His love for her had never diminished, yet he questioned the depth of her feelings beneath the anger. His concentration was broken by a hand on his back.

'I'm so sorry I'm late. The traffic was awful. Did you get my message?'

Toby looked down at his phone. No signal. Probably why there was so much conversation taking place in the restaurant. He had an intense dislike for people who sat on their phones when in the company of others. The antisocial element of it all was something he could never understand. He smiled knowing he wasn't contactable. There would be no distractions.

'No signal,' he said, turning his phone towards her. 'You look great,' he added.

He felt as awkward giving compliments as he did receiving them. She blushed and pointed her hand towards him.

'You scrub up nicely, Toby. Very suave indeed.'

A waiter came over and directed them towards the table that would be housing them that evening. It was a booth towards the back corner of the restaurant, which offered a little more privacy than many of the other tables. Though he had purposely chosen a place out of town that he hadn't visited previously, he couldn't risk anybody here recognising him. The guilt of dinner with another woman had been so acute, that he had vomited before leaving the house. Every voice inside his head had screamed at him to not pursue this, but there was something there. Something had sparked an interest in her, and he was struggling to deny its existence.

'Nice place. I've never been here before.'

'I've driven past it a few times. You know, admired it from afar,' Toby replied.

She smiled at him. It was a warm and genuine smile as she loosened her shoulders. Her body language provided a very clear message. She was interested in him and had little intention of hiding it. She reached for his hand.

'You've taken your wedding ring off,' she said rather nervously.

A pained look spread across his face.

'Beth has made it clear she isn't coming home. My wedding ring was a constant reminder of what I'd lost,' he answered rather sombrely.

'I'm sorry.'

'Of the two people seated at this table, only one is to blame for the state of my marriage, and you're not that person,' he said through a forced smile.

'Let's order some drinks,' Natasha said, searching for a member of the waiting staff.

As the waiter walked away with their order, Toby caught sight of him speaking to the barman, who was gesturing towards their table. The conversation was brief, but as the waiter began making his over to their table, tray in hand, Toby locked eyes with the man behind the bar who had just poured the drinks. He was well dressed, perhaps a similar age to Toby. His dark hair was swept back off his forehead, and he had a Latino look to him. His shirt sleeves were rolled up revealing a Polynesian tattoo on his forearm. Toby imagined he'd have some stories to tell, but wasn't able to dwell on that thought as the drinks arrived. Natasha picked up her glass of wine and raised it.

'Here's to good food and hopefully great wine,' she laughed.

The two glasses clinked together, the tone for the evening set.

'I have to be honest. I was quite surprised when you called me. Perhaps even more surprised when you suggested dinner,' Natasha said.

'I figured we both needed it. Besides, I wanted to say thank you for Abigail Crookes.'

'I didn't do much,' she replied waving away his gratitude.

'You called in a favour, that you didn't need to call in.'

'I just have a close friend who's still in the police. Really, it was nothing,' she insisted. 'Did you go to see Abi?'

Toby felt an uncomfortable feeling in the pit of his stomach. Perhaps this wasn't a path he wanted to tread. Natasha noticed his reticence.

'Do you know how difficult it is to be talking about rape victims knowing your own brother was the one responsible?'

Toby shook his head.

'All of those girls will have been left with emotional scars that will never heal.'

Toby was gripped by a sudden bout of sadness as he realised Natasha was speaking from experience. She knew what it was like to feel powerless and have your own body taken against your will. She felt the pain of each of his victims, yet she was also feeling grief over the death of the man who had inflicted that pain. The conflict she was confronting must have been torturous. She picked up her drink and took several sips. Her glass was emptying much quicker than his, and he knew why. She flicked her hair out of her eyes and studied the menu.

'The steak looks good.'

'It depends on how you have it cooked,' Toby replied trying to lighten the evening's mood.

'Will you judge me if I answer rare?'

'Anything more is disrespectful to the animal,' he laughed.

Natasha finished her wine and ordered herself another. Toby was still making his way down his first glass. He'd relaxed, but only a little. This still felt strange for him, as he continued to question his presence at a restaurant with another woman.

'This is nice,' she said.

'I must admit, it feels nice to step away from the social recluse I'd become,' Toby replied.

'You have an excellent reputation, Toby.' She froze. He could see she wasn't finished. 'So, you'll have already picked up on the fact that I like you. I have no expectations, but I felt it was important to be honest with you.'

Toby felt his pulse begin to race. He couldn't deny there was an attraction, and he was flattered by her attention, but this hadn't been his intention at the beginning of the evening. He suddenly felt the need to clarify this.

'I know you're in a difficult position, Natasha, and I would never dream of exploiting your vulnerability. I hope I haven't given you any impressions to the contrary.'

She smiled at him, gently gripped his hand, and placed her finger on his lip as he was about to say something else.

'No need to say anything further,' she whispered. Let's just enjoy the evening.

The arrival of the food was accompanied by the inevitable drop in conversation. This came as somewhat of a relief to Toby who had begun to feel awkward since Natasha had opened up about her feelings for him. The awkwardness was perhaps compounded by the fact Toby was unsure of his own feelings right now. He wondered whether he too was vulnerable. As the plates emptied, Natasha ordered them both another glass of wine, her third. She was relaxing into the evening, seemingly unphased by his reaction to her disclosure.

'I hear they've got Dylan Sampson in custody.'

The sudden change in direction of the conversation caught Toby by surprise.

'So, it wasn't Olivia after all?' she added.

'I'm not privy to the thought process of the police.'

'You must have an opinion,' she probed leaning forward, resting her arms on the table.

Just then the waiter collected the empty plates and served them with their drinks. It was a welcome distraction for Toby, but only momentary, as he felt her eyes resting on him in expectation.

'Dylan, Olivia and George all had motives, and each had opportunity. Out of those three, two would have been prepared to kill, but only one capable, given the circumstances.'

'So, you think it was Dylan?'

'I don't think it looks good for him right now. The evidence must be compelling, but being an ex-police officer, you'll be much more versed with the protocol than me.'

'You didn't answer my question. I want to know what you think.'

'Dylan is a complex character with a temper. His sheer size in addition to his levels of training in combat, make him a very dangerous individual to the wrong person.'

'My brother was that wrong person?'

'As I said, Dylan had a motive.'

'They have more than just motive.'

Toby wondered if she was speculating, or whether she knew more about the case than she was letting on.

'Where do you see your career going from here?' he asked.

'This feels like a job interview,' she grinned. 'And I would much rather talk about Dylan Sampson.'

It was natural she would take an interest in a suspect in her brother's murder case, and though Toby remained indebted to Dylan, he would indulge her...for now.

'They tell me he died of blunt force trauma, yet they don't have the murder weapon.'

Toby contemplated his response, wondering how much faith he had in his ability to read people.

'They must feel confident they can build a case without one.'

She shook her head but looked distracted.

'Mike told me he was struck on the back of the head with the bronze statue. The thought of him lying there on his own is heartbreaking. I know he did wrong Toby, but you have to understand he was still my bother.'

'Grief isn't a selective process, it's innate,' Toby replied.

The evening was passing by quickly, the drinks even quicker, certainly for Natasha anyway. Toby wondered whether this was long overdue for her. It wasn't just about the death of her brother. It was about losing her partner and sacrificing her career. It was about her own rape and how she could identify with each one of Eric's victims. He couldn't begin to imagine the inner turmoil she must be experiencing.

'You seem to enjoy your wine,' he said trying to avoid the evening from descending into a sombre occasion.

'It's not often I get to let my hair down. It's been too long.'

'And a fine Rioja is a lovely companion.'

'We're drinking Bordeaux, Toby,' she giggled. Sounds like you've had too many.'

'My mistake. I think you may be right, he agreed,' as their laughter rang out through the restaurant.

'Excuse me for just one moment,' Toby said as he headed towards the bathroom.

He didn't need the toilet, but he did need to gather his thoughts. Things were progressing at a rate he was less than comfortable with. He had an idea of how this would end, and it wouldn't be without consequences. He splashed water on his face and stared into the mirror. The reflection was somebody he no longer recognised. His physical appearance remained the same, but his personality had transformed into something he disliked. Most importantly, Beth disliked it, and that's why she had left. He looked down at his watch and saw it was now after ten. He wasn't sure whether that was early or late; it had been a while since he had done anything like this. One thing he did know, however, was that his night wasn't over yet. As he approached the table, he noticed his glass was full. Natasha had made her intentions clear.

'I took the liberty of topping up your glass.'

'Thank you,' Toby said tentatively.

She moved in closer to him.

'Tell me how you ended up consulting for the police.'

'Mike and I go back. I think he took pity on me,' he joked.

'Mike always thought highly of you. That day we left your house, he said you were one of the smartest people he knew.'

'That doesn't sound like Mike.'

'He also said you could be infuriating.'

Toby laughed heartily.

'Now that does sound like Mike.'

She reached for his hand and squeezed it. He blushed but didn't retract. The truth was the companionship felt nice.

As he looked down at his hand, enveloped by hers he noticed his phone light up, clinging to a weak signal. There was a voice-mail. This provided him with a reason to slow things down and remove himself from the situation.

'Forgive me, I'll only be a moment.'

True to his word, Toby returned quickly, but his demeanour had changed.

Natasha picking up on this, stood up to greet him, though she was a little uneasy on her feet due to the volume of wine she had consumed.

'Toby?'

He breathed in slowly and took his seat.

'They've charged Dylan with the murder of Eric.'

'I'm not sure how to feel. I guess I'm relieved it's over.'

'They found the murder weapon.'

'Where?'

'The field next to Eric's house. Apparently, there's an old well which is camouflaged by overgrown brambles. Do you know of it?'

'No, and I've been up there many times. That corner of the field has always been unsightly though, so it's probably been well hidden for a long time,' she replied.

Toby took a sip of his drink.

'What was Eric like as a child?'

'Believe it or not, he was relatively quiet when he was younger, but when we began to get older, our relationship soured.'

'I'm sorry to hear that.'

'There's an age gap between us, so by the time I was growing up he was ready to move out. By that time, I'd already seen something in him I didn't like.'

Toby relaxed back into his seat waiting for Natasha to continue.

'He saw the way our father treated our mother and took the wrong side.'

'He identified with your father?' Toby asked.

She lowered her head slowly nodding.

'He was exposed to more than I was, but he was very impressionable. Our father was controlling and our mother screwed around. He used to get physical with her on occasion. I don't think Eric idolised him, but he was able to convince him over time that he was merely reacting to her infidelity, though I don't know whether Eric truly believed that.'

'What makes you say that?'

'He grew to resent them both. I think ultimately, he saw fault on each side, but it's undeniable he shared certain traits with his father.'

Natasha stopped and ran her hand through her hair, but Toby couldn't tell whether she was uncomfortable or flirtatious.

'Why don't we continue this conversation back at my place?' she said with a grin. 'I have wine,' she added, giggling.

This was the moment he'd been dreading, yet perhaps not for the reasons he would have believed. The fact there was temptation left him with extreme feelings of trepidation, and of course guilt. Natasha had been open with her feelings, which meant that were he to accept the offer, it would send a very clear signal to her and raise her expectations. He had enjoyed her company, but it had been the conversation that had proved most rewarding...so far at least. Detecting his awkwardness, she leaned over and placed her hand on his arm.

'Relax, it's just drinks and conversation in a place a little more private than this. I know you're married and would never take advantage of that.'

Toby sat in silence for a few moments, silently processing his situation. He couldn't quite put his finger on why, but he believed whatever decision he made, would have consequences. He had been clear in his mind what this evening was about, but now there had been doubt cast on this. She looked radiant, in a classy way. Like Beth, she had a natural beauty about her and carried herself well. She was elegant and had no genuine need for makeup. Toby looked around the restaurant and noticed the once packed room was now sparse on diners. The clock told him they'd outstayed their welcome, yet the voice inside was telling him the night was still young. He called the waiter over before settling the bill and grabbing his coat. He then pulled out his phone and dialled for a taxi. As the voice on the other end asked for his destination, he removed the phone from his ear slowly and looked at Natasha expectantly, his heart knocking at the walls of his chest. It wasn't said with conviction, but his words were clear.

'Where to?'

CHAPTER 37

Wednesday 17th May...16:00pm

The scene was like something out of a movie, several police cars and vans placed strategically around the small hotel. Mike was taking no chances with the suspect, but this was no ordinary suspect. Dylan Sampson was a very dangerous individual. His size and military training made him a force to be reckoned with, and if they got this wrong, people could get injured. He wouldn't underestimate the suspect. A small part of him felt disappointed; disappointed his gut had been wrong. Everything about the murder seemed to point towards Olivia Stanton as the killer, but Toby had shed fresh doubt on this theory. Dylan had motive, he was at the scene on the day, and he certainly had the capability. They still didn't have the murder weapon, but it would only be a matter of time. They certainly had enough to bring him in. Then it was up to them to build a case which the CPS would move forward with. Mike thought about how difficult it must have been for Toby to turn Dylan in. Had he known all along and his conscience had been pricked, or had he been telling the truth and Dylan had admitted it to him more recently? Toby knew he would get called to the stand, meaning he would have to face Dylan in the courtroom. Between Toby's testimony, Dylan's presence at the crime scene, and the knowledge that Eric had raped and kidnapped Dylan's sister, Mike felt they had a strong enough case to pursue. But thoughts of any criminal proceedings were in the future, and right now they needed to ensure that he was apprehended with minimal disruption. The hotel was in a quieter part of the area, its geographical positioning presenting as the perfect place to lie low. Mike thought it would be difficult for a man of Dylan Sampson's stature to remain inconspicuous, however, he had remained just that up to this point. Mike made his way in through the main entrance, closely followed by six officers. He approached the front desk, where an older gentleman greeted them with a smile.

'How may I help you, officers?'

'We are looking for a guest by the name of Dylan Sampson.'

'I'm sorry, I'm not able to pass out any information on hotel guests. We have a duty to protect any patron's privacy.'

'Mr Sampson is wanted for questioning relating to a very serious crime. I'm wondering whether your duty to protect extends to guest safety?'

The man regarded Mike with a smile, but it felt disingenuous.

'Perhaps if you were to come back with a warrant?'

'If I leave here now, when I return with a warrant, and I will get one, I will also return with the media and give you your five minutes of fame as the man who obstructed a murder case and placed his guests at risk. I'll personally name you and defame this place to the brink of reputation ruin. You won't be able to give your rooms away by the time I'm finished. Now, do I still need that warrant?' Mike asked angrily.

The man behind the counter had lost his smile and was instead looking rather nervous.

'I'll go and speak with the manager. Please excuse me, for one moment.'

'You go and do that,' Mike replied, feeling frustrated he'd even had to make the threat. He had more important things to focus his attention on than an overly ambitious smart arse who hid behind a desk all day. Because the hotel was relatively small, a door knock wasn't out of the question, though it wasn't ideal. The difficulty with that, of course, was that they didn't want to create a panic, which may alert Dylan to their presence. Minimal disturbance was their priority, though, with the number of police vehicles in the car park, he wondered how inconspicuous they could remain. As with all arrests, his hope was that it would be a smooth process, but in this instance, he expected confrontation and resistance. As he looked around the reception area, he noted how quiet it was. Post-check-out and pre-check-in, he thought. Just then, the staff member returned with a tall man, wearing a dark suit and a dark blue tie. He was very well presented. Mike assumed he was the manager. He approached Mike and offered his hand.

'My name is Marcus, and I'm the hotel manager. May I ask what this is all about?'

Mike studied him for a moment, wondering whether there was going to be any hostility.

'We have reason to believe you have a guest staying here by the name of Dylan Sampson.'

'We take the privacy of our guests very seriously...'

'I'm going to stop you there,' Mike said casually, raising his hand. 'Your underling here made your position very clear. Now let me make mine. How many officers do you see here?'

The man looked behind Mike.

'Seven,' Marcus replied rather sheepishly.

'And do you think that the police would deploy seven officers for somebody wanted in connection with petty theft?'

'No.'

'Precisely. I'm going to explain to you the same thing I explained to your assistant there. We can do this with minimal disturbance and I can commend the hotel for its cooperation. Alternatively, I can come back with a warrant, every media crew I can get my hands on, and let the whole of the country know how you did everything you could to obstruct the police from taking in a murder suspect. Now tell me. Is guest privacy still your priority here?'

Mike's tolerance levels were diminishing rapidly. Normally, people were clamouring to get murderers off the streets. Yet here he was faced with two individuals who had other priorities. He didn't like making threats, but he didn't want anything to hamper this investigation. Eric Stanton's murder had garnered national interest, which inevitably brought pressure. He was seen as a local businessman who had worked hard for the community and undertaken various types of charity work. Of course, he had kept his darker side very well hidden, which meant the view of him was myopic, based solely on the man he presented as, not the man he was.

'We don't have anybody staying here by that name, officer, I'm sorry,' said Marcus, who had been scrolling frantically through the computer screen in front of him.

The colour drained out of Mike's face. Toby had been adamant this was where Dylan was staying. There had to be a mistake.

'That's not possible. Can you check again?'

Marcus returned to the screen, and this time scrolled slowly. Mike noted the concentration on his face.

'I've searched the name and we have never had a guest stay here under that name. I'm sorry you've had a wasted trip, and wish we could have been more help.'

'Excuse me for one moment,' Mike said before swiftly moving to a quieter part of the reception area.

'He's not here, Toby. Do you think he was tipped off?'

'Have you spoken to anybody about our conversation?'

'No.'

'Neither have I. There's no logical reason as to why Dylan would have his suspicion aroused.'

'Then where is he? There's no record of a Dylan Sampson ever having stayed here.'

'He's there, Mike,' Toby reaffirmed. 'He has to be.'

He sounded panicked, and Mike wondered whether a part of him feared that Dylan knew he'd given away his location to the police. Toby had taken a risk. If this went wrong, if they couldn't make the charges stick, Dylan would almost certainly seek out revenge and would be heading in only one direction.

'Pete Quinn,' Toby suddenly shouted.

'Pete Quinn?'

'Dylan once told me that's the alias he uses when he is lying low.'

Mike rushed back to where the group were situated and held the phone down to his chest.

'Try Pete Quinn,' he said hastily.

'Pete Quinn?' Marcus repeated.

'Do you know him?'

'I checked him in myself. The only reason the name resonates with me is because of the size of the man.'

'That's him,' Mike replied. 'Now where can we find him?'

Room 202. You can either use the lifts over there, or the stair-well through the doors opposite them.'

'We'll use both, to cover all bases.'

'Do you need me to ensure the area is clear,' Marcus asked nervously.

Mike looked around at the deserted area.

'I don't think we'll have a problem on that front,' he replied with a grin.

After the third knock, the door finally opened. Dylan stood in the doorway surveying the scene in front of him. Recognising Mike, he laughed, but it seemed less than friendly.

'How can I help you fine gentlemen?'

Mike stepped forward. Though eagerly awaited, the moment also filled him with dread.

'Dylan Sampson, I'm arresting you on suspicion of the mur-der of Eric Stanton. You do not have to say anything. But it may harm your defence if you do not mention when questioned something which you later rely on in court. Anything you do say may be given in evidence.'

Dylan's smirk disappeared as he took a step forward into the corridor.

'Seven officers, just for me? I think you're a little short on numbers.'

'Are we going to have a problem here?' Mike asked.

'We had a problem the moment you came to my hotel room to arrest me on some bullshit charge with no evidence.'

'If we had no evidence, we wouldn't be here right now. Place your hands behind your back please.'

'And if I don't?'

'I wouldn't recommend the alternative. Either you walk out of here under your own volition, or you're carried out on a trolley. Your choice,' Mike replied sternly.

Dylan put his hands behind his back as the cuffs were placed tightly around his wrists. As he was led down the deserted corridor, he ground to a halt and turned around to face Mike.

'How did you know I was here?'

'We're not at liberty to disclose that information.'

'This wasn't random, and it wasn't a stroke of luck. You were tipped off. Only one person knew my location.'

His anger grew.

'This was Toby Reynolds. That son of a bitch.'

'I suggest you calm down,' Mike said firmly.

'I'll calm down when I wrap my hands around that fucker's neck,' Dylan screamed, ignoring Mike's suggestion.

'That sounds like a threat.'

'Threats often go unfulfilled. Believe me when I tell you, this won't. Toby Reynolds has just put a target on his back, and someday soon, I'll be taking aim at it.'

The commotion continued until they reached the reception area. The handful of people now gathered, desperately trying to avoid eye contact with the giant of a man who had been apprehended and was being led out of the building in handcuffs. Dylan was more subdued on the ride to the station, but Mike, who had decided to accompany him in the back of the van, believed this was quiet contemplation rather than acceptance. He was plotting his revenge, and Mike felt certain that revenge was going to be on Toby. He leaned back and closed his eyes. Things had just gotten more critical. If they couldn't make the charges stick, Dylan would be free to roam the streets. He was the type of person who could kill somebody and make it look like an accident. Mike couldn't put a twenty-four-hour surveillance on him. He could no longer guarantee Toby's safety.

As the van came to a halt and the doors swung open, the sight of the police station seemed to antagonise the detainee further. Moving inside, Dylan quickly perused his surroundings, focusing his attention on the woman sitting behind the counter. She was smiling, but looked a little anxious, as he stared at her name badge.

'Are you going to process me, Cathy? My name is Dylan Sampson and I've been stitched up for the murder of a vile piece of shit I wish I actually had murdered. Perhaps you've heard of him? Eric Stanton. His sister was one of your lot.'

Dylan was pushed down the corridor quickly and taken to a holding cell. The less time he was in the view of others, the better. Mike turned to one of his officers, as an angry Dylan banged on the walls.

'Leave him in there for a while. We can't interview him in this state.'

The banging eventually began to subside, the room's occupant now more serene. There was a good chance he was smouldering under the surface, like a volcano ready to erupt after lying dormant for some time. Mike all the while sat isolated and deep in thought in the interview room where he would soon be facing Dylan Sampson. He thought about Toby and the sacrifice he had just made. He was relying on Mike to get a conviction, offering himself up as a sacrificial lamb in the process. Yet it wasn't the fact Toby had placed himself in danger, that bothered him. It was why? Why was Toby's level of investment in catching the killer so high that he was prepared to antagonise one of the most dangerous men Mike had ever encountered? Suddenly, this didn't make sense. Toby loathed Eric, so why was he risking his life to find his killer? That uncomfortable feeling never left Mike for the rest of the day. It was still with him as he closed his eyes to go to sleep later that night, just hours after he had conducted one of the most difficult police interviews of his career.

CHAPTER 38

Tuesday 16th May...22:00pm

It was late in the evening, but the timing had been necessary. The scarcely lit, secluded area was ideal for a conversation that in itself, was less than ideal. The sporadically placed trees causally swaying in the soft breeze, the only witnesses. Toby was perched on a wall, which backed onto a large field. He waited patiently, yet anxiously for the arrival of Dylan. Toby had thought extensively about what he was about to ask of Dylan, but even the most detailed planning still carried a high risk. Dylan had agreed to meet in person, but Toby wondered whether his suspicion outweighed his intrigue. The occasional passing car broke the silence in the night. Toby looked down at his watch. Dylan was late, which was unusual. His time in the military had taught him the importance of punctuality, which meant you could usually set your watch by him. Just as Toby began to wonder if he'd had second thoughts, out of the corner of his eye, he caught sight of a figure walking down the road. The man wore a dark jumper, which had the hood pulled over. Toby smiled, the thought of Dylan trying to remain inconspicuous causing him amusement. As he drew closer, Toby's nerves began to surface. Dylan took a seat on the wall next to Toby, who could feel his pulse beginning to race.

'Remind me again why this couldn't be done over the phone,' Dylan said rubbing his hands together in what had descended into a chilly evening.

Toby smiled, not expecting anything other than a direct conversation with the man seated next to him.

'Do you trust me?'

Dylan turned to face Toby, looking perplexed.

'What?'

'It's a straightforward question. I need to know if you trust me?'

'I struggle with trust, Toby, but as far as people go, I have more faith in you than most. Does that answer your question?'

Toby relaxed a little. Regardless of their differences, he had time for Dylan. He was loyal, to a fault sometimes, but family and friends meant a great deal to him, and Toby respected that. Whilst it was difficult to grasp at times, Dylan was one of the good guys in life. His methods were questionable, but his disdain for injustice and those who hurt innocent people was something you couldn't help but admire. But he was also dangerous, and not somebody you wanted to cause harm to. It was that which made what Toby was about to ask him even more challenging.

'I think I know who murdered Eric, but I need your help.'

Dylan's eyes widened with intrigue.

'Who is it?'

'That's not important right now.'

'You're asking me to trust you, yet you don't seem to trust me with the identity of the killer.'

'Suspected killer,' Toby corrected.

An awkward silence ensued as Toby knew Dylan was right.

'Dylan, I need you to trust me, but I also appreciate what I'm about to ask of you is something of great magnitude.'

Dylan didn't respond. He knew there was more.

'Have you ever heard of drawing a criminal out?'

'I'm familiar with drawing the enemy out.'

Toby considered how he could articulate this in such a manner that would convince Dylan. He'd been over this so many times in his head, but still found what he was about to ask almost inconceivable.

'Sometimes Dylan, people tell you much more than they believe they are telling you.'

'You've lost me.'

'If somebody is being deceitful, and you listen hard enough and long enough, you'll uncover their lies.'

'You can tell when somebody is lying?'

'It's not quite that simple. People will have subtle changes in their body language when they are being disingenuous. To be able to identify these, you first need to get a detailed perception of their body language when you know they are telling you the truth.'

'That sounds complicated, and I'm still not any closer to understanding where I fit into this little criminal profiling lesson,' Dylan replied.

Toby took in a deep breath and then looked Dylan directly in the eye.

'How would you feel about being arrested for murder?'

'This is a joke, right?'

Toby shook his head.

'Holy shit, you're serious,' Dylan raged in disbelief.

'The case against Olivia is sketchy at best, and I believe the real killer knows this. If new evidence comes to light and another suspect is arrested in connection with the murder, I believe it will push the real killer into making a mistake.'

Dylan began to laugh.

'You call me out here late in the evening, to the middle of nowhere, to ask me to give myself up for a murder I didn't commit? Are you fucking serious? What the hell made you think I would go for this?'

'Because you want Troy Galen.'

'Troy Galen killed Eric?'

'No, but the woman who is currently facing charges for a murder she didn't commit, has links to him. If we find the real killer and exonerate her, she will provide us with that link.'

'You made a deal with the devil, Toby.'

'There's a mutual incentive for the real killer to be brought to justice.'

'Even if I agreed to this ludicrous idea, what the hell makes you think it will draw out the killer, and what happens to me?'

Toby put his hands to his lips.

'Believe it or not, I'm the one who is taking all the risk.'

'How the hell do you figure that?' Dylan snapped.

'Because I'll be the one to give you up. If I'm right, Mike will know that I played him. If I'm wrong, Mike will also know that I played him. Either way, you walk free, and I deal with the fallout.'

'Unless you betray me.'

Toby froze. It hadn't even crossed his mind that Dylan would be suspicious of betrayal.

'I think you know I'm not that person. My sister-in-law was raped by Eric, and that destroyed my marriage. I have little interest in who killed him. Like you, I want to locate Troy Galen, and I believe the best way to do this is by unmasking Eric's killer so the charges against Olivia are dropped.'

Dylan stood up and walked around for a few moments. He looked up to the skies and ran his hands over his head repeatedly before walking back to where Toby was seated.

'You realise what you're asking, right?'

Toby nodded.

'Why would they believe you, without evidence?'

'Your prints were at the scene and you had a motive, but that's circumstantial. However, if you add to that a confession, it makes the case more compelling.'

'You're expecting me to confess?'

'As far as the police are concerned, you already have... to me. I will agree to testify in court.'

'Then what?'

'When I have what I need, I'll recant and present them with the real killer.'

'They still don't have the murder weapon.'

Toby sat stationary as he thought about what he was about to reveal.

'No, but I do.'

'Jesus Toby. What the hell are you doing?'

'Olivia told me where to find it.'

'She knew where the murder weapon was? Doesn't that make you suspicious? Surely the police can get prints from it?'

'The killer didn't leave their prints on it.'

'How do you know all this?'

'I'm asking you to trust me.'

'You're asking a lot more than that.'

As expected, tensions were now running high, and the atmosphere was becoming increasingly more volatile. Toby was worried he was losing Dylan, and he needed him. He placed his hand on his shoulder and flashed him a smile steeped in anxiety.

'You saved me from an intruder and entrusted me with the images you discovered at Eric's. Your sister is somebody I care for a great deal, somebody whom we worked tirelessly to rescue. Those are the reasons why you should trust me.'

Dylan looked him up and down before closing his eyes and inhaling loudly through his nose.

'How would this work?'

'I'll reluctantly confide in Mike that you confessed to me.'

'Then?'

'I'll tell him you're staying at the small hotel on the outskirts of town.'

'But I'm not.'

'You will be. Naturally to make it convincing you'll need to offer some resistance, but not so much that it lands you on further charges.'

'So, make a little fuss, have a little fun, and then what? Just let them take me?'

'Exactly that,' Toby smiled casually.

There was a small part of him basking in the excitement of what was about to come, though he wouldn't bear witness to it.

'I'm the only person who will know your location. Keep that in mind when you're arrested.'

Dylan sat deep in thought.

'There's something else.'

'What's that?'

'When you arrive at the police station, there will be a desk officer on duty called Cathy Benson. It's vital you provide her with as much information about your injustice as possible. Make sure she knows your name.'

'Why is she so important?'

'The more you know, the more likely this will look contrived. I promise I will explain every last detail to you once this is over.'

'And how does this end, Toby?'

'With the real killer being served up to the police, accompanied with irrefutable evidence.'

'How sure are you that we can pull this off?'

'Honestly? There are no guarantees, but I believe it to be our best chance.'

'We could always beat a confession out of your suspect,' he said with a smirk.'

'I won't need long.'

'And what happens to me in the meantime?'

Toby grimaced as he prepared to push Dylan just that little bit further.

'It will be one or two nights in the holding cells, along with an uncomfortable interview.'

'Jesus, Toby. You're the gift that keeps on giving,' Dylan said sarcastically.

'There's one more thing. If you're trying to remain hidden, you wouldn't check in under your own name. You'll need an alias.'

'Pete Quinn,' Dylan smirked.

Toby pulled his phone out of his pocket and made a note of the name, though still unsure whether all of this would be in vain. What he was asking of Dylan was unthinkable, but this needed to look authentic. Olivia could locate Troy Galen, but she wouldn't give up his location without getting something in return. She needed Toby, and Toby needed her, but they both needed Dylan. The question was, had he done enough to convince Dylan this was their best chance of finding the sexual predator who had dehumanised his victims? He turned to Dylan, who had been standing quietly for the last few minutes, staring into the night sky.

'Are you in?' he asked.

Dylan continued to stare up at the stars, slowly inhaling the crisp night air. He had a calmness about him; all anger seemingly now dissipated. He remained deep in thought for some time, with neither his expressionless face nor his stiffened posture giving his intentions away.

CHAPTER 39

S aturday 20th May...12:00pm

Toby had been staring at his phone for over an hour but had come no closer to making the call he knew he would inevitably have to make. He was about to blow a hole in everything the police thought they knew about Eric Stanton's murder. This had never been his intention, but tracking down Troy Galen had become his priority, consuming him like an obsession. It had become personal, and though Eric had been the one responsible for Lara's attack, he was under no illusion of Troy Galen's danger to women. He'd played high-risk stakes, but it had paid off. His suspicions had been confirmed. He knew the identity of the killer, and very soon, so would the police. Yet that in itself presented a whole new set of challenges, Toby knew it didn't end here for him. He debated internally on the morality of his actions, questioning if the outcome validated the approach. He'd not only played a senior police officer; he'd played a friend. Toby worried their friendship wouldn't survive this. Another lost relationship to add to the growing casualty list. Then there were the legal implications. Wasting police time, falsifying a witness statement.

Becoming increasingly frustrated at his own hesitation, Toby dialled Mike Thomas.

'Mike, I'm going to text you an address. Can you come and meet me?'

'Now?'

'It's urgent.'

'Slow down Toby. What's so urgent that you need me to drop everything?'

Toby paused. This was proving infinitely more difficult than he'd anticipated. His next words were irreversible. A turning point that would alter everything.

'I know the identity of Eric Stanton's killer.'

'We have Eric's killer in custody.'

Toby didn't like Mike's tone. He sensed a nascent anger simmering beneath the surface. The full force of Mike's wrath was imminent, a prospect that filled him with dread.

'Toby?'

'I need you to trust me, Mike.'

'I've given you nothing but trust. In return, you gave me a killer who I'm almost certain you're about to tell me isn't a killer. You know I could charge you with obstruction of justice, right?'

Toby's heart began racing erratically. Of all the implications he had considered, being arrested for obstructing justice wasn't one of them.

'Can you come?' Toby asked.

'Where are you?'

'Springdale Gardens. There's a café at the end of the road where it meets Blossom Lane. I'll be there in five minutes.'

There was a silence on the other end of the line, which did little to quell Toby's nerves.

'I'll be there in fifteen minutes. That will give you ten minutes to have a think about how you're gonna convince me not to throw you in a cell.'

This was as stern as he'd ever heard Mike. He went to hang up.

'And Toby?'

'Yes?'

'Screw me around this time, and I promise you there won't be a next. Are we clear?'

'I understand,' Toby answered in a barely audible whisper, but Mike had already hung up.

Toby imagined him red-faced, barely able to contain his fury at being played by somebody he had supported. This whole situation left Toby with a bad feeling, prompting him once more to consider whether the results were worth the methods he had used. He reminded himself that whatever happened from here, there were no winners. Everybody had lost something. He and Beth had lost trust; George had lost her innocence; Jack, his peaceful existence; Olivia, her freedom, and Eric his life. Lara had also lost so much, but still, he struggled to process that. The killer would be brought to justice, but even they had lost, on more than one level. Unsure whether Mike would ever trust him again, Toby began the short walk to the café. It wasn't just his integrity and reputation on the line. Toby's very freedom could hinge on his ability to convince Mike to arrest somebody who hadn't even cropped up on the police radar. Someone who they would never have suspected. Toby's disclosure on its own wouldn't be enough. Mike had to arrest the suspect and agree to take forward the case to the CPS. If he didn't, all of this was in vain, and Dylan was in trouble. As he entered the café, he pulled out a seat and sat down, as far away from the door as possible. He looked down at his hands, which were now shaking. The last time he recalled being this nervous was when he was sat in the interview room. He was about to face the same person but in very different circumstances. This wouldn't be recorded, and he had no legal counsel. Toby's composure began to give way as he looked up and saw Mike walking past the window and entering the café. The timer had begun.

Toby stood up to greet Mike.

'Sit down,' he said sternly. 'All I want to hear from you is why I have the wrong person in custody. And Toby, don't even think about bullshitting me.'

Toby swallowed, but before he could begin, Mike took him by surprise.

'Who killed Eric Stanton?'

'Somebody who has flown under your radar.'

He stopped upon realising he needed to be very careful with his choice of words here. The last thing he wanted was to imply that the police were in any way inept.

'Toby? Who do you believe killed Eric Stanton?'

Toby froze for a moment, before looking Mike directly in the eye.

'Natasha Jenkins.'

Mike laughed.

'His sister? The ex-cop? The ex-cop who sacrificed her career for him?'

'Yes.'

'I'm assuming you have sufficient evidence to substantiate this claim?'

Toby placed his hand on his chin and rubbed gently.

'Okay, let's begin with the motive,' Mike pressed.

'She discovered her brother was the very thing she despised the most. It was the one thing that resonated with her on a personal level. When she believed he may have been dealing marijuana, she was able to turn a blind eye, but when she uncovered the truth, it hit her hard. I believe she could have forgiven most things, but not that.'

'Natasha was a rape victim?'

'She was gang raped when she was younger, initiated by somebody she thought she could trust. It's not wholly dissimilar to what her brother was doing, but strangely he was guilty of sexual coercion, not rape.' Toby paused for a moment, struggling with his feelings. 'Except in one case,' he continued.

'One case?'

'My sister-in-law.'

Mike's facial expression softened, his anger seemingly reducing. He placed his hand on Toby's shoulder.

'I'm sorry, Toby.'

Toby waved his efforts away as he struggled to hold on to his emotions.

'You know sexual coercion can be difficult to prove?'

'Yes, and so did Eric. He sought out vulnerable women who could be easily manipulated. He studied them and found their weak point to exploit. None of the women would have felt like they had a choice.'

Mike clenched his fists together; Toby could see this was difficult for him to hear, but this conversation wasn't about rape.

'Toby, Eric wasn't short of enemies. Natasha discovering her brother to be a rapist isn't sufficient evidence to prosecute. I'm assuming you have more?'

I met with Natasha on several occasions. On each of those occasions, she lied to me.'

'Go on.'

'When I first met her, I asked her why she changed her name. She said she got married, yet her finger showed no sign of a wedding ring. Of course, not everybody wears a wedding ring, but she later told me that marriage was never her thing.'

'So, she lied to you about being married,' Mike said matter-of-factly.

'The more important question you should be asking yourself is why would that particular, seemingly insignificant detail, change? The answer is it wouldn't unless you'd forgotten the narrative. If you sit with a liar for long enough, they will expose their own deceit. You just have to know what you're looking out for.'

'I'm assuming there's more?'

Toby leaned forward in his seat, placing his hands on the table.

'At what point did you call Natasha to deliver the news that her brother was dead?'

'I can't remember the specific time, but as the time of death was into the evening, it would have been later that night. Why?'

'Because Natasha revealed to me, she had learned of Eric's death at teatime, on that day.'

'His body was still in the house at teatime. I was the first on the scene, and that was around eight in the evening,' Mike interrupted.

'I know.'

'How could you possibly know that, Toby?'

Toby looked uneasy. He couldn't lie, not now. He was already in over his head, regardless.

'I was at the scene.'

'What is it with you and that place?' Mike shouted angrily.

Toby held his breath for a moment, before opting not to reveal the truth. He couldn't risk the police going after Jack.

'I was in the neighbourhood and heard the sirens. Morbid curiosity you could call it.'

Mike shuffled back in his chair, but the look in his eye told Toby he didn't believe his story.

'The only way she could have possibly known at teatime that Eric was dead, was if she was at the scene.'

'Or she knew who was.'

'I did consider that, but when you piece it all together, all roads lead to Natasha. What do you know about Natasha's previous work?'

'Not a lot, why?'

'She worked at a rape crisis centre. She knew one of Eric's victims, though at the time she didn't realise. When I mentioned the name, I saw her flinch. She then later referred to the victim by a nickname, something you would only do through familiarity. I believe, realising Abigail was one of Eric's victims may have been what pushed her over the edge. As I said, this was the one crime that she deplored above all others.'

Mike, having taken out a notepad, was sat busily scribbling away. Noticing Toby had stopped speaking, he looked up expectantly.

'She also lied about her relationship with Olivia. Natasha claimed she and Olivia hadn't met until a year into her relationship with Eric. Olivia contradicted this.'

'You believe her?'

'Olivia wasn't lying; she had no need to.'

Mike put down his pen and stared at Toby.

'What you have, granted is compelling, but it's not enough.'

'Olivia told you she used the key from under the bronze statue to let herself in, but placed it back, right?'

'That's correct.'

'And when you arrived at the scene, that statue was gone?'

'Yes.'

'Olivia also said that she distinctly heard two voices, one female and one of her late ex-husband, Eric. There was no sign of forced entry, which means he let the killer in willingly. Olivia said after the sound of the argument, everything went quiet. She then went downstairs and saw George.'

'Right.'

'So in between the arguing ceasing and George arriving, the killer was able to make their escape with the murder weapon.'

'The statue?'

'The statue.' Toby took a deep breath. 'The very same statue that points to this being spontaneous as opposed to premeditated.'

'How so?'

'They get out of the car and an argument breaks out. He walks inside, whilst something snaps inside of her. She looks around and sees the statue. She picks it up and hits him over the head with it.'

'We don't have the statue.'

Toby looked at Mike, eyes glazed. It only took a moment to see Mike's whole demeanour change.

'Toby?'

'There's an old well in the field next to the house. It's almost entirely covered by brambles. You wouldn't know it was there unless you went looking.'

'And you went looking?'

Toby could see the disappointment in his eyes.

'I knew where to look.'

'How?'

'Olivia.'

'The suspect in a murder investigation told you where to find the murder weapon? Did that not set off alarm bells for you?'

'The opposite. Olivia knew it was the only thing that would exonerate her.'

'You're confident it will have Natasha's prints on?'

'No. I'm certain it won't. Natasha has Raynaud's. She wears gloves a lot of the time to control it. I don't believe she deliberately wore gloves that day, but she was perhaps grateful in the end. That's why she presented with such a confident demeanour. She knew there was little chance of the weapon being found, and even if it was, it wouldn't have her prints on it.'

Mike who had recommenced his frantic note-taking, paused for a moment, pen in hand, tapping away on the table.

'How sure are you that if I go to Natasha's house now, I am arresting the right suspect?'

'After last night, I am now certain.'

'Last night?'

'I know you're angry at me for the Dylan situation, but I couldn't see any other way. I had my suspicions of Natasha, but I needed that final piece of the jigsaw. I thought if she knew there had been an arrest, it may entice her into opening up a little more.'

'Did it?'

'We met at a restaurant, but the evening provided very different experiences for each of us.'

'How so?'

'Natasha was drinking, heavily. I'd spoken to the barman before she arrived and stipulated that regardless of what was ordered, my drinks were to remain non-alcoholic. She thought we were both getting inebriated, but the truth was only one of us was.'

'What was that missing part of the jigsaw?'

'She had been very keen to turn the conversation to Dylan at the beginning of the evening. But it was something near the end of the evening that gave her away.'

Mike leaned into Toby, the suspense clearly getting the better of him.

'I asked her if she knew of the well in the field. She said she didn't but then proceeded to describe its exact location to me. Eric's killer was known to him, had knowledge of the area, and had the motive and opportunity to kill him. Natasha Jenkins fits all those criteria.'

'What happened after you left the restaurant?'

'I went back to Natasha's house.'

'Why would you deliberately go to the house of somebody who you suspected was a killer?'

'To see if I could find anything else.'

'Did you?'

'Confirmation of what I already knew. Natasha was being fed information from inside the station.'

Mike shook his head before placing it between both hands.

'You mean to tell me I have another staff member who I can't trust.'

'Cathy Benson. Dylan was very specific in disclosing just enough information to her.'

'I don't even want to know how you uncovered that, but it appears the police need to be much more selective in their re-cruitment process. Right now, though, that's the least of my wor-ries.

Toby sat upright, his heart now racing at an uncontrollable rate. It was no longer through fear. This was adrenaline.

'That's not all.'

'There's more?'

'There's still the small matter of the knife,' Toby said slowly.

'You don't believe it was Natasha ensuring he was dead?'

'No. It doesn't fit. There were three other people at the scene that day.'

Toby suddenly realised he was lying, yet not intentionally. There had been a fourth, but the police had never found any trace of Jack at the house. Toby would ensure it remained that way. He didn't need any further complications.

'Olivia, George and Dylan,' Mike confirmed.

'But only one of them did it. This wasn't collusion.'

'I take it you have a theory?' Mike asked smiling.

'There was no evidence of Dylan having been in the house, right?'

'So that leaves us with Olivia or George.'

'The knife belonged to George, but you already knew that.'

A smile suddenly appeared on Mike's face as he seemed to know where this was leading.

'And so did Olivia.'

'Precisely.'

'But why?'

'It was the final act of taking back control, but I think she also saw an opportunity.'

'To do what?'

'Take revenge on me.'

'How?' Mike asked, intrigued.

'By implicating George. She still holds me responsible for her incarceration. It's also worth noting that George tried to frame Olivia for her kidnapping. The two don't like one another, regardless of the impression they may have given.'

Toby placed his hand on Mike's shoulder.

'You may not have Olivia for Eric's murder, but if my knowledge of the law is correct, desecrating a body is considered a criminal offence.'

Mike looked at Toby, and couldn't help but break into a smile.

'You know Toby, you're bright, and if you weren't such a maverick...'

'I'd make an outstanding police officer, right?' Toby interrupted, returning Mike's smile.

'I'm not sure I'd go with outstanding, but you'd certainly be an asset,' he replied with a grin.

Mike crouched down on the floor, head gripped firmly between his hands. He closed his eyes tight. The colour in his face appeared to have drained, his pulse beginning to race at an alarming rate. He ran his fingers through his hair slowly as he struggled with his emotions. This wasn't the first time he'd been faced with a sight like this, but experience was no consolation, particularly not in this instance. As the sound of the sirens drew nearer, he opened his eyes, more out of respect than anything else. The ambulance was a mere formality; it was too late. Helpless, he could only stay with the lifeless body hanging from the beam while waiting for the emergency services to take over. Glancing around the room, he noticed how ordered it was. She had clearly taken pride in her home. He didn't feel he was the right person to comb through the scene; he would leave that to others. Unfamiliar with her life beyond the workplace, his fondness for her made the decision to let her go particularly painful. He bowed his head and felt a stray tear begin to make its way down his cheek. Mike didn't usually get emotional at crime scenes, but this felt different. He had worked with and mentored her. For a while, she had been one of them, before an error in judgement brought her career crashing down around her. She had been young and ambitious but had ultimately veered onto the wrong side of the tracks,

which had cost her dearly. He felt a deep sadness for her demise
and regretted not being able to do more. Moving towards the
door, Mike reached for his phone.

'Natasha's dead.'

The words cut through him. The woman who yesterday had
been in his company at a lavish restaurant, now gone.

'Toby?'

'I'm here. What happened?'

He felt numb. Regardless of what she had done, she didn't deserve this. Her troubled life had been cut short under tragic circumstances. Another error in judgement. This time fatal.

'I'll spare you the details, but it looks like she took her own
life.'

Toby felt sick, his mind swimming with questions he would
likely never get the answers to.

'It seems the burden was too much to live with.'

'Unless this wasn't about guilt.'

'If it wasn't about guilt, then what?'

'Fear.'

'Fear?' Mike asked, seemingly perplexed.

'If she thought the net was closing in on her.'

'When was the last time you spoke to her?'

'Is this official?'

Though he said this with a smile, that smile disappeared as he
came to realise there would be an inevitable police interview to
follow. He may have been the last one to see her alive, not leaving
her home until the early hours, and with that would surely come
questions.

'Some people will say she took the easy way out.'

'Those people are ignorant. Suicide is never the easy way out,' Tony snapped back.

'She wasn't a bad person,' he added.

'Somewhere she took a wrong turn and got lost.'

'I don't believe she ever intended to kill him. This wasn't pre-ordained.'

'How can you be sure?'

'Because Olivia heard arguing which began as Natasha and Eric exited the car. I think the argument she overheard was Natasha demanding answers from Eric regarding his transgressions which she had recently uncovered. His denial would have only served to further infuriate her.'

'Or perhaps he admitted it to her, and that's what tipped her over the edge.'

Toby shook his head, not that Mike could see this.

'I don't think so. Eric conveyed a public image, and it mattered a great deal to him. He would never have let the mask slip in front of his own sister.'

'There's one thing I need to understand, Toby.'

'What's that?'

'How does Natasha go from an evening out with you to dead in less than twenty-four hours?'

Toby didn't answer. The truth was he couldn't answer. Natasha had shown no signs of anything bubbling away underneath the surface. It had been an enjoyable evening and remained that way even after he had spurned her advances. He suddenly stopped as he realised he had his answer.

'She planned this,' he muttered.

'Pardon?'

'She planned this, Mike. She knew the evening would be her last. She propositioned me because she had nothing left to lose. Natasha wasn't looking for a reason to live. She was looking for company before she died alone. You were right. The burden proved too much, but I still believe she still had an inkling that she had somehow aroused suspicion.'

'Jesus Toby. How can you be sure?'

'I can't. It's just an unsettling feeling,' Toby answered.

He lowered his head and removed the phone from his ear. If, as he thought, Natasha had planned her final meal with him, she had known he was on to her. He wondered why she would seek comfort in somebody who she believed was working to expose her. In a strange sense, he felt like he had betrayed her, and couldn't shake the feeling he was responsible for her death. She, like most others, had also been a victim, but her story would likely never be told. Natasha Jenkins would be forever remembered as the disgraced former police officer who murdered her brother. Her struggles and her trauma would never see the light of day. Toby felt a deep sense of injustice that while Eric's reputation remained intact upon his death, Natasha's would be forever tarnished upon hers.

'Go home, Toby,' Mike said affectionately.

'To what?'

He felt defeated. Again, he reminded himself there were no winners; everybody had lost something. Hanging up the phone, Toby trudged slowly down the road, immersed in his own thoughts. Mike's case may now have been closed, but Toby's was still wide open. His thoughts slowly made the transition from

Natasha to Troy Galen. A seed had been planted, and that seed was now growing at an alarming rate. Troy Galen may not have been directly involved in Lara's attack, but Toby was now becoming more convinced he knew about it. Eric was dead, but Troy was still free to offend. He'd used up Mike's goodwill, and the friendship card had disintegrated. As long as Troy was out there, Toby would never sleep easily. He'd not only proved he was a danger to women, but he had also shown he could get to Toby and wouldn't think twice about hurting him, should he get too close. It was simple really. Troy Galen couldn't see Toby coming. With that thought resting in his mind, Toby reached his car, which had been parked close to the café, and entered it tentatively. As he drove away slowly, he feared his emotional resistance was weakening, and questioned where he would be when the dust settled and the adrenaline dispersed. Physically he was running on empty, emotionally he was already in reserve. Rounding the corner onto his street, the emptiness washed over him again. He felt increasingly isolated and wondered whether every passing day was a step closer to reconciliation or a step closer to divorce.

CHAPTER 40

Thursday 18th June...17:30pm

As the door swung open, Beth regarded him, open-mouthed. She looked surprised to see him, something he never thought he would say about his own wife. They had been together for years, yet this had a first-date feel to it. He wasn't naïve and knew this wasn't going to be easy, but he had to see her. Right now, she was the one person he needed to be around. He felt exposed, desperately needing somebody to put their arms around him and say everything was going to be okay. But it wasn't just anybody he needed. It was Beth. Before she could say anything, Toby collapsed into her arms under a wave of emotion. She stroked his head gently and kissed his cheek.

'Toby, what is it?'

'I've missed you.'

She smiled at him and reached for his hands.

'How long have we known one another, Toby?'

'A long time.'

'Right. So, you realise that when you're keeping something from me, I know?'

Toby laughed, which alleviated any tension he was feeling. He also knew, not for the first time, that Beth was right. He looked her straight in the eye not letting go of her hands.

'I'm sorry'.

Beth didn't respond at first. She stared deep into Toby's eyes with a look he hadn't seen for quite some time. He caught a glimpse of the love they had once shared. A love that had once burned so strong, but had been recently suffocated by anger.

'I believe you,' she finally replied. 'No more lies, Toby,' she stated firmly. 'If we're going to work through this, we need honesty. The trust will take some time to rebuild.'

'I need you, Beth. I didn't realise how much until the last few weeks.'

'I know you were working with the police on the murder case.'

'It's more than that.'

'Then perhaps it's time you caught me up,' she said, leading him by the hand into the house.

Beth poured them both a drink and sat down beside Toby on the sofa. He looked around nervously.

'Lara's gone to the cinema with a friend. She doesn't blame you, Toby.'

The words should have come as a relief to Toby, yet they delivered a blow to his stomach as he wrestled with his conscience. It would have been easier had Lara been angry with him. Her reaction further highlighted the sweet and forgiving girl she was. Of everything that had happened over the last year, Lara's brutal attack was the thing he regretted the most. It had served as a cruel reminder that altruism didn't give you a free pass when it came to being subjected to heinous crimes. This was perhaps owing to the fact that quite often, trusting meant unsuspecting.

'I blame myself,' he replied.

Moving closer, she rested her hand on his and smiled lovingly at him.

'They identified Eric's killer.'

'So, they've arrested someone?'

'Not exactly.'

'Toby?'

'She died before she could be taken into custody.'

'She?'

'Natasha Jenkins. Eric's sister.'

Beth looked confused. There was so much she didn't know. It would be unfair to expect her to be able to join the dots from the little he had fed her.

'I met with her on several occasions. We went out for dinner.'

Noticing the smile disappear from Beth's face, he felt the urgency to clarify.

'The first time I met her was by accident. I'd come across a quaint little café out of town and she had been there. We got talking, and she seemed pleasant.'

'But?'

'There was just something about her I was unsure of. When I met her the next time, there were inconsistencies, but at the time I had no idea what she was hiding.'

'Yet you continued to see her?'

'She helped me to locate one of the victims. Little did she realise that by doing so, it actually drew me closer to discovering her crime.'

He stopped for a moment, taking in Beth's body language, before continuing.

'Throughout the dinner, I was plagued by guilt, though I now believe she knew I was suspicious of her, and had planned the whole thing. I had given up Dylan to the police in the hope she would give me enough to confirm my suspicions.'

Beth jerked back, wide-eyed.

'You gave Dylan up to the police? What the hell were you thinking?'

Toby smiled at her.

'Dylan and I planned it beforehand. You know he's not a bad guy. He placed a lot of trust in me. Had I got it wrong...'

'But you didn't,' she interrupted.

Toby finished his drink, placing his empty glass down on the table in front of him.

'How did you know it was her?'

'You only look in someone's direction when they give you cause to. Once I started looking, things became clearer. She had motive, she had opportunity, and she had somebody on the inside feeding her information. It all began to make sense.'

'What was her motive?'

Toby gulped. The answer to the question was going to resonate with Beth who had experienced the emotions of a rape victim vicariously through Lara. Yet holding back on her now wasn't an option. He had kept enough from her and lied to her on too many occasions. Anything other than transparency now would almost certainly end his marriage. She wouldn't forgive him again, assuming she would forgive him this time.

'She discovered her brother to be the one thing that she despised more than anything, due to her own experience. Couple that with the fact she had sacrificed her career for him, and suddenly things become a lot clearer.'

'How long do you think she'd been planning it?'

'She hadn't. This was a spontaneous act. Her unchecked rage got the better of her.'

'Your ability to read people is something I have long since admired in you, Toby. It's also the very reason I was so shocked at how you were blindsided by Olivia Stanton.'

Toby flinched at the mention of Olivia's name. She was the one enigma he had been unable to solve. Hours of reflection had yielded nothing. She had been his Achilles heel, yet he still wasn't able to identify why.

'Olivia, inadvertently, confirmed my suspicions about Natasha.'

'You've been to see her?'

She didn't sound angry, but Toby could see she was sceptical.

'Olivia was charged with her ex-husband's murder. She asked me to help clear her name.'

'And you did?'

'I'm not fond of Olivia, but I knew she wasn't the killer.'

'How could you have been so sure? She's manipulated you before.'

Toby felt hurt by her words, and his face couldn't hide it.

'I'm sorry,' she said reaching for his hand. 'It's just when it comes to that woman, the heckles are raised.'

'She gave me the location for the murder weapon. She also cast further doubt on Natasha's integrity, though I didn't go specifically to speak about her.'

'Did the fact she knew where the murder weapon was not raise doubts?'

'No. Last time she caught me off guard, but this time I knew where to look. It would have been a dangerous bluff for her to make.'

'What did she tell you about Natasha?'

'Though nothing specific, it cast doubt on the veracity of Natasha's statements. She had said that it was around a year into Olivia and Eric's relationship when she had finally met her, yet Olivia mentioned her being a regular visitor from day one. As a truth it's insignificant, but as a lie, it carries much greater relevance.'

Beth sat back, a curious look cast on her face.

'It must have been difficult helping the one person who has caused you so much pain.'

Toby scratched his head and smiled, wearily. Beth still harboured a deep resentment towards Olivia, and Toby understood it. Yet he also knew their marriage wouldn't work with three people in it. Whilst ever Beth carried this level of bitterness towards her, Olivia would remain a permanent fixture in their relationship.

'I didn't see it that way,' he finally replied.

'Then how did you see it?'

'I never chose my clients, Beth. It didn't matter who was sitting in the chair opposite, I worked professionally and diligently, remaining committed to helping those who sought it. Do I like

Olivia as a person or agree with the methods she uses to get her own way? No. But do I believe she should be punished for a crime she didn't commit? Also no. We don't choose the person; we choose the narrative.'

Beth stood up and walked into the kitchen to pour them both another drink. Toby decided to follow. His last visit here had been some time ago, which filled him with guilt considering the relationship he had enjoyed with Lara. She was the daughter he'd never had, though there weren't that many years between them, and he had always felt enormously protective of her. Beth noticed the nostalgic glint in his eye and smiled warmly at him.

'I remember the day she moved in,' he said, reminiscing.

'Pizza to celebrate if I remember correctly?'

'You do remember correctly,' Toby replied playfully.

His smile disappeared as the reality of what had happened bit hard. Suddenly the photographs strategically placed in chronological order, became a painful reminder of how her purity had been cruelly ripped from her. He thought about Olivia, George and Natasha, and how their ordeals had not shaped them, but changed them as people. Each had carried a deep-seated resentment, which had cost each of them in different ways. George had lost her trust in people; Olivia had lost her freedom; Natasha had lost her life.

'Why did you do it, Toby?'

Her tone had changed. A look of pain washed over her as if a sudden rush of memories from the past twelve months had overwhelmed her. Toby looked at her confused by the ambiguity of the question.

'Olivia, Dylan, George. Chasing kidnappers, getting into altercations, keeping things from Mike, lying to me, and going to client's houses. What was it all for?'

Toby looked up at the ceiling before focusing his eyes on Beth. He was finally ready to be honest with her; he was ready to be honest with himself.

'I know you think this began with Olivia, but it didn't. Olivia discovered something in me that I didn't know existed. The only career I ever considered once my mother passed, was psychotherapy. Yet it left me unfulfilled, I just didn't realise it until that moment.'

'Toby, you loved your work, and you loved your clients. It was always enough for you.'

'Until it wasn't,' he replied.

'What are you saying? This is who you are now?'

'Consulting with the police has given me something I haven't felt in my career for quite some time. It's given me a sense of direction. It's given me that excitement I've been lacking.'

'So, it's the adrenaline?'

'The day we located George after her kidnapping. I've never felt so alive. I can't explain it.'

She placed her hand on his shoulder and rubbed at it gently.

'Where does this leave us, Toby? Because you know I can't endure any more drama. I yearn for the quiet life we once had together.'

Toby looked dejected. It felt like she was asking him to choose between her and his career. That choice wasn't quite as straightforward as he would like it to be.

'I don't believe a quiet life and a stimulating career have to be mutually exclusive,' he replied, taking her by the hand.

'That scar looks nasty,' she said pointing to the wound over the corner of his eye, which still hadn't fully healed.

'I'd like to say the other guy came off worse, but...'

'You're not a fighter,' Beth laughed.

'You know, the first time it was Dylan who saved me. He arrived and chased off the intruder. I was grateful he was there. However, the thing with Dylan is I never know how far he'll go.'

'You've been attacked more than once?'

Toby peered over Beth's shoulder at the digital photo frame placed above the fireplace. The glass he had been drinking out of fell out of his hands and smashed into tiny pieces. His face contorted in horror. His heart felt like it had stopped before thundering back into action, announcing itself with vigour. His face was ashen, and he felt an overwhelming sensation of repugnance. For a moment, his grasp on reality slipped, with the entire room feeling like it was a surreal image he just happened to be part of. Beth by now had a look of concern on her face and gripped his hands tightly.

'Toby, what is it?'

How could he even begin to explain this? Lara's nightmare was supposed to be over, but it may only just be beginning. The guilt returned and Toby felt panic setting in. He wanted to be wrong. So badly, he wanted his eyes to have deceived him, but he knew what he'd seen. Getting up out of his seat, he walked over to the photo frame and picked it up. Frantically clicking, he retrieved the previous image and hit pause.

'This picture,' he said pointing directly at the image. 'When was it taken?'

'I don't know, why?'

'Who is this man with Lara?' he replied ignoring her question.

'That's Grant. She's only known him for a few weeks, but she seems really taken by him. He's a little older than her, but I think she feels secure around him. He is of German descent which I think she is quite enamoured with. Oley, I believe his surname is.'

'Have you met him?'

'Once. He came to pick her up, and I happened to answer the door.'

'He's been here?'

'You sound like an over-protective father,' she laughed, but the laugh soon faded when she noticed the look of horror on Toby's face.

'Toby, what's going on?'

Toby gripped his hair with both hands, before screwing his eyes shut so tightly, that when he reopened them he was seeing white flashing objects for a moment. He'd spent the last few weeks trying to piece back together his life, rediscovering a routine that depicted as close a resemblance to normality as possible.

'Toby?', she asked again, her voice now raised.

He wondered how he could tell Beth that her sister may be in grave danger. This was the ripple effect he'd feared. People close to him had been hurt. These people would use anyone they could to make their point and stave off detection. It was only a matter of time before Beth was targeted, but this had already gone way too far.

'How much do you know about the man in that picture?'

'Just what I told you, but the look on your face tells me you have something to add.'

Toby let out an anxious breath knowing Beth wasn't going to like what he was about to say. He worried that he was about to burn any bridges they had built, but still, he couldn't lie.

'Do you remember when I told you that Eric had an accomplice?'

Beth nodded but remained silent.

'Dylan got a name from somebody who had worked for Eric. Troy Galen. I believe it was Troy Galen who attacked me in the car park. Except he wasn't known in the pub as Troy Galen.' Toby stopped for a brief moment and looked up, trying to remember his conversation that day. Suddenly he was back in the pub, the charming and mysterious Roger White seated in front of him.

'There was this one night, however, where I walked in on an argument between him and Tony Regal over there,'

As he returned his gaze to Beth, he noted how pale her face had become. She began to shake her head.

'No, Toby. Please don't continue. You can't.'

Overcome with grief, her tears flowed freely, the intensity of her sobbing increasing with each tremor. Toby reached out to console her, but she pushed him away.

'You did this, Toby. All of this is because of you. How can you live with yourself knowing what you've caused?'

Already emotional, the words cut through Toby with precision. He was devastated at what had happened, but hearing Beth hold him responsible served as a chilling reminder of the true consequence of his actions over the last year.

'We have to call the police. Mike will know what to do.'

She paused, but her demeanour was anything but rational.

'No, I'm going to call Lara.'

Toby reached for her hand.

'When are you expecting her home?'

'Around eleven, she said. Why?'

'You don't want to panic her. More importantly, you don't want to panic him.'

'How can you be sure it's him?'

Toby pondered for a moment. He'd only really seen the barman briefly, and the attack had taken place from behind, with the perpetrator's identity not revealed at any point. Perhaps he had this wrong. Perhaps the man in the picture had a striking resemblance, and nothing more.

'Maybe you're right,' he conceded.

A deathly silence enveloped the room, both its occupants deep in thought. The change in atmosphere was now palpable, neither willing to meet the other's gaze. Toby hoped he was wrong; Beth feared he was right. He could see it in her eyes. The hope he had seen when she had invited him in had now been extinguished. Finally, he met her stare, and as he looked deep into those eyes, he saw the pain. Her former life was now a distant memory. She had actively withdrawn from her life with Toby, refusing to accept the lack of stability that came with his career change. Though he had felt abandoned, he understood why she had taken that decision. Her life with Lara was supposed to be simpler, but Lara had been used as a mere pawn in a vengeful vendetta against Toby. Leaning against the breakfast bar, he studied the room. It had been decorated since the last time he'd visited. It had a fresh look to it and somehow looked bigger. There was a hint of modernity, a hint of tradition, and also some chic aspects. It had several personalities like it was playing to its audience. Suddenly Toby looked up, startled.

'Toby, what is it?'

'Several personalities.'

'Several personalities?'

'What did you say the name of Lara's friend is?'

'Grant Oley,' Beth replied wearing a look of confusion.

'And the barman went by the name of Tony Regal. I can't believe I never realised this at the time.'

'Realised what?'

'Grant Oley and Tony Regal are the same person...Troy Galen.'

'How do you know?'

She now sounded panicked.

'They're anagrams. Grant Oley and Tony Regal are anagrams of Troy Galen. He's been playing with us the whole time.'

'Jesus Toby, what are you saying?'

'He's left subtle clues, but he believes he's too smart to be caught. The chase is part of the fun for him.'

Ignoring Toby's plea, Beth had picked up her phone and dialled Lara while he had been talking.

'Straight to answerphone,' she said, now sounding more frantic.

Toby went to comfort her, but she again pushed him away.

'All I see when I look at you is the reason why Lara is in danger.'

'Beth, I didn't mean for any of this to happen.'

'But it did Toby. You were warned, but still...'

She broke down in tears before she could finish the sentence. Toby's heart sank at the sight of Beth in so much distress. This still didn't make sense to him. Lara had been attacked by Eric alone. She had confirmed there had only been one attacker. Troy Galen was involved somewhere, but he wasn't sure where. Perhaps he had been involved, or perhaps he had known all along but had played no active role. Or maybe that wasn't his angle at all. It wasn't entirely implausible that he in fact knew nothing about the attack, but had simply identified Lara as being somebody close to Toby. Unless...

'What if Lara isn't the target?'

Beth wiped away her tears with her sleeve.

'Sorry?'

'What if this isn't about Lara, but she was a stepping stone to get to somebody else?'

'Like who?'

The words were there but he couldn't bring himself to say them. Verbalising what he was thinking made it real, and he didn't want any of this to be real.

'Toby?'

'Like you, Beth.'

'What would he want with me?'

'It's not about who you are. It's about your worth. These people will find the weak spot and apply pressure until they get a submission. So far, they have gone after Jack, George and Lara to protect their secret. If they can make me believe that you're next, they have me. In a game of poker, this is where I'd be expected to fold.'

Beth looked at him wide-eyed having now stopped crying. The distraught look she had worn just moments earlier had been replaced by a look of intent. Considering she had just discovered her sister was in the company of a sexual predator, and was now out of contact, she suddenly looked remarkably calm. Too calm, he thought. He was unrecognisable to her, she'd said, yet now it was she who felt like a complete stranger. The look in her eye didn't worry him, it frightened him. She stood up and walked over to the cabinet in the kitchen, reaching for the bottle of gin.

'Something a little stronger?'

Toby shook his head. Beth rarely drank, and certainly not during the daytime.

'This is the part where you try to convince me we shouldn't call Mike,' she said taking a sip out of her freshly poured drink.

'Something tells me you don't need much convincing.'

She looked at him with a face that gave nothing away. She looked devoid of emotion, but that meant one thing. She was sitting on a rage which, for now, was being kept in check, but it would only be a matter of time before it broke through the surface and began quenching its thirst.

'There's a reason he has flown under the radar all this time. Sexual coercion is difficult to prove. None of his victims will see him as a rapist. They will simply see him as a manipulative and vile individual. All have too much to lose to come forward, which means there is a distinct lack of hard evidence.'

'So, are you saying he's untouchable?'

'Perhaps to the police.'

She looked at him with intrigue.

'There are certain advantages we have over the police right now, Beth.'

'Advantages?'

Toby reached for his bag and slowly removed an old grey book from it. He held it out to her.

'What's this?'

'Before you open it, you need to know how it came to be in my possession.'

She pulled back her hand having reached out to grasp it.

'The night I had dinner with Natasha Jenkins, we ended up at her house. Actually, we didn't simply end up there, I'd planned it beforehand. I was already fairly certain she was the killer, but I just needed that final piece of the jigsaw.'

'And this is it?'

'Yes. It's what Eric and Troy argued over in the pub that day. I believe Natasha somehow came across it and it confirmed her suspicions of her brother. I imagine she confronted him and that's when the argument spilled into the house and her temper got the better of her. She picked up the statue and hit him with it before quickly disappearing.'

'You took this from a crime scene?'

'No. I took it from Natasha the night before she died. I didn't enter the house on the day of her death.'

'Why doesn't Mike know about this?'

'Because Troy Galen will disappear into the wind, the moment he knows the police are looking for him. We can't risk that.'

'We?'

'Dylan and I.'

Beth looked at him scornfully. The whole conversation was so far removed from what they were accustomed to, yet he felt unapologetic.

'Troy Galen and Eric Stanton ruined so many lives and created so many victims. This was a game to them, the women nothing more than pieces. It was about control and humiliation. They took enormous pleasure in what they did and showed not a hint of remorse. Eric is dead, but Troy is alive and free to continue his sickening desire for the degradation of women.'

The sound of a car disrupted them. Beth dashed to the window and saw Lara getting out of the back seat...alone. She closed her eyes, the relief visible.

'This didn't end with Eric Stanton, but it can end with Troy Galen. We have to be smart and make sure we hand unassailable evidence to Mike, but that's going to mean removing yourself from your comfort zone and heading to a place you've never been before. It can be dark, it can be confusing and it can push you to your limits. There's nobody to hear you scream and nobody to catch you if you fall. Now you know how I obtained the book, you need to ask yourself if you're prepared to open it because the content is harrowing. Whether you open that book or not will tell me whether you're prepared to use everything you have to go after Troy Galen and get justice for each one of his victims. I have no expectations.'

Beth sat deliberating, one hand placed on the book, the other clutching her glass tightly. The house fell silent, only the ticking of the clock breaching the tranquillity. She looked tired and beaten, and Toby was left wondering if she had finally reached her limit. He wasn't sure whether coming here had been the right decision, but whatever happened between them moving forward, he would savour the brief closeness they had shared this evening. A closeness they hadn't experienced for some time. For that, he had no regrets. Moments later Toby recoiled in his chair as Beth rose up out of her seat and kissed him gently on the forehead before leaving the room, closing the door firmly behind her. He had his answer.